Lust
The Bad Earl

CHRISTI CALDWELL

The Bad Earl

Copyright © 2024 by Christi Caldwell

All rights reserved. No part of this book may be reproduced in any form by any electronic or mechanical means—except in the case of brief quotations embodied in critical articles or reviews—without written permission.

The characters and events portrayed in this book are fictitious. Any similarity to real persons, living or dead, is purely coincidental and not intended by the author.

This Book is licensed for your personal enjoyment only. This Book may not be re-sold or given away to other people. If you would like to share this book with another person, please purchase an additional copy for each recipient. If you're reading this book and did not purchase it or borrow it, or it was not purchased for your use only, then please return it and purchase your own copy. Thank you for respecting the hard work of the author.

For more information about the author:
www.christicaldwellauthor.com
christicaldwellauthor@gmail.com
Twitter: @ChristiCaldwell
Or on Facebook at: Christi Caldwell Author

For first glimpse at covers, excerpts, and free bonus material, be sure to sign up for my monthly newsletter!

Printed in the USA.

Cover Design and Interior Format

Other Titles by Christi Caldwell

ALL THE DUKE'S SINS
Along Came a Lady
Desperately Seeking a Duchess

ALL THE DUKE'S SIN'S PREQUEL SERIES
It Had to Be the Duke
One for My Baron

SCANDALOUS AFFAIRS
A Groom of Her Own
Taming of the Beast
My Fair Marchioness
It Happened One Winter
Loved and Found

HEART OF A DUKE
In Need of a Duke—Prequel Novella
For Love of the Duke
More than a Duke
The Love of a Rogue
Loved by a Duke
To Love a Lord
The Heart of a Scoundrel
To Wed His Christmas Lady
To Trust a Rogue
The Lure of a Rake
To Woo a Widow
To Redeem a Rake
One Winter with a Baron

To Enchant a Wicked Duke
Beguiled by a Baron
To Tempt a Scoundrel
To Hold a Lady's Secret
To Catch a Viscount
Defying the Duke
To Marry Her Marquess
The Devil and the Debutante
Devil by Daylight
My Heart Forever

THE HEART OF A SCANDAL
In Need of a Knight—Prequel Novella
Schooling the Duke
A Lady's Guide to a Gentleman's Heart
A Matchmaker for a Marquess
His Duchess for a Day
Five Days with a Duke

LORDS OF HONOR
Seduced by a Lady's Heart
Captivated by a Lady's Charm
Rescued by a Lady's Love
Tempted by a Lady's Smile
Courting Poppy Tidemore

MCQUOIDS OF MAYFAIR
The Duke Alone
The Heiress at Sea

SCANDALOUS SEASONS
Forever Betrothed, Never the Bride
Never Courted, Suddenly Wed
Always Proper, Suddenly Scandalous
Always a Rogue, Forever Her Love
A Marquess for Christmas
Once a Wallflower, at Last His Love
Endlessly Courted, Finally Loved

Once a Rake, Suddenly a Suitor
Once Upon a Betrothal

SINFUL BRIDES
The Rogue's Wager
The Scoundrel's Honor
The Lady's Guard
The Heiress's Deception

THE WICKED WALLFLOWERS
The Hellion
The Vixen
The Governess
The Bluestocking
The Spitfire

THE THEODOSIA SWORD
Only For His Lady
Only For Her Honor
Only For Their Love

DANBY
A Season of Hope
Winning a Lady's Heart

THE BRETHREN
The Spy Who Seduced Her
The Lady Who Loved Him
The Rogue Who Rescued Her
The Minx Who Met Her Match
The Spinster Who Saved a Scoundrel

LOST LORDS OF LONDON
In Bed with the Earl
In the Dark with the Duke
Undressed with the Marquess

SEVEN DEADLY SINS
Wrath: The Devil Duke

BRETHREN OF THE LORDS
My Lady of Deception
Her Duke of Secrets

THE READ FAMILY SAGA
A Winter Wish

MEMOIR: NON-FICTION
Uninterrupted Joy

"The sweetness of love is short-lived, but the pain endures."

Sir Thomas Mallory

PROLOGUE

They say blood will let. It is true. As such, my children, each of them, are as cursed as I, their mother. They are destined to be lovers of vice. Sinners. Slaves to lust.
~ *The Duchess of A*

London, England

AT ELEVEN YEARS OF AGE, Lady Raina Goodheart was entirely too old to believe in ghosts. That did *not*, however, prevent her from fearing them.

Lying alone in her chambers, with her nursemaid, dead to the world, snoring away in the connecting room, Raina stared at the floral canopy overhead.

She swallowed loudly.

Dead to the world hadn't been right

Her only brother, Gregory, the future Duke of Argyll had assured Raina spirits returning from the dead, weren't real. And that if they *were*, those haunts would have far grander, more enjoyable things to do upon their return to earth than go about bothering eleven-year-old girls attempting to sleep.

But also, now that he'd gone off to university, Gregory didn't come 'round like he once did.

Alone, in her rooms, with only the night's shadows and a recurring forlorn wail for company, Raina wasn't altogether sure that where ghosts were concerned, her brother had the right of it.

Another distant, broken sob, whispered in the midnight silence.

Her teeth chattering, Rain snatched her chintz coverlet and tugged it all the way to her chin.

They aren't real.

They aren't real.

"Whyever would a spirit spend a night here when he could be out to all manner of mischief at some wild masquerade?" Gregory's gently spoken reminder echoed around her mind.

In a bid to escape the terror tugging at her, she did as he'd once told her to do if he weren't about; to repeat that conversation over and over in her mind.

She focused on breathing—just like he'd said. "They wouldn't." She'd answered him. "Whyever would ghosts wish to spend the evening at the Goodheart residence?"

"Precisely," he'd reassured.

A long, forlorn moan broke once more into the quiet.

Raina squeezed her eyes shut.

If they weren't real, then what else could possibly account for those piteous wails that came and went on various nights?

"There are no monsters," she whispered to herself. "There are no ghosts."

Another piercing sob spilled into the quiet.

Before her courage deserted her, Raina swung her legs over the side of the bed and stood.

The cold came up to meet her bare feet.

Shivering, Raina first fetched her wrapper, then a candlestick, and made her way from the room.

With the way Mrs. Bossley drank her gin before bed and then slept, the older woman wouldn't have heard a mail coach were it to come crashing through her lone window.

As if to highlight that very point, the moment Raina brought the door shut behind her, an enormous, bleating snore spilled through the white-painted panel.

Only, now alone in the long, empty, corridor, she looked around.

The lit tapers within the gilded sconces dripped beads of clear wax like sorrowful teardrops. Dark shadows flickered off the peacock-painted wallpaper; turning those sapphire and emerald majestic birds into sinister beasts.

Raina's hand trembled violently, and the abrupt movement sent the tiny flame out so that the only light remaining came from within the handful of sconces still lit.

As she inched deeper down the hall, she took care to keep her gaze directed forward.

How had she failed to appreciate before now, how unnaturally quiet it was in the dead of night. Or how eerie the halls were?

Perhaps they'd always been?

Raina attempted to swallow around the large knot in her throat.

"Gr-Gregory," she called out. "I know you said there are no such things as ghosts and monsters, and I believe you because you never lie to me, so I'm hoping it is just you and Rex and Edward who are here and just being noisy." She paused to take a deep breath. "*Is* it you?"

He always *did* return at the most unexpected times and made the grandest show when he arrived.

Silence, however, served as her only answer.

Raina stilled.

Wait. Those wretched wails which had penetrated her sleep and dragged her awake were no more.

If she'd even heard them, at all.

Raina glanced about the empty corridor.

Some of the tension eased from her shoulders.

"It appears you were right, Gregory," she grudgingly admitted. "I have a colorful imagination and hate sleep because I don't want to miss anything. That's what you always say, isn't it?"

She didn't need a reply, his already existed in her head.

A duke's daughter lived a lonely life. The servants did not permit their children to play with Raina. The village children did, but only for those short times her family retired in the summer. As such, Raina took the one friend whom she did have in her brother and relied on him, even when he wasn't around.

He—

A ragged sob punctured the quiet.

With a gasp, Raina bolted and took off running back from the same direction she'd just come.

"Why-wh—why?"

Crying softly, Raina, grappled with her door handle. She made to wrench the panel open and looked with a frantic gaze for the monster. When, from the distance, through her panic, she registered that single word uttered over and over.

Monsters and ghosts didn't speak the King's English.

Did they?

Only—Raina's pulse continued to hammer away in her chest— she recognized that hoarse, lyrical, voice.

"Mother," she whispered.

Her mother's cries echoed in return.

"No. No. No."

She hesitated a moment; considered finding Papa or screaming down the household for a servant.

When presented with dashing off alone, again, Raina opted for the latter. She opened her mouth to get help for her mother but stopped.

Some twenty paces ahead, a tall, graceful figure, emerged from the shadows like some wispy specter in flowy white silk skirts, so sheer as to be see-through.

She blinked. "Mother?" she repeated, this time more loudly.

As the duchess trailed the halls, she gave no outward reaction she'd heard Raina. Mother and daughter existed in some strange plain; like they were trapped in a dream, but separated by a screen.

Her earlier fear aside, Raina frowned.

Where was she...going?

With her gaze, she followed her mother's meandering path, until the duchess reached the South wing.

Springing to life, Raina took off, sprinting after her. Winded and out of breath, she stumbled around the corner.

They continued on that way.

The duchess wandering. Raina following. Until at last, Raina's chase brought her to a wing of the house she'd never been before. Strange that. She'd lived in this household; played in every corner of it, only to discover there were still uncharted places for her to explore here.

Her mother's shoulders sagged, and then she let herself into a room.

Click.

Alone once more, her unease and hesitancy of before returned, it was this time, with more cautious steps that Raina made the rest of her way over.

She hovered at the entryway.

Dampening her mouth, Raina pressed her ear against the door and listened.

There came more of her mother's tears; her mother who never cried and who always wore a smile. And as much as Raina yearned to find her way back to her corner of the household and forget everything she'd seen and heard, she couldn't. How many times had Mother wiped Raina's tears? Or held her when she cried.

Bringing her shoulders back, Raina caught the handle, and let herself inside. It took a moment for her eyes to adjust. As she walked slowly inside, Raina moved her gaze throughout.

"Mother?" she called quietly.

There was no answer.

Then she found her.

She lay beside an ink pot, turned over on its side, the small pool of black continued to leak out toward an empty crystal decanter.

Raina's frown deepened. She knew what an empty bottle meant. The last time she'd discovered one so, she'd also discovered Gregory and Edward raucously inebriated and outrageously loud.

But the duchess wasn't loud.

"Mother," Raina whispered.

It was her mother, but at the same time, it wasn't.

Curled on her side against the corner.

Raina fell to a knee and touched her lightly on the shoulder. "Mama?" she repeated.

Weeping softly, the duchess rolled onto her back.

Raina started at the sight of her: her glazed, vacant, eyes bloodshot and swollen as they'd never been. Her lips covered in rouge.

"I hate h-her," the duchess slurred, "b-but I hate him more." A gurgling half-laugh, half-sob escaped her. "But I l-love him even more than I hate him."

Her pulse picked up again. "Wh-who, Mother?" Fear burgeoned in her belly.

The duchess lifted her tear-ravaged face. She moved a drunken gaze over Raina's. "Why can't I be enough?"

"I don't know what you mean, Mama," she implored. "You are enough."

Father. Where is Father?

Raina desperately longed to search for him. He always made Mother smile.

"I-I hate all of them," her mother's words rolled together so badly, Raina struggled to make out what she was saying.

When she did, a chill went through her. "Wh-Who do you hate?"

But Raina's voice didn't seem to penetrate the faraway misery and hate in the duchess's eyes. "She is for us. *They* are for us," she spat. "It's never for us. It's for him." Another crazed laugh burst from her lips. "And I do it for him but then...I love it, because I'm just as d-depraved."

Raina's teeth clanked together. *I don't understand.*

Did she even voice her question aloud? Maybe not, because she didn't want to understand whatever it was Mama spoke about.

Suddenly, through whatever hell kept the duchess in its snare loosened. Lucidity glimmered in her tear-filled eyes. "We are a family of sinners, Raina. Your father. His father before him. The entire line is corrupted to the core. Me." Her features twisted. "*Gregory*. My beautiful boy is n-no different than him."

The duchess's shoulders slumped. "I-It is in our blood, Raina," her mother said, her voice steady and sober and all the more chilling for it. "You'll see."

"What is?" Raina urged, her fear redoubling. She gave the duchess a slight shake. "What is, Mama?" she repeated.

"It is in our blood, Raina. We were cursed...to be sinners. Or blessed to be sinners..."

With unsteady movements, her mother collapsed upon her back on the floor.

She's dead.

Raina cried out. Tears ravaged her cheeks the same way they did Mama's.

Except, the duchess fumbled her arm about, and then muttering something, she fetched a small book from the floor. "Here," she slurred, tossing the leather tome.

Raina caught it against her chest. Confused, she fanned through the pages. Upon inspection, it wasn't a book, but rather, a journal, kept in her mother's hand—a diary.

"I protest the wicked acts he proposes we take part in, but shamefully, wickedly, and secretly, I am intrigued and…aroused. I—" Raina's eyes widened as she read the remainder of the sinful words her mother recorded. She slapped the book closed.

"Here," she said, gruffly, and attempted to hand it back to her drowsy mother.

The duchess gave Raina a sad smile and rejected those attempts. "Better you know now than when you are a hopeful young woman with stars in your eyes, my dearest Raina."

Her eyes slipped shut. A moment later, a snore to rival Papa's favorite hunting dog, aptly named, Thunder, filled the room.

Falling back on her haunches, Raina stared at the stranger before her. Not taking her gaze from her mother's slumbering form, Then, glancing about, she grabbed a blanket off the bed. Raina looked at the cool fabric in her hands.

The crimson red satin wouldn't keep any person warm. Still, she gently covered the duchess, and then, Raina resting her back against the bed, stayed with her mother while she slept.

The diary her mother had pushed into her hands stared tauntingly back—the book dared her to pick it up. To read.

Raina bit the inside of her lower lip hard enough to draw blood.

Then, squeezing her eyes tightly shut, she grabbed her mother's private diary as she'd urged Raina to do.

Raina read.

And read.

And continued reading until a coldness lived within her and she'd reached the last page.

Heart pounding, Raina slammed the leather volume shut and tossed it on the other side of the duchess's still sleeping form.

Not taking her gaze from her mother, this stranger before her, who'd revealed the past Raina hadn't known, and prophesied Raina's future, she came to her feet and backed slowly away.

She continued backing away until she'd put the room and her mother behind her.

But not the thoughts. Those horrid, hideous things she'd read, followed Raina, as she wound her way back through the maze of a household.

When she reached the corridor connecting to her hall, Raina stopped.

Why did I go seek out the source of those wails? *Why?*

Because then, she wouldn't know. Then, she wouldn't know that her parents' love wasn't the grand, devoted one she'd believed, or that wickedness ran in the veins of all Goodheart's—Raina, included.

A large hand settled on Raina's shoulder.

Crying out, she spun to face—

"Gregory," she whispered.

"Hey, what is my favorite sister doing—" The usual cheer-filled grin on her brother's face faded. His gaze moved from Raina's swollen and bloodshot eyes to her tear-stained streaks.

"Who do I have to kill?" he asked quietly, with a lethality she'd never before heard from him.

Raina scrubbed a hand over her face. "N-No one." She gave her head an uneven shake.

He narrowed his eyes.

And through the haze of her misery, she noted details which she likely wouldn't have otherwise noted—until her meeting with their mother.

Her brother's rumpled garments. The rouge stain on his also wrinkled white cravat. The stench of spirits on his breath.

"It is in our blood, Raina. We were cursed...to be sinners. Or blessed to be sinners..."

Her mother's half-mad sobbing laugh pinged around Raina's head until she wanted to clamp her hands over her ears.

She wrenched her arm free of Gregory's grip. "Let me *go.*"

Surprise flared in his eyes. "*Raina?*"

And as she bolted for her bedroom, leaving Gregory behind, she discovered too late—

If she'd been allowed to choose between a world where monsters and ghosts freely roamed or where her parents weren't hopelessly, and desperately in love with only each other, she'd far prefer the former.

CHAPTER 1

Today is to be my debut—I dream of a grand love. I yearn for a grand love. I will settle for nothing less.
~AA

London, England

SEATED IN THE PRIVATE OFFICE of one of England's most powerful peers Severin Cadogan, the Earl of Kilburn, former agent with the Home Office and current private assassin for hire, gave the understatement of his life.

"I don't play nursemaid, Your Grace."

The Duke of Argyll flashed Cadogan a genial grin.

"Ah, but I don't require a nursemaid." The duke, and also head proprietor of Forbidden Pleasures, a premier club in London, reclined in his leather armchair. "What I'm *looking* for is a guard. More specifically, a *body*guard."

"You can dress a pig in a gown; it's still going to oink, Your Grace," Cadogan said candidly. "I don't *guard* bodies."

What Cadogan *did* do was make men *disappear*.

"I'm well aware of your reputation." Argyll flashed another smile. "It's why I intend to hire you."

"I'm not interested in the assignment you're selling, Your Grace." In fact, he was even less interested in this particular job than the last one put to him, not long ago by this same, dogged nobleman.

"Come now, Cadogan. You haven't even heard the details of this proposal. At the very least, you can entertain me."

Cadogan inclined his head. "I'm listening."

"First, may I interest you in a brandy?" The man was already on his feet and heading for the liquor cabinet.

"No, thank you, Your Grace."

As a rule, Cadogan avoided liquor. With the other man's reputation for lacing spirits, Cadogan would sooner slit his own throat than partake in any food or drink in this gilded and marble rococo palace.

The duke's eyes glittered with the first hint of annoyance, which he swiftly masked.

"Are you certain?" the duke persisted. "The bottle I have in mind is not just *any* cognac. It is from the first case sent from France enjoyed by King George III after he allowed Martell Cognac an import license."

The man couldn't have been more obvious had he attempted to pry Cadogan's mouth apart and poured his *fine* libations down his throat.

Cadogan met that irrelevant story with silence. He didn't repeat himself for anyone.

With an irreverent shrug, Argyll poured himself a snifter and rejoined Cadogan.

The duke, his glass framed between his hands, studied him in an assessing way. "You and I, we have much in common, Cadogan."

"Oh?" he said, genuinely amused.

"You don't think so?" Argyll lifted a sardonic brow. "You and I are both men born to one station but are far more comfortable pursuing *actual* work. Our businesses, each in their own way, result in the demise of unsavory sorts. Neither of us suffers from the bothersome effects of having a heart."

As the lofty nobleman tossed back a long swallow, Cadogan resisted the urge to shake his head. Did the gentleman truly *believe* he could appeal to some imagined similitude between them? Cadogan hadn't even entered *the* world that naïve.

Argyll set his drink aside. "I will get to the point. I care about my sisters. I will do anything to protect them." He locked a flinty gaze with Cadogan's. "*Anything.*"

Anything, that was, *except*, watch them himself. Then, Argyll wasn't unlike other nobles in that way.

"That's where we're different, Your Grace. Where your responsibilities include a family, mine do not." Nor would it ever. He had siblings. They shared blood, and that was about all.

Drumming his fingertips together, Argyll contemplated Cadogan. The gentleman abruptly ceased that grating tapping. "*Everyone* can be persuaded, Cadogan."

Such were the words of a lionized lord who'd never been told 'no' in his entire vacuous existence.

And though Cadogan didn't fear any man, he'd built his new career on working for the most powerful lords. Therefore, when it came to rejecting a duke's assignment, Cadogan had to tread *somewhat* carefully.

"If it's a bodyguard you seek, Your Grace, I'd be more than happy to assign you one of the men who works for me. They're capable. They're—"

All hint of the duke's earlier good humor vanished. "It has to be you."

"Why me?" Cadogan paused. "You have seventy-five guards. Why not one of *them* to watch over your sisters."

The duke failed to mask his surprise.

"I see you've attained very specific information about my club," Argyll murmured. "You mustn't leave me to wonder how you ascertained those details and what *else* you may know?"

In other words: Did Cadogan work for the duke's former business partner—now business *rival* and enemy—the Duke of Craven.

"If there's something you want to ask, Your Grace," he said coolly. "I suggest you ask it."

"Very well." The duke let his hands drop to the arms of his chair. "This isn't the first time you've rejected an offer from me."

No, it wasn't. Just a fortnight ago, the duke had paid Cadogan an unexpected, morning, visit and made him a *very* generous proposition.

"I asked you to take over the security detail for my club in exchange for a large stake in the business and a sizeable fortune no other man in his right mind would have turned down." Through his recounting, Argyll sounded as peevish as he had the day of the rejection. "Which leaves me no choice except to ask: do you serve the Duke of Craven?"

"I don't *serve* any man," he said, with a tight smile. "I work for myself."

Had Cadogan recently handled a case for Argyll's former friend and now rival club owner the Duke of Craven? Yes.

Did that mean Cadogan possessed any allegiance to the other man? No.

Argyll sharpened his gaze on Cadogan's face, undoubtedly in search of his sincerity.

Throughout that scrutiny, Cadogan remained motionless. The imperious lord could look until the cows came home—he wouldn't find even a hint of Cadogan's thoughts.

"You claim you aren't working for my enemy, Cadogan," the affable gentleman remarked, this time in his good-natured way. "How is it then, you know the precise count of men in my employ?"

"I make it a habit of finding out everything about potential clients, Your Grace."

The pretend war the two dukes played, was just that—a game. These fancy lords? They knew less than shite about real conflict. Cadogan, on the other hand? The things he'd done to preserve peace and prosperity for king and country…and now his private work, would make even the duke's evilest act look like a trip to Gunter's ices.

"I'm honored by your continued attempts to hire me in some capacity," he said, lightly steering his meeting with the gentleman to a conclusion. "Given your recent reservations, Your Grace, I believe it is fair to conclude I am *not* the man to watch after your sister."

Giving a little laugh, Argyll shook a finger his way. "You are a baffling one, chap."

Cadogan displayed no outward reaction.

The duke's expression grew serious once more. He joined his hands together and continued his scrutiny of Cadogan.

"What will it take for me to tie you down?" he mulled his question aloud.

"I can't be tied down, Your Grace." Not by anyone or anything.

"You are the best, Cadogan," the duke persisted, his tone growing peevish. "And I only employ the best. I'll give you a fortune and more if you trade your role of assassin for the very temporary role of protector."

For an assignment Cadogan had absolutely no intention of taking, the exchange had continued on long enough. He already possessed a fortune and had the luxury of accepting or passing on assignments.

"Your Grace," he began, walking a careful line between making an enemy and making himself clear. "I trust you do not need me to point out your close *friend* and partner, Lachlan Latimer would be a sufficient *alternative*."

A tic pulsed at the corner of the duke's right eye. "I am not questioning Latimer's abilities."

"I did not say you were." He didn't need to. The duke's continued requests of Cadogan spoke to the contrary.

He could practically see the wheel's churning in his mind. Argyll worried about that slight getting back to his partner.

"I'm not a man who talks, Your Grace," he said, alleviating at least one of the man's worries. "As for your sister, if not Latimer, I trust you're more than capable of providing her with the protection she requires." Cadogan stood and dropped a short bow. "Good evening, Your Grace."

He turned to go.

Wood scraped wood as the duke shoved his chair back. "There must be some way I might entice you."

The coy knowing tone stopped Cadogan in his tracks. Narrowing his eyes, he faced the desperate gentleman.

"I don't want for anything, Your Grace," he said curtly. He'd built a fortune out of corpses. "I need even less."

The duke fixed a calculating gaze on the jagged scar running down Cadogan's cheek—that same mark which ended Cadogan's career at the Home Office.

Argyll's lips tipped up in a smug grin. "Sometimes the things we *want* are very different from the things we need, eh, Cadogan?"

God, how he'd love to kick the everlasting life out of the pompous, self-assured fuck.

"*I* have something you want." There came a slight, and obvious pause. "That is, I should say, I have *someone* you want."

The duke stared unmistakably at the telltale scar marring his face.

Cadogan went still. Surely Argyll hadn't discovered the identity of the one who'd ended his career. His own searches into that question had all come up empty.

"Not at all curious?" the imperious gentleman lifted a brow. "Very well."

Argyll sauntered out from behind his desk.

"What would you say," he enticed, "if I told you I can offer you not only the name of the one behind that mark on your face, but also tell you *exactly* where you can find him."

There it was; Argyll had called checkmate, after all, and it was a match Cadogan found himself all too happy, nay, eager to lose.

For the duke possessed the one thing—no, the one *person*—Cadogan not only wanted but needed.

Hate singed his veins. The man who'd stolen his career and confined Cadogan to the unfulfilling future of settling frivolous conflicts of pompous lords deserved to pay.

Now, he would.

"Can you provide me that information, Your Grace?" he asked evenly.

"I can and I will." Argyll flashed a white grin. "That is, if you do me the favor of guarding the eldest of my sisters."

The thrilling promise of revenge fed his blackened soul.

Cadogan turned a slow, cold smile of his own. "It appears you *do* have something I want, after all."

First, however, there were details to sort out.

"I'm not committing an endless amount of my time ensuring your sister's well-being," he said, laying out the terms.

"My sister is well-behaved, innocent, and beautiful. She also happens to be the Diamond of the Season, and not simply because she is my sister." Argyll grinned. "Though that certainly improves her stock with some. She'll be wed before you know it. I need *you* until she's betrothed."

In other words, until the lady was some other gentleman's problem.

With that emotional detachedness, maybe Cadogan had more in common with the duke than he'd previously credited.

"I want an *exact* timeframe."

"Based upon how sought after she is? A fortnight."

By the speed with which the lady's brother delivered that answer, he'd not only already put thought into it, but was exceedingly confident in Lady Raina's prospects.

"Two weeks, then, Your Grace. And the *fortune* you spoke of?"

"Ten thousand pounds."

"You and I have very different opinions on what constitutes a fortune," Cadogan said drolly. "Either your club is not as prosperous as you let on, Your Grace, or you don't value your sister's life and virtue as much as you let on."

The Duke of Argyll's left brow twitched. "Twenty thousand pounds. The first half to be paid now, in full. The second installment you'll receive the day of Lady Raina's wedding. I want you accompanying her wherever she goes."

In short: Cadogan could anticipate shopping outings. Fittings. Walks in the park.

God help him. *That* is what he'd be doing for the next week. He was almost ready to slit his own throat just *thinking* about tedious assignment he'd agreed to take on.

"Your Grace?" Cadogan sharpened his eyes on the other man's unreadable face. "If I discover you've lied about the information, you'll be sharing with me when the fortnight is up, that'll be the last thing you ever do. Am I clear?"

The duke lifted his head in acknowledgment. "I don't lie."

Again, Argyll sent a brow up. "Is there anything else?"

"I want to meet the lady."

"Yes," Argyll said. "We will schedule a time for you to—"

"Now."

That way, Cadogan could determine for himself just how obedient and predictable his charge would be.

CHAPTER 2

This evening, I fell in love. I saw him from across the ballroom and I knew. Our gazes met and the room, the people, the entire earth stood still.
~AA

RESTLESS, LADY RAINA GOODHEART, DAUGHTER of the late Duke of Argyll and sister of Gregory Goodheart, 9th Duke of Argyll took another look out her bedroom window.

A bewigged, crimson-clad servant remained at the head of the enormous black mount whose rider had arrived nearly an hour ago.

Daughters of dukes enjoyed all manner of luxuries.

Such *esteemed* ladies were bequeathed ancestral jewels and bestowed sizeable doweries. Every door in the kingdom—including that of the King and Queen of England, themselves—remained open. Their presence sought by all the leading hostesses. Their hand in marriage desired by all the most eligible bachelors.

The one *luxury* her station could *not* provide was any true, meaningful friendships. At best, they had acquaintances or people seeking to curry favor with their family

Regardless, ducal daughters and ducal sisters had no one whom they could really trust. Which likely accounted for why she'd been impatiently—and sadly—awaiting the ducal summons.

It'd been more than an hour. Where was he?

Perhaps her younger sister Millie hadn't heard correctly. Or maybe—

"I'm not wrong."

"You could be," Raina pointed out, her gaze still on the streets below.

"I never am," Millie, all too happily reminded her.

No, she wasn't. She caught her lower lip between her teeth. "You're certain you heard—"

"Mr. DuMond told Gregory that they'd both be wise to take even greater caution with you and Lady Violet because Craven intended to ruin Lady Violet's reputation," the little girl said, with all the exasperation of a weary governess being asked to repeat herself for the hundredth time. "And I'm not sure how you go about ruining a lady. It is not like we're a sheet of parchment or embroidery frame."

Millie gave a confused little shrug of her shoulders and resumed her work.

To some men they were. Someday, she'd explain to Millie all about their parents' relationship. She deserved to know, but Raina would preserve her sister's innocence as long as she could.

For nearly the dozenth time, she tugged back the airy linen and lace curtain, and peered out at the gated front drive.

"If I didn't know better," Sarcasm dripped from Millie's voice, "I would say you are actually looking forward to one of Gregory's goons watching after you."

Glancing back, Raina waited until her sister looked up, and then smiled.

Millie's blue eyes went big. "Are you *mad*?"

"The opposite."

"Sane?"

Raina frowned. "Elated."

"Well, I wasn't asking if you were upset, I was asking if you were off your head, Raina." Millie tossed her sketchpad down. The disregard she showed that coveted book indicating the level of the little girl's disbelief. "Here I am, put out with a lax governess and you want your freedom restricted."

Raina bristled. "I do not want my freedom *restricted*." She paused for emphasis. "Just the opposite."

"I'm only a child, Raina," her sister said dryly. "But it would seem in my opinion, *wanting* independence and being happy about having a *bodyguard* assigned to you don't really seem to go together."

Raina folded her arms. "They could."

"In what world?" Millie's question contained a genuine inquisitiveness.

Raina hesitated a moment. "Turn around."

Millie frowned.

"*Millie.*"

When her sister grudgingly complied, Raina hurried to the right corner of her room. Raina, not taking her eyes from Millie, got onto her knees, and reached under her painted armoire for the loose floorboard underneath.

An exasperated Millie released a long sigh. "Can I turn around?"

"Not yet." Swiftly bypassing the diaries she'd taken and hidden after their mother's passing; Raina fetched the leather folio inside the secret panel she'd personally created years earlier.

"All right," she said, when she'd gotten to her feet and met Millie back at the side of her bed.

With great care for the aged papers inside, Raina gingerly slipped the one out to share with her sister.

Showing a like regard for the yellowing sheets, Millie set aside her pencil, and read.

"Lady Diana Verney," Raina murmured after several moments. "She, too, was a duke's daughter and she found herself assigned a bodyguard by her brother, Mr. Black, who also happened to own a gaming hell." Or he had when Raina's parents were alive and attending those dens of sin.

Eager to finally be able to share her plans with, Raina hurried to explain. "Lady Diana's bodyguard also happened to be Mr. Black's brother and despite that, and despite her father's title, Mr. Marksman's loyalty belonged to Lady Diana."

Looking up from the page, Millie eyed her dubiously. "They were in love."

"Yes, but that is beside the point."

Her sister gave a dizzying shake of her head. "No. That is exactly the point. And you are missing a key difference, Raina… Mr. Marksman was not hired to do a job. He watched Lady Diana because she was his partner's sister."

"When did you become so cynical?" Raina muttered.

"I'm not cynical." Millie smiled widely. "I am clever."

"Yes, you are." Raina affectionately tousled the top of her sister's blonde girls.

"Very well, now that we've ascertained your hopes for Mr. Gaoler—"

"May we call him something different?"

"We can." Millie nodded. "The moment he proves he's a 'Marksman' and not one of Gregory's goons."

Dropping onto the mattress, she brought herself up onto her elbows. "I intend to…do things."

Millie's curiosity became fascinated intrigue; she flipped over onto her stomach, bringing her and Raina face to face. "*Things*, you say?"

This time, Raina carefully weighed her words. Given Raina had no friends, no confidantes, and no *older* sisters, there wasn't really anyone whom to truly confide in. Millie was the closest she had but given her tender years, Raina couldn't share completely with her young sister.

Millie flicked her on the forehead. "Raina?"

"Ow!" Raina scowled.

"*What things?*" Millie pressured.

"I should have said places; Places to visit." Ones written about in her mother's diary. Establishments the late duchess had patronized and enjoyed attending.

Wide-eyed, Millie urged Raina to share more. "Do tell?"

"I can only say they are places Gregory would never permit me to go," she confided on a whisper.

"Like Forbidden Pleasures?"

She gasped. "Millie!"

Her sister wrinkled her brow. "What? Is it really much of a leap to believe you'd be curious to see his club and what actually happens there?" Millie answered in Raina's stead. "*I* am and someday I intend—"

"*Millie!*"

"I don't understand you, Raina. If you aren't curious then why are you even going."

Unless she went, she'd never know the truth...

Are you sure you even want to know...

"It is in our blood, Raina. We were cursed...to be sinners. Or blessed to be sinners..."

Forcibly thrusting away her mother's long-ago profession from her mind, Raina moved closer to your sister. "I'm not going to Gregory's club," she whispered.

"Yes, that might not be the wisest place to visit." Her sister reluctantly conceded. "It would be extremely difficult to get in without someone recognizing you." The little girl chewed at her lower lip.

Suddenly, Millie's eyes lit; she sat up more straightly. "You'd be wiser visiting Craven's place."

Oh, hell.

"I hear his hell is even more wick—"

"Can we stop focusing on where I'm going," Raina quietly begged. "It's better for you knowing as little as possible, in the event Gregory grows suspicious."

Her sister snorted. "*Gregory* would have to be paying attention to either of us to be suspicious about you or me. In fact, that's the reason he's hiring someone to watch you in the first place, because he doesn't want to be bothered with you."

"From the mouths of babes," Raina muttered under her breath. The days of Gregory being the best friend, older brother always about had ended long ago, and where his defection would never not sting, knowing Millie had never before witnessed that side of him would never not hurt.

"All right, how does Mr. Gaoler configure into your plans?"

She went on to explain.

When she finished, a dubious Millie stared back. "So as to clarify: You have a list of places you wish to go. You intend to share this list with your *guard* and ask him to accompany you."

Raina nodded.

"I trust you intend to share with Mr. Gaoler this evening." Her sister stretched out a hand. "May I see this list?"

"A-Absolutely not," Raina sputtered.

"I won't even look at it." She gave a little waggle of her fingers.

"Then, why would you need—"

"Just give it over, Raina." Millie gave her a hard, determined look.

Rolling over, Raina fished the folded sheet from within the clever pocket sewn along the side of her dress.

The moment it appeared, Millie wordlessly rescued the sheet from Raina.

In one fluid motion, Millie hopped up, headed for the hearth.

Just as Raina realized what her sister intended, the girl tossed it into the flames.

"Millie!" Raina jumped to her feet and rushed to join Millie. The fire had already blackened the edges and curled the pages. In an instant, the page she planned—or had planned—to give Mr. *Gaol*—whatever the guard's name was, went up in smoke.

With a grunt, a pleased Millie wiped her palms back and forth.

Raina stared incredulously at her smiling sister. "Why would you do that?"

Instantly, Millie's expression grew serious. "I love you, Raina," she said, concern glittering in her revealing eyes. "But your plan? To ask the bodyguard, our brother, Gregory, *the duke*, hand-selected for you to escort you to places Gregory won't allow you to go…"

"I don't have any other options, Millie." Not wanting to see the pity in her sister's eyes, she glanced away. "The servants would never do anything to displease him, nor could I even ask them to." Frustration built in her chest. "It is not as though I have…" Raina's skin went hot. She stopped herself before completing that humiliating admission.

A small hand touched hers.

Raina looked at her and Millie's joined fingers and then shifted her gaze to her young sister's.

Somber, Millie peered at Raina. "Friends to help?" she ventured tentatively.

She made herself smile. "Well, with the exception of you, of course, Millie." Raina lightly squeezed the small hand in hers.

"I am not offended. I know you love me. I have Paddy." Paddy being Lord Rutherford's young brother-in-law, near in age to Millie, who'd become her best friend. "You don't have a Paddy, though. I understand."

Rap-Rap-Rap.

They both looked to the door.

Raina's heart jumped.

From the moment she'd caught sight of a formidable, dark, stoic stranger being admitted to Horace House, she'd been prepared for Gregory's summons. Even having been secretly aware of her brother, the Duke of Argyll's plans to sic a bodyguard on her, didn't diminish the eager anticipation when the knock finally *did* come.

A slight tug on Raina's hand brought her back to the present.

"Do not tell him too much until you know you can trust him and even then, still don't trust him." The girl fired off those advisements like a seasoned military commander. "And when you do, test him. Do not give him—"

Rap-Rap-Rap.

"Lady Raina?" Raina's maid, Lucy, called from the other side of the panel.

"For St. Peter's sake," Millie cried out. "Will you please wait a moment?"

That silenced young Lucy.

Millie lowered her voice. "When you do test him," she repeated, in hushed tones, "do not share with him one of the actual locations you intend to go. Pick some other slightly scandalous, but not outrageously scandalous place like the ones on your list."

Another blush heated her cheeks. "I didn't say they were scandalous."

"You didn't have to."

Rap-Rap-Rap

This time, both young ladies ignored Lucy's more incessant knocking.

"If he allows you the freedom to explore and accompanies you for protection, then you'll know, Raina."

Rap-Rap-Rap

"But I don't have much hope in one of Gregory's minions," Millie tacked on. "As such, my advice for you?"

Raina stared, waiting for her wise-beyond-her-years sister.

"Make him fall in love with you."

With a sound of annoyance, Raina jumped up.

"What?" Millie protested. "That's the only way—"

"Enter," Raina called over her sister's argument.

Raina's lady's maid entered. She cast a deservedly wary glance between the sisters.

From the corner of her eye, Raina caught a glimpse of the mischievous grin on Millie's lips.

With a devilishly naughty grin for the maid, Millie sent both eyebrows lifting twice. Anyone who lived in the Goodheart residence with Millie—no, anyone, familiar with Millie—*also* knew that look meant trouble.

Raina nudged her elbow lightly into Millie's side. "Behave."

"What?" Millie grumbled.

The maid dropped a curtsy. "His Grace has requested you join him in his office, Lady Raina. He's asked that you dress in your—"

"In my *finest*?" Raina spread her arms indicting the white silk organza dress, adorned with pale green, yellow, pink, and blue silk flowers, she'd selected. "I trust this will suffice?"

Lucy's gaze lingered on the light wrinkles from when Raina had lain down earlier. The pretty servant cleared her throat. "Aye, my lady."

Skipping over to the windows, Millie nimbly twirled the Italian lace curtains about her little frame and rapidly twirled herself free. "Always in your finest," she said, with a dramatic arch of her back.

A pained-looking Lucy wrung her hands together. "Lady Raina, His Grace is waiting."

"We mustn't leave the duke waiting, Raina," Millie chided, giving a wag of her finger.

Taking mercy on her poor maid, Raina ended she and her sister's fun. "Good night, Millie."

"Sending me away." Millie sighed. Pausing to collect her things from Raina's bed, she filled her arms. "I see how it is. I shall go, for now."

After Raina's sister left, Lucy cleared her throat. "His Grace *also* requested you don your tiara, my lady."

She frowned. "My tiara?" The twenty-four karat gold rose-gold crown dripping with gemstones Gregory insisted she wear to the most important *ton* functions and meetings?

Why would he have me wear it for this meeting?

"I'm afraid I cannot say, my lady," Lucy demurred, confirming Raina had spoken her question aloud.

With a forced smile, Raina took up a seat at the gilded, bronze-mounted Louis XVI Sevres-style dressing table. All the while, her maid tended to an arrangement befitting a duke's sister, Raina stared distractedly at her reflection.

Everything about Raina's brother, every part of his existence revolved around appearances. For one of London's most powerful, most sought-after bachelors, his entire existence had to shine— and that included Raina.

Maybe this is what it had been like for her mother. Just like the late duke had expected the duchess to garner the world's notice, so, too, did Gregory put Raina on display for all society to see.

Nor was Raina naïve. It wasn't just about appearances. Millie had been correct when she'd said Gregory neither wanted nor needed sisters about. Between their brother's single-minded obsession with his gaming hell and the current feud he had going with his former business partner, the Duke of Craven, Raina and Millie were nothing but an albatross about his neck.

Millie could be left to governesses—for now. Raina, on the other hand, needed to be squired about London.

"My lady?" Lucy's tentative voice cut across her musings.

"Hmm?"

"Your hair, my lady. Is it... acceptable, my lady?" Lucy ventured.

Raina followed the girl's gaze to the looking glass. Time and time again from servants and members of society alike, Raina heard just how much she'd come to resemble the late duchess. The portraits on display in various halls throughout the household confirmed daughter and late mother's shared likeness.

A burning started in her throat.

She wrenched her gaze away.

Lucy made a nervous clearing sound with her throat. "I can redo it, my lady," she offered. "Maybe something a touch more elaborate?"

The young woman was already reaching for the gilded crown she'd placed upon Raina's head.

"No, Lucy." Raina offered a smile for the young woman's

benefit. "It is lovely. His Grace will be *most* pleased with your efforts."

After all, the duke's approval mattered most to all.

"The duke will be waiting," Raina murmured.

Lucy's deep-set eyes flared. "Yes, my lady. Of course, I did not mean to take so—"

"It is fine," Raina spoke the same way she did when soothing her younger sister.

Desperate to escape yet another reminder she was viewed as more an extension of her brother than her own person, Raina quit her chambers.

She made her way below stairs. When she reached the ducal office, Raina took a moment to arrange her features into a smooth, serene mask—the proper, regal lady persona, she adopted for the world. Then, with a steadying breath, she let herself in.

"*Hello*, Greg—" Her cheer-filled greeting cut out, as her gaze slid away from her brother to the imposing figure standing just to his right.

Raina's heart sped up.

She didn't know what she'd been expecting of the guard who'd been assigned her. But she'd not been expecting *him*

Breathing became an onerous chore.

Dressed in the black finely cut garments of a gentleman but scarred like a fighter who'd grown up on the streets, the dark-haired stranger was a compelling figure.

With her hedonistic parents, libertine brother, and the long line of debauched Goodheart's before them, Raina prided herself on being in full control of her senses and sensibilities. Except, she realized now, she'd never faced a true test of her temperance until this dark stranger.

In fairness, the warrior who stood before her, however, was unlike anyone she'd ever set eyes upon.

An enigma.

A sorcerer.

A dark devil.

Between his bronzed skin and the vicious scar bisecting his noble brow and cheek, the guard put Raina in mind of a savage ruler of old; the kind of warrior whose only thought and goal was cutting down his enemies and drinking those lesser men's blood.

Possessed of a hawkish nose and heavy jawline, the gentleman wouldn't be considered handsome by conventional or even *unconventional* standards.

A fluttering sensation started in her belly; the one she'd never experienced before now—before this man. The same tingling her late mother had written about in her diaries.

Her brother's voice cut across her musings. "Raina?"

Heart pounding, Raina pulled her attention from the compelling stranger.

Raina cleared her throat. "My apologies. I did not realize you had company," she lied. "I will return—"

"No. No." Her brother motioned her over. "Please, join us. Allow me to present, Mr. Cadogan," he said when she reached them. "Mr. Cadogan. My sister, Lady Raina Goodheart."

Mr. Cadogan bowed at the waist. "My lady."

Three years earlier, back when Gregory had time for them, he'd escorted Raina and Millie to the opening of The Rotunda Museum in Scarborough. Raina had wandered about, taking in all the various stones—until she'd caught sight of a large piece of cobalt. That deep blue-grey mineral had shone with a metallic gleam that'd mesmerized. She'd never before gazed upon such a magnificent shade of blue—until this moment.

Gregory cleared his throat. "Raina?"

Dazed, Raina forcibly pulled her attention away from Mr. Cadogan. "Hmm?"

Her brother stared concernedly at her.

Oh, hell. *Introductions.*

"Forgive me." She sank into a belated curtsy for the nighttime visitor. "How do you do, Mr. Cadogan?"

He inclined his head.

Up close, the guard her brother had chosen for her somehow managed to radiate an even greater aura of menace and mystery.

"You are likely wondering why I've requested an audience."

"I confess to some curiosity," she murmured, the lie slipping out easily.

She knew why. She'd known long before this late-night

summons. Her brother could never imagine a world where when he was off all hours of the night, she had free reign of the entire household—his office included.

Gregory clasped his hands behind him and rocked forward on his heels. "As you are aware recent developments at my business resulted in...tension with the Duke of Craven."

While he revealed details she already knew, Raina made a show of paying close attention.

His mouth formed a grim line. "DuMond and I learned Craven intended to ruin DuMond's sister-in-law, Lady Violet."

In pretend shock, Raina touched a hand to her mouth in pretend shock. "Surely not."

Gregory gave a brusque nod. "I am afraid so. Craven is not the same gentleman you, or I, or DuMond, once knew." Then, he went on to furnish additional details—all of which Raina, also already possessed.

Feeling a prickling sensation on her skin, Raina stiffened.

She made the mistake of glancing at Mr. Cadogan.

The square-built guard regarded her; his unswerving gaze incisive; the kind that could see through a person, and extract their deepest secrets and—

"As such, I've made the decision to assign you to Mr. Cadogan's protection," Gregory finished.

This is where she needed to tread carefully. He'd expect her to meet his announcement with indignation.

First: the protestations.

"Protection, Gregory?" She pressed a hand to her heart. "*Surely* that isn't necessary."

"Where Craven is concerned," her brother said, regretfully, "I'd rather be cautious than taken by surprise."

Momentarily forgetting her objections were merely for show, she frowned. "You don't *truly* believe *Edward* would harm me, Gregory?" The two men may be rivals now, but they'd been best friends since practically the nursery.

All the while she and Gregory spoke, the guard's piercing gaze moved between them. It was all Raina could do to keep from squirming under his unflinching scrutiny.

"Edward wouldn't have," he said. His expression grew grim.

"As the Duke of Craven, now?" He shook his head. "I no longer recognize the man he's become."

"I'll have a moment alone with Lady Raina, Your Grace."

Raina whipped her gaze back to the one who'd remained quiet—until now.

Gregory stiffened.

With the title of duke, no one offered him anything less than fawning respect. Raina had never believed she'd see the day someone went ordering *him* about.

"A private meeting is hardly necessary, Cadogan." Her brother in a clear attempt to reassert control of the exchange motioned to the seats situated near the hearth. "We three can speak."

"I wasn't *asking*, Your Grace," he said, the ghost of a smile on his lips.

Her brother frowned. "I am not leaving you to speak with my sister alone, Cadogan."

"On the contrary. Isn't that exactly what you are proposing to do, Your Grace?" the guard drawled. "Unless you are planning to guard me while I guard her."

She found herself spellbound at the way he commanded power—and she envied him more than a bit.

Mr. Cadogan clasped his hands behind him. "I'm laying out the terms here."

"We already did," her brother gritted out between tightly clenched teeth.

"If you're trusting me to on this assignment," the formidable bodyguard continued over her brother's outburst, "you're going to trust me to conduct my business the way I do."

As the Duke of Argyll, everyone was beholden to Gregory, and he knew it, too. From, the men who courted Raina. To the servants who tended her. To the modistes who dressed her. Everyone answered to Gregory.

Here, though, stood an implacable Mr. Cadogan, the only person who'd not bowed to the duke's demands; who'd instead gone toe-to-toe. Perhaps she was a rotted sister for a complete lack of sibling loyalty, but in this moment, she found herself reveling in Mr. Cadogan's power over the duke.

The hope Raina carried for her relationship with the guard

assigned to her flourished bright and vibrant. That was, if Gregory's ridiculous male pride didn't get the best of him first and he sent Mr. Cadogan on his way.

Fearing just that, Raina touched her brother's sleeve. "Gregory," she murmured. "It is fine."

A muscle ticked at the corner of her brother's eye. "I'll be right outside this door, Raina."

She nodded.

Gregory leveled a warning look on Mr. Cadogan. As if her brother, a duke, let alone the king himself would be any kind of match against the lethal, dominant guard.

Raina trembled—and not, with fear.

Fear, she suspected would be far less dangerous a response to Mr. Cadogan than whatever *this sensation* he stirred inside her.

CHAPTER 3

I have never known anyone like the Duke of Argyll. He's clever, witty, and he manages to make me feel like I'm the only lady in an entire room. He consumes my waking and sleeping thoughts.
~ AA

IT HAD TAKEN CADOGAN LESS than a handful minutes to know one important fact about Lady Raina Goodheart: the chit was going to be trouble.

If he let her.

Not because, with the lady's enormous breasts and trim waist that flared to generously curved hips, the ice-blonde beauty had a body made for bedding. No, if Cadogan *were* the type of man ruled by his cock, Lady Raina would have been his empress. For him, however, lust was nothing more than a physical need—no different than eating and drinking—to be slaked.

No, it'd been that less than impressive performance she'd put on for the duke, and more about the ease with which Argyll *believed* her, and the effortless way in which she'd steered the gentleman out of his own office.

"That was quite a show, my lady," he drawled.

Lady Raina cocked her head, and that slight tip sent her glittering tiara sliding. "Mr. Cadogan?"

He kept his voice quiet when he spoke. "His Grace's announcement didn't come as any kind of surprise to you."

Her generous mouth moved several times before any words

came out. "I'm afraid, I don't know what you're talking about, Mr. Cadogan."

He sent an eyebrow shooting up. "Don't you?"

"I do *not*." Lady Raina managed to somehow stiffen her already painfully looking straight spine.

"Hmm. I see."

A fiery sparkle lit the lady's eyes, and in an impressive display of strength, she held his gaze. He'd give her a three count. A lady with her spirit wouldn't be able to resist his challenge.

One-two—

"What exactly is it you think you see, Mr. Cadogan?"

He opened his mouth to reply, but she proved all too happy to answer for him.

"That I somehow *knew* about being assigned a bodyguard before *this* meeting."

She absolutely had. "No?"

The lady shook her head so hard; her tiara came tumbling forward. She caught the sparkling piece and set it down haphazardly upon the side table near to her.

Cadogan fought a sudden and unexpected urge to laugh. He'd always loved—and still did—the thrill of complex assignments. For him, beautiful liars were the easiest—and most *pleasurable*—to read. Shockingly—or, maybe the better choice, *appallingly*—Cadogan found himself enjoying Lady Raina's especially inferior acting.

Alas, like all other bad liars, his *charge* couldn't sit with silence.

"How *could* I have known, Mr. Cadogan?"

Oh, because the duke was lax and underestimated her.

Only when it appeared she'd truly finished did Cadogan address the artless miss.

"Are you finished, my lady?"

"Yes." Lady Raina gave another uneven nod. "Yes, I believe I am."

She darted the delicate tip of her tongue out and traced the seam of her crimson cupid's bow lips. In any other woman, that glide of pink flesh over her moist mouth would have been a deliberate gesture and a bold invitation. From this one? There wasn't a worthwhile bit of artifice in her virginal body.

Strangely, his cock stirred anyway.

"When I noted His Grace's announcement didn't come as a surprise," he said evenly, "I didn't refer to my hire but rather to the conflict between His Grace and the Duke of Craven."

Lady Raina blinked slowly; the languid up-and-down glide of her lengthy blonde lashes accentuated the biggest eyes he'd ever seen; a dozen shades of blues and greens, like the sky and sea had struggled for supremacy and ultimately came together as one.

"Oh," she said weakly. "Indeed?"

Indeed. Those enormous eyes could be as big a problem for a man as the lady's lush mouth.

He nodded.

A warning bell chimed in his mind. He'd said something here, done something, that'd lowered the lady's defenses and led her to reveal this softer, more vulnerable side of her. Though that goal practically defined his career, in this particular case, this assignment, watching over this lady, represented a potential problem.

As always, his patience and silence were awarded.

"Very well." Lady Raina stole a quick peek at the heavy oak panel that stood between them and the duke. She lowered her voice to a ridiculously loud whisper. "I *may* have known His Grace intended to bring someone into the household to serve as my bodyguard."

"*May* have?"

His mischievous charge nodded. "I *did* know," she mouthed.

"You don't say." Only a lifetime of service to the Crown allowed him to deliver that with a straight face.

She couldn't have appeared prouder at her profession had she earned a spot in the Queen's court.

His ears pricked up at a noticeable note he detected.

"And you don't believe you're in need of protection, my lady?"

Lady Raina shook her head. "I believe, given my brother's business, he sees threats all around."

There *were* threats all around.

In just five minutes alone with Lady Raina, Cadogan: one, understood just why the innocent chit needed looking after and two, why Argyll wanted to pass that onerous task on to another.

With her naivete, the only thing which had kept her from peril, thus far, were the fortunate circumstances of her birth. Otherwise, she'd have been raped, dead, or worse long before now.

She dampened her lips again, and this time, it took everything he could to keep from staring at that seductive sweep of her tongue and imagining all manner of uses he had for that innocent mouth.

"May I confide in you?" she asked in that lyrical way of hers.

The lady didn't wait for an answer. "My brother expected I would be annoyed at being saddled with a bodyguard."

"And you're not."

She shook her head. "Are you familiar with Lady Diana Verney or her husband, Mr. Marksman?"

The speed with which she changed topics, it was a wonder he didn't wrench a neck muscle. "Should I?"

"He is a bodyguard, too. Or he was."

"I'm not a bodyguard," he said flatly. "I'm *your* bodyguard."

Her face scrunched up. "Do those not mean the same thing?"

"They don't."

"I see." The slight uptilt at the end of her statement indicated she did not.

Nor did he expect her to, this sheltered woman who openly conversed with him like they were bosom friends.

As for Cadogan? In all his thirty-one years, he'd suffered neither friend nor family and was privileged to not find himself weakened by actually caring about anyone.

Lady Raina drifted closer. She stared so long, had Cadogan been another man, he'd have shifted under that unswerving focus. With the intensity in which she peered at Cadogan, the only thing she needed was a microscope.

"Tell me," she tentatively put forward.

He was being interviewed by the lady.

For what purpose? To what *end?*

"Yes," he gently encouraged her to finish her question.

"Do you believe it possible for us to possibly become friends, Mr. Cadogan?"

Of anything she might have asked, that'd certainly not been the question he'd expected.

What the hell reply did he give for that?

Friends.

My God, he'd not believed there to be a soul as unsullied and snowy white as this chit—until this very instant.

He'd have laughed—if the wholesome beauty's expectations for him—for them—hadn't been so alarming. For all the various sorts of women Cadogan had experience with, virgins were not included in those ranks.

His work hadn't required it. His commitment to bachelorhood dictated it.

Without careful navigation on Cadogan's part, what'd promised to be an agonizingly dull assignment, threatened to become a hornet's nest.

"Perhaps we might sit and talk, Lady Raina?" He motioned them over to the seating Argyll had indicated earlier.

The duke's sister went with a ladylike artlessness and claimed a spot on the sofa. Folding her hands primly on her lap, she smiled up at Cadogan with a candor he'd not even known before now people were capable of.

Each person was driven by their own wants. Everyone had motives; no persons were the same. Argyll: wanted his sister safe and didn't want to see to the chore himself. Given Lady Raina didn't fear for her safety meant some other reason accounted for her barely concealed anticipation at his being here.

Now, to find out *why*.

"It is important for me to understand your expectations for our arrangement," Cadogan said when he'd taken the chair nearest hers.

Lady Raina eyed him a moment. "And that matters, Mr. Cadogan?" she finally asked. "*My* expectations?"

"Absolutely."

Those sea-green pools of her irises softened. "Why?"

Most people wouldn't have put much thought into the lady's inquiry. For Cadogan, every word a person uttered revealed something deeper into what they thought. How they felt. What they cared about.

As such, he took care before answering. "Given your question, I take it you're not accustomed to people asking your opinion?"

"*Given* my brother's standing, Mr. Cadogan," she said softly, "do you truly believe anyone in my circle *asks*, let alone, *cares*?"

"No," he answered sincerely.

Cadogan wasn't any different. He had a job to do, and when he finished, he'd get the information he sought.

Cadogan gentled his voice. "I expect you find that frustrating." He said the right things, because he knew the right things to say.

She snorted. "Infuriating, frustrating." Lady Raina waved her long, graceful, fingers. "You may take your pick."

"What if we agree to settle on both?"

Lady Raina's laugh, the sultry, husky sound of her mirth, filled the office, and the air and hit Cadogan with an uncomfortable stab of lust.

Bloody hell. The sooner he disabused the lady of her aspirations for their relationship, the better they'd both be.

Her expression turned solemn once more. "We're very similar, Mr. Cadogan."

They were about as similar as a doe and a dragon.

"Are we?" he said non-committal.

"You don't think so," she noted, proving accurate at least one assertion.

Her eyes twinkled like a thousand stars; the gold flecks within those pools, mesmerized.

She put a different question to Cadogan. "Whom do you answer to, Mr. Cadogan?"

Cursing himself for being distracted by nothing more than a pair of pretty eyes, he gave his head an indecipherable shake and focused on his back and forth with the lady.

"I don't answer to any man," he answered truthfully. There'd been a time he'd served the king, but no more. "Only to myself."

A smile, both sad and somehow still beautiful, formed on her lips. "But that isn't really true, is it?"

He frowned. Had she been an adversarial viper, he'd have believed she intentionally sought to nettle him.

"Granted, you certainly enjoy far more freedoms than I do," she allowed. "But you answer to my brother."

The pitch of her voice changed ever so slightly enough that

whether she knew it or not, had transformed her words into a question.

"I already told you," he repeated evenly, "I don't answer to anyone except myself."

She peered even more intently at him.

Lady Raina was looking for something—what exactly that was, remained to be seen.

"What about your clients," she persisted. "If you are in any way successful, which given the duke hired you, you are likely the best, you must also find yourself many times, answering to people whom you'd be all too happy to send to the Devil but find yourself having to hold your tongue instead."

Bemused, he stared at Argyll's sister.

"That's what you are asking?" he asked gently. "Or is it what you are wondering? Whether I'll do whatever my client says?"

Which he would—as long as the directives pertained to the assignment and didn't break his two rules: no rape. No murdering children.

"Lady Raina, are you questioning whether my loyalty is to you or your brother?"

Shock sent the lady's eyebrows up. But, wearing a pleased smile, Lady Raina nodded.

"And that is why you ask about the possibility of our becoming friends?"

The duke's sister seemed to hear his deliberate detachedness. She went quiet and stayed quiet.

"It…appears, Lady Raina, you aren't exactly understanding what His Grace hired me to do."

"I believe we've already gone over this, Mr. Cadogan."

Oh, without a doubt, the lady *thought* she knew.

"If anyone who shouldn't go near you, does, and puts you in any harm, my lady, I'm to kill them," he said bluntly. "That's what I'll do." That's what he did, and he did so as naturally as other men took meals, drank, and breathed.

The pretty color slipped from her high, pointed cheeks, leaving her vibrant, unblemished skin a sickly, ashen hue.

"This would be a good time for me to make several other things clear, my lady," he began. The sooner he disabused her or any fanciful imaginings she had for their time together the better they'd both be. "First, His Grace hired me for your protection. That is my assignment; to keep you safe. You are a job to me, and nothing more," he said, without inflection.

Had he not been studying her so closely, he would have missed the way she flinched, but he did see.

It does not matter. It does not...

Cadogan made himself plow ahead in the same straightforward way. "Also, to clarify, I am not your friend. We never will be. I'm not here as some confidante you can talk to about your hopes and dreams and wishes or gossip."

He'd not issued the statement to intentionally hurt but rather to lay out facts about their *relationship* as long as he resided here, so she didn't get herself hurt. But as pain filled her eyes, damn if he didn't feel like he'd kicked her kitten.

Cadogan gritted his teeth, bloody annoyed at himself for caring either way.

"This arrangement is nothing more than a business one, Lady Raina. I'll exist in the shadows, so much so you'll forget your brother assigned me to watch after you."

"If only I could be so lucky," she fumed under her breath.

He cupped a hand around his ear. "What was that?" He cocked a brow but continued. "As for the rules—"

Her gasp cut across his prepared speech. "Rules?" she sputtered. "*Rules?*" Her voice climbed several octaves.

"Yes, as in, *an accepted principle or instruction that states the way things are or should be done, and tells you what you are allowed or are not allowed to—*"

"I know what a rule is!" she shouted.

"—do," he finished.

If looks could kill, she could have hoisted Cadogan's lifeless body around for all his living enemies to spit upon.

But the fire in the innocent chit's eyes blazed to life once more, and that profound misery faded, and he preferred her this way. After all, he didn't *want* to destroy her spirit.

"I know what a rule is, Mr. Cadogan," she repeated, more calmly but still seething.

"One: I'll have your daily plans turned in for me the night

before. In them, you'll include the places you intend to visit, when you'll do so, the people you intend to see. *Everything.* The hours you'll sleep. When you get up. I want your every routine laid out, and I want no deviation from what you submit."

"And would you also have me include those details of when I have my menses?" she spat.

His brows shot up at her unexpected mettle. He swiftly masked his surprise and regained his footing.

"Two, you are not to go anywhere alone. Three, *I'm* to accompany you at all times."

A fiery anger blazed from her eyes. "Is there anything *else*, Mr. Cadogan?"

He inclined his head. "That is all. As long as you obey me, Raina, I trust we'll get on just fine."

With the regal bearing of a queen, the spirited beauty sailed to her feet.

Cadogan stood.

Holding his gaze, Lady Raina tipped her chin up. "People are not automatons, Mr. Cadogan. A living, human being cannot exist with an unbending schedule that doesn't allow for spontaneity. No one can live like that."

"My life is ordered exactly that way," he said. "And as long as I'm charged with your care, you will do the same. Are we clear?"

Her eyes glittered. "*Abundantly* so," she said

Lady Raina sank into a curtsy. Cadogan dropped a bow.

And with that, she sailed from the room.

Cadogan rolled his shoulders. In terms of his meeting with Lady Raina, it hadn't begun as he'd expected, but it'd certainly concluded as planned.

The parameters had been set.

Soon enough, he'd be done with this nothing assignment and on his way to killing the first—and last—person to triumph over him.

CHAPTER 4

*I never knew such splendor existed until my husband
claimed my body and made me his in name and body.
~The Duchess of A*

THE FOLLOWING MORNING, SEATED AT her violet and amaranth writing desk, Raina glared at the same empty ivory sheet of paper she'd been glaring at for the past thirty minutes.

If the Great Bard believed sleep to be Nature's soft nurse, then Severin Cadogan was that same soft nurse's assassin.

Last night, Mr. Cadogan pretended he genuinely cared about Raina's opinion on his being personally assigned to her. He'd made it seem like he wanted to allow her a voice in outlining her expectations for their time together. All the while, he'd been attempting to cozen out anything that would interfere with *his* and *the duke's* intentions for her.

Just as it had done while sleep eluded her, she and Mr. Cadogan's interaction continued to repeat in her mind.

She'd been so thrown off balance by his challenging Gregory, and then sending him out, so he could speak with Raina *alone...*

"*...Perhaps we might sit and talk, Lady Raina...*"

In a world where men and women weren't permitted those liberties, there'd been an added layer of intimacy to both his demand and their audience.

"*...It is important for me to understand your expectations for our arrangement...*"

Then, he'd spoken about her expectations for 'his and Raina's arrangement'. Not: his arrangement with the Duke of Argyll.

No one cared what Raina thought. For a sliver of a moment, she'd been seduced by the illusion that this stranger capable of ordering a duke around *did* see her as a person with whom to speak as an equal.

How utterly mortifyingly naïve she'd been. Why, he must take Raina for the world's greatest ninny and that she should care either way what Mr. Smooth-Smiling-When-He-Wanted-To-Be Cadogan, surely made her one.

A white-hot anger held her firm in its grip, and Raina embraced that rage.

Anger was good. That way, she didn't give in to thinking about how utterly humiliated she'd left that meeting with Mr. Cadogan.

Like a child. No, he'd treated her *worse* than a child. Forget the friend and confidante she'd hoped to have; he'd made it clear he didn't so much as view her as a person.

What was it he'd said? *"...You are a job to me, and nothing more..."*

Reflexively, her fingers curled tight around her pen.

Snap.

Ink went splattering all over the desk and exposed sheets of parchment.

Raina stared blankly at those blotches that dotted the page like black teardrops.

What do I care what a stranger thinks? I don't.

A swell of emotion formed in her throat, and Raina swallowed several times to clear that sensation.

She didn't give a jot that the person she'd be expected to spend her days with was yet another subservient to the duke. That'd always been the way and it would *always* be that way.

How then to account for this sharp twinge in her breast?

Raina gave her head a tight shake.

She'd already allowed him more time in her head than he deserved. He wanted a detailed accounting of her day and where she intended to go, and not a thing more. She'd give him exactly what he wanted—the job Gregory had promised him—and everything that went with it.

"I dare not forget you want my daily plans, and nothing more," she said tersely into the quiet. "What was it you said? Ah, yes."

"...I am not your friend. We never will be. I'm not here as some

confidante you can talk to about your hopes and dreams and wishes or gossip…"

This time, the echo of his blunt statement of facts brought her lips up in a tight smile.

Well, she'd give him precisely the assignment the Duke of Argyll assigned him—guarding a duke's unmarried sister.

Bringing her shoulders back, Raina fetched another pen out of her center desk drawer, along with clean sheets of paper.

She dipped the tip into the crystal inkpot. She tapped the excess ink gently against the edge, lightly tinkling the crystal.

Lady Raina's Plans

With the heading marked, Raina stared at her list for Mr. Cadogan.

"…Two, you are not to go anywhere alone. Three, I'm to accompany you at all times…"

With a hard smile, Raina began to write.

She poured herself into her task, including absolutely everything he'd requested—commanded—and more. She included such detail; filling up every single space to be had on the page and then setting it aside to dry, so she could go right on to the next.

"If you're thinking to burn a hole through those pages with the look you're giving them, might I suggest using the fireplace as I did last evening."

Gasping, Raina's hand slipped, and her pen went sliding off the top of the page.

She glanced to the entrance where her sister Millie who, with her sketchpad tucked under her left arm, had at some point let herself in.

"Millie," she greeted dumbly as the little girl kicked the door shut with the heel of her boot. "I didn't hear you."

"Mr. Gaoler, that bad, eh?"

"Worse," she mumbled as her sister hastened over.

"I'm listening." Millie slapped her sketchpad down on the desk, rattling the inkpot. "What is he like?"

What is he like?

Uninvited, another memory of her bodyguard slipped in—as he'd been when she'd first caught sight of him.

Darkly enigmatic. Provocative. Built and scarred like a warrior, and unlike the milksops of the *ton*, more handsome than any man had a right to be.

Provocative?

She buried a sound of disgust. More like provoking. How to describe crafty Mr. Cadogan who—if he wielded a weapon with the ease he did his charisma—was surely unsurpassed as far as guards went.

"He is rude," she finally supplied a child-suitable response.

Is he really rude or just brutally honest?

"Arrogant," Raina added.

Fine, she'd allow confident— and clearly for good reason.

"And..." She searched her mind.

"...As for the rules I expect you to follow..."

"And overbearing!" she exclaimed.

That, he absolutely was. No ifs, ands, or buts about it.

"And cold-hearted!"

Why, because he flatly rejected her offer of potential friendship?

"I didn't even say 'be friends'," Raina muttered, to herself. "I said, 'possibly be friends'."

A low, drawn-out groan cut across her fuming and reminded her of Millie's presence. "Oh, saints in heaven, Raina. When I said 'do not tell him too much until you know you can trust him', you took that to mean mention *friendship?*"

"I know. I was..." Enthralled. Entranced. Bewitched. *Brainless.* "*Not thinking.*"

Close enough.

"It does not bring me any comfort saying I was..." The girl's blonde eyebrows came together. "*What is this?*"

"*...the people you intend to see. Everything. The hours you'll sleep. When you get up. I want your every routine laid out, and I want no deviation from what you submit...*"

Raina set her mouth in a grim line.

"Mr. Cadogan demanded I provide him with a daily schedule, detailing my plans for the day."

Before Raina knew what she intended, her sister picked up the still-damp page.

The girl's eyes bulged. "*Raina*? Egad, what are you *th-thinking*? Surely, you've not allowed them to do—" With her little fingers, stained from playing in the gardens, she shook the page. "*This* to you."

"Would you have a care." Ever so gingerly, Raina slipped her notes for Mr. Cadogan from her horrified sister's fingers. "I know what I'm doing, Millie."

She went on to fetch her silver pounce pot. While her sister sputtered, Raina sprinkled powder upon the still-damp ink.

"Are you certain, Raina, because filling out that *sheet* for your gaoler and…and those places you…"

Millie finally caught the playful glimmer in Raina's eyes and her worrying trailed off. The girl's lips curled in a slow, puckish grin that dimpled her full cheeks. "Brava, big sister."

"I haven't done anything, *yet*."

"Yes, well, if you *do*, well, there may be hope for you yet."

Popping up, Raina dropped a kiss on the top of Millie's head. "I need to try and reach Gregory so that I might ask him a few questions."

Questions about Mr. Cadogan. One needed to know one's opponent, after all.

Millie snatched up the sketchpad she'd arrived with. "I want to help. There has to be something I can do," she protested, following close at Raina's heels.

"I don't…" Raina's steps slowed.

"*…I'll exist in the shadows, so much so you'll forget your brother assigned me to watch after you…*"

She frowned.

She'd made one misstep where Mr. Cadogan was concerned, once. She'd not make another.

"There is something you can do…"

A short while later, Raina sailed into the breakfast room, just in time to catch Gregory as he was about to quit the table.

"Dear brother," she greeted, with a smile, enjoying herself even more this day.

Surprise filled her brother's classic features. "You are awake."

"Disappointed?"

When he didn't reply quickly enough, Raina playfully waggled her eyebrows.

Gregory slapped a hand against his chest in mock affrontery. "How could you *ever* believe I'd ever be disappointed by your company?"

Oh, only because he'd rather hand her over to a rude stranger than squire her about London. "How, indeed?" she drawled

As Raina made her way to the buffet, she couldn't help the wave of poignancy.

Older and bigger than her, he'd loomed larger than life. He'd always entered every room with a wide smile and told jokes that left Raina, her sister, and their parents in stitches. When had he ceased trying?

Making herself a plate, Raina, from the corner of her eye, caught Gregory just as he pushed his chair back.

"And yet," she drawled, adding two pieces of toast to her plate, "for someone who is not disappointed to see your beloved sister, you certainly appear to be in quite the hurry to leave."

This time, a very real frown flashed across his countenance. Did his displeasure stem from his having been so transparent or because she'd prevented him from leaving a second time? Most likely, both.

His grin returned in an instant. "In a hurry to leave one of my favorite sisters? *Never!*" he scoffed.

With a snort, Raina helped herself to a scoop of eggs.

Dish in hand, she made her way over to the vacant chair on the right side of the head one which her brother stood behind. She placed her dish on the table and sat.

"You're still standing, devoted brother," she said dryly, giving her linen a light snap, Raina rested the white fabric upon her lap.

Like a troublesome lad who'd earned himself a knuckle rapping, Gregory plopped back down into his previously vacated seat. He motioned for a refill on his cup of coffee.

After the servant had gone, Gregory contemplated Raina over

the steaming cup. "Forgive me, Raina. I understand I've not been as attentive as I should be. I've been preoccupied."

She gave him a look.

"More preoccupied than usual," he grudgingly conceded. "These times, however, are not ordinary ones."

Raina nibbled at the corner of her toast. "Are there new problems with Craven?" she asked after he'd taken a sip of his coffee.

Such hate blazed from Gregory's eyes; Raina shivered.

What did it say about her own brother's ruthlessness that he could so easily sever a lifelong bond?

"You needn't worry your head about it, Raina," he promised.

That condescending way in which he spoke to her, like she was a babe to be protected, set her teeth on edge. After all, Raina wasn't the one feuding with a good friend like two boys quarreling over spillikins.

"That wasn't an answer, Gregory."

He must have mistaken her terse response for worry.

"I promise you will be safe, Raina," Gregory added. "Especially with Mr. Cadogan to care for you."

With her napkin, she dusted at the corners of her mouth. "About Mr. Cadogan," she said, having adroitly shifted them to the real reason for catching him before he disappeared.

Gregory took another sip of coffee. "Yes?"

"He is not one of your usual guards." That much was clear. "Where exactly did he come from?"

Her brother's relaxed demeanor vanished. "Has he—?"

"Oh, do stop," she scoffed. "He's been here but a day or so and I've barely seen him."

But you were captivated when you first caught sight of him, the devil in her head taunted with that indecent reminder.

Raina's face went hot, and that same heat scorching her cheeks fanned her entire body.

Gregory pinned a calculating gaze on Raina. "Why all the questions about Mr. Cadogan?"

Oh, hell. Her brother was too perceptive by half. Perhaps it was actually for the best he wasn't underfoot.

"If our roles were reversed, and I assigned some stranger to follow *you*, would you not have questions about the man?" At that, one she now shared a roof with.

A frown played at his lips. "I..."

God, give me the strength, ego, and boldness of a man, accustomed to power.

"I trust you did not think about that, dearest brother," she ventured all false innocence.

Gregory set aside his drink. "Fine. I'll tell you all you need to know about the gentleman."

"You will?" she batted her lashes. *He'd* decide what she needed—or didn't need—to know about Mr. Severin Cadogan. "How very *good* of you, Gregory." The high-handed way in which everyone treated her, would never not grate.

"Do I detect sarcasm?"

"Likely only because you'd rather avoid talking to me about anything..." *Important.* "else." Something her brother said earlier, registered. "You referred to Mr. Cadogan as a *gentleman?*"

"Cadogan is the son of a late marquess and Cadogan's eldest brother is the *current* Lord Carnell."

"How...absolutely..." Her heart dropped. "Reassuring." Horrible.

A gentleman who'd been born into the *ton*. No *wonder* he'd been so horrified at her mention of friendship.

"You are correct, Raina," her brother said somberly. "I've been remiss. I should have alleviated your worries long before this. As a genteel young lady, you deserved to know. He's known as *Mr. Severin Cadogan* but comes from quality."

From quality? He thought *Raina* cared about Mr. Cadogan's station?

Severin. Raina rolled that name around in her mind. Austere. Stern. *Severe.* It suited him perfectly.

"Certainly, knowing Mr. Cadogan comes from a noble family would have greatly eased my *fears* at having him, a *stranger*, residing under the same roof and accompanying me about," she remarked.

Unlike before, her brother completely failed at picking up Raina's sardonicism.

Her brother shook his head. "Cadogan was recognized for acts of service and bravery to the Crown. For his efforts, he was made the Earl of Killburn. The gentleman, however, does not go by his title."

Despising one's origins was an all too familiar state for Raina. As such, she found herself developing a kindred—but unwanted—connection with the enigmatic lord.

"What kind of acts of bravery?" she asked, all too happy to chip away at the aura of danger and mystery behind Mr. Cadogan.

"He did intelligence work for the Home Office."

Her stomach plummeted. "Intelligence work?"

Gregory nodded.

Bloody fabulous. A spy. Not only had Gregory hired a gentleman—a nobleman—to guard her, he'd stuck her with a blasted *spy*.

She fought the urge to groan.

Unbidden, Mr. Cadogan's visage whispered to the front of her mind; the opaque set to his angular features. The ragged scar that bisected his face. The incisiveness of his stare. The smooth, gentle way in which he spoke. That emotionless way in which he spoke.

It all made sense.

And here, had it not been for her ten-year-old sister, she'd have handed him over a list of the haunts she intended to visit.

All the pieces slowly began sliding into place.

Such a cold-blooded figure should terrify, rather than intrigue, and yet, the fact remained, something in him…roused her curiosity.

Curiosity.

That was all it was.

That was all it could be.

What else would it be?

Nothing.

"Is that all?"

Raina whipped her gaze over to her forgotten brother so quick she viciously wrenched her neck muscles. "Hmm?"

"About Cadogan?" Gregory said. "Are there any other concerns or questions you may have so that I can alleviate you of some of your worrying."

"No." She flashed a smile. "No. I believe that is all, at this time." At least by way of her brother's usefulness. "You've provided me with everything I needed to know."

Absolutely everything.

Raina smiled.

CHAPTER 5

How can I ever be enough for a man of
his appetites and desires?
~ The Duchess of A

AFTER A SINGLE DAY IN the Duke of Argyll's employ, Cadogan had been to hell and back again and then repeated the same godforsaken trip.

All thanks to Lady Raina Goodheart—the *ton's* Diamond, darling, and ducal daughter in every way.

A walk in Hyde Park. A visit to Lady Jersey. Tea with Lady Cowper. A visit to Lady Sefton. A visit to the milliner. A visit to the modiste. A visit to a *different* milliner. And now…

"A Dialogue Between Clara Neville and Louisa Mills!" Lady Raina turned her latest selection around for her audience of two. "Well? What say you?"

He'd say after sitting through Lady Raina's reading of yet another selection—having been all but forcibly persuaded by the youngest Goodheart girl to join them in the drawing room hours earlier—the day appeared nowhere close to a bloody end.

Cadogan wasn't a drinking man, but if he were, this bloody day merited the entire bottle of Argyll's prized cognac.

"Oh, please do!" Lady Millie, the other Goodheart sister, seated near Cadogan's feet, appeared to be of a different opinion entirely. "Read that one, *please.*"

In fairness, it was easy for the girl to condemn them both to the latest miserable reading material Lady Raina selected, she'd spent the better part of the evening, seated next to Cadogan, *sketching*.

Her unflaggingly energized charge turned on Cadogan the same serene smile she'd worn all day. "Your turn, Mr. Cadogan. What say you to the selection?"

"Stimulating, as all your other selections, Lady Raina," he murmured.

He couldn't say what he truly wanted to say about her latest choice of literature. What he'd begun to think, however, for the first time since he'd taken a blade to his face, was that revenge might not be worth *this* special hell.

Her smile brightened, and she made to open her latest book.

Cadogan consulted his timepiece. "The hour is, however, advancing, Lady Raina."

"Ah, but, it is fortunate then, is it not, that one is never too tired for a book?" She inclined her head and the lone curl, artfully placed at her right shoulder, bounced.

And damned if he didn't find his gaze drawn to the crevice between those generous cream swells where that pale curl finally came to lay.

"Isn't that right, Mr. Cadogan?" she asked softly.

Perched six feet away on the stark white armchair across from him, he caught the glimmer in her expressive eyes, and damned if he didn't find himself battling the better place to stare—those siren's irises, or her ample breasts.

Lady Raina's smile slipped. "Is everything all right, Mr. Cadogan?" Concern filled her query.

Bloody hell, I need a woman. It'd been too long if he was lusting after a virgin with a taste for bad books.

He found himself saved by Lady Millie's yawn.

"Though I do concur about your opinion on literature," he put forward smoothly, "I believe the hour grows late for Lady Millie."

"Not at all!" Millie cried. "Please, Raina. *Please*, read."

Young sister batted nearly identical eyes at older sister.

Cadogan didn't stand a bloody chance against that.

Lady Raina beamed like the Diamond she'd been christened. "If you both insist."

He hadn't. That detail didn't appear to hold any water, as Lady Raina snapped her book open and began to read. *"A Dialogue Between Clara Neville and Louisa Mills. Clara Neville..."* The young beauty cleared her throat. *"I am happy, Miss Mills, in having an opportunity afforded me, to have an hour's conversation with you..."*

What'd begun as a lesson in restraint when she'd first opened her mouth to read, and her husky, throaty contralto filled the room, had since become a lesson on an entirely different form of restraint.

While Lady Raina droned on and on, he used it as a further opportunity to study his unlikely assignment.

This delicate lady who spent her days shopping, paying visits, and reading pious works, fit precisely with everything the papers had written about her being a model of ladylike perfection. It also gave credence to the duke's confidence that the girl would be married off any day now.

He grimaced. God, help the poor man.

But then, with her naiveté—all her hopeful talks yesterday of their striking an accord—

And there was also the matter of her glorious form.

His gaze, unbidden, locked on her ample breasts. God, they were made for a man's mouth, hands, and cock. The things he'd do to them. They were also the manner of debauched things some staid, proper, lord would never think of doing to the lady.

What a shame.

That you won't be the one to bury yourself ballocks deep inside her? Or that some other undeserving chap will?

Cadogan frowned. What the hell?

Mad, the inanity of this day had turned his mind to rot. There was no else accounting for his lusting after a bloody ingenu.

From over the top of her book, Lady Raina's eyes briefly found his. "Do you disapprove, Mr. Cadogan? You wear quite the scowl."

Oh, he disapproved of his body's response, all right.

Cadogan held her surprisingly, and impressively direct, gaze. "You just gave me something to think about while you were reading, Lady Raina," he said simply.

An experienced woman would have pinkened at the suggestive quality of his murmurings and tone.

His impeccable charge gave a pleased little nod.

She resumed her reading; effectively dousing his ardor. *"A virtuous man will be contented anywhere; and he who is not virtuous has no right to expect the great blessing of contentment let him be where ever he may…"*

Someone tugged his coat sleeve. "Look at my latest drawing."

Ah, that's right. The assault on both sides.

Cadogan glanced at the other Goodheart sister.

Lady Millie turned around yet another picture for his consideration.

"This is my rendering of Paddy."

This one sketched with the same passion her sister read tedious literature.

"Another exceptional piece, Lady Millie," he said.

"Paddy is—"

"The Marquess of Guilford's adopted son who is near your age, though the actual date of his birth is a mystery as there are no records on his birth or birthparents," he recited those details with the ease he'd once shared reports with his superior: no nonsense. Simply facts. In doing so, one needn't get pulled into discussion or reveal anything more than one ought. Such had been a guiding principle taught him at the Home Office.

Alas, the powers that be within the agency hadn't met Lady Raina's ten-year-old garrulous sister would have given a magpie a run for its proverbial money.

"What I was *going* to say," the girl impressively managed to rebuke both with her gaze and tone, "is that Paddy is visiting the Royal Armories and I've been invited to join him."

Lady Raina paused in her recitation to give them a disapproving look.

Both he and Lady Millie inclined their heads in apology. When the impeccant beauty returned her attention to her torturous selection, the youngest Goodheart retrained her scowl on Cadogan.

"Forgive me," he murmured. "It was rude of me to interrupt before, Lady Millie. Do you have an interest in weapons?"

"You might say, more of an interest in using them, Mr.

Cadogan," she whispered, and lifted her pencil toward her throat in a slight, slow stabbing motion.

He blinked slowly. Had he just been threatened by...a child?

The fire's glow played with the light in the girl's eyes, giving them a menacing glimmer.

He blinked.

The candles flickered, and illuminated Lady Millie's bright, innocent, expression as she now used her pencil to scratch at her lace collar. "Would you care to join us when we go?"

He glanced over to where Lady Raina still read.

Oh, all Satan's sinners, let her be married by then. "If I am still here then, I would be honored."

"In a private family what discord and confusion reign, where there is no proper governor, or director, one who has the command of..." Lady Raina's droning cut off as she yawned loudly.

Apparently, she'd begun to bore herself, too.

She opened her mouth to pick up once more.

Cadogan surged to his feet. "Lady Raina, this has been most stimulating."

Lord, help me.

Never having had a reason to believe in God, he'd never been the praying sort, but after this day, with Cadogan's next request, He'd make an exception.

"I trust given the," vapid, "*full* day you've enjoyed, and the equally full day you have scheduled tomorrow, it might be wise if we both retire?"

For a moment he thought she'd protest; for an even longer one, he feared she would.

Then, another yawn she swiftly buried behind her fingers, spared him. "Perhaps you are correct, Mr. Cadogan. It was a fun day, was it not?"

He'd let any number of lies fall from his lips, over the years; the following proved the hardest to make believable. "Most stimulating, Lady Raina."

There came a choking sound from the sofa behind him. When he looked over his shoulder, however, Lady Millie remained a study of concentration in her sketch.

The lady stood and sank into a deep, graceful curtsy. "Good evening, Mr. Cadogan. Millie."

Millie who'd stayed buried in her latest artwork, lifted her hand. "Night, Ray."

As Ray sailed by, Cadogan bowed. He watched her go.

Ray.

That moniker, though, suited to an effervescent diamond didn't extend beyond the lady's handsome looks.

Cadogan turned to extend a goodnight to the last remaining Goodheart sister who still needed to retire. Then he'd be free. One night done. Thirteen more to go.

If he survived.

Cadogan cleared his throat. "I trust it has also been a long day for you, as well."

Lady Raina's sister bestowed a giant smile on him. "Oh, no. I do not go to bed early, like Raina." She patted the place on the sofa beside her. "Sit. When I finish drawing Paddy, I'm going to sketch you, Mr. Cadogan."

Fuck.

As he found himself remarkably without a choice, Cadogan followed the ten-year-old Napoleon's orders.

Perhaps, this, his being made to shadow a colorless, naive miss about Town during the day and play nursemaid to her insomniac replica at night, was his personal hell for all the lives he'd taken.

CHAPTER 6

The Fight Society. I search for accurate words to describe such a bloodthirsty arena. There the men, naked from the waist up, they battle like savages.
~The Duchess of A

As Raina's hired hackney bounced along the uneven cobblestones, she contemplated the Mayfair Streets giving way to the western boundary of St. Giles Parish.

The windowpane reflected back Raina's softly smiling visage. Why, it wasn't *every* day a young lady outmaneuvered a veteran agent with the Home Office.

Had Raina managed to do so?

Yes.

Had it been easy?

No. It had been ridiculously simple, and enjoyable—for Raina, anyway.

Well, with the exception of herself having to suffer through the tediousness she'd put the both of them through today. Trips to the modistes, milliners, and leading societal patronesses? The world's worst, dullest, reading materials.

She pulled a face.

No, Mr. Cadogan hadn't been the only to one suffer for her efforts.

And yet…

Raina nibbled at her lower lip.

She didn't want to think about how easily he'd conversed with Millie; how patient he'd been with her young sister. He could have very easily rejected the girl's request to join them in the Drawing Room. Instead, he'd allowed Millie to persuade him to not only do so but to sit beside her, and consider all her drawings.

Raina shut her eyes.

Given her own brother's apathy for his own female relations—and any respectable woman—Raina discovered a dangerous weakness for gentlemen who didn't merely indulge young ladies, but instead, who actually listened to them.

That was the manner of man she yearned to have in her life.

Raina's eyes went flying open.

Are you mad? Woolgathering over Mr. Cadogan because he'd entertained your younger sister? She made a moue with her lips.

It is his job.

You are his job and nothing more, pointed out that same voice of reason which had pulled her out of her fantastical musings.

She'd not feel guilty or give the man some kind of credit for being in anyway decent. As she'd learned during his interview, Mr. Cadogan, bodyguard extraordinaire, smooth-talking spy, put up a façade with the ease of once renowned actor, Mr. Edmund Kean.

Proud and driven, Mr. Cadogan would be a whole lot less magnanimous were he to discover he'd been duped.

That pebble of unease in her belly grew.

Fortunate for Mr. Cadogan he need never worry about discovering how badly he'd been hoodwinked.

Because if he did ever find out…?

A small, promontory shiver traipsed along her spine.

Do you truly believe a man of Mr. Cadogan's caliber and resolve won't? the devil in her head delighted in pointing out.

Raina let the curtain go, and the faded ivory fabric danced back into place.

It was too late, she'd allowed a crack; thoughts of Mr. Cadogan finding out he'd been duped, and the floodgates opened.

Her protector, with his granite-hard jaw, nearly obsidian-blue eyes, and forbidding stare fixed on Raina. They'd glint with the promise of punishment.

Thump-thump-thump

Raina gasped. Her heart pounded painfully against her ribcage.

"Arrived we 'ave, sir."

They'd arrived.

At some point, she'd reached her destination, somewhere between Shaftesbury Avenue and Oxford Street.

She'd been so focused on the thrill of her triumph and then the niggling of worries about sneaking out from under Mr. Cadogan's watch, that she'd not thought about just where she'd ordered the hackney driver to take her.

Raina took a deep breath. "A moment," she called, deepening her voice.

Maybe she'd deliberately focused all her energies and musings on thwarting stern, stoic, Mr. Cadogan, to keep herself from thinking about where she was going.

But now she was here, and there could be no pretending or letting herself think about anything other than *this*.

By the din outside the carriage walls, for all intents and purposes, Raina may as well have arrived midday for the fashionable shopping that took place near this side of the Dials. The loud exchanges and boisterous laughter of passersby combined with calls of women and men hawking whatever goods they were selling.

With fingers that shook, Raina reached into the jacket she'd pilfered from one of the stable hands and found the sheet she'd tucked away there.

She stared blankly at the page for a moment, worrying the already wrinkled corners with her fingers. If she didn't step outside this carriage, if she ordered the driver to turn back, and never stepped foot outside, then she'd never know.

She'd never know if her mother had been right and that Raina was the same as all the other Goodheart's before her, and the ones that would come after her.

With a quiet curse, she unfolded the new list she'd made to replace the one Millie burned.

The Fight Society

When all respectable noblemen in Polite Society notoriously fought at Gentleman's Jackson's, of course, her late father and brother would frequent a ribald, lawless, boxing arena, where women were granted access.

Raina edged the curtain back enough to steal a peek outside. With the streets dark, and dimly lit by the lampposts, she needed to peer closely for the place in question.

Her mother's diary contained entries throughout about her attendance at *The Fight Society*. Those dates had ranged widely from the late duchess's first mention Raina could find, being the third of March in 1800. In her writings, the duchess also indicated the duke frequented the boxing arena many years before their courtship.

As such, it was entirely possible such a crude *enterprise* ceased operation years a—

Her gaze caught on a building some fifteen or so yards away.

Maynard & Bragger's Fight Society

Raina sneered.

"Society," she whispered, into the quiet.

Maybe that harkening to the institution—as names and titles mattered most to the ton—alleviated all the deserved shame and guilt these lords and ladies felt over spending their nights at such a barbaric place.

Thump-Thump-Thump

"Time is money, sir," her driver called out impatiently.

Raina warred with herself.

"I said, 'time is money.'"

She glanced once more at her list.

"I've got other pass—"

Not permitting herself to coward out, Raina opened the door.

The driver gave a startled look.

"Here," she tossed him a small purse. "You'll find the agreed-upon fare, and I've doubled it for the time you've lost. Wait for me, and there will be far more than that." She nodded at the velvet sack his eager fingers were already sifting through.

"Aye, sir."

Adjusting the big, brimmed hat she'd buried her curls under, Raina jumped down.

Keeping her head down, she made her way along the pavement, ignoring as she went, the crude invitations for 'him' to join the prostitutes along the street. A proper lady would have been shocked by the sights and sounds, and offerings being made.

A wave of bitterness constricted her throat. The innocence Raina *once* possessed as to what took place between men and women, and to the debauched extent they did, had been shattered when all good ladies were still playing with dolls and marbles and kites.

Raina reached the front doors of *Maynard & Bragger's Fight Society*.

Dubious, she contemplated the crude oak door, with its even cruder engraving of the title, flanked between two skulls.

On the other side of that panel, ceaseless, bloodthirsty cries rang out. On occasion, from within the cacophonous noise, emerged perfectly obscene and quite descriptive curses that raised a blush on her cheeks.

Who would want to come to such a place?

Your mother, who by her own written admissions, loved every minute of her time here…

Nauseous, Raina, shook her head hard.

Except if it'd been that easy to get rid of the repulsive secrets she carried about her parents, she would have succeeded years ago.

Very well, let us see what this establishment is about, and just why Mother spent so much time coming back to it.

Raina grabbed the handle and let herself inside.

A deafening roar rolled through the jam-packed arena like a wave and poured out into the streets.

A barrel-chested guard, well-dressed in surprisingly fine black garments blocked her entry. The hard gaze he moved over Raina proved as incisive as Mr. Cadogan's, and for a sliver of a moment, she froze in fear that he'd identified her as a young lady disguised as a man.

Greed, she'd learned, however, proved to be the great equalizer.

Raina snatched another purse from within her jacket and thrust the generous offering at the formidable impediment between her and the establishment she needed to visit.

"If you'd be so good as to show me to a private box," she shouted to make herself heard over the din.

"A private box?" he yelled. Surprise—and something akin to

amusement—lit the good-looking worker's hard brown eyes. "This way, my lord."

With an unexpected regard, he carefully escorted her through the arena.

People of all stations stood so close their arms touched, and one couldn't wedge one's body through, except when they cheered on the prized fighter they had their money on. As her
personal escort shoved men apart to make room for the two of them, she squinted to adjust her eyes to the thick haze of cheroot and cigar smoke that hung over the dimly lit arena.

Until, at last, the big fellow brought her to a stop at the curtained alcove in the furthest right corner of the arena. He pulled back the curtain and motioned her inside the crude, makeshift private box.

Raina eyed the space dubiously.

"Wait here," the worker said, pulling her attention his way. "And for your safety, don't leave."

At that stern order, she frowned. And here she'd believed gentlemen weren't treated in the same high-handed manner ladies were.

The curtain fluttered into her place, and the brusque worker took his leave, Raina looked around the box which, with the wood crates and mismatched chairs scattered about, had the look more of a storage area.

"We bring you our next match," a voice boomed over an impressive quiet that'd managed to fall over the stadium. "Born in St. Giles to Mac Diggory and…"

As the crowd erupted into another round of thunderous applause and cheers, Raina settled herself in. She'd taken her fate into her own hands and set out to find out answers—no matter how horrible they may be—about the type of woman she was.

It was time to find out.

CHAPTER 7

*I did not want to leave, and I cannot wait to return. I fear
this means I'm wicked.
~ The Duchess of A*

"...Fucking kill him..."

Ladylike horror and disgust were, of course, the very much deserved and appropriate response from Raina over the vulgar gladiatorial calls thundering through *Maynard and Bragger's Fight Society*.

"...break his throat..."

From the center of her makeshift box, Raina parted the crude curtains wide enough to catch another look at the latest fight, this one between Mr. Bragger and Mr. Maynard themselves.

Her viewing area set away from the grandstand, as it was, afforded her an unobstructed view of the two men, naked from the waist up, still locked in battle.

Thus far, it'd been the longest match of the night.

Under the immense candlelight filling the arena, their bare chests gleamed with sweat. With every punch thrown and every blow landed, each man's sleek, well-defined, muscles strained and bulged.

The pair had been fighting for the better part of what seemed like thirty minutes, and neither appeared to be flagging.

"...hit him in the ballocks..."

Even as the audience screamed their demands for that brutal assault, when Bragger slammed his knee hard between Maynard's legs, a collective groan rolled through the stadium.

Heart pounding, Raina released her grip on the curtain. As either side of the fabric fell into place, the material danced, leaving a slit between them and revealing flashes of the savage match still unfolding.

Raina closed her eyes.

Between the frenzied cries for violence coming from the arena and the primitive, hand-to-hand fight, it hadn't taken long for Raina to make her first discovery about herself.

Where the Fight Society was concerned, Raina's heart did race—but it was an outrageous thrill of excitement. Having stolen glimpses of three matches now, her attempts to will away that shameful eagerness had proven futile.

Instead, the crowd's wild shouts of encouragement for their favored boxer mocked her efforts; the ribald cries only deepened Raina's longing to view for herself the strong, sinewy, men fighting like warriors of old.

When it came to matters of boxing, there was nothing predictable about the sport. Two, equally matched, men entered onto a stage, and who emerged triumphant in the primitive battle changed every second of every match. One minute a fighter was one blow away from defeat, and the next, he'd felled his opponent with a lucky, unexpected shot.

The world Raina knew, on the other hand, was a predictable one. In it, ladies were sheltered and shielded from everything except dull, proper, activities like the ones Raina had spent doing with Mr. Cadogan.

Mr. Cadogan.

For the first time since she'd pulled back the curtains to reveal the mesmerizing fights on the other side, thoughts of her gaoler slipped in.

Between his muscle-bound form and ferocity, Mr. Cadogan fit in this primal world. A provocative image took root of Mr. Cadogan. Naked from the waist up. Emotionless and cold and powerfully built, she'd put money on his being able to take down all the fighters who stepped into the ring—even several of them at once.

Proud, hard, and unpredictable, he wasn't a man who'd accept defeat.

Once again, her pulse took on a quick, erratic, beat. This time, it wasn't excitement which drove the rhythm.

For this night, with her actions, she'd made herself a foe to Mr. Severin Cadogan—if he discovered what she'd done. Though the gentleman didn't know it, Raina had declared him an opponent to be outsmarted and outmaneuvered.

Her reasons for doing so would never matter to a man such as he.

"Stop it," she spoke quietly to herself. "You are here, and he is not." He was likely retired for the evening and remained none the wiser of her first outing. "There is nothing to fear."

Even uttering that reassurance didn't ease the ice that traipsed along her spine.

"Oh, I wouldn't be so certain of that, Princess." That quiet voice, loaded with mockery, sounded from somewhere behind Raina.

Her entire body recoiled in shock. At some point, like she'd conjured him of her thoughts, Mr. Cadogan had entered the box and availed himself of a chair. He now sat upon that gilded, high-backed, imperial seat, sat like he was the King of England, himself.

Nay, Raina's *protector* wore his power with a greater ease than William IV did his cloak and crown.

At her continued silence, Mr. Cadogan sent a dark brow arcing up.

Say something.

Raina's dry mouth made it difficult to get out a full response. "*You.*"

He smiled coolly. "*Me.*"

"Bloody *hell*," she whispered.

"No. I fear we're both still here on this Godforsaken earth," he drawled, with an amusement that threw her further off-balance. Ice glinted in his eyes. "Though, I'd very much like to send you to hell right now."

Yes, that confirmed it. No actual amusement there. Not that she'd expected there to be. Not after what she'd done.

Still, she feigned a laugh. "How *funny* you are, Mr. Cadogan." Her heart tripled its beat and knocked wildly against her ribcage.

"I don't make jests, my *lady*," he said flatly taking in her boyish clothing.

That she believed. She almost felt badly for this man incapable of mirth. Almost. The fact remained, he sought to bark orders and expected Raina to listen like some obedient dog.

You are not a coward. You are the daughter of a duke and now sister to one. You don't answer to anyone—certainly not this overbearing man.

Finding herself fortified by that reminder, Raina lifted her chin and looked him dead on. "Then, it would behoove me to inform you, Mr. Cadogan, that *gentleman* do not go about cursing so at ladies."

"Then we are an unlikely match, Princess," he said frostily. "As *ladies* don't visit fight clubs," He gave her a derisive once over. "At least not respectable ones."

Raina felt like she'd been slapped.

Her stomach muscles seized into painful knots. "You bastard," she whispered. "How—?"

"Dare I?" he finished for her.

Is he really wrong, though?

"And on what grounds are you calling my character into question, Lady Raina? Hmm? From our meeting yesterday, I've been nothing but straightforward with you."

He gave her another derisive up-and-down sweep. "*You*, on the other hand, fed me a pack of lies and dragged me all over London as some sort of childish game."

"It was not a game."

"No, because you're a grown woman. What, you didn't like that I rebuffed your calls for friendship, so you sought to punish me?"

"That isn't why." Maybe a little bit it had been. She just hadn't acknowledged as much until Mr. Cadogan called her out.

"I truly don't care what your reasons were," he said with more of his cool bluntness.

Her lower lip quivered, and she hated that telltale tremble.

"What I *do* care about," he continued, "is that you sneaked off and recklessly took off and would have likely been raped, killed, or worse, had one of my men not shadowed you."

Realization dawned. "The guard who escorted me to this box, he works for you."

Slowly, he unfurled nearly six feet of thick, raw strength. What her fearsome bodyguard lacked in Gregory's height, he more than made up for in muscle. On sleek, silent steps, he started over to Raina.

"This *box* is a storage area he hid you inside and guarded until I got here. Otherwise, I don't have a single doubt, Princess, you'd not be standing here before me now."

Her heart sped up. "Would it have mattered, Mr. Cadogan?" she ventured. "If something happened to me?"

Given he'd gone as gruff as the grizzly bear she'd observed at the Royal Menagerie years earlier, hope stirred that there was some tenderness within Mr. Cadogan, after all.

His next brusque response swiftly killed *that* delusion.

"If something happens to you, I don't get paid."

A vise gripped her heart.

In the end, that's all she meant to *any* man—what value she had. What she could bring them. And she hated that be it her brother or a near stranger, that both should so viciously sting.

Mr. Cadogan cut into her mournful pondering. "Who are you meeting?" He did a glance about.

"What?"

"According to the guard I had watching you, whoever the gent is, has yet to show."

A muscle at the corner of his left eye twitched…as if he were annoyed with some imagined sweetheart who'd abandoned her.

She had to tamp down a snort at that improbable thought.

"Why do you believe I'm meeting a suitor, Mr. Cadogan?"

"Lover," he crudely corrected.

Heat blazed across her cheeks. "Fine. Why do you believe I'm meeting *any* man?"

"Why *else* would you be here?" he asked, his brow as puzzled as his deep baritone.

Raina twisted her fingers in the jacket she'd borrowed. Before her courage left her, she spoke on a rush. "I came to watch a boxing match."

She immediately tensed and braced for more of his mockery.

They stared at one another.

Raina looked away first. "I trust you are going to drag me off," she said, not bothering to disguise her bitterness.

"And deprive you of the pleasure of witnessing the evening's entertainments? Hardly, Lady Raina."

His tone revealed nothing of what he was thinking.

She eyed him dubiously. "You're making…light."

"I've already told you, Princess, I'm not capable of joking."

"That I believe," Raina muttered under her breath.

Mr. Cadogan narrowed his eyes. "What was that?" The lethal look he leveled on her, knocked her briefly off-balance. "I believe the next match is beginning."

Raina lied. She had no idea *what* was unfolding on the other side of that crude wool curtain that stood between she, Mr. Cadogan, and the hundreds of spectators.

The hard grin he wore said he knew it, too.

In clear challenge, Mr. Cadogan dragged the chair he'd previously occupied over and set Raina up near the center where both curtain edges met. "Sit."

Raina made a show of staring straight ahead.

Strange how a ruthless fight club should be far safer than making eye contact with Mr. Cadogan.

Alas, he'd not let her have that.

"Here," he said. "Put this on."

Raina forced her gaze his way.

She shot her hands up just in time, catching the cap he'd flung her way.

"Your hat conceals next to nothing," he explained, while she examined the wide-brimmed, John Bull cap he'd provided. "Your disguise is shite, by the way."

"Thank you," she said, wryly.

"It wasn't a compliment."

In addition to not *making* jests, he couldn't detect droll humor, either. Raina added that detail to Mr. Cadogan's growing list of *attributes*.

"In fact," he remarked, "you look like a bawd dressing herself up for her male clients with a taste for—"

"Mr. Cadogan!" she exclaimed, slapping her hands to her burning cheeks. "If you'd *please*."

"Please clarify?" His hard features were a perfect expressionless mask. "Or, please stop?"

"The latter!" she exclaimed.

Outside the window, the crowd cheered.

"And I *assure* you," she continued when the spectators quieted enough that she needn't shout, "I am *well aware* yours was not a—"

She caught the distinctly devilish gleam in his hard eyes.

The look went as quickly as it'd sparked to life.

He grunted. "Put it on."

Oh, no. She'd not abandon this that easily—no matter how much he clearly wished it so.

"It appears you *do* have a sense of humor—"

"Put it on, Princess," he snapped.

"Very well." She'd pushed his rare show of agreeableness too far. Raina hurriedly switched out her hat for the one he'd given. "*There.* Anything to make you happy, Mr. Cadogan."

"If that were the case, I wouldn't have spent my day in hell and my night chasing after you."

She wrinkled her nose. "I was being sar—"

"I know," he said, dismissive once more.

The stoic guard headed to the front of the boxed room and drew the curtains wide enough to reveal the two fighters still in their respective corners, preparing for their match to begin.

"You've come to satisfy your craving for bloodshed, don't let me stop you, Lady Raina. So *sit*."

The incisive warning in his low baritone compelled Raina to scramble into the seat like some docile terrier.

He bowed. "Now, please, enjoy the blood sport to your heart's content."

Mr. Cadogan went and fetched himself a chair.

He returned and set the oak dining chair next to Raina's more extravagant seat.

She'd never been alone with *any* man. Now, she found herself in the Seven Dials, on the fringe of an arena of hundreds of drunk, screaming spectators, and with a sinister Mr. Severin whom, other than his previous work and familial connections, she knew nothing about.

Everything is scary in the dark.

And that truth extended to her irate guard.

Raina, however, was no longer a girl afraid of imagined monsters and mysterious, and dark shadows. Such was the reason she'd set out in search of answers about herself.

Mr. Cadogan seated himself.

He'd positioned himself so close, his knee touched hers; a fierce heat emanated from him. It penetrated the fabric of her trousers and for the way Raina's skin radiated there may as well have been no material barrier between her and Mr. Cadogan's flesh.

Oh, she'd seen any number of legs in the course of her life. Not a single, living, breathing male, not even the skilled fighters she'd witnessed firsthand this night, possessed the oak-hard, muscularly contoured limbs of Mr. Cadogan.

Raina closed her eyes and concentrated on breathing slowly and evenly. She fought—and failed—to reign in this shameful awareness of her primal bodyguard.

In the whole of her nineteen years, not once had any boy or man been so close she could feel *any* part of his body.

With the whispers she'd heard behind her mother's back from disapproving servants, Raina didn't so much as let herself think about touching any man, in any way.

And maybe she hadn't because, deep inside, Raina had known to do so would have revealed parts of herself and her morality, that she didn't want answers to. When she'd grown up and fully confronted her origins, out of fear of what it would reveal, she'd ran as far and as fast away from any real introspection.

"If you came to watch, opening your eyes would be a good place to begin, sweetheart," he drawled.

Her eyes flew open.

Damn him and damn him for the amusement he'd find at her expense.

And worse, damn her body for being so bloody aware of him, a man who saw her as a job; at that, one he immensely despised.

Desperately attempting to quash her illicit response to Mr. Cadogan and his nearness, she carefully edged her leg away from him. When she'd managed to do so, she inched over to the far corner of her spacious chair.

"Funny, that."

At Mr. Cadogan's deep, gravelly baritone, she looked at her unlikely *companion*.

By the way he intently studied the match, which during some point of her self-ruminations had begun, she thought for a moment she may have imagined his curt utterance.

"What is that, Mr. Cadogan?"

"It's just ironic, a fancy lady such as yourself, who's got a hunger for blood-sport should be repulsed brushing up against the man hired to protect her."

A hard grin, one that looked like it'd been even harder to achieve, graced his stern, smooth lips.

That's how he'd perceived her attempts?

"Well, it appears between that and your suddenly discovered sense of humor and ability to detect sarcasm, you've learned two new things this night, Mr. Cadogan," she said pertly and with all the regal haughtiness he believed she possessed.

He scowled.

Good, let him despise her for the denigrative image he'd painted of her in his mind. Better that than his discovering she sat here lusting after him.

"Are you wanting to wager, Princess?"

"What kind of wager, Mr. Cadogan?"

Her heart sped up as she thought of any forbidden number of challenges, he could put to her.

"The match, Princess. The one that was so important for you to see you risked life and limb to attend."

Oh.

"Er…yes?"

Mr. Cadogan stretched his right leg out. The tip of his boot sent the crude wool fabric into a slight flutter.

An instant later, the back flaps opened, and Raina looked at the familiar figure who'd earlier escorted her through the boxing hall.

"Who are you placing your wager on?" Mr. Cadogan quizzed her.

She slid her gaze to the opening and her stare landed on the pair of fighters, just as one of the bare and barrel-chested boxers sent his right fist flying into his opponent's cheek.

Blood and teeth sprayed from the man's mouth, but somehow, lankier and leaner by several stone, the fighter kept his feet and returned with an even more powerful blow.

Raina recoiled. With fists held close to their faces, the fighters circled one another, and each searched for their next opening.

"Are you wagering or not?" Mr. Cadogan's impatient question barely penetrated her engrossment.

"The tall, slender, fellow," she said, unable to glance away as the boxers exchanged another set of punches.

The fight dragged on. Both men, their bodies slicked with sweat and blood, appeared willing to die before they conceded.

The crowd's deafening cries created a hum in Raina's ears and added surrealism to the grisly scene at play in the arena.

Breathless, she angled her body in time to her fighter's sleek movements. Each hit he landed was like a victory of her own.

Suddenly, an infinitesimal shift occurred.

Then, a hungry grin formed on her fighter's bloodied mouth. He came at his opponent with all the fury and speed of a tempest, and with a like energy, Raina exploded to her feet.

"Go," she cried. "*Go*," she repeated over and over until her voice grew hoarse.

At last, the bigger, but lesser contender faltered.

Raina's fighter pounced; with a final, lethal-looking blow his adversary's collapsed onto his back.

Raina joined her excited scream to the ear-splitting shouts that flooded the arena.

She'd always felt trapped; both by her birthright and having been born a woman in a world controlled by men. In the thrill of this moment, however, a dizzying freeness left her buoyant. Here, she didn't belong to anyone or anything other than this untamed arena.

When the referee stepped forward, raised the man's swollen and bloody fist, and declared him the winner, Raina joined her hands together and shook them over her head.

CHAPTER 8

*I have done my duty by the Argyll line. I've provided my
dearest love, Wallace, his heir. A more beautiful
boy there never was.
~ The Duchess of A*

HE'D BEEN CORRECT IN HIS initial assessment of Lady Raina—she was going to be a problem. He'd just underestimated all the different *kinds* of trouble she'd be.

Women knew how to use their wiles on weak men. In Cadogan's case? His willpower had always proven greater than the greatest temptation.

Until now.

Now, with Lady Raina jumping up and down—and in her enthusiasm setting her big, poorly bound breasts bouncing—Cadogan was only just beginning to realize how much a threat she posed to *him*.

Lady Raina, thankfully, remained too heady from her win to notice either Cadogan or the enormous, and more enormously inconvenient, erection he'd sprung.

Between Raina's slim waist, wide hips, and supple arse, she would make a dead man cum. That lush body of hers made for sinning, in marked contrast to her big, innocent, blue eyes, and flushed cheeks was enough to have made a monk abandon his oath of celibacy.

As badly as he'd welcome the opportunity to claim her body and mark her as his, it wasn't her siren's figure that challenged Cadogan's willpower.

Still outraged and annoyed at being tricked by Lady Raina, now that he'd found the minx safe and had her under his watch once more, he found himself able to appreciate the bold, defiant, and clever way in which she'd outmaneuvered him.

And now, she not only watched a violent sport in action, she'd thrown herself into the revelries of London's most brutal fight club.

Simpering women were something Cadogan was all too accustomed to having dealings with. Those same coquettes who batted their eyelashes and turned away in revulsion at society outside their cultivated crystal palaces.

In contrast, Lady Raina made no attempt to minimize or conceal her enthusiasm or, for that matter, feelings. That much had been true when he'd interviewed her.

Oh, she'd put on quite the show during the day, but when she'd found herself confronted, she'd faced Cadogan and his displeasure head-on.

With her still engrossed in the action, Cadogan drank his fill of the sight of her. The lady's high, defined cheeks were flushed a rosy red and her full mouth—that lower lip slightly larger than her upper—trembled with feverish excitement.

With a squeal, Lady Raina brought her clasped hands to her chest, and sank backwards into the folds of her seat. "Did you see that?"

He certainly had.

"How magnificent!" she exclaimed happily, like they were the friends, she'd naively expected they'd become. "He was smaller and lighter, and it mattered not that he appeared in every way at a disadvantage. He won, Cadogan."

As she continued prattling, he flexed his jaw.

Her happy chatter snapped Cadogan out of his moment of insanity. With the words she spoke, she may as well have been talking about the two of them; it centered him on a detail he'd be wise to never forget—she'd proven herself a crafty opponent not to be trusted or underestimated.

The curtains parted and Cadogan spun to face Scar, who'd returned with the lady's winnings. As Cadogan took the money from him, Scar's gaze slipped an appreciative eye over to the still zealously jubilant beauty.

At some point, during her rejoicing, Lady Raina lost her hat. From within her previously tight plait, flyaway, ethereal white strands had become loose.

Cadogan knew precisely how the lady looked and how she looked to Scar.

His man passed an appreciative gaze over the lady's figure.

Something primal and raw and real reared to life inside Cadogan's chest; a sensation born only of the role he'd been hired to do Raina's protector.

As if feeling Cadogan's caustic stare, Scar bowed quick, and wisely took his leave.

Once gone Cadogan put his attention back on the vexatious hoyden. Raina, in her gaiety, still remained oblivious to the fact not only someone had come and gone, but a whole unspoken exchange occurred.

Rage filled him all over again at the danger she'd put herself in and the way she'd imperiled Cadogan's revenge.

"Do you have any idea…?"

The rebuke he intended to deliver withered on the vine from which it was born.

Lady Raina remained oblivious to his censure. Bouncing on her toes, she joined the crowd in, clapping and yelling the triumphant fighter's name.

Cadogan stared, transfixed.

Lady Raina chose that moment to recall his presence.

She spun about; her eyes sparkled like a thousand stars. "Did you see…?" Her joy-filled voice trailed off. That radiant light in her eyes went out.

"What is it?" she asked haltingly.

Madness on his part, was what it was.

Swallowing a curse, Cadogan stomped over, swiped her hat off the floor and set it atop her ethereal blonde hair.

"Let's get something straight, Princess. This will be the last time you defy me."

Spots of furious color entered her cheeks. "I did not defy you,

Mr. Cadogan," she raged. "Furthermore, you aren't my nursemaid or gover—"

"If you aren't a child, then start acting like it."

She gasped. "You…you…"

"Yes?" He stared at her jeeringly. "What do you have for me, Princess?"

If her cheeks turned any redder, the lady was going to go up in flames.

"Smug, pompous, condescending, stodgy, old-fashioned *man*," she exclaimed, those insults all rolling together as one great disparagement.

Old-fashioned? *Stodgy*? That'd been the first time in his miserable life *those* slights had been tossed his way.

He kept his features even and let Raina to her fury.

Raina shot back, jabbing a long, slender, finger against his chest. "From the moment we met, *you* set up terms. You expected my obedience and set demands like I'm a girl. I'd say doing precisely *what* I want and *when* I want, are the actions of a grown woman."

She took a breath.

But wasn't done.

"And if you think I'm going to allow you to bully me, you are certain to be disappointed, Mr. Cadogan."

God, with her pluck, Cadogan didn't know whether he wanted to kiss the lady mindless or turn her over his knee and spank the impertinence out of her.

Both prospects sent a bolt of lust through him.

He flashed a grim smile. "From this point forward, there'll be no escaping me. You can count on me being your shadow."

The long, graceful column of her throat moved rhythmically in a smooth glide. "Is that a threat?"

"No." It was about protecting her. "I don't go around making idle threats."

The air crackled.

Lady Raina darted her tongue out and as she trailed that delicate tip of flesh over her lush mouth, his gaze automatically followed those movements.

In his years of work, a large number of women attempted to break him of his secrets before he broke them of theirs. They'd been skilled, inventive, nubile beauties but he'd been a master of restraint.

Except, ironically, with that seductive glide of a virginal Lady Raina's tongue and imagining the endless uses he had for her mouth, all those taxing lessons and belief about his willpower were suddenly called into question.

"Here." Desire along with frustration at himself, made Cadogan's voice emerge gruff.

He stuffed the lady's winnings into her hand.

Raina dipped her gaze to those crumpled notes, but before she did, he caught more of that pious sadness creasing the corners of her eyes.

Good, she'd took his brusqueness for anger. Better that than were she to know the real truth—he wanted to fuck her senseless, here on the fringe of a bloodthirsty crowd.

Lust. That primal urge was the closest thing to emotion that Cadogan came.

His beautiful charge delicately folded her money and tucked it away inside the front of her snug-fitting jacket.

"Thank you," she murmured, and perched herself primly in her chair.

A duke's sister who expressed gratitude to her inferiors. This certainly marked a first among the nobility.

Cadogan remained standing. This intolerable awareness of his tempting charge required he have some physical distance from her.

He grunted. "Another wager, Princess?"

"I…" She tipped her neck back, at an awkward angle, that'd give her a hell of a crick. "Won't you sit, Mr. Cadogan?"

His shaft stirred, and at nothing more than Lady Raina's innocent, lilting invitation.

Evading her attempt to get him in that chair, Cadogan quirked his lips in a wry half-grin. "I'll stand."

Lady Raina ran her gaze over his face. "I see."

Cadogan waited.

"I'm well aware of how you view me," she said melancholily.

"Oh?" he asked, genuinely curious.

"You think me capricious, reckless."

Correct. Correct.

"Imperious," she added.

Also, correct, but not in the negative way her tone suggested.

The lady continued her enumeration. "Bothersome. Vexing."

Also, both accurate. In fairness, depending on a given moment, he varied between admiration and annoyance.

"And," Lady Raina's lower lip quivered, "you do not like me," she delivered that final one.

"Does that matter one way or another?" He didn't *dislike* her but let her think that.

The lady quickly averted her gaze, but not before he caught the glossy sheen in her eyes.

Over the years, countless women—and men—had employed that desperate *weapon*: Great, gasping sobs. Quiet weeping. Silently falling tears.

All efforts had proven futile. Cadogan couldn't be moved by small, salty drops of water.

He frowned. This woman, on the other hand, she carefully guarded her tears like they were the crown jewels.

Cadogan grunted. "I don't like anyone."

"That I believe," she said under her breath as he effectively killed her sadness and restored her spirit.

"I expect it matters very much to you whether you are revered."

"I don't need to be revered," she said tightly.

He ignored that. "Given you are the darling of the *ton*, I expect you become confused when receiving anything less than complete and total adoration, but not being the recipient of those sentiments, you've come to expect isn't necessarily the insults you take them for."

Her entire body jerked; her perfectly beautiful features spasmed.

Cadogan tacked on 'uncomfortable with blunt truths' to the lady's personality. Though, invariably women of all stations were.

"It appears I was right about your opinion, after all," she said, her voice barely a whisper. Her earlier joy at being here now faded, stared not at the latest match unfolding, but at her lap.

Strange, she appeared to *truly* care what he thought.

As soon as the fantastical possibility slipped in, Cadogan frowned. An ethereal beauty such as Lady Raina didn't give two shites what a man such as him thought about her very-near-royal self.

This beauty dripped artlessness and innocence but had already proven herself to be a most cunning schemer.

As he waged a silent battle with the randy fellow inside his trousers bewitched by the spirited chit, he forcibly reminded himself—once a duper, always a duper.

And he'd never underestimate a soul, a second time. Not even if the minx possessed the body of Aphrodite and the spirit of a Spartan warrioress.

CHAPTER 9

*The duke is a most devoted Papa. He is also eager to bed
me again…and oh, how I have missed being in his bed.
I can tell by the frenzied way he makes love to me
that he missed me, too…*
~ *The Duchess of A*

SEATED AT THE LONG, WOOD table in the Duke of Argyll's empty kitchens, Cadogan broke a cardinal rule.

He drank.

Aside from those assignments which required he sip some for-pretenses sake, Cadogan hadn't drank liquor since the year he'd started his work with the Home Office.

Funny, in the name of King and Country he'd slashed the throats of men while they'd been sound asleep—even sometimes having done so while those traitors slept beside a spouse or mistress who'd slumbered on through those murders.

He'd witnessed men who'd served with him, face cleverly gruesome ends at the hands of adversaries.

He'd dispensed of too many bodies to remember.

And in the end, it hadn't been those acts of barbarous violence which had driven him to drink, but rather, the lush, generous crimson lips of a woman who was brave one minute and trembling next.

His lips quirked in a grim smile.

All he knew was he wanted her.

Oh, he wasn't one of those fellows to get bogged down with

a sense of guilt or shame for lusting after a lady—sex was sex. A beautiful woman was a beautiful woman.

And there was no doubt, Argyll's pert-mouthed, saucy sister with her big, doe-like, innocent eyes, and whitish-golden blonde hair aptly bore her Norse goddess's name, of gold and beauty.

It was a shame her spirit would eventually be extinguished by whatever fancy lord her brother married her off to.

Either way, Cadogan neither cared nor would he be around to see the day.

On the Marriage Mart, she'd go quick and fast, and Cadogan? Cadogan would be free to get back to that which really fired his blood—*work* that didn't involve *governessing* an innocent miss with a spirited streak, but actual, mercenary business only a beast like Cadogan was capable of doing.

And not least of all, he'd have the identity of his assailant.

He raised his mug to take another swallow—and stopped. Though not a whisper of sound split the quiet, Cadogan sensed her presence before she even spoke.

Fuck.

"Are you hiding, Mr. Cadogan?" Lady Raina asked softly.

He dragged a hand discreetly over his face. God, she moved stealthily. Yet another attribute to add to the list of things that both infuriated and impressed him about the lady.

"If you are operating under some misguided hope, I don't see you," she said in an appallingly bad whisper, then I regret to inform you, hiding in plain sight in the middle of an empty kitchen is a most ineffective hiding spot."

Was the chit mad? Strike that question. He already knew the answer. "If you think I'd be so inept when it came to evading you, then you clearly haven't realized the manner of opponent you're—" Cadogan finally turned to look at her.

The lady's full lips twitched. "I was teasing."

"Teasing," he repeated dumbly. What the hell was that even?

Apparently misinterpreting that as an invitation to join him, Raina seated herself.

"*Teasing.* And, as I know you enjoy *helpful* definitions, it means to laugh at someone or make light of them in order to embarrass, annoy, or upset."

He stilled. Why, the gall of the chit tossing his previous elucidation at his face.

He thinned his eye into even narrower slits. "It appears—"

"As though, I've proven cleverer than you, again?" Lady Raina batted her endlessly long, golden lashes at him. The glimmer in her eyes devilishly impudent.

His mouth moved, but nothing came out.

The crafty minx, on the other hand, had words enough for the both of them. "Worry not, Mr. Cadogan." She patted him on the arm like he was a petulant child. "I'm merely teasing." She paused. "*Again.*"

Lady Raina folded her hands primly before her on the tabletop and smiled.

He snorted. "Do you truly take me as a man who'd hide from *you*?" Or, for that matter, *anybody*?

"I don't know, Mr. Cadogan," she mused. "You did pass the role of watching me to the handsome gentleman outside my door and are all the way down here in the kitchens. You, one, wish to avoid me. Or two…?"

Hardening his gaze, he dared her to finish that short list.

"*Two*," she said, taking up his unspoken challenge. "This day proved entirely too long and exhausting for you; as such you required the handsome guard outside my chambers take on your responsibilities."

His nostrils flared. "*Handsome gentleman?*" She'd call fucking Phillips *handsome.*

Lady Raina hesitated. "Uh, I…assume he's one of yours? He's not quite as tall as you. Loose, ash-blond curls," she said, gesturing to her own much blonder than ash head. "He's also very muscular."

Her very detailed description indicated Lady Raina had studied Cadogan's man *very* closely. Too closely.

Cadogan suppressed a growl.

"Not that I believe it is the latter as you don't strike me as one who suffers from a weak constitution," she hurried to assure him, completely—and thankfully—missing the reason for his inexplicable rage.

This was bloody enough.

"You think I'm avoiding you?" he asked on a steely whisper.

"I…do."

The corner of his right eye twitched.

The gall of this impudent wench.

What was worse? The blasted lady was as *clever* as she was spirited and daring.

She was the first to look away. Unlike all the times before when she'd boldly met his gaze, now Lady Raina studied her lap. "Do you believe I'm wild?"

Cadogan barely heard her whisper.

He leaned in. "*Wild?*"

She peeked up at him with luminous eyes. "Depraved?"

Her?

From under his lashes, Cadogan contemplated the woman before him, as much as her fear-filled question.

She'd asked if he thought her depraved.

This hesitant, guileless ducal sister didn't have a hint of wicked in her body. She was a veritable Eve before the apple. A caged tigress lived within her, and God, how hot it'd be when she set that side of her free. As a rule, he wanted the women he fucked to be experienced and as ruthless in bed as Cadogan was in his every day dealings.

Yet, for some reason the idea of having this particular *debutante* under him, and then burying his cock in her tight, virginal sheath, sent blood rushing to that randy organ.

The fact remained, only one of them possessed a corrupt soul, and it was decidedly not the artless miss stealing glances up at him.

"No," he finally said, his voice harsh and hoarse with desire.

A bitter-sounding laugh spilled from her lips. "A prevaricator you are not."

A prevaricator was all he *was*.

"And you're someone who cares about being proper?"

Unlike the blush of before, this time her cheeks flared with crimson color.

She'd taken offense at his blunt question. Not that he'd expected anything else. A regal princess like Raina Goodheart would only be outraged at someone thinking of her as anything less than a lady.

"Are you always this loathsome?" she whispered.

Confusion wreathed her sweet, dulcet tones.

"Usually more so." After all, there wasn't another way a man built for murder could be than reprehensible to normal men and women.

"My...mother visited that club, once," she confided.

When he said nothing, Raina lifted her gaze to his. "She enjoyed watching those fights," she said softly.

Her color deepened.

"And this is relevant to me, why?" he asked, more curious than impatient.

To Raina, however, the query may as well have been the latter.

Fury blazed within the green pools of her expressive eyes. "I hate you."

"Yes, you've said as much two times now," he taunted. "And yet you still continue to seek out my company. Therefore, what does that say about *you*, Princess?"

A hiss exploded between her teeth, and as hesitant as she'd seated herself before, was as fast as she stormed to her feet.

He expected her to run.

She stunned him by staying.

Standing over Cadogan's still-seated form, she glared at him. "Let us be clear, *Severin*," she said, teeming with rage. "My being here has absolutely *nothing* to do with you. I have a habit of visiting the kitchens."

By God, she was breathtaking in her spirit and fury. Perhaps he'd been wrong all along in wanting his women obedient.

"*Furthermore*," she jabbed a finger in his face, "you are the one who followed *me* tonight."

Growling, he caught her by the wrist and held her trapped in his hard grip. "No one," he whispered, "I repeat, *no one*, puts a finger in my face. Am I clear, Princess?"

Raina gave a juddering nod.

"As for my following you," he mocked. "Until you go and get yourself married to some dull chap, you're my responsibility," he coolly informed her. "If getting yourself into the kind of trouble that makes you unmarriageable, then *I'm* stuck for God knows however long."

Her hand trembled. A glassy sheen filled her revealing eyes.

Bloody hell.

Tears.

With every fiber of his unfeeling being, he despised those crystal drops which denoted weakness.

"I'm not c-crying," she said, the break in her voice made an even worse liar out of her.

Cadogan grunted. "I didn't say you were."

Fuck. He didn't have the time or energy for mollifying a young miss.

"Well, I knew what you were thinking. I-I saw it in your eyes."

He stiffened.

With a slow, but deathless fury, he stood, denying the lady the advantage she seemed to think she had over him and this exchange.

"There is nothing in my eyes," he whispered, as she hurried to put several paces between them. "And you know nothing about what is in my head."

"Maybe normally, and with other people, Severin."

He may as well have imagined any weepiness from this one. The lady was all fire, again.

Raina lifted her delicate shoulders in a flippant shrug. "But with me, and this particular time, *yes*. You were *horrified* by my tears, Severin," she charged, spreading her arms wide. "They disgust you—*I* disgust you," she amended. "I make you uncomfortable."

With the exception of that disgusted with her part, she'd landed unerringly on the mark. She disconcerted the hell out of him. Other than that, the only person he was disgusted with was himself.

That same annoying muscle pulsed at the corner of his eye.

First, this pert lady who knew precisely what he'd been thinking, and now this goddamned tic to give him a way; what in hell was wrong with him?

Raina, however, proved infuriatingly in control of her emotions and this exchange.

"Another thing, Sev—"

He shot a hand out and the rest of his name ended on a gasp, as he again caught her by the wrist.

This time, he reeled her slowly in, until her soft, full breasts were pressed against his chest.

As close as they were, he heard the way her breath came faster, and lower. He felt each shiver that raced through her.

"You are afraid, Raina. Good." He curved his lips into a cold smile. "You should be."

He'd give credit where credit was due—she didn't even try to lie. But then, with her body shaking and her chest rising and falling like she'd just completed a race, how could she do so convincingly?

Leaning down, he put his lips near her temple. "You have me mistaken for some servant or inferior lady you can defy and disrespect."

"I do not treat people with disrespect," she said, still breathless. "That is, I don't treat anyone other than *you*, that way."

She'd decided *Cadogan* was somehow the man she'd treat with irreverence? He looked her over, searching for insanity in her eyes, but found only deadly serious determination.

He whistled. "You are either daft or dumb, Princess."

Raina wrinkled her perfectly symmetrical, Greek nose. "Why, because you're unaccustomed to people being unafraid of you? You go about life being treated like some sort of god not to be crossed."

This further show of her undaunted spirit should infuriate rather than enflame him. Anger with her, and her effect on him managed to cool his ardor—some.

"A mortal man," he bit out. "A dangerous one. I'm no mythical, non-existent entity, people have never seen or who they convince themselves is real."

Raina's sky-blue eyes went wide. "Did you…are you suggesting you are more powerful than the Lord?" Her question ended with her laughter.

He allowed the lady her amusement.

Cadogan knew the moment the chit realized her mistake.

Raina attempted to tug her hand free; he retained his hold.

With a deliberate slowness, he brought his face close to hers. The spark of spirit in her eyes dimmed and fear flared.

"From this moment, going forward," he snarled, "know *this*, Raina; I am not a man who'll be ordered about by anyone or disobeyed. You have taken your last midnight jaunt."

She gasped. "I've already told you, I'll not be treated like a child."

He gave her a scathing once over. "Do you know what you are?"

Raina gave her head a small shake.

Cadogan lit into her. "You're a duke's pampered sister. You *think* rules don't apply you, Princess. This time, however? They very much do. Be warned; you do not want to face my wrath." He narrowed his eyes. "Have *I* made myself *clear*?"

When Raina failed to respond fast enough, in want of an acknowledgment on her part, Cadogan applied a light, but firm pressure to her delicate wrist.

The spitfire darted the tip of her tongue out and traced it along the generous seam of the most gorgeous lips he'd ever had eyes on.

His cock swelled to the point of pain as he imagined all the things he could do—and wanted to do—with her sensual mouth.

"What will happen if I disobey you, Severin?"

Her breathtaking challenge broke through his lustful imaginings.

"You are not my master," she shot.

"Something tells me, sweetheart," he taunted on a husky whisper, "you would welcome me as your master. In fact, you'd beg for it."

She gasped. "I most certainly would *not!*"

He smirked. "By your explosively indignant reaction, you certainly have yourself convinced. Not me. I *know* what you want."

Her cheeks blazed bright as the setting sun.

Cadogan found a perverse relish in provoking her with the wicked things he knew to be true about her.

"That is why you snuck off tonight," he continued.

When she gave a furious shake of her head, Cadogan pressed

her further. "You went to the Fight Society because you have a taste for strong, powerful men. Primal ones."

The color on her cheeks flamed all the brighter. "You don't know anything," she said between clenched teeth.

"I know everything," he purred, sliding closer.

Backing away, Raina, darted her wild gaze about.

Cadogan continued his slow, deliberate approach until he'd backed Raina around the other side of the table. There she stood before him, trapped front and back.

"You hate that I know every wicked thought you're thinking," he taunted.

She lifted her chin. "Do you really, Severin? If that were true, how did I manage to get the better of you this entire day?"

They locked stares in silent, heated, battle.

God, she was breathtaking in her strength and courage.

And infuriating.

More infuriating than breathtaking.

Bloody liar.

"Unless you don't want to be kissed senseless, Princess, I suggest you run," he whispered, dipping his head, lower.

Raina edged hers back. Her lashes fluttered and her head fell back in invitation.

"Don't say you weren't warned." With a growl, he tugged her into his arms and mated his mouth with hers.

She stilled, and then gripped his lapels. With more of that innocent desire that enflamed him, Raina attempted to match his kiss.

He swept his tongue inside and consumed of the sweet, fruity hint of wine on her breath. He nipped her tongue. Drew that flesh deep and sucked, until she was moaning and undulating against him.

With a grunt of approval, he snatched Raina's skirts up in one swift move and lifted them high around her waist.

As he edged her back and perched her sweet arse on the table, she let her legs splay in an invitation as old as Eve.

Cadogan stepped over the bench, and with the heel of his boot, he shoved that seat backwards, so he could more easily get himself between the lady's slender, lightly muscular thighs.

With an intuition as old as Eve, Raina pushed her hot center flush against his rock-hard cock.

"You don't really care, do you, sweetheart?" he said between each angry slide of his mouth upon hers. "You don't care what the world thinks about or expects of you." Cadogan rocked his hips in a slow, undulating circle so she could feel each steely inch of his erection. "You just want this."

Moaning low and long and hungrily, Raina's head fell back.

As greedy a lover as he'd always been, Cadogan took advantage of her reflexive offering. He kissed a path down the long, graceful column of her throat.

While he worshiped that satiny soft skin, suckling and biting until he'd marked her, Cadogan reached between their bodies and cupped Raina at her center.

What'd begun as a taunting lesson had morphed into something else.

But then, with her full-figured, voluptuous body against yours, what did you expect? the devil in his head taunted.

"Your curls are drenched with desire," he praised.

She whimpered, a sound steeped in shame and longing.

Cadogan slipped two fingers into her hot, tight, sheath, so wet it eased his way inside.

He gave another grunt of approval.

"Do you feel how wet you are, Princess?" he whispered. "This is not the body of a lady who cares what I or anyone thinks about her. This is the body of a *woman* who *knows* what she wants."

He placed his lips at her ear. "And what my Princess wants and craves is my thick cock, isn't it."

With a whimper, she burrowed her face against his shoulder.

Ah, yes, she'd fight the spoken truth about her desire. Whereas her body didn't lie.

She rode his hand, panting and gasping.

Breathing heavily, he continued pleasuring her with the rhythm she needed, and exactly how she needed it.

"You're going to come all over my fingers, my love," he promised, adding another digit to her quim. "When you're done, I'm going to suck them clean."

Raina stiffened; her sheath gripped tight about his fingers buried in her.

"Take it, Princess. Come, before I change my mind and punish you for sneaking out of the goddamned house."

Either that domineering threat, or the mockery in his voice, or maybe both, sent her soaring to her climax.

Cursing and crying, Raina bucked and thrashed her hips as she came undone in his arms. "S-Severin," she wept, turning his name into a plea. "S-Severin."

At the sound of her begging, his cock wept. Sweat beaded at his brow, and he, the master of restraint and self-control, found himself fighting the need to rip his placard open, release his shaft, and bury himself inside her.

He didn't. He couldn't.

But God, how he wanted to.

Cadogan clenched his teeth so hard his jaw ached, and he welcomed the pain as a distraction from the unceasing agony of his painfully tight ballocks.

He was stronger than his basest hungering. He was capable of giving a woman relief but taking none for his own.

That'd always been the case.

This time, with *this* woman, however, wanting to fuck her as he did, challenged every long-held belief he'd carried that he was more powerful than his wants.

Gritting his teeth against an all-consuming lust, he poured his attention into servicing Raina, bringing her off, for the first time in her life—that is, with the touch of any hand other than her own.

He intended to give her a quick second.

Cadogan returned to petting her.

Soon, she was panting and gasping.

"Have you touched yourself before?" he rasped harshly, already knowing the answer, but wanting Raina to utter it anyway.

Whimpering, she bit her lower lip and gave her head a jerky shake.

"You wouldn't lie to me," he whispered. "Not when you know I'll punish you mightily, by stopping."

"No!"

"No, don't stop?" he jeered. "Or are you saying you've never touched yourself this way?"

Raina chewed at her deliciously full lower lip. "I…"

God, he wanted to consume that pouty flesh.

When Raina still did not answer, Cadogan stopped giving her what she needed.

She cried out; her entire body jerked like she'd been shot.

He looked at the flushed beauty in need of the mindless surrender he'd given her and would give her again—if she obeyed.

"Open your eyes," he demanded gruffly.

At his directive, Raina's lashes fluttered open. Her passion-glazed eyes shone with a mix of virginal shyness and shame.

That this woman who'd just come undone in his arms moments ago should also still possess the eyes of an innocent proved an unlikely aphrodisiac.

"You don't have to answer me," he said huskily. "I already know you've stroked your quim."

"No!"

Raina's inner muscles clenched around the fingers Cadogan still had buried inside her; making a liar of the lady.

"And you loved it," he whispered,

Her eyes flared. "I didn't!"

The minute Raina's revealing declination came flying from her mouth, she blushed.

Cadogan chuckled.

"When do you stroke your pussy?" he continued his onslaught. With the mental image he painted in his own mind he'd have to toss himself off tonight. "No answer, hmm? You'll make me guess. Very well. You do so while you bathe."

Her needy little whimper was all the confirmation he needed, but he continued to torment her anyway.

"After your maid tends your hair and washes your back, you send her away, because you do not want her there as *you* tend *yourself*."

As he spoke, he drove his fingers inside her faster and harder, until tears coursed down her cheeks.

"When she's gone, you place a washcloth between your legs

as a barrier and clean yourself, but as you do, you also caress yourself." Lust hoarsened his voice. "Until you reach that great peak."

Panting, Cadogan drew from the most vigorous lessons he'd been dealt by the Home Office, in restraint.

"You want to scream with pleasure, but you bite your lower lip," as was her way, "to keep anyone from hearing and knowing precisely what you are doing to yourself. But today you learned you want a real man's hand on you, instead. *My hand.*"

With that, Cadogan touched Raina in the precise spot to send her over the brink.

Then, she was coming again. She wept, as he pleasured her with his fingers; frenziedly she lifted her hips and bucked against his hand.

Until, with a last, agonized gasp, Raina collapsed once more.

Cadogan waited until she finally looked at him. Then, as promised, he licked the remnants of her orgasm from his fingers.

A blush added a deeper color to her cheeks already flushed from her latest La petite mort.

With her dreamy expression, heavily-lidded eyes, swollen and bruised mouth, she had the look of a sated Aphrodite who'd been well-pleasured by Ares, God of War.

"Did you like that, Princess?" he asked, already knowing the answer. He'd loved it a thousandfold more. But he hated, and worse, *feared*, how half-mad with lust he was by this woman's innocence.

The instant she fully opened her eyes, Cadogan wished he hadn't asked. It was the way those big, blue, pools of her irises, glittered.

Bloody fucking hell, this was dangerous. Each minute spent in her company, Lady Raina Goodheart, London's darling Diamond, was proving to be the weak link he'd never known he possessed; his body's response to her, potentially fatal.

He needed to disabuse her of any fanciful musings that'd already sprung in her beautiful head.

Cadogan stepped away, depriving the flimsy cover she sought in his arms. Stoical, he shoved Raina's skirts back into place.

Lines of confusion creased her regal brow.

"You forget, Raina," he said on a silky warning, his unrequited lust made his voice ragged and even rougher than usual. "I've made a career of identifying liars and getting answers from them. My very lengthy list of malefactors includes women whom I've given great pleasure to, in exchange for information I want."

Joy faded and hurt flickered to life in Raina's eyes.

"Is that what this was?" she moved her gaze haltingly across his face, in search of answers she'd never find. "A...lesson."

No.

When he didn't speak, she asked, again, this time her voice pitchy. "Was it some kind of *test*?"

No.

"Yes." He lifted his shoulders in a lazy shrug. "Though, if it would alleviate any virginal guilt, this," Cadogan motioned between them, "can be whatever you *want* it to be."

Hurt bled from every exquisite plain of her features, which twisted in an intolerable, all-consuming grief.

Through his work, he'd been required to lie too many times to count.

This was the first, he'd ever felt...some peculiar way about it.

Raina inched her chin up another notch. "You are a bastard," she whispered.

"Yes." He'd always known it.

Cadogan smirked. "In the *figurative* sense, at least, I'm *very* much a bastard."

Raina's lower lip trembled.

That slight quivering caused his stomach muscles to seize.

"Now that we've squared all that away," he said, emotionlessly, detached on the outside, even as he wanted to part her legs again, bury his aching cock deep inside her, and restore her sadness with mindless bliss.

Raina stared at him with stricken eyes. No, her eyes weren't just those of a wounded woman. Within those revealing depths blazed hatred. Good, that was the correct sentiment the lady should feel for him and about him. Not whatever it was he'd spied too many times now.

He made himself meet her stare with an opaque one.

When she made her exit, she did not run. Instead, Raina, like the regal queen she was, marched away from Cadogan, her lowly subject.

And 'lowly subject' couldn't have been a more apt descriptor for Cadogan. For in this moment, he'd never felt lower than he had because he'd hurt Raina Goodheart, a proud, and daring, goddess.

CHAPTER 10

How is it possible to crave a man's kiss more than food and drink and the very air I breathe?
~ The Duchess of A

SEATED ON HER BLUE, VENETIAN style bed; her back against the painted headboard, Raina stared out as rain battered the crystal windows. Earlier in the week, the skies had opened up in a deluge that would not quit.

The whole while, she stared absently out the window.

All future *tests* could likely be called off. The question she'd set out with, hadn't necessarily been answered at any public venues, but right here, in the kitchens of her family's house.

She was...wicked.

She'd allowed Severin Cadogan, the fearless, all-powerful, Earl of Killburn to do the most shameful things to her. What was worse? She'd loved every single moment and thought only of Severin and that night.

She'd *also* actively and successfully avoided him. The rain, certainly *helped*. Though, arrogant and clever as he was, he'd absolutely suspect the extensive amount of time Raina spent in her rooms had more to do with him.

"Oh, you are probably loving this, you great dunderhead," she muttered.

It was improbable. Her attraction to Severin Cadogan defied logic. He clearly didn't like her. He delighted in tormenting her. He didn't smile.

But in being in his arms carried with it a feeling of rightness and also, absolute wrong.

"*...Did you like that, Princess...?*"

No, she'd *loved* it.

Raina closed her eyes to silence the voice—*his voice*—persisted.

"*...you've discovered you want a real man's hand on you... My hand...*"

The place between Raina's legs quivered. She pressed her thighs together to ease the growing ache there.

"*...My very lengthy list of malefactors includes women whom I've given great pleasure to, in exchange for information I want...*"

That last avowal managed to do what all previous remembrances had not—it cooled her ardor.

It'd served as a reminder—then and now—nothing he'd done with her had been special. While she'd believed he'd shown her heaven, Severin's feet remained planted firmly on Earth.

Raina hugged her arms close.

She *didn't want* to endure a wretched marriage like the late duke and duchess. She *didn't want* a husband who could separate himself from his emotions.

She'd read her mother's journals enough times. The late duchess began as a respectable lady who'd lost her heart, pride, and then all happiness.

Now, if there'd ever been a man who epitomized, *divorced from emotions*, it would be Severin Cadogan—former spy turned hired mercenary and who—

"Oh, dear."

Raina let loose a squeal and looked to the happy, spritely, source of that interruption.

"Millie!" she greeted her youngest sister.

The girl, with fay footing to rival any fairy, sprinted across the room and launched herself onto the bed. That sudden disturbance sent the feather tick mattress bouncing. Millie laid on her stomach so that she and Raina faced one another and then kicked her legs up behind her.

"It is horrendous what Gregory has done to you, assigning that horrid man to you."

That horrid man who did the most wonderful things to me...

"Imprisonment is driving you mad, Raina."

"Imprisonment?"

Millie nodded. "That is what the servants are calling it."

"Yes, well, it certainly feels that way," she said under her breath.

Just then, thunder rumbled, the same time a flash of lightning lit up the sky.

Millie scurried closer.

Automatically, Raina grabbed the nearby throw and. Lying next to her sister, Raina pulled the blanket over them. Then, sliding an arm under the girl, she drew her close. While the storm raged, they two remained that way.

For as long as Raina could recall, her young sister feared storms. Whenever Mother Earth whipped up a tempest, Millie took sanctuary with Raina.

Stroking the top of Millie's curls, Raina held her young sister, until the storm let up, and then stopped altogether.

"Where did you go?"

Pulled from her musings, Raina glanced down. "Hmm?"

"The last time you snuck off," Millie clarified. "It must have been wonderfully scandalous if he locked you in your rooms for days."

She frowned. "He didn't *lock* me in."

Millie's eyes rounded. "You locked yourself in?" She whistled. "It must have been a *very* bad place."

Raina troubled at her lower lip. How excited her young sister had become. Perhaps they truly all did possess their family's corrupted blood.

Millie tugged the bottom of Raina's plait to get her attention. She touched the back of her head. "*Ouch.*"

"Well?" Millie persisted. "Surely you don't believe I'll tell *Gregory*?" Hurt laced her sister's voice.

"No, Millie! *Never.*"

She and her sister only had each other.

Raina lowered her voice. "I went to Braggert and Maynard's Fight Society. It is a..."

"Boxing Arena," her sister finished on an awed whisper.

Raina frowned. "You know about—?"

"*Of course*, I do," Millie said, as if it were the most natural thing in the world for small girls to know about such violent establishments. "What was it like, Raina?"

Raina searched for a way to explain such a spectacle.

Then, the thrill of last night came rushing back. "It was appallingly violent and loud and dangerous and compelling. The fighters, they were like gladiators of old and bare from the waist up…"

And it is why you were the only woman present, an all-knowing voice in her head jeered. *Unlike the other young ladies who've just Come Out, you aren't proper, respectable, or good.*

Millie, free-spirited as Raina had always been, remained innocent and naïve to their family's dark history.

For now.

Raina intended to keep it that way for as long as she could.

"*Yes?*" Millie urged. "Do go on."

She registered her young, impressionable sister hanging on the story like it was a dangling thread of licorice.

Raina cleared her throat. "And it was something *no* proper lady should ever bear witness to."

A whispery soft sigh escaped Millie's lips—a dreamy little expression of wonderment that would have better suited a younger sister learning about her big sister's first ball. "I wish I could have joined you."

Warning bells went off; the loud, chiming, clanging ones that indicated that Raina needed to watch Millie closely. The same, bold, independent Goodheart streak, existed in her, too.

Millie shook Raina's arm. "What is next?"

"*Next?*"

Millie looked at her incredulously. "You must have *other* exciting places to visit?"

She did. But those were certainly not ones she could ever or would ever speak to her innocent sister about.

She ruffled the top of Millie's wild curls. "That is all, poppet." Given Severin's furious response and dogged determination, it would be the last time she could freely sneak off.

The younger girl swatted her hand away. "That is *all*?"

For as horrified as Millie was, Raina may as well have committed treason against the Crown.

"Surely not—" An understanding well beyond her innocent years, lit Millie's eyes and she growled. "*Your gaoler.*"

My gaoler. It turns out he'd become just that, after all.

"I won't be able to slip off again." Raina managed a smile for her sister's benefit. "Mr. Cadogan is not a man who'll be fooled twice."

"The bloody Sard," Millie muttered.

A sharp bark of laughter exploded from Raina's lips. "*Millie.*"

"Well, he is," her sister scoffed. "We are permitted to *speak*, however, we please. Just as *you* can *go* wherever you want."

"You know we do not have those freedoms," Raina gently reminded.

The younger girl didn't have a mother, and much of her influence came from their older, rakish brother. Raina had to at least try to be a proper influence.

Millie pulled a face. "It is not fair."

"No, it isn't." Where women were concerned, life usually wasn't.

A maudlin silence fell between them.

Even though her sister wasn't wrong in thinking women *should* enjoy the same freedoms as Gregory, the fact remained their movements were monitored and restricted.

"Psst, Millie?"

Her glum sister looked up.

"We aren't allowed to do the same things as the gentlemen." Raina lowered her voice to a whisper. "In private, however? When we're with our friends, women enjoy our own freedoms."

Millie's spine grew three inches. "Then as your friend, *I* am here to help you evade Mr. Sour-Face."

Another short laugh burst from Raina and prevented her from repeating that very apt moniker for Severin.

She sighed. "I fear I cannot evade him, poppet. He has a number of men stationed at various points inside *and* outside the household."

"Seven."

Raina stared confusedly at the younger girl.

"One at the entrance to the kitchens. One in the foyer. One at the hallway that leads to the main suites. One that leads *away* from the master suites." With each location mentioned, Millie shot a finger up. "One at the stables. One outside the front gates. One at the servant's entrance."

"You know all that?" Raina let all her awe and admiration shine through.

Millie snorted. "Do you *truly* believe any man is a match for me?"

"Forgive me." Raina bowed her head. "I have *greatly* underestimated you."

"Better."

They shared a smile.

"What of Mr. Cadogan?" Raina strove to make her question as casual as possible. "Where precisely is he stationed?"

"Oh, *he's* the floater." Millie hopped up and did an impression of a ghost flitting about the room.

"He's like a phantom who moves from one spot to the next."

A shiver traveled along Raina's spine. A phantom. There couldn't be a more apt description of the powerful, emotionally deadened bodyguard.

But ghosts weren't capable of physical touch and doing all the wondrous things Severin Cadogan did to her body that night in the kitchens.

Millie jumped in front of Raina, startling her.

"*We*, in contrast," she dropped her hands on the edge of the mattress, "are far stealthier and more dangerous than any *phantom*."

Millie gave her eyebrows a little wiggle.

If only Raina possessed the same confidence as a young girl.

"There is no evading him, Millie," she said, regretfully.

"Bah, we've already done so once," her sister scoffed. "*Plus*, you have our big-headed brother, wrapped about your finger. *Plus*, when have *you* ever allowed any man to bully you?"

Raina frowned.

Never.

Until enigmatic Mr. Severin Cadogan had come along.

Her scowl deepened. Here she sat, hiding away in her chambers because of one overbearing gentleman.

Do you fear Severin or your body's response to him, a voice in her head prodded.

Raina steeled her jaw.

Either way, she'd not stay here any longer, letting him think he'd gotten the better of her.

"Do you know, Millie, I believe I will be going out, after all." Whether Severin liked it or not.

Millie sprung to her feet and jumped wildly about Raina's mattress. "Huzzah!"

Quietly laughing, Raina touched a finger to her lips.

Not. Severin would *not* like any further displays of defiance. She smiled. That would make it all the more enjoyable.

There was but one problem. "How do you propose I slip past Mr. Cadogan's minions? They're stationed all over the corridors."

"You won't slip *past* them, silly."

Raina stilled.

As one, they looked to the closet with its secret panel that led through the interior corridors.

Millie grunted. "Now, let us sneak you out."

Nearly an hour later, with the assistance of her impish sister, Raina exited through the basements, and slipped along the grounds until she reached the nearest neighbor's properties.

Then, Raina was on her way.

Heart thundering, Cadogan bolted upright in bed.

"Fuck," he muttered.

How the hell long had he been asleep?

Cadogan scrubbed a hand over his eyes and fumbled around the nightstand looking for his watch fob.

Squinting, he consulted the time. An hour and sixteen minutes. After she'd snuck off to the Fight Society, in the event she got it into her fool head to try and run off again, he'd put more men on her.

He trusted his men, but he trusted himself more.

Who he didn't trust, was Lady Raina Goodheart.

She'd been…too quiet.

Is it that she's quiet or is it the fact you wounded her with the crude, hate-filled words you hurled after pleasuring her?

The latter. It was definitely the latter. And that truth, didn't make him feel better.

Cursing roundly and blackly, Cadogan got out of bed and went through his morning ablutions.

What was it about Lady Raina Goodheart that mesmerized him? Yes, she was beautiful and clever, but he'd had any number of beautiful, clever women in his life. And duplicitous. They'd been that, too.

Closing his eyes, he dunked his head into the full wash basin that'd been set out. Cadogan held his breath, waiting as long as he could, until the water fully wakened him.

With a gasp, he straightened.

Maybe that was the difference, he thought, as he toweled off.

Raina was more innocent than he'd believed a person *could* be. Oh, she'd been wild in his arms, but that was the expected response, and her release, always the outcome. He'd mastered the weaponry of desire.

Not a single one of his past lovers wore the glitter of awe in their jaded eyes that Raina had that night in the kitchens.

"What the hell is wrong with you?" he muttered, tossing his towel aside.

Cadogan went to fetch his boots.

Sex.

That's all that accounted for this mindless fascination with the Impertinent Incomparable.

Before now, he'd never had a taste of someone like her, and now that he'd sampled Lady Raina Goodheart, he'd not be content until he ate his fill.

Fully bathed, shaved, and dressed, Cadogan headed off to check in with his staff, when a tingling at his nape froze him in his tracks.

Frowning, he strode over to the window and, gripping the sill, Cadogan did a quick check finding each of the men he'd hired in the spots he'd stationed them.

Everyone from this vantage was in position.

He kept scanning the rain-covered cobblestones.

Then, from the corner of his right eye, he detected a flash of movement—the same moment one of his men did.

A spritely figure flew from the shadows and bolted as if Satan himself were after her.

The others in Cadogan's employ immediately set in pursuit of the lady.

"Bloody hell," he gritted out.

God, she was a level of trouble he'd never anticipated.

With a curse, Cadogan made to go after the damned chit but abruptly stopped.

There was something too outrageous, too obvious about that small figure.

Sure enough, while his men continued in pursuit of someone who was most certainly *not* the troublesome wench Cadogan had been tasked with looking after, a slender figure slipped through the front gates of the neighboring properties.

She stole a furtive glance about before stealing out and heading for a hired hack some yards ahead.

Cadogan took off running.

The minute he arrived outside, Raina nearly reached a hackney.

Cadogan increased the length and speed of his strides.

"By God, I'll stop the damned thing with my bare hands if I have to," he gritted out, from between clenched teeth.

Except…

Bypassing the hackney altogether, she crossed to the opposite side of the street and continued heading north.

What the hell?

As annoyed as he was intrigued, Cadogan followed close enough to ensure the lady didn't come to any harm, but with enough distance to not alert her of his presence—at least, not until he discovered the reason behind her latest rebellion.

She moved with a sprightliness better suited to the mincing steps of a quadrille.

Cadogan gritted his teeth. Did the chit *want* to get herself raped in some alleyway and left with a slit throat for her efforts?

Where in blazes are you going, princess?

A short while later he followed close as she headed with determined steps for…

Lucifer's Lair.

He drew his eyebrows together.

This is where she was headed, alone, in the early morning hours?

At that, she'd had the help of someone he'd wager his black soul to Satan was, in fact, her younger sister—the closest person she had to a friend.

Cadogan dealt in the business of shady souls and cutthroat men and women working against the Crown, driven by money, power, and influence. He'd discovered people of every station capable of any level of evil and cruelty to get what they wanted.

What he'd not expected, however, was the dogged determination and stealth of a virgin intent on sinning.

Raina didn't learn.

Or she hadn't.

After this latest transgression, however, she'd know better than to make the mistakes she had, again.

Oh, she'd learn.

In a single, quick move, Cadogan was upon his naughty charge. Instantly, he had Raina's slender frame stuck between his body and the solid brick wall.

Anticipating her scream before she could even breathe that plea for help into existence, he clamped a hand over her mouth.

In a bid to free herself, Raina whimpered and moaned and bucked against him.

The lush globes of her buttocks thumped against his cock, and he went as hard as a schoolboy with his first whore.

Cadogan gritted his teeth; and for the first time, he found his fury with this woman to be greater than even his desire.

Is this what she needed? To be scared bloody straight.

His breath came as ragged and fast as her own inhalations and exhalations.

Were he another man, a decent one, respectable and good, he'd have been horrified at being aroused by her struggles. He'd ceased to be a gentleman—if he'd ever even been one to begin with—and now, only a primal hunter, who subsisted on lust, and bloodlust raged within him.

Cadogan lowered his lips close to the shell of her ear.

"We're going to need to work on your fighting skills," he said, his voice sharp and hoarse. "That is, unless you're *trying* to get a man hard."

Even with his vulgar jeering, the sound of his voice had a calming effect on the lady. She instantly ceased her struggles and went soft and supple in his arms.

"Sefferin," she mouthed into the palm he still had over her lips.

Slowly, he removed his hand from her mouth, keeping it close enough lest he need to silence her once more.

He needn't have bothered.

The moment she wheeled around, she stretched up on tiptoes and gracefully looped her slender arms about his neck. "Severin," she breathed.

Never before had a single person looked upon him with the relief and joy this woman did now.

Cadogan grunted. He attempted to disentangle her arms from his person, but she remained as tenacious and clingy as stubborn ivy. "I told your brother," he whispered sharply against her ear, "I am not your goddamned nursemaid."

Her eyes twinkled. "I should *hope* a nursemaid wouldn't bring a babe to *Lucifer's Lair*."

Cadogan remained unamused. Granted, he'd never had grounds for laughter—and that absence of light extended far back, long before his work, to his bastard of a father.

The lady wrinkled her nose in that ridiculously adorable way of hers. "Do you ever laugh, Severin?"

Severin. There it was again. His bloody Christian name. The bold, little imp used it to get a rise out of him.

Proving tenacious, Raina brushed her palms over the lapels of his black, wool coat. "I asked if you ever laughed."

"No," he said flatly. Nor did he smile. "I don't have any reason to."

The lady moved a saddened gaze across his face. "How sad," she said softly, a woman speaking to herself, who didn't realize she'd spoken aloud.

Discomfited as he was furious by her pitying utterance, he grunted. "What are you doing here?"

"I think that should be obvious, Severin."

"It isn't," he said flatly.

She folded her hands as if in prayer. "I'm visiting *Lucifer's Lair*."

The nun-like way she carried herself against the backdrop of her intentions nearly pulled a laugh out of him.

"Why?"

She rolled her eyes in exasperation. "I can't very well visit *Forbidden Pleasures*."

Cadogan searched for some indication she was making a jest but found none.

He didn't know what he wanted more: to bend her across his knee and spank her for the latest trouble she'd set out in search of, or get her home...where he'd very much like the opportunity to do the same thing, there.

Home.

Home was the priority.

"Your brother would not be pleased were he to discover you've been to Craven's, Raina."

The lady wavered. "Yes, well, it is a good thing he shall not find out."

"He won't."

The obvious tension she carried in her shoulders eased some.

"That is, he won't as long as you accompany me home. *Now*."

Severin reached for her wrist.

Raina backed away. "I'm *not* leaving."

"One of us is correct, Raina, and the other, is you."

"I'm going inside, with or without you."

"How adorable you are," he jibed. "You thinking you have any control over me or what I decide."

She wrinkled her nose in a guileless way that should disgust Cadogan, but instead captivated.

Jaded by death and murder and all the dealings he'd had over the course of his career, Cadogan discovered a strange and unexpected appeal in this innocent woman and her absolute lack of artifice.

He made another attempt for her hand.

"I expect my brother will be *most* displeased to learn I've escaped your watch. Nor is this the first time. Given that, I trust whatever payment your expecting will go unpaid."

Fury sent his nostrils into a full flare. "My God, you insolent wench." She'd come between him and the only thing he sought in life.

The lady gave an impudent toss of her head. "If an insolent wench is a woman who knows what she wants, and won't be ordered about, then *yes*, I'm an insolent wench."

He heard Craven's men when they were still nothing more than a distant shadow, seven or so yards away.

Fucking hell. This was the last bloody thing he needed.

Cadogan buried his mouth against Raina's, covering her lips in a hard, punishing kiss, and as her innocent body melted against him, he became briefly lost in the taste and feel of her.

A pistol cocked and jolted Cadogan from the lustful hold this maddening woman had over him.

"What have we h—?"

The rest of that icily mocking query came to a sudden stop.

"If it is not, Severin Cadogan," the Duke of Craven drawled, sounding more than faintly amused at discovering just who it was who'd been intending to enter his clubs.

"Craven."

The ruthless proprietor lingered his gaze on Raina's hidden form.

She slid closer to Cadogan.

"You invited me to sample your clubs," Cadogan said bluntly, recalling the duke's attention. "I'm here."

After he'd saved Craven's wife, the duke offered Cadogan an open—and generous—invitation to frequent as often as he wanted and to fuck as many of Craven's Cyprians, whenever he wished.

Suspicion flickered in Craven's eyes. "You've also brought company," the duke remarked. He gave Raina a longer look. "Though I confess, I expected you'd enjoy the services of my Cyprians, instead of bringing your own."

"As you may remember when you presented me with an invitation," he said coolly, "I have specific requirements about the women I fuck."

"I recall." With a tight smile, the duke made a grand gesture with his arm. "Then, please, do not let me keep you any longer from your pleasures."

Craven glanced to the flinty-eyed, towering fellow who watched Cadogan with a deserved amount of suspicion.

A moment later, with Raina at his side, Cadogan followed the guard inside *Lucifer's Lair*.

CHAPTER 11

*I wondered so long how Wallace could
enjoy this. I believe I now, know…*
~ The Duchess of A

…As you may recall when you presented me with an invitation…I have specific requirements in the women I fuck…

Severin's frosty reminder to the Duke of Craven echoed in Raina's head as he guided her inside *Lucifer's Lair*.

How…emotionless he'd been in speaking about something as intimate as lovemaking, and how pathetic that Raina found herself wondering about those requirements, and whether she met them.

He gripped Raina's forearm through her silk cloak so hard, it was certain she'd wear his marks upon her skin. Now, he used her limb to steer her through the gaming hell floors.

Raina would have taken his grip as violent, but it hadn't escaped her notice the way Severin used his body to deliberately block her from the male patrons eying her like she was a new cut of veal brought to Cook in the kitchens.

In so shielding her, he also kept Raina from seeing any of the activities which transpired on the other side of him. While the tall, enormous body of the guard who served as their personal escort prevented Raina from taking in much in front of them.

As such, with her view limited, she attempted to take in as much as she could to her left.

Alas, Raina found herself ushered so quickly in and through *Lucifer's Lair*, the scenes of bare, undulating bodies as they unfolded around her, passed in a blur.

Within moments, she found herself ushered into a private, dimly lit room, ahead of Cadogan.

It took her eyes a moment to adjust to the darkness, and while Severin spoke to the Duke of Craven's man who'd escorted them, Raina evaluated the room they'd been shown to.

Done in gold from the carpets to the wide, awkwardly positioned armchair to the centerpiece of the room; a gilded tester bed sans curtains and resplendent in gold sheets.

But for a center portion of the front wall with a large wood panel and the back wall which featured a variety of riding crops, whips, and other peculiar devices she could not place, the rest of the walls were made of mirrors.

At that moment, her gaze caught upon the tall, menacing figure contemplating her with inscrutable eyes. She searched for some sign or hint of warmth or affection and found absolutely none.

Wordlessly, he stalked over.

Heart thumping, Raina hastily backed out of the way. "I know you are…" *Angry*.

Angry would be an understatement. As rigid his control over his emotions, fury poured off his big form.

Ignoring her like she hadn't even spoken, Severin stopped beside the armchair. Then, as effortlessly as if he lifted a newborn babe, he hauled the leather seat over his head and carried it closer toward the front of the room.

He deposited the chair in front of that peculiar panel.

Disquieted, Raina, in a bid to break the tension, trilled a laugh. "I don't believe the Duke of Craven will appreciate you rearranging—"

He jabbed a finger at the seat. "Sit."

"—his furniture," she finished weakly. "I—"

"I said, *sit*."

Raina wanted to snap his head off for daring to order her about, but he was an enigma who could bend God to his will if he so wished it, and so, she found herself doing as he bid.

He collected a brass knob she'd failed to notice on that front panel. Without warning, he yanked open a small door and stepped aside so that Craven's club stood on full display.

Gasping, Raina instantly shrank.

The same tableaus she'd attempted to take in moments ago, were clear for her to observe, conversely, while she and Severin remained invisible to the other patrons all in various states of dishabille.

Unbidden, her gaze roamed the Duke of Craven's establishment: where some men with barely clad women on their laps, alternately sipped brandy and toyed with their partner's breasts.

The sight of one gentleman compelled her. This dark-haired lord, a stranger, feasted on the pebbled tip of a plump, masked woman. That lady twined her fingers in his black hair, and they may as well have been two performers who acted out the earlier scene between Raina and Severin in the breakfast room.

Where the things Severin did to her breasts had felt magical and special, seeing this same act performed left her feeling tawdry. It left what they'd done that day feeling dirty.

What you and Severin did? Raina's inner voice mocked her.

She'd assigned something meaningful to something that'd been purely lust-filled, but she...didn't want just that. Staring at all those other couples out there engaged in salacious acts, did stir a desire somewhere in her belly, but...she wanted more.

She didn't want just a physical satiation any man could bring.

She yearned for love, and an intimacy, the physical kind to be had with a man who was her partner...just like her mother had wished, hoped, and expected it would be with her husband, Raina's father.

At what point did women compromise in their dreams and hopes for life and settle for something less?

Raina found herself looking down at her lap.

Severin rested a hand on her shoulder and massaged Raina through the satin fabric of her cloak.

His touch, proved quixotic, somehow tender and hard, all at the same time, and her eyes slid closed as he rubbed and caressed her.

"You wanted to come here, Raina," Severin purred like a feral cat. "You wished to see scandal and sin and maybe you even wanted to take part in what's at play out there."

She gasped. "No!" She'd *wondered* if this manner of wickedness appealed to her as it did her family. That was different…wasn't it? Please, let it be different.

He chuckled.

"Look," he said, the low, husky quality of his baritone surely that which had earned the secrets he'd sought from those women he'd mentioned while in the kitchen.

Look.

He was right. This was certainly the reason she'd come to the Duke of Craven's hell. She'd sought answers about her morality and whether she possessed the same wicked streak of all the Goodheart's.

Instead, she found herself lost to this man's touch; thinking about the way he'd worshipped her breasts and brought her to climax, and she wanted that with him again.

"Look," he enticed, and his voice compelled.

Raina forced her eyes open and glanced out at the debauchery before her, she shivered, not at the wicked sights but from the compelling sound of Severin's voice.

She stilled and the haze left by Severin's touch lifted.

Raina's gaze locked in on an exquisite titian-haired woman, on her knees, and with her head bowed over a gentleman's lap.

Raina glanced away. Cold, unspeakable, dismay held her in its grip.

Still, this is why she'd come. Severin had been correct, just not in the reasons he'd thought.

Raina made herself sit and observe the Duke of Craven's club.

She watched married lords betray their wives.

She observed gentlemen who openly courted her, wagering a small fortune at gaming tables, at the same time women pleasured them.

All of it appeared mindless. *Empty.* All these people here were reduced to primitive beings, who mated like animals and knew no emotion other than lust.

Raina found herself unmoved. Unlike earlier that morning

when Severin had perched her on the edge of the kitchen table and deftly touched her.

For the first time since she'd arrived, an ache developed between her legs.

Even as her gaze caught on a young dandy playing with a stunning brunette's nipples, Raina's vision grew clouded.

In her mind, Raina saw herself and Severin as they'd been.

"*...Lovely. Your curls are drenched with desire....*"

Her breath quickened.

"*...You're going to come all over my fingers, princess,*" *he whispered.* "*And when you do, I'm going to suck your juices from me like the sweet nectar it is...*"

As she relived her petite morte in her mind, Raina's eyes slid shut. There'd been something profound and poetic and so very extraordinary that a single man had brought her to such heights. Her longing for him then—and now—proved so great that it wasn't merely the act her mother had written about, but a single man who'd made her feel those things.

She didn't want to have a string of lovers. She didn't want a husband who didn't mind sharing her with another man. She wanted to love so fiercely and be so fiercely loved in return that they two were enough.

This was too much.

Raina surged to her feet and took several jerky steps away from Severin, retreating to the other side of the bedroom.

What it was not, however, was enough space.

CHAPTER 12

It has been so long since we've partaken in the wicked.
Dare I hope, we are at last content with only one another?
~ The Duchess of A

SEVERIN WATCHED RAINA PACE LIKE a caged lioness. She wanted to flee. Not the sights which she'd boldly taken in, but rather, Severin.

She didn't.

The minx was too daft, bold, or courageous for her own good.

As if to reiterate his very thoughts, Raina angled her chin up a smidgeon, and looked him straight in the eye.

"You're afraid," he purred.

She scoffed. "What could I possibly f-fear?" That slight tremble ruined her otherwise impressive attempt at nonchalance.

He slipped slowly towards her. "Did you not sneak off a second time?"

"That you *know* of anyway."

Cadogan stopped and looked at her a long moment. An unexpected snort of laughter burst from him.

The lady bristled. "You find something amusing?"

"Not something, Princess," he managed in between his amusement. "Your poor attempts at lying."

Raina stuck her tongue out, and that playful display stilled. How, strange. Perhaps it was being with Lady Raina Goodheart was like no other experience he'd ever known or had, but there came a welcome warmth inside, and another laugh slipped out.

It was hard for them to say who was more surprised: him or the wide-eyed beauty across the room.

"Mr. Cadogan," she whispered, a twinkle in her eyes. "Are you—?"

"No." His heart thumped weirdly in his chest.

Her lips twitched. "I didn't say anything."

"I'm not," he gritted out.

She smoothed her features. "You're not what?"

"Laughing," he snapped.

Raina blinked with an overabundance of pretend innocence. "I never said you *were*, Severin."

"Are you making light of me, Princess?" he hissed.

"I rather believe you're carrying on this entire *conversation* by yourself."

He brought his eyebrows together. The lady played a dangerous game. The sooner she realized that the safer she—and Cadogan—would be.

"I know why you're here," he whispered in lethal tones.

She wavered. "You d-do?"

Not so confident now.

"You came here to Craven's club because you know everything there is to know about *his, DuMond, and Latimer's* establishment."

Raina appeared to find her footing. "We've discovered yet another thing you are wrong about, Severin."

"I know everything," he purred, sliding closer. "You are aware Craven caters to those most depraved; that the entertainment featured at his club shocks even the most jaded rakes."

Her skin blanched; she scrambled and tried to put some distance between them.

Cadogan closed it in a second.

"Where are you running, love?" He jeered. "Hmm? Away from me? Away from the truth? Or both?"

Her throat jumped wildly.

He wasn't even close to done. "You also know where *Forbidden Pleasures* offers those with a proclivity for voyeurism, a more private place to take part in that depravity, Craven's club has every possible sin—and then some—on full display for his patrons."

Raina held his gaze and said nothing.

Lust sent his nostrils into a full flare. God, even with her defying him time and time again, with her spirit and courage, the lady was utterly magnificent.

"You'd be wise to run, Princess," he whispered.

She lifted her elfin chin a notch more, a defiant fraction. "Is that a threat?"

"It is a promise, sweetheart," he said huskily. "If you don't go now, I'm going to do things to you that you'll both love and regret."

Her breath caught on a soft, audible intake—but she didn't leave as she ought.

"I'm not afraid of you, Severin."

Severin.

The sultry way she owned his given name in this moment, sent a wave of lust rushing to that randy organ between his legs. It would bring Cadogan the utmost pleasure to educate her as to why she'd be wise to not provoke him.

"Don't say you weren't warned," he jeered.

Cadogan tugged her into his arms.

Growling, he buried his mouth on Raina's. She went immediately soft and pliant against him.

With an unexpected, but welcome, boldness, she twined her fingers about his nape and kissed him back with all the skill of a maiden and the ardor of a debauched beauty.

The blend of her hesitancy and wild enthusiasm drove him wild, and what'd begun as a lesson in fear morphed into something far more dangerous—for Cadogan.

"Open for me," he demanded.

His defiant princess immediately complied.

Cadogan slipped between her parted lips and plundered the hot, sweet, warmth of her mouth. He buried his tongue inside and devoured her. Consumed her. Until she was moaning and writhing against him, incoherent utterances spilling from her lips.

Mindless with lust as he'd never even been with the most inventive Cyprian, Cadogan darted his tongue repeatedly inside Raina's mouth. Theirs engaged in a violent thrust and parry, over and over, simulating the way he wanted to bury his hard cock hard, deep inside her.

She met him passion for passion.

Breathless, urgent gasps shook her beautiful body.

Grunting like the animal he was, Cadogan sat on the bed. He scooped Raina under her generously curved arse and perched her on his thigh. The wicked scenes unfolding on the other side of the curtains could have stopped and Craven's club emptied out for all Severin noticed.

He guided Raina's hips, teaching her how to ride him in for her pleasure.

Raina's head fell back. "Severin," she keened his name like a prayer.

Cadogan clasped her by the nape and kept her mouth where he wanted it; he swallowed her long, hungry moan.

A chuckle rumbled in his chest. "If you love this, sweetheart, you'd love having my cock buried deep inside you."

He didn't bother to gentle his language. Tender talk during sex wasn't something he'd ever had need of.

Instead of being repulsed, Raina whimpered and rode his thigh with greater intensity; she rocked her sweet quim against him.

Perspiration built at his brow.

In the scheme of the acts he'd performed with and on women, this was as innocent as it came. So why then, was he enflamed in ways he'd never been before this moment, before this woman?

Cadogan consumed the pillowy-soft flesh of her mouth as he'd wanted to do the instant she'd first stepped into the room in her diamond-studded tiara, yesterday.

Ravenous as he'd never been, Cadogan sucked her lower lip, and then lightly bit her.

"I want to fuck you while you wear nothing but that high, haughty crown of yours, love," he rasped in between kisses.

She moaned into his mouth.

The hungry sounds of her desire drove him mad with lust; his ballocks drew up tight and painful.

Cadogan continued rocking his hips against Raina.

A small, mournful whimper eased past her full lips.

Deciding to give her overworked senses a taste of another source of wickedness, Cadogan tugged the bodice of her dress and chemise down and bared her resplendent flesh.

He stopped long enough to work a hungry gaze over the most magnificent breasts he'd ever set eyes—or hands—on in his life; which given the experience he had compliments of his work, was saying a tremendous deal about Lady Raina's attributes.

Her beautifully formed, cream-white breasts and enormous pink nipples belonged on canvas, a visual masterpiece of lush carnality to be memorialized and worshipped for all time.

"Pretty," he growled.

He'd lied for so long in the name of King and Country, that understatement slipped out of Cadogan with an ease. All the while, the hardness of his sex him mocked him with that understatement about Lady Raina, as the biggest fraud.

Cadogan cupped the ample mounds, so bountiful, even in his large palms, the flesh flowed over.

"Have you ever had your breasts touched, Princess?" he asked huskily, already knowing his hands were the first to brush the silken, soft orbs.

That wasn't all he intended to be the first to do to them.

Raina whimpered, and, like a bashful nymph, she buried her head against his shoulder.

"Tell me," he purred, wanting her to say the words anyway, wanting her to admit he was the only man who'd touched her, thus far in her sheltered, pampered, life. "I want to hear you say it."

When she still didn't speak, he tweaked her nipples, hard.

The innocent in his arms cried out softly and arched her into his rough play. "You are the first man to touch them, Severin."

He'd not be the last. The very nature of his arrangement ended with her marriage to some fancy toff; a staid fellow who wouldn't pleasure her in all the ways she needed to be pleasured.

An unpleasant taste settled in his mouth, and he thrust thoughts of her with another away. He'd never liked sharing. That's all it was.

"There's something you'll love even more, Princess," he both promised and tempted.

She shivered—with anticipation. He felt it in the way she undulated her hips

Lowering his head, he hovered his mouth near the swollen tip of her right breast and picked his gaze up.

"Are you curious to know what that something is?"

Flushed like she'd been kissed by the summer sun, Raina nodded frenziedly.

Keeping his eyes directed upward and on her, Cadogan captured a turgid, pink, tip between his lips and sucked deep.

Raina hissed. Tangling her fingers in his hair, she gripped him hard and anchored Cadogan in place.

He alternately licked and sucked the peak, until she was moaning and writhing in his arms.

As the tension began to build in her body, Severin came off her nipple with a wet little pop that he knew would drive her wild.

As anticipated, Raina splayed her legs wider and lifted her hips up in supplication.

"I've been remiss," he murmured, and reclaiming the thrusting point in a more savage sucking, he lavished his attention on the previously neglected, tip.

He caught the crest in his fingers and rolled the flesh—gently at first.

"Severin," his innocent temptress moaned, turning his name, into a plea.

Enflamed by the sultry siren's sound of her voice, Cadogan's cock throbbed to the point of pain, and only the years of training he'd endured prevented him from releasing himself and wrapping her long, graceful fingers about his length.

Strangely, the smug, savage satisfaction found in showing the intermate beauty a taste of sex proved just as gratifying.

Liar. You want to fuck her senseless.

Growling, he pinched the hard tip, at the same time he sucked the other.

A broken gasp erupted from Lady Raina's lips.

Cadogan continued working her nipples, biting them, sucking them harder, until the innocent beauty rocked her hips frenziedly.

She ground herself against his thigh.

Bringing her enormous breasts together, Cadogan simultaneously licked the lady's nipples.

"Mmm," she keened. "Mmm."

Sweat beaded his brow.

God, had he ever had in his arms a woman as responsive as this one?

No.

Cadogan could say with an absolute certainty, he hadn't. All the lovers he'd fucked for work, or just slaked his lust with, had known exactly what they were doing. There'd been no artifice. They'd been women trained in sex and masters of restraint in their own right.

Cadogan lapped Raina. He licked her. Bit her.

She gasped.

"Not all women like having their breasts roughly handled," he said, his harsh breathing at odds with his otherwise, matter-of-factly spoken tone. "Some women love having their nipples squeezed hard, Princess. Some love it harder."

He tugged her peaks gently and then wrenched them both, sharply.

His beautiful spitfire bit her lip and moaned, with a different sort of anguish.

"What of you, sweet?" he teased. "Do you like when I'm rough with them?"

Again, he knew the answer. But would the lady herself own her truths?

"Yes!" She sucked in great, heaving gasps of air which set her chest shaking. "I love it."

"Good girl," he harshly praised and rewarded her by giving her precisely what she hungered for.

He squeezed her nipples and continued tightening his hold until the lady's gyrating hips took on a frenzied, almost broken rhythm.

Cadogan gritted his teeth. His massive erection strained the front of his trousers and challenged his restraint in ways not even the fiercest test with the Home Office had.

Raina bit her lower lip hard; her undulations grew erratic.

"Aww, let me help you, love." Cadogan gripped her hips and continued to guide her up and down. "You crave something hard between your thighs." He rolled the engorged tip of her right breast between his tongue and lips.

"Mmm," she keened, her speech now fully dissolved into the wild sounds of a primordial creature in the throes of fucking.

He arched his hips up in time to Raina's downward thrusts. Sweat slicked his brow.

This had to stop. It was too much. His senses were afire; his head clouded.

"You're going to come, Princess," he ordered sharply, in between suckling her, preparing her for her impending orgasm. "And from nothing more than having your breasts played with and riding my leg like it's the cock you truly crave."

With a growl, he bit her hard.

That, together with his filthy talk pushed Raina to her peak.

"Severin!" she wept his name over and over; grinding her core against him as she came.

Cadogan kept on suckling her until she went limp as a puddle in his arms.

He caught her as she collapsed against him and drew her body close.

Their chests heaved with a like intensity and time; she from the little death he'd just brought her, and he from the agony of unslaked lust.

"Good?" Cadogan murmured against her damp temple.

Her face still buried against his shoulder, Lady Raina gave a tentative nod, and then inched her gaze up to meet his.

Cadogan found himself irritatingly mesmerized by those irises and a question as to how long it would take, and what things would he have to do to her that would drive the purity away.

The blue of her eyes sparkled with wonderment, but that effervescent light faded out. "I trust if you had doubts before as to my wickedness, we have an answer now," she said softly.

An odd sensation squeezed his chest, one that deprived Cadogan of his usually smooth tongue. When it came to assignments as an agent, words he'd uttered hadn't mattered. Why should they now with this woman?

"Why are you so concerned about whether or not you're wicked, Raina?"

A bitter-sounding laugh spilled from Raina's full lips. "It does not escape my notice you didn't answer the question, Severin."

She discreetly wiped at her eyes.

Oh, hell.

"In fairness, it didn't strike me as a question," he spoke haltingly. "More of a statement?" *Why am I struggling here?*

Raina gave him an odd look, and then, averting her gaze, she drew herself off his lap and seated herself on the side of the bed.

Cadogan sat shoulder to shoulder beside her.

This is why he didn't deal with virgins because they flagellated themselves for enjoying life's greatest pleasures.

You know it's not that…

He gnashed his jaw. What the hell else would it be, then?

"My parents were scandalous," she confided in quiet tones that penetrated his jumbled musings.

"Were they?" he asked, continuing to tread carefully.

Looking at her lap, Raina nodded. "They were *very* much in love," she said softly. "But they were notorious for their," her color deepened, "proclivities."

"*Proclivities?*"

Raina hesitated. "They would visit wicked clubs where debauched things took place, and from what I've read and heard…" She grimaced and opted to not complete the rest of that revelation. "My mother was often the center of those *displays.*"

"And this is relevant, why?" he asked, more curious than impatient.

To Raina, however, the query may as well have been the latter. A fresh wave of tears swelled in her eyes.

Tears.

No, *Raina's* tears. Hers made Cadogan feel strange inside. *Weak.*

His palms grew damp and—

It was too much.

Sort this out.

Then she'll finally stop running all over London for him to chase.

To put distance between them, he stood and backed away from Raina.

A pair of crystal drops wound a sad little path down each of her cheeks.

Tears were a sign of sadness, which indicated Raina spoke sorrowfully about the late duchess and duke's sordid marriage. But the mother proved the main subject of her recounting.

Then it hit him. "You believe you're like your mother before you." His wasn't a question.

Raina's shoulders came up in a little shrug. "What else am I supposed to believe? I enjoyed the Fight Society just as she did. I love being in your arms, and…"

He froze.

I love being in your arms.

His heart thudded at a sickly beat against his ribcage. This was bad.

"This is why you've been sneaking off," Cadogan filled in for her, neatly sidestepping the part involving him. "To visit the places the duchess frequented?"

She gave a small nod.

All right. This was a good deal safer. Some of the tension left him.

"Raina," he said gently. "If we were the same as all our kin, I'd be a stuffy, pompous, lord with a wife, an heir and a spare, and a mistress, on the side."

"You're speaking about your family," she murmured. "Your father? Or do you have a brother or broth—?"

Cadogan interjected. "And who gives two shites if your mother did enjoy carnal pleasures? Where's the shame in that?" he asked, gruffly.

Raina slid neatly back to the topic they'd been discussing and not his personal life.

"My mother loved my father." She touched a hand to her heart. "She loved him desperately and ached for his love, and he *did* love her." Her features spasmed. "As he was able. Not enough to not give up his debauchery or other bed partners. My mother believed if she joined her husband in sinning, she'd win his favor and he'd forsake all others."

A half-mad laugh burst from her lips, and he knew it marked the moment she ceased to see Cadogan.

"She yearned for his love and wanted only him." The fight

went out of her. "By contrast, the duke found pleasure in sharing the duchess, his wife, *my mother*, with his friends and strangers."

Raina hugged her arms around her middle. "What do you make of all that, Severin?" she asked, grievously.

Cadogan frowned. What did he make of all that? *What did he make of all that?*

He didn't couch his language. "What I believe is, you shouldn't revile the late duchess for finding pleasure, but rather the caddish, contemptible, reprobate, duke, who'd share his bloody wife with others," he said bluntly.

At last, his words seemed to penetrate the haze of misery surrounding her.

Raina slowly picked her head up.

He wished she hadn't.

Her features went soft, and her eyes positively glowed with unmistakable adoration, gratitude, and warmth.

Inside, Cadogan recoiled.

First, he'd accidentally revealed details about his life. Then, he'd been caught up in her pain, the same way a sailor did a siren's song. He'd sat silent while she lamented her mother's life and her parents' marriage.

All the while she'd shared her fears and sorrows with him, Cadogan, who didn't speak to anyone about anything not related to work, had sat and *listened*.

At some point, he'd allowed the same woman he'd been assigned to guard to feel like she could open up to him about her life.

Good Christ.

He needed to put a bloody end to this—*now*.

"Raina—"

"Severin—"

They both stopped.

She cleared her throat. "You may speak first, my...Severin."

My Severin.

At her accidental ownership of he and his name, a fresh wave of lust rolled through him.

He gritted his back molars. How swiftly she'd shredded his restraint.

"This is the last time you'll sneak off, Lady Raina," he said coolly.

Dismay filled the lady's every feature.

She shook her head. "I…don't understand?"

"Of course, you do. You're clever enough to slip past my guard twice," he said flatly. "You want to know how I can be all business after I had your beautiful breasts in my mouth and your hot cunny on my thigh."

All the color bled from Raina's cheeks. "Why are you doing this?" she entreated.

"As a reminder for you." *And me.*

They needed a wall between them, and this marked the easiest way to construct that barrier.

"*Everything* between us," Cadogan slashed a palm back and forth between them, "*is* business, and the sooner you realize that the easier this arrangement will be."

For both of us.

After a profound and unending silence, Cadogan narrowed his eyes. "Have I made myself clear, Lady Raina?"

"*Abundantly* so, *my lord*."

Hate and hurt warred in her expressive eyes. Cadogan shouldn't give two shites about either. The knot in his chest, however, taunted him with the unpleasant reality that it *did*.

"Tell *me*, my lord," she sneered. "Does making love with the women you've been assigned to protect constitute business?"

Cadogan donned the falsest smug grin he'd ever worn in his entire career. "Yes."

Her entire body jerked.

"Didn't expect that, did you, Princess?" He took a stalking step closer, and instead of fleeing as he'd hoped, Raina held her ground. "I've bedded countless women, in service to the Crown."

"How *noble* of you," she said archly. "Weaponizing lovemaking."

She was adorable when ruffled.

Cadogan lowered his lashes. "You'd be surprised." He hardened his features. "What we did here does not constitute *lovemaking*, my lady."

Another innocent blush spilled across her cheeks. "Thank you for that inestimable clarification, *my lord*."

"I don't make love to women," he said frostily. "I fuck them."

Raina inhaled sharply.

At the sign of her suffering, he clasped his hands behind him and balled them into tight fists.

Her eyes grew stricken.

"Oh, and, Raina?"

She stared blankly at him.

Cadogan dealt the final death blow.

"Next time you have an urge, I'll be more than happy to take that on as another job. Just so you don't have to go dashing about London to get your itch scratched."

When she let her palm fly, he didn't bother to stop the blow. He let Raina hit him, as he deserved.

His skin stung—and, by the way she cradled her fingers close to her chest, her palm smarted.

Still, prepared as he was for that strike, he wasn't expecting the impressive strength she packed.

Silent as he'd never seen her, Raina stared at him with stricken eyes. He made himself meet her stare with an opaque one.

"Have you seen enough, Princess?" He nudged his chin toward the couples engaged in all manner of lewd acts outside the windows. "Or perhaps, you'd like to *experience* more?"

Her throat wobbled. "I'm ready to leave," she said, her voice thick.

Wordlessly, Severin waited until she'd drawn her hood into place and straightened her skirts.

Then, without exchanging so much as a glance, they quit *Lucifer's Lair*.

CHAPTER 13

The duke blindfolded me and took me to a surprise location. I couldn't have been more stunned…and anguished. Wallace brought me to the Hellfire Club.
~ The Duchess of A

Raina STARED OUT AT THE passing Mayfair streets.

The moon's glow combined with the light shining from the lampposts illuminated the busy cobblestoned roads. The route they traveled to Lord and Lady Rutherford's was teeming with carriages as the ton made their way to various events.

It'd been five days.

Five days since she'd fallen in love with Severin Cadogan at *Lucifer's Lair*.

Five days since she'd had her heart swiftly broken.

And five days since she'd seen him.

Oh, wherever she went, without fail, he was always there, but he'd since become the shadow he'd vowed he would be.

They'd not exchanged a word.

A glance.

Not even a good morning.

Even while she'd made a point to avoid him just as he'd clearly done Raina, she couldn't stop herself from remembering, in its entirety, their meeting together.

When she'd revealed to him the worst secrets about her parents' marriage, he'd sounded and looked so horrified by the late duke passing the late duchess around to his friends, that Raina fell more than a little in love with him.

As she'd predicted from before, and then caught glimpse of in his eyes that night, he'd never share whatever lady did capture his heart.

And I despise whoever that woman is out there. Raina fisted the fabric of her vibrant peacock green and blue skirts. She herself yearned for a man who'd pledge himself, body and soul to her.

"Here, my dear sister has spent years dreaming of attending a masquerade, and this is the night, and you couldn't appear more miserable than when I'd pilfer your desserts when you weren't looking."

She finally forced her gaze away from the window and looked to the bench opposite hers.

From over the top of his black domino, Gregory sent a brow shooting up.

Raina gave him the only smile she could manage. "Ah, yes. Those good old days," she said dryly. "When you, a grown man away at university, managed to visit your young sister, only to then steal my treats. How could I ever forget?"

Her brother looped his foot across his opposite knee. "*That*, dear sister, strikes me as an *evasive* answer."

Yes, it had been. She didn't want to discuss the reason for her misery, and certainly not with her big brother.

Gregory's expression grew serious. "What is it, Ray?" he asked, in one of his rare moments of solemnity.

Her throat grew tight. *This* was the brother she'd loved. The one who'd genuinely cared.

Slowly, he uncrossed his leg. "Has someone hurt you?"

Ice glazed his usually convivial eyes.

"With Mr. Cadogan as my shadow?" she said, not bothering to contain her causticity.

If her brother discovered she'd been intimate with Severin, he'd duel him; one man would survive and that man was definitely not her brother.

He skimmed his gaze over her face. "You are angry with me still for assigning you Mr. Cadogan to protect you?"

Raina shook her head.

I'm upset that I've fallen so hard and so fast for a man who brought me exquisite heights, only to then reveal it'd all been a game, meant to teach me a lesson.

"It'll all make sense to you someday, Raina," Gregory said quietly. "Why I hired Cadogan to look after you. It is my hope you'll understand."

Turning her attention back to the window, she absently nodded.

They rode the rest of the way in silence.

When the carriage finally reached the front of Lord and Lady Rutherford's drive, a servant knocked.

"A moment," Gregory called.

Raina looked questioningly at her brother. "Is there a problem?"

"Clearly there is," he said. "But in failing to tell me what said problem, in fact, *is*, as your devoted brother, I'm obligated to remind you that you've been looking forward to this moment for years, Raina."

The duke dropped his voice. "As such, you have my permission to evade any pesky chaperone who'd interfere in your pleasure."

Slowly registering those words, that permission to spread her wings some, she looked wide-eyed at her brother. "Are you suggesting—"

"Eh-eh." Gregory clamped his hands over his ears. "I know nothing."

For the first time since Severin splintered her heart, her lips twitched up into a smile. "I love you, Gregory."

Color suffused his cheeks. "Yes, well, well. None of that. Just… be good."

A short while later, after they'd made their way inside, Severin followed close behind them.

He couldn't have been clearer as to how little he desired her. At every turn, he went out of his way to remind Raina she wasn't anything more than a work assignment.

Resolved to enjoy herself, as her brother encouraged, she looked about Lord and Lady Rutherford's dimly lit revelries.

As Gregory pointed out, for years, Raina had been eagerly awaiting this moment.

She'd imagined the costume she'd have designed and all the sets she'd take part in.

She'd dreamed of forbidden exchanges and stolen kisses.

And she'd be damned if she allowed *him* to prevent her from enjoying the evening's festivities.

Raina looked out over the crowded ballroom.

The dashing lords in their black dominos and highwaymen's guise flirted shamelessly with masked ladies.

Gentlemen with the most built physiques used the evening as an opportunity to don nothing more than Roman or Greek robes, sandals, and olive branches in their hair.

She gave her head a wry shake.

Severin would *never* be caught dressed so or conduct himself thusly.

No, because Mr. I-do-not-smile-or-laugh would never do something as trifling as don a costume and join in a masquerade. And what madness possessed her that she spent this night she'd been looking forward to for years lamenting his disinterest in her?

Since when had she become a woman with so little pride to go woebegone?

A flute of champagne appeared before her, startling Raina from her thoughts.

She glanced over her shoulder to see the one who proffered that glass.

A spritely, dark-haired beauty, cleverly dressed in a fitted, feather gown smiled back.

La Chouette—the owl.

Raina had heard the Marquess of Rutherford refer to his beloved wife to recognize the intimate symbolism of the marchioness's costume.

"Lady Rutherford," Raina greeted the other woman.

"Oh, dear," Lady Faith said as Raina took the glass from her fingers. "I hoped you would have led with '*who* are you'?"

Despite the misery of these past days, Raina laughed. Lady Faith, married to Gregory's partner, Rex DuMond, who with her effortless smile and kindly eyes couldn't be more different than her always scowling, menacing, husband.

"I fear my costume has not been as effective as I'd hoped," the other woman mused, casting a glance down at her luxuriantly crafted piece.

"My lady, any discovery has less to do with the effectiveness of your disguise and more to do with the formidable gentleman, nearly a foot taller than the rest of the guests, who's only just allowed you out of his sights," Raina assured her.

The marchioness leaned in and whispered in Raina's ear. "Were it not for your brother, he still would be."

Together they looked over to where Gregory and Lady Faith's husband conversed. Each man wore a somber, sober expression at odds with the flushed cheeks of the already tipsy guests.

But then, neither the duke nor the marquess were ones who'd built their reputation as the ruthless gaming hell proprietors, by being blithe fellows.

Oh, Gregory usually wore a grin, but Raina well knew that expression to be empty and jaded.

With the feud having escalated between the men and their former partner, Gregory and the marquess had intensified the efforts with which they looked after their kin.

"I am not the only one of us being closely guarded, I have heard," Lady Faith murmured in such hushed tones, it was a moment before Raina heard and registered them.

"My lady?" she said hesitantly.

"Is he as horrid as I've heard my husband and your brother discuss?"

It was on the tip of her tongue to say 'worse', but Raina managed to call the spiteful words back. She wasn't so petty as to speak ill of him, for the simple reason he did not like her or want her.

"He is not horrid," she said, unable to keep the defensive edge from creeping in. "He is skilled at what he does, and the fact that he is grave, and no-nonsense isn't a mark against his character." But rather an indication of the difficult things he'd done and seen. "In fact—"

Raina stopped, suddenly *very* aware of the *very* interested look the marchioness directed at her.

Raina instantly went close-lipped. Friendly though the other woman may be, the marchioness's loyalty first and foremost belonged to the Marquess of Rutherford, and the Marquess of

Rutherford's loyalty belonged—just like everyone else's—not to Raina, but to her brother.

"You may rest assured, Raina, if there is ever anything you'd like to speak about," Lady Faith paused and gave her another pointed glance, "or *anyone*, I would never break your confidence." Lady Faith gave that quiet assurance.

"I thank you, but there is *nothing* to discuss, my lady."

"Or…if there is anyone you'd like to speak about, Mr. Cadogan, perhaps…" the marchioness gently put forward.

Raina stilled. Her heart knocked against her ribcage. Had she been so very transparent?

"I promise you, my lady, there is *nothing* between us," she said, making an emphatic slashing movement with her hands. "He is my bodyguard and I'm merely the woman he'd been hired to protect. There are absolutely no feelings between—"

She registered too late, the growing shock in the other woman's eyes, and stopped mid-sentence.

Raina's stomach fell.

Oh, hell.

Lady Faith hadn't been talking about romantic feelings between Raina and the bodyguard.

Mortified, Raina took a long, slow, swallow of her champagne, nearly draining the glass. As long as she drank, she didn't have to field any—

"You…care for him," the marchioness ventured.

"I most certainly d-do not." Raina finished the remaining contents of her drink and in a bid for nonchalance, she trilled a laugh. "I hardly know him."

The other woman did allow Raina's weak attempt at mirth to put her off.

"I knew Mr. DuMond but one evening when I allowed him liberties that I'd never allowed another man," she said gently. "And Mr. DuMond was not living in the same household as me, Raina."

"Well, I have not," Raina said, her voice coming out sharper than she intended, and certainly sharper than the friendly marchioness deserved.

The other woman inclined her head. "Forgive me," she demurred.

Sighing, Raina glanced out absently at the dancers concluding the latest set. "No, forgive me. I appreciate your willingness to speak with me about…personal matters." Particularly as there wasn't any other female Raina could rely upon. "But…it's just not the same."

Raina wasn't the marchioness. Lady Faith came from a respectable, morally upright, family. Her mother hadn't done the shameful things as Raina's late mother.

The lovely noblewoman looped her arm through Raina's and gave her a gentle side hug. "It often seems that way when we are in the midst of it," she said softly.

She gave her a quizzical look. "My lady?"

A twinkle lit Lady Faith's pretty brown eyes. "You'll see." The marchioness's gaze caught on someone in the crowd. "It appears business matters have been concluded for the evening."

Raina followed her stare. Gregory and the marquess made their approach.

In all his ducal arrogance and pomposity, Gregory hadn't bothered with a disguise beyond his domino. His presence at her side would steal the anonymity her costume afforded. And he'd of course use the opportunity as he did at every affair they attended to introduce her to potential spouses—and not at all thinly veiled in his attempts.

"I trust spending a masquerade with one's brother is not what you had in mind when you set out tonight," Lady Faith whispered, relieving Raina of her empty flute. "Go. I'll distract him long enough for you to lose yourself."

With a grateful smile, Raina headed in the opposite direction.

As she meandered through the ballroom, perhaps it was the speed with which she'd consumed the fine French champagne or the thrill to be had in anonymity, but her steps grew increasingly quicker and lighter as with every stride she felt freer and freer.

Here, no one knew who she was. Here, she could be anyone. Here, she wasn't Lady Raina, Daughter of Eve, as her mother had been referred. Here, there was no judgment.

She'd let Severin make her despondent to the point she'd nearly cost herself the joy of this night. Now, she imagined him suffering through the merriment and frivolity of the night and having to keep close eye on her amidst the disguised guests.

An awareness trickled along her nape; delicious little tingles she'd only ever felt when his hands and mouth were on her.

He is near.

Raina briefly stilled and did a sweep of the crowd.

Sure enough, from across the room, and over the tops of the heads of the guests, her gaze locked with Severin's.

He wore his usual somber, dark, expression. His hard mouth sported a scowl.

He didn't like that she'd managed to escape him.

A man of his caliber and ego wouldn't.

Raina lifted her fingers and gave a little waggle.

He narrowed his eyes and even with the length of the ballroom between them, she caught the glint of displeasure.

The idea of giving him, the all-powerful Severin Cadogan, keeper of her life, chase, propelled Raina into flight.

As she wandered through throngs of guests, a laugh spilled from her lips, and that heady lightness melded with the like sounds of revelry around her.

Raina continued running and, crashing past a stag and lamb in the entryway, she stumbled into the hallway.

Breathless from her exertions and the exhilarating enjoyment she found in thwarting her keeper, Raina cast a glance back, more than half-expecting to find Mr. Cadogan, the scepter and ghost he proclaimed himself to be, had discovered her.

She ducked her head around the doorjamb and silently cursed.

Severin, some ten yards away, caught sight of Raina.

Laughing once more, she bolted. She felt like a child again, playing hide and seek. When had she last enjoyed herself so?

Granted, if he finds you—when *he finds you*—*you aren't going to feel so triumphant,* the voice of reason needled.

She shivered.

Then, all the better to not let him find her any time soon, and certainly not alone.

Raina ducked into a nearby room and drew the panel shut.

After the din of the ballroom, the silence here rang loudly in Raina's ears.

Heart pounding, she pressed her back against the wall, and gave her eyes a moment to adjust to the darkness.

Lord Rutherford's offices.

She more than half expected Severin to burst into the room, and yell 'got you', but when that didn't immediately happen, Raina quit her place beside the entryway, and began a slow turn about the room.

Furnished with all the Chippendale mahogany pieces, leather armchairs, leather button sofas, the room may as well have been those belonging to any gentleman.

With the exception of Gregory who'd taken input on the redesign of his office from Raina and Millie.

Raina paused at the sideboard, stocked with decanters and bottles of various spirits.

Along the way, Gregory had become so lost in the empire he'd built that he'd stopped seeing her and Millie or caring about them.

Oh, she didn't doubt he sought to protect them at all costs. She just missed before he'd viewed her as nothing but another responsibility, among a long line of them.

The work he did, the life he lived, one similar to the debauched one their parents once lived, had changed him—and in no ways that were for the better.

As for Raina, she wanted no part of that existence. She'd explored enough these past several days to have all the answers she needed and to know that wickedness, as she'd feared, did live within her, but she'd not allow those worst attributes to define her as it had her parents—and now, her brother.

She just wanted to be loved by a man who desired her and only her. She wanted to be enough for him so that he'd sooner slay a man than allow anyone to touch her. She wanted to matter more than her husband's proclivities or passions or pastimes or work.

And she'd sooner die a spinster than settle for anything less.

There could be no doubting, the man who'd held her spellbound these past days and coaxed her body to exquisite pleasure, could never be that man, which made this unwitting fascination with him so untenable.

Raina stared vacantly across her host's library.

Severin didn't see people, and as he'd reminded her time and time again, he didn't see her. He saw work and only his work and would never put a woman before the career he'd built for himself.

What then accounted for this…untenable fascination with him?

No, she knew. Members of the *ton* maintained a veneer of politeness, but it was nothing more than a façade. Lords and ladies of the peerage were ultimately vipers who sneered or whispered about Raina—and others— behind their backs.

Severin, on the contrary, was a man who spoke his mind. Oh, she may not like, and even be hurt, by the things he said to her, but he did not dissemble. He didn't pretend to be something he was not.

What was more, in rejecting the title he'd been granted by the King, he carried the same derision Raina did for their ordered and civilized society.

Alas, Severin didn't much seem to recognize or care that they were in some ways, the same.

The men she was destined to have in her life were invariably those whose energies, love, and passion, belonged to their professions.

And she hated that realization should eat her up inside.

He's not really part of your life, though…

The heavy tread of footfalls sounded somewhere in the corridor, interrupting her thoughts.

Unsteady and loud and accompanied by boisterous laughter and discourse, there could be no doubting it wasn't Severin who approached.

Swallowing a curse, Raina did a frantic sweep of the room.

"…finest collection of cognac, our generous host would absolutely wish us to…"

Raina raced behind Lord Rutherford's desk, dropped to all fours. She scurried under the broad piece of furniture when the door opened.

She carefully dragged her skirts close, so they didn't spill out from under the desk, and held her breath that the crunch of organza and gossamer didn't give her away.

Alas, the ebullient revelers wouldn't have heard much over the commotion they made; pouring drinks, talking loudly over one another.

There came the tinkling sound of the corner of a glass being struck, which proved surprisingly effective in silencing the group.

One gentleman—his voice, unfamiliar—spoke up. "If I might suggest we begin with our official business so that we are free to return to this year's festivities."

She puzzled her brow. *Official business?*

Lord Rutherford's guest continued. "Which of the many ladies in disguise do we think is the delectable, Lady Raina."

She froze.

"The lamb." That suggestion by one fellow was met with a bevy of laughter and ribbing.

They were…discussing *her*.

"What?" the gentleman protested. "Though she covered up all that gorgeous blonde hair, the trollop's got the same big breasts and large hips ."

Her stomach clenched.

"She also has a waist I can span with my hand," the Earl of Sandwich—she recognized his voice—drawled.

When he was met with boos and hisses, the earl laughed. "I'm merely stating a fact, gentleman."

As if, on cue, several men spoke at once: "The peacock."

Then, like they'd solved the world's greatest mystery came the slap of hands hitting backs.

"I'd like to show that delicious peacock a different cock," one man piped in.

"Given the lady's wanton family, she will welcome it, too."

There came the tinkling of more crystal as glasses touched in an obvious toast.

Humiliation turned Raina's entire body hot, and she curled into herself, feeling incredibly small and wanting to make herself even smaller.

She didn't know how long she remained there under her

host's desk while they skewered her with their opinions and commentaries about her body and morality and family history—or how long she remained after they'd trailed from the office and closed the door in their wake.

When she finally climbed out from under the furniture, her neck, back, and shoulders ached from the cramped position she'd found herself.

She wanted someone different than her father and brother and the clients at Gregory's clubs, but perhaps in truth, there weren't any really good men. Perhaps, they were all driven by lust and greed and wickedness. Perhaps—

"You, wicked minx, have given me quite the chase."

Raina stiffened.

In her misery, she'd forgotten she was being hunted—that was, hunted by another man, for entirely different reasons than the carnal ones driving those others.

"Do you know how long I've been searching for you?" he purred like the king of the jungle who toyed with his prey.

For someone who professed to not feeling anger or emotion—his smooth, low, baritone contained a wealth of barely suppressed rage.

Severin.

CHAPTER 14

It has been days since we've spoken. My love believes he's offended me, and I'm content to let him to that opinion.
~ The Duchess of A

Good God, he didn't know which he wanted more: to throttle the lady or kiss her.

The goddamned chit really didn't have a bloody idea the fucking danger awaiting a woman of her beauty, connections, and spirit.

Time and time again, she'd rush off, without a care for her damned well-being. The minute he'd caught her making her escape, he'd been on her, but, with them being separated by a crush of costumed guests and her being fleet of foot, he'd lost her.

"I asked you a question," he bit out.

If he were being honest with himself, the unbridled anger raging through Cadogan was more with himself than her. But he wasn't being straight with her. He wouldn't be—*couldn't be*—and give her the idea that he was soft and would tolerate her continuing to put herself in harm's way.

"I heard you," she said, the husky quality of her lyrical voice doing maddening things to his thoughts, driving his lust and self-annoyance to impossible heights.

"Look at me when I talk to you," he snapped.

He braced for her customary defiance, instead she quietly and calmly heeded his command.

No doubt so that he'd go easier on her.

To hell with that manipulation.

"Are you determined to get yourself killed or raped or—"

The blistering tirade he'd prepared on his way to her froze on his lips as he caught sight of her. At some point, the elaborate mask she wore had come free and the blue-green feathered silk turban had slipped loose so that the pale glow of the full moon cast a light upon Raina's face.

Her cheeks, usually bright with color, were an ashen hue. Tears gleamed in her eyes.

Rage briefly blinded him. Rage that had nothing to do with this woman and everything to do with the work he'd been hired to do. Even as he reassured himself of that, a growl he couldn't control shook his chest and taunted him with the flimsy lie he'd tried to make himself believe.

"Who?" He didn't bother to conceal the lethality within his whispered query. "Who hurt you? I want his name."

He'd kill the bastard. First, he'd cut his vocal cords out while he slept and forever silence him so he couldn't cry out for help as Severin tortured him to death slowly, and painfully.

Raina hugged herself in a sad, little, lonely embrace. "No one h-hurt me." The tremble there made a liar out of a terrible liar. "Not really."

That visible evidence of her melancholy from something *someone* had done and said had an unpleasant effect on his stomach muscles.

In this instance, 'not really' was the same as: Someone hurt me.

Filled with a primal, unrelenting rage, he opened his mouth to, this time, *demand* the name of her offender—but managed to retrain himself.

As much as he wanted to snarl and roar like an angry animal, doing so would only cause Raina to further retreat within herself.

"Do you want to talk about it?" he asked, infusing a softness into his query.

As he'd intended with his tone, his question penetrated whatever tumult she remained locked within.

She turned her head. The wistful expression she wore hit him square in the gut. "And here I thought I wasn't to come to you as a friend or confidante."

A bemused smile teased her cherry-red, bow-shaped, lips.

Cadogan let his gaze linger on her mouth a moment. Had Wellington had her on staff, he could have avoided the Battle of Waterloo altogether.

"Or, for that matter, I wasn't to seek you out over—how did you say it?" she asked softly. "Whatever it is I got in my silly little head about our time together."

"That's true," he granted. "You're right."

She gave him a sad, little, look.

"But technically, you didn't really seek me out as much as *I've* come to *you*." He flashed a wry half-grin.

Raina's lovely arched eyebrows flared slightly, and she moved her stunned gaze over his face. "Mr. Cadogan, are you…*making a jest*?"

"I'll deny it to my grave," he said with false solemnity.

Raina laughed, a wholesome, merry, snorting laugh that made her, a woman so exquisite in her beauty as to be a piece of art, *real*. Even had she not possessed a grandeur to rival Helen of Troy, Raina's laugh alone had the power to not only launch a thousand ships, but to breathe a lightness into his black, jaded soul, as well.

His response to her gaiety along with her artlessness left him uncomfortably lopsided and annoyed with himself about his own weakness.

"What man hurt you?"

Raina's mirth faded as quick as it had begun.

Her expression grew shuttered.

"He is no one," she said, with an air of finality that indicated, she didn't intend to speak any further on the 'matter'.

Cadogan silently cursed himself to hell, that underworld that would one day be his final resting place.

He is no one…which meant, there was a 'he' that she wouldn't speak to Cadogan about.

His impatience had cost him.

Raina's features grew serious once more, and he knew the moment she'd stopped seeing Cadogan or thinking about him.

He frowned.

An unpleasant question whispered forward in his mind.

He thought of the noticeable efforts she'd made to avoid him these past two days. Her silence when they did see one another—her looking through him like he was invisible, which Cadogan *should* prefer, but which instead, rankled.

Her running away from him at this goddamned masquerade and giving him chase.

He drew back.

Was he the one who was responsible for her bleak, unadulterated misery?

Of course, that made the most sense.

I don't care. I don't care. I don't care.

That phrase rolled around as an unending litany in his head. For maybe, if he continued to silently repeat those words, he'd eventually come to believe them.

Fuck.

"Is this because of what happened between us at Craven's?" he asked bluntly.

Raina gasped. "My God," she breathed. "You *are* hateful."

Absolutely he was, but it wasn't because of the honest question he'd just put to her.

"Well, the truth remains, as disgusted as you are by me, I am a thousandfold so with myself," she hissed, with a bitterness he'd not believed her capable of, until now. "Panting for you. *Begging.*"

With every husky whispered reminder she gave of their exchange, his previously flaccid cock swelled to new and painful heights.

"Coming," he supplied gruffly. "You came." And loudly. She'd omitted that best and most important part.

Color blazed across Raina's high, slender cheekbones.

"Very well, Severin." Hurt filled her expressive eyes. "You want me to say it—you were right all along. I'm a whore, just like..." Her voice broke and she spun away from him.

He reeled. *A whore?* That was what she thought?

Maybe with the words you'd spoken after pleasuring her; because you gave her every reason to believe that.

His frown deepened.

No. Hers were merely the emotional musings of an untried lady.

That knowledge didn't stop him from stepping out of the

moment subjectively and silently going over every exchange he'd catalogued away.

He'd mocked her as a bored Princess, with a hungering for the forbidden. He'd never found her less because of her wants—those desires were normal cravings. They were sexual urges that were as natural to a man and a woman as breathing.

A debutante, just out in Society, however, wouldn't view it in that light. She'd see herself as immoral and debased.

With the regal grace of a queen, Raina started a march across the room and made a graceful beeline for the door.

Still stunned, Cadogan stared at her retreating figure.

That is truly what she believed he thought? She, a pixie-like beauty who wore her innocence in her eyes for all the world to see, should espouse her wickedness.

For the first time in the course of Cadogan's existence, he found himself wrong about something. He was capable of *real*, unchecked amusement, *after all*.

A rusty-sounding rumble shook his frame.

Raina whipped about so quickly her turban toppled, and her pinned hair tumbled loose and cascaded in a waterfall of whitish-blonde tresses that danced and swayed about her trim waist.

He dimly noted her marching back to him.

The back-and-forth wave of her hips as she walked, held him spellbound. God, she was magnificent. She could have coaxed the secrets out of the world's greatest informants with nothing more than a look, the sway of her hips, and smile.

Raina stopped several paces from him.

"I hate you," she seethed.

The tremble to her full, lower lip muddied the lady's clear attempts at rage and did more uncomfortable things to an area of Cadogan's chest—which felt dangerously close to his heart.

"You, who by your own admission a liar and killer, should pass judgment on me?"

"No one passes judgment on you, Raina," he said, calmly, attempting to de-escalate her rapidly spiraling response. "Most certainly not me."

She laughed. This cynical explosion of false mirth was unlike any other he'd heard spill from her lips. It contained none of the clear, bell-like, peal of real amusement.

She winged an eyebrow up. "*You* haven't judged me?"

Cadogan paused. *Had* he?

Then, the fight left Raina. The spirited lady sank into the folds of the leather button sofa near her and waved her hand as in dismissal.

"You're not really like them," she said tiredly. "In the way you make no attempt to hide your disgust and ill opinion of me, *you* are at least honest."

He frowned. "Not like *who*?"

She gave a slight shake of her head, as if trying to clear her thoughts. "It doesn't matter…"

He didn't need a lifetime of service in the Home Office to recognize *her* flimsy lie. But this vulnerable, hurting side of her was something he didn't know what the hell to do with.

Why, *why* should he suddenly feel *anything* about her suffering when he'd not been so moved by a single person in the course of his career?

No, in the course of his *life*.

Suddenly, an exit seemed easier, and he briefly eyed the doorway out. No need to stay. Plenty of reason to go, and wait for her in the hall, until she collected herself and was ready to return to the festivities.

Then he heard it…the faintest little sniffle indicating the lady cried.

Fuck.

Bloody fuck.

Cadogan, wishing just once he could choose the coward's way out, but knowing it wasn't in his blood, made his way slowly, and more, *reluctantly*, over to Raina.

Without seeking permission, he availed himself to the place beside her; close enough to confer support, but far enough to not startle her into fleeing.

He reached into his front pocket, withdrew his handkerchief, and then, without so much as looking at Raina, he silently offered her the scrap.

There was a slight hesitation before she finally plucked the article from his fingers.

Don't look at her. For some reason, her tears were like Medusa's serpent-tendrils to Cadogan, but instead of helping him maintain his stony veneer, they made him something far worse. Her tears, nay, this *woman*, made him—*human.*

They sat a long while in silence; neither one of them speaking. Nor was this quiet the deliberate kind he often employed.

Oddly, he knew *precisely* what to say to ferret out the most abominable secrets of even the most adroit emissary, but sat tongue-tied next to a virgin who'd just had her Come Out.

From the corner of his eye, he caught a flash of white fabric as Raina wiped at the corners of her eyes.

Bloody hell.

He'd looked.

Why had he looked?

Sweat slicked his palms.

Never again. When all was said and done with this goddamned assignment, he wouldn't let himself within two hundred meters of the bloody chit. She was more dangerous than Boney's best spies and more tempting than the decadent beauties who'd carried secrets he'd needed.

How did a woman such as this glorious goddess come to believe herself a victim of society's nastiness?

Bloody, bloody hell.

Cadogan grunted. "Raina, you are the Diamond, of the first water. Your favor is sought by all."

"My *brother's* favor," she said bitterly before Cadogan completed the thought.

"Yes, your brother," he conceded. "*And* you. There are certainly those desperate, weak, fellows who seek to curry the duke's favor or aspire to link their family to yours. But you are written of favorably in even the most rubbish newspaper."

Raina drew back. "*That's* how you know of me," she said, her discovery emerging as a soft exclamation. She stared at Cadogan with those wide, unblinking, doe-eyes of hers. "You *read* about me before you accepted the duke's assignment."

"Of course, I did," he said gently, and strangely the tone he adopted with her in this moment wasn't the practiced one he used to slip past the nemesis of his quarries. "And with everything I've read, there wasn't a single bad or even faintly disapproving thing recorded."

The big blue-green pools of her eyes radiated joy and Raina clasped her hands close to her chest. "Not a single one?" she whispered.

Good. He'd slowly managed to erase that woeful look of before.

Cadogan nodded. "Not a single one. You are the toast of the *ton*." He left out the obvious part, which though true, would only insult the lady—she was mad to believe she was anything less than respected and revered.

He resumed his efforts to break through to her. "Praises are sung to your beauty, Raina."

And he'd pushed too hard.

She let out a frustrated sound. "I don't care if people find me beautiful."

If? There was no 'if'. Not a single soul would or could gaze upon Raina Goodheart and see anything other than an unparalleled, ethereal beauty.

Cadogan found his footing. "The point being, Raina, are there those who are jealous of you? I'm certain of it. But you are descended from one of the oldest, most respected titles in the kingdom. People clamor for *your* family's approval, not the other way around." As she somehow thought it was. "There is not some grand number of people speaking ill of you behind your back."

Finally, he looked at her.

She stared at him with a peculiar expression; he resisted the urge to squirm.

Then, she bowed her head. "Thank you, Severin," she said softly. "Thank you for opening my eyes to see all this."

And for the first time since he'd entered this hellish office, a wave of relief washed over him.

Thank God.

Some of the tension eased from him. He'd done his job. He'd secured his quarry and gotten her to a place where he could now be free of her.

"Are you ready to return to the ball?"

Her nod came so enthusiastically, and he should feel a great swell of relief at being done with her—for now. Why then, did he feel something damned close to regret at her flitting among those drunken lords, while Cadogan stood in the shadows and watched her all the while?

He quickly stood.

"Here," he said gruffly, and set to work tucking her blonde tresses back into place.

All the while he fixed her hair, removing pins, and rearranging pieces into their previous artful arrangement, Raina remained regally still.

Cadogan next saw to her shimmery blue and green feathered turban until finally all her glorious blonde locks were concealed.

He paused to assess his finished work.

What a shame to hide all that beauty.

Puzzling her brow, Raina touched a palm to the side of her head. "Is there something wrong?"

There was everything *right* about the lady. *That* was the problem. It was…*she* was…proving an unwelcome, and unexpected *distraction*.

"The mask," he said. "I was thinking what was missing. It's your mask."

Fortunately believing that prevarication on his part, Raina fished the article in question out of her organza pocket and held it up, so it danced in the air between them.

Wordlessly, Cadogan took the feathered disguise from Raina's bare fingers that were exposed by her open-cut black leather gloves.

Moving behind the lady, he lowered the mask over her face, so that his arms framed her, and affixed the disguise.

When he'd finished, he took a safe step back away from her, putting some healthy space between him and the nymph.

"There," he said, flatly, all business once more.

Cadogan stretched out an arm and motioned to the exit.

Raina eyed him a moment, and then took that silent cue and headed toward the front of the room. When she reached for the panel, Cadogan waved her aside and took her place at the entrance.

Once she was off to the side and safe from view, he ducked his head outside the door, and eyed the dimly lit hallway, several times. He waited a moment more.

Empty.

Glancing over at her, Cadogan jerked his chin.

Raina exited before him. She'd gone several steps when she paused to look back at him.

There was a question in her eyes.

He nudged his jaw. "Go," he mouthed.

They couldn't be seen together, and with Cadogan, undisguised, here at Argyll's behest as a visible reminder that none were to tamper with his sister, certainly not alone.

This time, Raina didn't cast another glance his way. She resumed her stately march, and he stared after her retreating figure, until she reached the end of the hall, and took a left toward the ballroom.

CHAPTER 15

It's been twelve agonizingly long days. My love and I have finally resumed speaking.
~The Duchess of A

THE MINUTE HE FOUND HIMSELF alone, Cadogan dragged a hand over his face.

Bloody hell. The chit needed to get herself married. *Cadogan* desperately needed her to marry some good, boring, safe, respectable fellow.

When had he ever been so fascinated by a woman—at that, a goddamned lily-white virgin.

Disgusted with himself, Cadogan quit the host's office, and, after he drew the door shut behind him, he started at a quick clip, the same path Raina had taken.

Perhaps he should take Argyll up on his generous offer. Perhaps he *should* have the duke select two—*no*, three—of his filthiest, most accomplished bawds for Cadogan. Cadogan could fuck them all senseless and do the wickedest things to them and with them. Then, and only then, in relieving himself of this unbridled, irrational lust that gripped him whenever he so much as thought about Lady Raina, could he think clearly again.

At least, when he'd been instructed to lure the secrets out of the mistresses, lovers, and wives of men who were enemies to the State, he'd been able to fuck freely with work being the ultimate driving force. In each of those many encounters, sex with those wantons had been an enormous benefit that kept his head clear.

But he couldn't fuck Raina.

Oh, he wanted to. He wanted to do the dirtiest, most debauched things to her gloriously curved body.

The Princess, however, was off-limits, and her being forbidden fruit, only made him hungrier for her.

She—

Footfalls and the low murmur of voices reached him.

"There's not been a sight of the peacock," one of the men was saying, his tone wreathed in frustration.

Cadogan's eyebrows dipped.

Their voices and steps grew nearer.

"What's the matter? Afraid, she's already busy servicing some other man's cock?"

"I'm sure she is," the friend said, sounding purely disgruntled at the thought as if he had some right and possession of the lady in question.

The lady in question being…

From a place deep within, where the greatest evil and darkness dwelled inside Cadogan, a growl built.

Raina.

Balling his hands into tight fists of fury, Cadogan ducked into the nearest room, and waited.

"Worry not, old chum," the other fellow said, his voice growing nearer. "Given the stories of the late duchess's exploits, the fact someone's in her cunny right now, hardly means she wouldn't be more than happy to be stuffed full a second, third, or fourth time, right after." The gentleman paused. "In fact, maybe even at the *same* time," he added, as they passed by the parlor where Cadogan stood, stationed.

The pair erupted into ribald laughter.

A breathtaking and boundless rage coursed through every nerve ending in Cadogan's being.

Caught up in their crude discourse on Raina, the bastards never heard him coming.

Cadogan caught each man by the side of their necks. He sank a finger into their pressure points which held them paralyzed.

Leaning in, Cadogan placed his lips between them. "Speak of her again? Next time, you die," he vowed on a low, graveled whisper.

Their previous levity gave way to matching whimpers.

Without another word, Cadogan brought the men's heads colliding at the temple.

They crumpled into a noiseless heap; their hilarity of before silenced.

It wasn't enough.

His chest heaving, Cadogan stood, the savage beast that he was, looming over them; his fingers curled into claws as the monster he'd been transformed into. He itched, ached, and yearned to rip their throats out and kill them.

The urge to murder was strong as it'd ever been. Filled with a primal urge to silence them forever, Cadogan could taste their blood on his tongue like he'd already spilled it.

With a growl, he brought his heel back and kicked first one, and then the other, in their sides, over and over again.

The cloud of black rage hung like a curtain still over his vision.

The need: to leave some visible mark he left this day to remind them of the fate awaiting them were they to defy his orders.

Snarling, Cadogan crowded over the unconscious pair and unleashed his full wrath upon them. He slammed a fist into the lanky fellow's face first. The bastard's nose crumpled under that blow until blood gushed from that broken appendage and coated Cadogan's knuckles.

As he delivered the man an unforgivable beating, Cadogan's chest heaved from the thrill of punishing the ones who'd dared breathe her name.

A moan from the other prig penetrated Cadogan's all-consuming, demonic wrath.

Perspiring from his exertions, Cadogan put all his attention on the prig just starting to come through. With a feral grin, Cadogan leveraged back to deliver the neglected bounder, the same fate as his chum—when a faint whisper reached him.

"S…Severin?"

He froze.

Fuck.

Straightening, Cadogan turned toward the owner of that softly lilting voice.

Some ten yards away stood Raina. The portions of her face

revealed by her mask were a stark white, her lush lips parted in a pretty moue…and those eyes. Those revelatory blues that were a window into her soul and thoughts.

His rapidly speeding pulse slowed to a dull, sickening, thump. Christ.

What had he done?

He'd been careless. He'd never been negligent.

But that isn't really true, is it? Cadogan's inner voice mocked him. *You were sloppy, once before and that slackness cost you a career.*

That silent reminder alone should propel him into movement. Instead, he loomed over his vanquished foes, as immobilized as those lesser men.

He'd vowed to never again be as weak as he'd been on that failed mission, and yet, frozen in this corridor across from Raina, with discovery imminent, he found himself more impotent than ever—because of a woman.

No, not just any woman.

Her.

This Siren.

His Achille's heel.

This enchantress who, with graceful, confident strides, now moved toward him, while Cadogan's own legs had been rendered useless.

As she neared, he drew his top lip back in a feral sneer. His blood coursed still with rage over the men who'd dared disparage her, at Raina for having caught him in a rare moment of weakness, and himself for having been so absorbed as to not have heard her approach.

By the time she reached him, that boiling pent-up frustration reached a crescendo, and he opened his mouth to blast her for returning.

Going up on tiptoe, Raina twined her slender limbs about Cadogan's neck and effectively silenced him.

Without missing a beat, his innocent, beguiling, temptress, pressed her soft, supple body against him. His entire body went stiff, and his randy cock responded to the feel of her.

His chest rose hard and fell in time to hers. Their breaths, his harsh, hers ragged, melded and meshed.

With their gazes, they searched one another's faces

"Thank you," she breathed against his mouth.

Cadogan took her hips in his hands; his fingers bit into her so hard, she gasped.

Narrowing his eyes, Cadogan squeezed her tightly. "You're nothing but an assignment, Princess," he ground out, that sharp, angry reminder for the both of them.

Raina, intrepid and stunningly strong-willed, held his gaze with a stunning directness. "I don't believe that, Severin," she said, so calm in that mellifluent utterance, it had the opposite effect on Cadogan.

Burned, he released his hold on her hips and made to step out of her arms, but Raina tightened her hold about him.

Sheer, mindless panic, the likes of which he'd never known, held him in its grip.

"You're wrong," he taunted. "*Desperate*, if you believe *that*."

Me, I'm the desperate one.

The fact Raina held him, and Cadogan made not the slightest attempt to shake free of her weaker hold, when anyone, at any minute could pass by, showed her wieldy power over him.

"You didn't save my life," she said softly. "You defended *my name*." The long, graceful column of her neck moved rhythmically up and down. "That was never part of your assignment, Severin. You could have let those two men continue on their way and forget you ever heard it, but you didn't."

He couldn't speak, because her words were truth, and effectively lying in this moment, to her, evaded even him.

Christ. How much had she witnessed?

Cadogan cast a frantic look back over at the still unconscious pair he'd silenced. Worse, what might she have overheard him say?

Raina brushed her fingers in a delicate, butterfly-soft caress along his jawline, and guided his focus back to her. Her tender, lingering, touch, burned Cadogan—in every way.

"You avenged my honor, Severin." Tears turned her eyes into shimmery pools.

With every word she spoke, his panic spiraled.

But the tears.

Her tears would be his downfall. Even when they glimmered from the joy expressed within.

"Why the hell are you here, Princess?" he rasped. "Why the fuck didn't you go back to the festivities like I instructed?"

Why, when by returning to this spot, she'd unsettled the universe's balance?

Raina moved her guileless eyes across his face. Suddenly, she went motionless.

Her neat, slender brows flared like some great understanding just dawned.

Cadogan tensed and reached up to untangle her graceful arms from about him.

Then, Raina lifted herself higher up onto tiptoe and brought herself close so her breath, an intoxicating blend of champagne and strawberries, teased his lips.

She pressed her mouth against his in a gentle, but full kiss.

All the while, she moved her lips over his, Cadogan remained rooted to the spot, fighting for restraint; digging deep.

She paused, with her lips a hairsbreadth away from his own. "Kiss me," she whispered, hers a plea and a command, so divergent, his shaft twitched at the unexpected—and unexpectedly, appetizing juxtaposition.

Then moaning, Raina parted her lips and gave him full dominion over her mouth, issuing an erotic invitation for Cadogan to sin and surrender—and he was lost.

He froze and then with a low, fierce growl he folded her in his arms. Without breaking contact with her lips, he drove Raina back into the previous parlor he'd secreted himself.

He didn't even dig down to salvage his habitually rigid self-control. Enflamed as he'd never been, he now knew fighting was futile. He'd not get back to a place of self-mastery until he slaked his lust with this woman.

It had to be her.

And, with his caution as fucked as Cadogan himself was, he kicked his heel back and shoved the panel shut.

In one quick movement, he drove her against the door.

The panel gave a noisy thump.

His body made a prison around her.

"They don't matter, Raina," he jeered. He bore his eyes into hers. "You spend so much of your life trying to conform yourself into some fictional, unflawed, colorless, lady to please a world that cannot be pleased."

Cadogan lowered his brow to hers. "All the while, love, you still haven't realized, there's nothing ordinary about you. You've an effervescence that cannot be dimmed, no matter how much you attempt to extinguish your own light."

Raina's breath caught; the shimmery, adoring, light that sparked to life, set off warning bells.

Refusing to focus on that deep reverence, he buried his mouth against hers.

He and Raina were both gripped by uncontrollable, mindless lust, for each other—that was it.

In life, everyone took what they wanted and needed. Cadogan did not take himself as any kind of exception to that rule.

His family, the Home Office, his clients, his bed partners, they all had wanted or did want something from him.

This innocent, firebrand, eagerly kissing him in return, was no different.

Steadied by those reminders, Cadogan glided his fingers all over Raina's shapely body. He cupped her high, buxom breasts in his hands; he squeezed and molded the plump flesh until Raina's heartfelt moans and breathy sighs filled his mouth.

Cadogan's pulse pounded in his ears. Sweat built at his brow.

Between each thumb and forefinger, he caught her nipples, and tweaked and squeezed.

Raina bucked her hips frantically into Cadogan.

A satisfied grin brought his lips up.

Yanking her flimsy skirts up, he shoved a knee between her legs, parted her, and drew her to rest on his thigh. In a rhythm as old as time, Raina, her breath coming as hard and fast as Cadogan's, sank onto leg and began to hump him.

A bead of moisture slipped down his cheek.

Gritting his teeth, Cadogan held her hips in his hands and guided Raina up and down. "Is this what you want, sweetheart?" he demanded, harshly in between each slant of his mouth over hers.

She whimpered and moaned her affirmation.

Cadogan grunted his approval.

Good, it was what he wanted, too—what he needed.

Then, he'd be fine.

She'd be well sated.

And he'd be free.

When Raina ground her core hard against him to find her climax more quickly, Cadogan tightened his hold on her hips and steered her rhythm.

"Slow, sweet," he urged, out of breath himself. "You don't rush lovemaking."

Raina's long, thick lashes fluttered, and she lifted desire-filled eyes to his. "I thought you didn't make l—"

Silencing the rest of that, Cadogan captured her mouth in a rabid kiss; he sucked her full, lower lip hard, alternately biting that crimson flush and suckling. Finally, he plunged his tongue inside and thrust wildly, angry in his desire.

Instead of maidenly fear, Raina moaned low and long; the movements of her hips grew faster and more frantic.

Pure, savage, lust consumed him.

Yanking the bodice of her gown down, Cadogan exposed her enormous breasts to his worship.

His mouth went dry at the bounteous sight before him. She'd the most beautifully formed titties he'd ever laid eyes on.

At his scrutiny, shy, virginal, Raina brought trembling hands up to cover herself.

Cadogan caught her hands in his and stopped her. "Don't shield yourself, sweet. You don't hide splendidness such as this."

Her eyes softened.

Disconcerted by the transparency in her every thought, move, and love, Cadogan threw himself back into his efforts of getting them both off this day.

He shifted his mouth; trailing a path of kisses, dragging his tongue along her heated skin, as he made his way to that place he had to taste.

Cadogan stopped with his lips a hairsbreadth away from her big, swollen, nipples.

"Look at these beautiful breasts," he praised, lifting the bounteous orbs in his palms. Her flesh overflowed even in Cadogan's large hands. "How could you ever think to hide them?"

"S-Severin," she implored.

Ignoring her pleas, he brought the heavy globes together, lowered his head, and flicked his tongue back and forth between the stiff peaks.

Exhaling a gasp, Raina sank onto his thigh and resumed grinding herself fiercely against him.

Cadogan sucked and suckled her; he kneaded and stroked her aching breasts until Raina's speech dissolved, and only incoherent utterances spilled from her swollen lips.

He stopped fast.

Raina cried out.

Her body crumpled against the door, and she stared at him with accusatory angry eyes.

Holding her desperate gaze with his amused one, he slowly, and deliberately shepherded her deeper into the room.

"Worry not, Raina," he teased, as she willingly went. "I'll give you another one of those delicious little deaths you so love." He brought her to a stop at the nearest piece of furniture. "This time," he said huskily, "this time, however, we'll *both* come."

She blushed as the virgin she was, even as her expressive eyes glittered with curiosity at the promise he'd made.

"Sit," he ordered sharply. "And part your legs for me."

At his crisp command, she stumbled slightly, and fell into the sofa.

Cadogan grunted his approval. "Good girl." He sank onto his knees and catching her by her hips, he dragged her to the edge.

Aside from the queen, he'd never knelt for any woman. He'd only serviced lovers in this way as a way to exact secrets from them, but never had he knelt. He'd lain in beds and placed his head between his partner's legs, making them come as he would this woman now.

Ultimately, however, he was the master of all his bed partners. They were weaker than him, so weak they'd do whatever he bid, and he'd never be so pathetic as to be submissive for anyone. Only to now discover a terrifying hunger for prostrating himself before this naïve, innocent, but eager, siren.

"Wh-What are you doing?" The sound of Raina's voice brought him back to the moment.

He glanced up.

At some point, she'd leveled herself onto her elbows and now stared at him with a question in her passion-glazed eyes.

Slaking his lust and surrendering to this lady was the only thing that would allow him to be free of this maddening, all-consuming hunger. Better to give in to his desire for her than be devoured by it.

Restored by that thought, he flashed a feral grin.

"What am I doing?" he purred. "I'm showing you pleasure like you've never known." His pledge emerged as a harsh, bestial, gnarl. "And after me, a pleasure you'll never know again," he warned, growing harder just by the thought of her unblemished fingers wrapped about his cock.

She whimpered, and she squirmed as if the idea of belonging to him this once drove her mad with desire.

This time, he took his time, lifting her skirts. Cadogan dragged the soft, silken fabric up slowly, inching it higher and higher. As he bared her lower limbs, he drank in the sight of each exposed swath of skin: tapered ankles, rounded calves, defined knees.

He paused at her thighs.

His nostrils flared. Her well-proportioned thighs were a blend of athleticism and voluptuous flesh, and there was no other place he wanted to be than between them.

Cadogan shoved her costume all the way up about her waist. His mouth went dry, and his ballocks tightened at the sight.

Under her costume, she'd not bothered with chemise and pantalets, and now, naked from the waist down, her cunny sat on full, libidinous display.

Raina's curly mound of pale blonde curls beckoned. He slipped his fingers through that tight nest at the apex of her thighs and tested her wetness. He chuckled at the discovery. "You're dripping for me, already."

Raina moaned and arched her hips.

"I want to feel you on my tongue, sweet Raina. I want to taste you and lap you up…and I'm going to."

As he'd intended with those salacious words, her guileless eyes widened.

"I'm not even going to ask if you want it, love," he whispered, caressing his hands along the outside of her slender, but voluptuous thighs. "By the way you're dripping wet and the heavy scent of your musk, I know you do."

Cadogan dropped a quick, harsh, hard kiss upon her inner thigh. That slight brush of his lips pulled a gasp from Raina's lips. Whimpering, she splayed her legs more widely, inviting him in.

"And I'm going to do it now, sweet," he growled.

Sliding his hands under her bare arse, he drew her closer, and then, Cadogan, buried his nose against her sodden curls, and slipped his tongue in that cleft between her legs.

Raina cried out. She gripped his head in her hands, anchored him to that hot place where she wanted him, and urged him on.

And Cadogan randy like a schoolboy, was all too happy to oblige the lady.

He threw himself into the task of servicing her. He sucked her swollen, sensitive, folds. He licked them, nipped them, until Raina was writhing and moaning.

Enflamed by the heightened state of her arousal, Cadogan slipped a finger inside her tight, wet, center.

A hiss exploded from between her lips and her hips shot up. "Severin!"

"Love this, do you, Princess?" he rasped, between each glide of his tongue in her slit.

"*Yes*," she moaned, stretching that one syllable into four.

The thrusts of her hips grew faster, more agitated.

Sweat beaded at his brow

She was so fucking wet and responsive. The way she moved and begged and gave of herself drove him mad. Unlike every single lover he'd ever taken or been required to bed, who'd known precisely how to move, and who'd been false in every way, there wasn't a shade of artifice to Raina Goodheart.

He stole a glance up, and it proved a fatal error.

Raina stared down at him, with soft, desperate, eyes. The depth of emotion in them, briefly paralyzed him.

What the hell are you doing? You aren't one of those pathetic men ruled by their cocks.

But then, just as he made to stop, Raina let her head loll against the back of the sofa, and she directed her gaze to the heavens.

Cadogan knew the moment she ceased to see him, and everything within her tunneled on the glide of his tongue in and out of her. That unwitting distance she'd put up also allowed him to carry on pleasuring her.

He buried his tongue inside her channel; alternately sucking at her swollen, slick folds.

Raina lifted and lowered her hips.

"Severin," she panted his name, over and over again. "Severin." It was as if all other words had left her, and his given one was the only one she knew. "*Severin.*"

He stopped again.

This time, she wept.

Taking mercy on his enchantress, Cadogan pressed a kiss against the inside of her silky soft, thigh.

She whimpered.

"Aww, my Princess is in pain." Cadogan burrowed his mouth against her sopping thatch. "We cannot have that..." He gave Raina more of what she liked—nay, *loved*.

Her breath grew shallower. Her thrusting quicker, more agitated.

His cock responded in kind. Cadogan gritted his teeth in pain and annoyance at how badly he wanted to fuck her.

"Are you all r-right?" Raina's hesitant whisper reached across his body's tortured misery.

He leaned back, balancing on his haunches. "I'm so hard for you, I hurt," he said bluntly, confessing something he'd never confessed to another woman, for the simple fact, he'd never known a desire like this for anyone before her.

Raina dampened her lips with the tip of her pink tongue. Instead of turning timid, she stole another bold peek at his trousers.

Curiosity and shock brought her eyes into a full flare. "It *grew*," she whispered, awe-struck.

A chuckle, equal parts amusement and desire, shook his frame. "It does that."

"Yes, I know," she prattled, her words coming quick, and filled with the excitement of one who'd made some great scientific discovery. "I just thought it grew and then...that was it." Raina renewed her study of his tented pants. "Does it just continue to grow?"

Her innocent query sent a fresh round of blood rushing to that randy organ. Cadogan attempted to tamp down a groan—and failed.

The minx scrambled to the edge of her seat. "Oh, Saint's preserved," she whispered. "It *does*. Will it eventually explode?"

A strained laugh exploded from Cadogan's chest, and he dropped his head forward.

She gasped. "Oh, goodness, Severin. You're in pain."

Then, before he knew what the lively beauty intended, she reached over and wrestled the buttons of his front flap free.

His cock immediately sprung free from the excruciating constraints, and he exhaled a slow, sigh of relief and he moved between her thighs again.

That allayment proved entirely too short-lived.

He felt her eyes upon him and glanced up.

Raina's puffy lips parted. She attempted to close them and failed. "You are...*huge*."

This time, when he drew away from Raina, gasped. "No," she wailed.

Her long, surprisingly strong, fingers spasmed in his hair—but the lady found her grip. Holding Cadogan's head in an almost punishing hold, she forced his head back to that place where she needed him most and the only place he wanted to be in this moment.

As such, Cadogan allowed Raina that false sense of control. He let her ride his mouth and tongue and grind herself into his face.

He was even amused by it.

His chest rose and fell hard and fast.

Even more, however, he was aroused by her attempts.

"Beg me," he taunted, his breath, ragged. "*Beg me*, my sweet, Raina. Tell me how badly you want me to suck you until you come. Tell me, and I'll give you what you want."

And then, finally, Cadogan would have what *he* wanted.

CHAPTER 16

*I still marvel at the fact he, the Duke of Argyll, believed I,
his wife, a good, respectable, lady would <u>ever</u> visit
a place so scandalous.*
~ The Duchess of A

SPRAWLED ON HER HOSTESS'S PRETTY sofa, with her rumpled skirts rucked about her waist, and Severin prone before her, Raina made a discovery.

She wanted Severin Cadogan.

She wanted him, not just as the skillful lover, and only man, who could ease the agonized throbbing between her legs.

She wanted *him*, Severin Cadogan, the Earl of Killburn—blunt, honest, and unapologetic. He wasn't the polite, proper, tender gentleman she'd imagined she wanted.

Where Raina had existed in a self-doubting state, worrying over people's ill opinions, and fearing who she might be, she'd simply existed and not lived.

Unlike Severin. Confident and self-assured, he made no apologies for the things he'd done, and in every way, owned he was, and it was impossible not to love such an impenitent man.

It was why she had no pride around him, and even less so when he had his hands or mouth upon her.

For years, Raina had wondered, and worried over the question as to whether she was a wanton like her mother. She'd feared society's opinion of her.

Now, however, with this bold, strong, powerful man, kneeling between her thighs, and pleasuring her so, she, at last, realized—

she didn't care what the world thought. She didn't care about what decisions her mother made.

The duchess's decisions hadn't been Raina's.

Raina's life was her own.

Cadogan had set her free of the chains she'd bound herself in.

Severin flicked his tongue teasingly over some over-sensitized place between her legs, bringing her back to the moment.

Raina cried out. Of their own volition, her hips shot up.

Severin paused his efforts and tipped his face up enough to flash Raina a smile.

"Where have you gone, sweet?"

The tender way he spoke and the grin he wore, was not the practiced, hard, empty one that too often grazed his lips.

She tipped her head to the side and contemplated him. This smile, so real, and teeming with benevolence and warmth, and it was as though, only during this love act that he could truly let his defenses down.

He grunted. "What?" he demanded, all harsh roughness once more.

Still off-kilter, Raina shook her head. "It's..." *This glimpse of you.* Only, she couldn't say that. Not without scaring him off completely.

An impatient growl rolled past his lips.

"Nothing," she murmured. "It is nothing." It was everything.

His sharp, angular features fell back into a familiar mask, and yet, he'd let it slip. He'd revealed that hidden inside, existed a man capable of warmth and tenderness.

It was like the shooting star she'd once seen flying across the Kent sky, one summer—so fleeting, but magical and magnificent—a chimerical sight too wondrous to ever be forgotten.

"Shall I stop?" he jeered.

Raina caressed her fingers along the jagged, puckered, red scar upon his cheek. "Do not stop, Severin," she said softly

Passion blazed to life in his eyes.

He pressed a fierce kiss against her inner thigh, and then took that flesh in his mouth, suckling so hard she knew he marked her in this most intimate place; a spot that only Raina would see, so that she could remember when he'd put his mouth upon her.

Raina briefly closed her eyes.

She wanted him to imprint her as his—even as he clearly wasn't a man who'd ever want anyone. She'd not think of that now. As he sucked and nipped that soft flesh, she allowed herself to lose herself in his full, open-mouthed ministrations.

Then, he buried his nose in the damp curls at the apex of her legs.

She inhaled sharply.

"I love the smell of you," he murmured.

Raina whimpered. With his face at the entrance of her womanhood, when Severin spoke, his chin brushed against her throbbing center and his low voice rumbled through her.

"You're earthy, and sweet like molasses. May I have another lick, sweet Raina?"

"*Yes.*"

Chuckling, Severin licked her slit back and forth over and over.

Her lashes were suddenly too heavy. Closing her eyes, Raina let her head fall along the back of the sofa, while he worshipped her.

"You taste even better than you smell, love," he murmured, between each glide of his tongue. "I could eat you all day. If you thought people talked before, imagine what they'd say if I dropped to my knees and lifted your skirts and ate you up in the middle of the ball."

Raina palmed his cheek.

At last, she had her answer. She didn't crave or want the exhibitionism that her parents made of lovemaking. She wanted to celebrate the wonder and magic of the wicked, alone, with the man she loved; their own, private, but most intimate, glorious secret.

"I don't want anyone to see us, Severin," she said softly.

He chuckled. "Good," he whispered, dropping a kiss of approval atop her damp curls. "Because then others would want a taste, and I'd have to kill them because I don't like sharing."

With that, Severin lowered his head between her legs and buried his tongue deep inside her slit.

As he attended her, she closed her eyes and lay in lazy surrender to his worshipping.

He bespoke the manner of relationship she ached to have—one with a man who'd sooner slay than share Raina with another. One where he'd love her and do the most salacious things with her and to her, in a way that left them both satisfied as to never need or want to stray.

Just like that, Raina lost another corner of her heart to him.

While he still serviced her, Severin lifted his head enough to slant a hard look at Raina. For a moment, she feared he'd been truthful before and that he knew all her thoughts.

For an even longer moment, she feared she'd driven him away, and he'd stop making love to her.

"You still haven't begged me," he purred against her throbbing folds.

He pulled away so quickly, a convulsion wracked her body. She cried out; the pain of his cessation couldn't hurt less than had she taken an actual bullet.

"Severin," she turned his name into the entreaty he sought.

He dipped his thumb between her folds and gave her several maddening strokes, then, her punishing lover showed her benevolence. He buried a long, powerful finger deep inside her.

She exhaled a soft, grateful sigh and began to move. Lifting and lowering her hips, Raina rode his hand, too consumed by her need for fulfillment to be ashamed of her wantonness.

Raina was so close. She pushed against his hand. If she just ground herself into him, she'd have that glorious surrender she'd known only with him.

"Tsk. Tsk. Are you trying to steal from me, Raina?"

In the worst form of punishment, Cadogan drew that long, callused finger out of her channel.

Words failing, Raina made an unintelligible sound of protest.

Cadogan lifted that long digit he'd stroked her with; it glimmered with the sheen of her juices. "Want a taste of life's sweetest dessert?" he tempted.

A stab of lust ran through her.

Even as a blush born of desire and shyness blazed across her cheeks, a stab of lust ran through Raina. She forced herself to shake her head.

He chuckled. "Liar." His expression grew feral. "More for me."

Riveted, Raina watched, wide-eyed, as he drew that finger deep into his mouth, and sucked her essence free.

Briefly, he closed his eyes, like a man who'd tasted the first apple in that fated garden. "Delicious," he murmured.

Suddenly, he opened his eyes and made to stand.

Raina gasped, and, scrambling to the edge of her seat, she caught his arm. "Wh-what are you doing?"

She didn't care about the desperation that rang out in her query. Surely, he wasn't this cruel?

He gave her a cool once-over. "You know the rules, Raina. I get what I want. *Beg* me."

Beg me.

Of course, he'd take nothing less than what he'd demanded—Raina, humbled and begging, with the words he wanted, and how he wanted them.

Severin didn't think she'd so lower herself. Undoubtedly, he took her as a woman too proud and too spirited to beg any man—and he'd be correct.

What he didn't know—and she was grateful for his ignorance—to her, Severin wasn't a mere man; he was a God among mere mortals; a king among plebians. When it came to Severin Cadogan, the Earl of Killburn, Raina had no pride.

The price he asked, her supplication, was a pittance.

She'd have handed him her soul in this moment.

Shifting back onto the sofa, she edged up her skirts that'd slipped, and splayed her legs wider, in a wicked and welcoming invitation. "I want your mouth on me, Severin, *please*," she beseeched.

His eyes dilated. "Good girl," he growled.

She'd never grow tired of his naughty praise.

Then, just as he'd promised, Severin gave her what she hungered for…what she needed.

He started slow; flicking his tongue back and forth over that extra sensitive nub at her center; grazing it, licking it until a little mewling, throaty incoherent sound built in her throat and bubbled from her lips.

"This is your clit," he said, while he pleasured her. "I'm going to suck it, sweet."

She cried out as he fulfilled that latest promise. That vulgar word combined with the wild dance his tongue played at her center, sent her body temperature rising.

Her mind had ceased to function. The tender, exquisitely, thorough love Severin made to her, reduced her to a bundle of heightened nerves.

Moaning, she undulated her hips, in time to each, long, slow glide of his tongue.

While he worshipped her womanhood, she stared, dazed, overhead at the mural of two lovers embracing amidst a lush garden.

She didn't want this to end. But more, she wanted him—*all* of him. His blunt honesty. His cool self-assuredness. His passion.

Raina forced her heavy eyes to Severin, and she watched as he worked her with his mouth.

When this man loved, he'd do so with the whole heart he swore he didn't possess. With his fiercely primal, possessiveness, he'd never use the women in his life—be it his wife, his daughter, a sister, or any female kin—as whores to grow his empire.

He'd not force her to don a crown and march her around like a piece of horseflesh as some sort of distraction that, in some way, furthered his wants.

And she wanted to belong to such a man.

Raina closed her eyes and allowed herself the fantasy, that Severin knelt between her legs, as the husband she'd like him to be; *her* husband.

The image was too much; the pull too great, and she lost all control.

"Severin!" Crying out, Raina's back and neck arched at the same time she wrapped her legs about his head.

Weeping and cursing, she ground her sex against his face.

He did not let up.

Severin lapped her and licked her and sucked her until every nerve in her body thrummed and tingled.

Only when she collapsed back into the folds of the sofa did Severin stop.

Panting and gasping, Raina lay there replete; her shoulders rising and falling fast, all the life drained from her.

She'd read naughty books, with even naughtier pictures. She'd read her mother's vivid, and also pitiful, journal. She'd been a voyeur to others in various states of dishabille, and also in various acts of lovemaking.

Never, *never* had she believed it could be like this.

Liar.

The muscles of her mouth, too tired to form the deserved smile, twitched, instead.

Each and every single love act coaxed her to new, soaring heights, so that, after each exchange, Raina wondered at how she could move through her life with her feet firmly on the floor.

Alas, all good things came to an end.

She felt a rush of cool air as Severin pulled his head out from between her legs, and she sighed at that loss.

Cadogan looked up. His mouth, chin, and jaw gleamed with her juices, and the sight of her on him sent a fresh flood of wanting to her core. "Good, Princess?"

Another dreamy smile played at the corners of her lips.

It'd been magical, wondrous, otherworldly, and she wanted to do it again and again with him.

With the cocksure glint in his eyes and haughty grin, the gentleman knew very well the havoc he'd wrought on her senses.

Raina gave his arm a playful swat. "You know it was far more than good," she said, her voice husky and thick as only it'd ever been in the earliest morning hour.

For as sated as Raina found herself, however, Severin's features were arranged into a pained mask.

She wasn't naïve. She'd read enough to know a man needed to spill his seed to stop hurting as Severin clearly did in this moment—because of her.

And for the first time without caring about legacy or being proper so as to not become like all the other Goodheart's before, she brushed her fingertips lightly along his shoulder.

His hard eyes, glinting with frustration and heat, bore through hers.

"You are hurting," she said softly.

He narrowed his eyes.

"I...I know that...not that I know-know it," Raina rambled,

but couldn't stop herself. "But I'm aware that what happened to my body, happens to yours. Not in the same way, of course." Her cheeks heated. "I just know you are hurting."

"It's not an emotional pain," he said sharply.

She drew back. "N-No. I'm aware." Severin took care to remind her at every turn that he wasn't capable of emotion, outside the physical.

"What are you saying then, Raina?" he jeered.

Severin still hadn't realized, she wouldn't be cowed by him. He thought to scare her off. No, he believed he could scare her off.

"I'm saying I want to pleasure you the way you pleasured me." That profession emerged far more timidly than she wished.

But just speaking those words aloud, sent a fresh flood of warmth and wetness rushing to her core.

His eyes bulged. His nostrils flared.

He had the look of a crazed man. The fact she had this power over him, rocked her with another wave of desire so strong she squirmed and shifted on the bench to alleviate herself of that unbearable ache.

Then, a mocking smile touched his lips. "You want to pleasure me or bring me off the *same* way I brought *you* off?"

Bring him off.

How crude.

How vulgar.

And how those utterances enflamed Raina.

That mocking grin he wore became all-knowing. Severin wrongly took her hesitation as second thoughts. How little he knew her.

Tipping her chin at a bold angle, she held his gaze. "I want to do whatever it is that makes you feel the way I do when you bring me pleasure, Severin."

He inhaled a sharp, noisy breath, through his teeth.

Getting up from the floor, he joined her on the sofa. "Then, let us begin, sweet."

Sweet.

She'd always dreamed of having a suitor and husband who'd refer to her by those little endearments, but how she preferred those rare times he called her his 'love'.

"You've never touched a man," he said, matter-of-fact. "Take me in your hand and I will show you how."

She didn't want to know for or because or how for any man—but him.

Humbled by that truth, she did as he bid, and wrapped her fingers around his enormous length.

A hiss exploded from between his teeth.

"I hurt you." She made to pull her palm back, but he wrapped his larger hand about Raina's.

"You hurt me in the best possible way, love," he said, his breath coming hard like he'd run a long race.

Severin's shaft pulsed and jumped, and she lifted her gaze, marveling that she had any power over this formidable, menacing lord.

He grunted. "Let me show you."

Severin guided her hand through the motion; teaching her exactly what he liked, and how he liked it. He showed her the right amount of pressure to exert.

And as she found the rhythm, he extolled Raina's efforts.

"Good girl," he panted.

There must surely be a deficit of her soul and character that just two casual words from this man could stir such pride within.

He helped her onto her knees, and she willingly, no, eagerly went.

"Now, take me in your mouth."

Raina didn't hesitate; she did as he bade, parting her lips wide, and lowering her mouth over his thick, long length.

"Slowly, love," he guided her, tutored her. "Less teeth."

As he instructed her, she modified her movements to match the instructions he gave her. He coaxed her, teaching her just how he liked it.

"Like that," he coached, breathing heavily as he did. "Relax your jaw so you can take me deeper."

And Raina knew by the relieved sigh that escaped him, that he approved.

Soon, Raina found the rhythm he loved

His head fell back. "Mmm," he groaned. "You're so good at this. Now, move up and down, Raina." All the while she followed his instructions, he stroked the top of her head like a beloved pup, whom he rewarded with a caress.

Emboldened, Raina took him deeper.

"Yes," he hissed, lifting his hips up and down to meet each stroke of her mouth.

Her center throbbed and dripped shamefully, as pleasuring him, fueled her own desire. In a bid to alleviate the agonizing ache between her legs, Raina rocked her hips, thrusting at empty air.

He chuckled. "My Princess is getting off on sucking me."

I am bad. I am wicked.

Those ugly, unwanted, intrusive thoughts that'd been with her too long, chose that moment to slip in and cast a darkness upon a previously only beautiful exchange.

Once they sank their tendrils in, there was no shaking free.

Do you truly believe other good, virginal, debutantes are off in a parlor, kneeling between a gentleman's legs?

I am my moth—

Severin cupped her jaw with an infinite tenderness and forced her to stop and meet his gaze. "You are perfection," he murmured, huskily. "Celebrate the joy of lovemaking; do not punish yourself for it, sweet Raina."

Her heart sped up and his rough, but gentle manner silenced those self-contemptuous ruminations.

"Tease me with your tongue," he encouraged, roughly.

Raina poured herself into his pleasure. She licked his length and swirled her tongue around the plump, round, tip of his shaft.

"Oh, fuck, that feels so good, love."

She continued that way, alternately sucking and licking him.

"Raina," he moaned, nothing more than her name, over and over again. "Raina. Raina."

She took him even deeper until he nearly touched the back of her throat.

His manhood grew impossibly big in her mouth, and she widened her lips to accommodate that stretching.

"You are so good," he panted. "How are you this good?"

While she learned the way he liked it, Severin groaned low and long.

"Christ," he rasped. "You need to stop. I'm going to come." Severin tried to shove her off.

"I'm going to spill myself inside your mouth, if you don't stop," he warned, sounding equally angry at her disobedience and desperate for her to defy him. "And it's going to be so much cum, Raina."

"I want you to," she moaned. With her mouth wrapped around Severin, Raina's avowal came muffled and distorted.

"If I were a better man, I'd insist you stop," he said hoarsely. "But I'm a blackhearted bastard so I'll take what you offer." Then, it was like a demon had been set free within him.

Severin tightened his hold upon her head, and as she bobbed her head up and down, he drove his hips up, to meet each downward stroke of her mouth. There grew an increasing urgency and harshness to his movements.

"Mmm. Yea. Fuck," he groaned.

His speech dissolved, and her body went ten degrees warmer as Severin's control slipped even further and further, and all because of the things *she* did to *him*.

His length pulsed and throbbed.

"Last chance," he gritted out. "I'm going to come, Princess."

What a low opinion he carried of himself. He, the same man who'd only just touted himself as caring more about his wants, gave her the choice, still.

Unlike before, Raina didn't offer words of assurance, she just sucked deeper.

"*Fuuck*," he gasped, stretching that vulgar one-syllable into four and a prayer.

Severin surged upward, repeatedly.

Then, his body went taut; his fingers spasmed in her hair, that'd fallen loose again from the force of his thrusting.

Cadogan readjusted the grip he had on Raina's head.

"Here I come," he rasped, and with a long, low, guttural groan he flooded her mouth with his seed.

She moaned.

He'd claimed she tasted like the sweetest dessert. But Severin? The taste and feel of him, there was nothing like it—salty, and so primitive and masculine, she could subsist on the taste of him alone.

All the while she swallowed, Severin groaned and ground himself into her mouth.

With what sounded like a last, dying gasp, he sagged into the folds of the sofa, as Raina herself had done when she'd reached her surrender.

Swallowing the last of his seed, Raina peeked up at him.

Severin lay sprawled like a sated king, with one arm stretched along the back of the sofa and his opposite hand resting on his flat stomach.

His broad, muscular chest moved fast and hard.

On the heels of his surrender, the intimacy of what they'd done, and what *she'd* just done to him, proved sobering.

Raina drew her mouth from his softening length.

What they'd shared had been wicked and depraved—and Raina had loved every single moment of what they'd done this night.

Between her family's lurid past and the business her brother owned, Raina had been surrounded by vice. As such, she'd viewed acts of carnality as sinful, wrong, and depraved.

Closing her eyes, Raina rested her cheek against Severin's oaken thigh.

With him, she'd discovered lovemaking wasn't just the meaningless couplings her mother had come to relish or that Gregory had made a fortune from. No, when shared with the one who'd bespelled you in every way, it was…

"Magic," she silently mouthed.

A sated smile played at her lips.

The touch of Severin's hand and the feel of his mouth on her and inside her had awakened Raina to something special and earth-shattering.

For *her*.

Raina's smile fell.

But to Severin? It'd been purely carnal and devoid of all reverence and beauty she'd ascribe to what they'd shared in this now, sacred-to-her, room—a room which belonged to Lord and Lady Rutherford.

Cadogan glided his fingers through her hair that now hung

in a tangle about her waist and massaged the back of her skull. He continued to rub those muscles and then the ones in Raina's neck—muscles she'd not even realized hurt until now. A soft grateful sigh eased past her lips.

The way he touched her now, however, so tender and considerate of her comfort after she'd pleasured him, didn't speak to a heartless man, focused only on his needs.

Or, the cruel devil in Raina's head taunted. *maybe you're just so very desperate to see something that isn't there because you are in...*

Raina stilled.

Oh, God.

Her pulse thudded at a slow, sick, beat.

I love him.

She wanted *him* and *only* him.

What Raina and Severin shared here, hadn't stirred his heart, or made him dream of and long for a future with her.

For Severin, any eager, willing woman, would do.

Nausea roiled in her belly.

She'd become her mother, in the worst possible way.

Not because of the wicked and wonderful things she'd done together this night, with Severin. No, finding she craved only the carnal would have been preferable to *this*.

A tear slipped down her cheek.

The irony wasn't lost on her. She'd spent her adult life disgusted at how her mother lived her life. She'd been repulsed at the details her mother kept of lurid acts she'd performed with men and women, all in an attempt to *please* her husband.

Now, Raina saw how love could break a woman.

At last, she understood and ached for what her mother had yearned for, and never experienced, in her union with Raina's father—true love. The kind of love where each person was enough for the other. A marriage where one who needn't change oneself into someone else, in a bid to have one's feelings reciprocated.

In her short, whirlwind relationship with Severin, Raina had also gleaned another truth—she was not her mother in another, very, important way.

Raina couldn't and wouldn't suffer such a cruel, tragic relationship. Her heart would be forever broken at not having

Severin in the way she wanted him in her life, but she'd never settle for anything less than complete and total devotion and love from her husband.

There wouldn't be that mythical husband she'd dreamed of. For she'd already lost *her* heart to a stonyhearted earl, married to his career.

Another tear slipped free, followed by another, and she'd never been more grateful for the still and silence from him.

God, what would Severin even *say* if he knew all the thoughts roiling in her tortured mind? Or worse, if she professed her love?

Except, she already knew. He'd remind her they'd merely *fucked*, and he couldn't love. What was worse, he'd either revile or pity Raina for being the naïve, romantic, fool who'd fallen for him.

A fresh onslaught of tears clogged Raina's throat and made it impossible to swallow. What had happened to him? What had made it so that he didn't believe himself capable of loving? Or maybe it was *he* didn't believe anyone could love him? Surely there'd been someone?

Surely…surely…surely, you're just desperate as to plant seeds of hope in a garden that cannot grow.

No. No. No.

Raina simply couldn't face him. How *could* she? How after doing something so foolish as to fall in love with him.

Severin concluded his gentle massage. Now, he stroked the top of Raina's head like she was a dutiful servant who'd pleased her master.

A panicky giggle bubbled past the emotion in her throat.

And in a way, isn't that precisely what you are where Severin is concerned?

Humbled and devoid of pride where he was concerned, she'd allowed him liberties she'd never allowed another, and for that matter, she'd performed acts with him and on him that she didn't ever want to do with anyone *but* him.

"Look at me, Raina," Severin urged, his voice husky, hoarse, and so gentle, fresh tears formed.

Oh, God.

Closing her eyes, Raina shook her head.

He'd been right that day they'd first met—Severin *knew* Raina's thoughts and the ones he didn't, he invariably ascertained, often, before even Raina herself knew what she was thinking.

She'd not survive the humiliation of his seeing how fast and how hard she'd fallen for him.

Only, being honest with herself, this vicious twisting at her heart had nothing to do with wounded pride.

No, when she lifted her eyes to his, she'd gaze upon a man whom she desperately ached for, in every way, and who'd never be hers, and who'd never want her in all the ways she wanted him.

I'm just like my mother. Just like her.

"I said look at me," he repeated, this time, harshly impatient.

Not even the king himself could deny such a decree.

Raina, in a futile bid to hide her misery, discreetly swiped the moisture from her cheeks, and then lifted her gaze to Severin's.

His hard, unblinking gaze instantly locked on her face. Anger flashed in his eyes.

Raina recoiled.

"I know what you're thinking," he purred.

Oh, God, this was unbearable.

A fresh sheen of moisture in her eyes further revealed her weakness.

With an animalistic growl, he reached for her.

Raina attempted to scramble away; needing space from him, needing to flee, to get as far away as possible from this room and his derision.

Alas, she was no match for Severin Cadogan in any way.

Severin hauled her from the floor and drew her, so her thighs were splayed on either side of his waist.

Still, Raina resisted, as she thrust and squirmed, his shaft grew hard and prodded the entrance of her woman.

Raina bit her lip hard as a warm rush of heat immediately flooded that place between her legs.

"D-Don't," she whispered, her voice catching. "P-Please."

She attempted to bury her face in his shoulder.

Severin, however, wouldn't allow her to hide. He drew her away just enough to pass his cold, punishing gaze over her face.

A terrifying anger burned from his eyes. "Do you think I'm going to force you?"

That's why he thought she pleaded with him?

Reeling from that discovery, Raina tensed as Severin, with a tenderness that belied his earlier tone, withdrew a handkerchief from his jacket, and lightly wiped the remnants of saliva and seed from around her mouth.

At his considerateness, Raina felt tears prick her eyes.

"I've already told you. I don't force women," he said bluntly.

Even as self-preservation urged her to let him believe his erroneously drawn conclusion, she couldn't.

"N-No," she said, her words muffled against his hot, slightly sweaty skin. "Of, course not. It's…just…it's…"

Raina renewed her struggles, and this time, when she hid her face against him, he allowed her shelter in his frame.

Severin, once again, proving to be a chameleon in every way, wrapped his arms about Raina and held her in a heart-wrenchingly tender embrace.

He pressed a gentle kiss against her temple. "I know why you're crying," he said quietly, and without judgment.

Her stomach muscles knotted. "Y-You do?"

She felt his nod.

"I do," he murmured, placing another kiss on her head, this time at her brow.

He did.

And he didn't sound horrified. He didn't mock Raina or give her blunt coldness.

Raina's heart thumped quickly.

Then, for the first time since he'd stormed into her life and she'd fallen hard and fast for him, hope kindled and blossomed in her breast.

Still shy that he knew, Raina edged slowly away from him. She draped her arms about his nape and met his gaze squarely.

"It happened so quickly," she began softly. "I didn't expect…" To fall in love so quickly. "I never thought I could…" Until him. "Or would—"

Severin took her lips in a gentle, but full kiss that silenced her ramblings and liquified her inside out. With a sigh, she surrendered herself fully to his embrace.

As he drew away with a palpable reluctance, Raina couldn't have concealed her boundless joy, if she'd tried.

"I thought you would be repulsed," she admitted, half-laughing, half crying.

His lips turned up in a charmingly crooked, grin.

"How could I ever be repulsed, love?" he murmured, the sough of his breath, soothing and warm against her skin.

Love.

His assurance, his endearment, brought her eyes sliding shut.

Raina's heart swelled. "T-Truly?" she whispered.

A chuckle rumbled from deep within his chest, and Raina's body shook under that gentle amusement.

Severin palmed her cheek, and with a dreamy sigh she leaned into his caress.

"You are a spirited, bold, clever woman, sweet," he said solemnly, and his profession sent a piercing warmth to her chest.

"I could never be disgusted at you for slaking your lust and being a generous lover," he said, his husky voice, filled with such warmth, it was a moment before his words registered.

Slaking her lust?

Her heart knocked hard and fast against her ribcage, and then that organ slowed to a dull, faint thud.

Being a generous lover?

She went cold inside.

This time as he seized her mouth, in a long, hot-blooded, she remained immobile. Raina couldn't have moved if she'd tried.

All the while she'd thought he'd gathered she loved him and not only accepted but embraced the fact, he'd taken her tears as signs that she'd been ashamed of having made love with him here.

I'm going to be ill.

"Even with all the naughty acts you enjoy, you'll always be my good girl," he breathed, between each glide of his tongue against hers.

His good girl.

Tears flooded her eyes.

God, what a bloody, dim-witted, pathetic, fool she was. Where everything they'd shared and done this evening had left her altered in every way, where Severin had been concerned, nothing could have been further from the truth.

As she'd feared all along, Severin, man of legend, so skilled in bed he'd seduced the secrets from the most experienced women, as part of his work to the Crown, saw what'd happened here as lust-filled exchange, and nothing more.

A low groan, born of the seeds of Raina's sorrow and watered with all that would never be between her and Severin, welled inside. And from her misery sprung an anguished sob.

Severin stiffened, and as he ended this, their last kiss, Raina didn't bother to keep her tears in check. For there couldn't be any more of this…or *anything* with Severin. She'd played with fire and gotten burned. Were she to continue doing so, all the pieces that made Raina, Raina, would go up in a conflagration that destroyed her forever.

All the life drained from her and she collapsed against Severin and wept all the harder.

He took her lightly but firmly by her upper arms and angled her back.

Even with her eyes blurred with tears, she caught the swirl of emotion in his dark-blue gaze he combed over her face: anger, frustration, and concern reflected back there.

"Raina?" he asked, his low, baritone steeped in worry.

This rare benignity he slipped in and out of, wrenched a sob from Raina.

Unable to reveal the depth of her despair, she sank her teeth into his shoulder to keep that cry from tumbling past her lips.

"What is going on, Raina?" he demanded, disquieted as she'd never believed he *could* be.

"Tsk. Tsk." An entirely too familiar voice sounded from the front of the room, cutting across Raina's misery. "I trust as the lady's elder brother, *I* am the one who should be asking *that* question."

No.

A sick sensation formed in her belly.

Gregory.

All Severin's muscles jumped under her.

Raina followed Severin's stunned gaze to the entrance of the room. Her brother lounged with his back against the ornate door panel. The tension emanating from his body, however, belied the casualness of his tone.

"I will say when I asked you to care for my sister," Gregory said coldly, "this is certainly not what I had in mind."

"Fuck." Severin surged to his feet. He angled himself away from Raina's brother and righted his trousers.

"Indeed," Gregory drawled. "Is *that* what happened here?"

"No!" Raina exclaimed, clenching her toes hard into the soles of her slippers.

While Gregory put his frosty attention on Severin, Raina rushed to right her own garments.

After she'd stood and shoved her crumpled and crushed skirts back into place, she found her brother's hard stare back upon her. A powerful emotion in those depths managed to slip past his rage-filled eyes—regret.

Raina curled into herself.

Oh, God, I'm going to die of mortification. Please, let me die.

"I'd ask what is going on," he said quietly. "Alas, the moment I discovered you gone, and your bodyguard missing, I'd already determined what was at play. And imagine my surprise when DuMond indicated he'd found two guests in this very hall, badly beaten, just coming to. He...happened to hear—"

Raina clamped her hands over her ears.

DuMond had heard her in the throes of passion with Severin?

Oh, God. And here she'd believed there could be no greater humiliation than falling in love with Severin Cadogan, only to discover just how very wrong she'd been.

Horror filled every corner of her humiliated and hurting being.

Wanting to hide, *needing* to hide, Raina took a step toward Severin.

Like a real-life Perseus evading Medusa, Severin practically bent himself backward to avoid Raina.

"The lady is a virgin," Severin bluntly stated.

In other words, he had no intention of marrying her. Numb,

Raina stared vacantly at Severin. He needn't have worried. She would *not* enter into a union with a man who didn't love her. So why did a fissure form in her heart?

Instead of taking offense, Gregory appeared more amused than incensed.

"Ah, yes," he drawled. "I trust her maidenhead is intact, though had I not arrived when I did, I'm confident you wouldn't be able to make that same claim."

Raina shrunk into herself, wanting to disappear, feeling so very alone.

Alas, there was no sanctuary to be had.

Gregory spared Raina a brief glance. "Given the red, swollen state of her lips, however, and the way you were stuffing yourself in your trousers when I entered the room, can the same be said of my sister's mouth, Cadogan?"

Heat singed her cheeks. "*Gregory!*"

Raina may as well have saved her breath.

Severin pressed his hard lips into an even harder line.

Strangely, it was that silence that managed to reach Raina's brother. His expression grew serious, almost sad. "I didn't think so," he said quietly to himself.

Former assassin and duke stared one another down.

"Fix your neckline, Raina," Gregory snapped, without breaking eye contact with Severin.

Raina jumped. Hands shaking, she struggled to adjust her bodice.

From the corner of her eye, she caught a hardening of Severin's heavy jaw. Did he take offense at her being ordered about so?

Of course, you did. Just as you ascribed more to his having pummeled those crude lords in the corridor, and then again when he made love to you with his mouth.

"Given all, *this*," Gregory swiped a hand between Raina and Severin, "a *discussion* is obviously in order."

She'd rather snatch out her own eyes than speak to Gregory about this. Nonetheless, she nodded.

"I'd expect nothing less, Your Grace," Severin said, making it clear he'd been the true recipient of Gregory's demand.

Pain clutched at her throat, and she turned tear-filled eyes on

Severin, even icier and aloof than when she'd met him in her brother's office. "I am s-sorry," she whispered. "I am s-so sorr—"

"Come, Raina," Gregory barked. He held an elbow out. "It is time to leave. You've had enough *fun* for this evening."

As she hung her head and approached her brother, she held her breath—foolishly, naively, desperately, willing Severin to call out. Wanting him to stop her overbearing brother and lambaste him for the crude jibes he'd made at Raina's expense.

Except, Severin didn't so much as exhale an audible breath.

What did you expect? Since her Come Out, Gregory had started seeing her not as a person, but a pawn to be moved about his game board of power.

And Severin? From the start, and at every turn, he'd told Raina she was less than nothing to him.

She bowed her head.

As she and Gregory quit the room and Severin remained behind in that space where she'd owned her feelings for him, that fissure at last, gave way, splintering into a thousand, different, jagged cuts about her heart.

CHAPTER 17

I finally agreed to join my love at the Hellfire Club.
This time, I'll make myself see what it is he craves. If I
understand, I can keep him satisfied.
~ The Duchess of A

THE IRONY OF THIS NIGHT was not lost on Cadogan.

He'd been taken down now twice in his life: the first time by a ruthless foreign adversary and the second, by his uncontrollable lust—for a *virgin*.

Thirty-seven minutes after being discovered with Raina straddling his waist, Cadogan found himself back at Argyll's home and ushered into the duke's office.

The butler bowed and backed out of the room, leaving the two men alone.

Reclined in his enormous leather armchair, the Duke of Argyll, sat with his fingers steepled, and contemplated Cadogan for a long moment.

Cadogan stayed stock-still.

"Please, please," Argyll finally said. "Do take a seat." Raina's brother motioned to the chairs across from him like he greeted an old, dear, friend, and not some stranger who'd just fucked his virgin sister's mouth.

Wordlessly, Cadogan crossed the long length of the meticulously designed space. All the while he kept a razor-sharp gaze on the man.

Cadogan tugged a chair out, took a seat, and folded his arms at his chest.

Cadogan had been weak enough to lose all self-control for a goddamned debutante, but he wasn't stupid enough to believe Argyll's genial attitude, or that there'd be anything cordial about the impending exchange.

Raina's brother and Raina's seducer studied the other.

Several minutes ticked by with the duke having uttered nothing beyond that initial invitation for Cadogan to sit.

This silence, however, was a peculiar one. Unlike the strained, volatile stillness back in Lord and Lady Rutherford's parlor, this quiet proved strangely placid, and the Duke of Argyll remarkably calm.

Given the state in which the elder brother had discovered his cherished sister and the man hired to be her bodyguard—with his cock still out of his trousers, and Raina's skirts rucked about her waist and his mouth marks all over her—the other man should be brimming with rage.

Hell, given the debauched things Cadogan had done with and to Raina, her protective brother

should have attempted to take Cadogan apart by now. He certainly shouldn't be relaxed and unwarlike.

By now, Raina's brother should've launched a loyal, brotherly response and, at least, *attempted* to kill Cadogan the moment he'd foot inside his ducal domain. That he should be so implacable and detached over Raina's ruin, unexpectedly stirred the inner beast inside him.

Cadogan sharpened his gaze on Raina's brother.

I am missing something. What am I missing?

The duke caved first. "Drinks?"

Cadogan just stared.

Drinks?

"Brandy?" the duke pressed. "Cognac? Sherry? Whiskey?"

Madness. Perhaps that's what accounted for Argyll's hell-backward nonexistent reaction?

"No," he said tersely.

Argyll gave another one of those infuriating ducal shrugs and stood.

Cadogan followed Argyll's lazy stroll to the sideboard crammed full of bottles and decanters. Humming to himself, Raina's brother, contemplated the vast collection of spirits to choose from.

The veins in the top of Cadogan's hands bulged.

My God. The duke put more thought into his drink choice than Raina's ruin.

The savage monster inside Cadogan reared its head again, and begged for freedom.

"Ah," Argyll settled on a decanter of brandy and as an afterthought, fetched a glass.

The duke tugged the Stoppard out and tossed it aside. "Some of the finest stock." He turned and displayed the bottle in question for Severin. "Are you certain I can't—"

"I'm certain."

Shrugging, Argyll devoted all his attention to his pour.

Over the course of his lifetime, Cadogan navigated any number of mystifying situations. Not a single one held a bloody candle to whatever the fuck *this* was.

There could be no doubting he found himself engaged in some game, with the duke.

"I confess, Your Grace," Cadogan remarked, trying to read his opponent. "Given the circumstances, I'd anticipated a violent reception."

Argyll arched a single blond eyebrow. "Were you thinking I'd demanded a meeting to call you out and have you name your seconds?"

Dead. I'm going to kill him.

Cadogan flexed his jaw. "Actually, given the state you found me with Lady Raina, that'd been the very least I expected. Had she been my sister, I—"

You would have done what? You haven't even seen your sisters in... years. Too many to even remember. The one key difference being: there were other brothers to see to them. Raina had this appallingly deficient libertine to rely on for her security.

"What was that, Cadogan?" The duke angled his head. "You would...what? *Hmm?*"

How bloody flippant. It took every ounce of Cadogan's self-control to keep from snapping his neck.

In one fluid motion, Cadogan unsheathed the double-edged

khanjali from inside his boot and launched it at Raina's bastard of a brother.

That deliberately aimed blade sailed past the duke.

Argyll dropped to the floor, a second before Cadogan's weapon struck the wall.

All the blood had leeched from the duke's cheeks.

Not so bloody smug now.

The slack-jawed nobleman, got onto his knees; his rounded eyes moved back and forth between the dagger buried into an ancestral portrait of one of the many dukes before him and Cadogan.

"Good *God*, Cadogan."

Horror and reverent awe bled from the nobleman's malediction.

He waited until the cad got to his feet before speaking. "If I did the things with Lady Raina you're accusing me of, why not face me at dawn, Your Grace?"

"Do I think I can kill you in a duel, Cadogan?" The duke's counter-question rang with humor. "*Possibly*," he acknowledged with a side-tip of his head. "Most likely not. I've done my research. You could put a bullet in whatever part of me you chose before I even got a shot off."

A roiling heat formed in his belly.

"Your sister isn't at least worthy of your trying?" Cadogan somehow managed to keep his voice even.

Amusement glimmered in the rake's eyes. "What good would I do either of my sisters if I'm dead, hmm?"

As Argyll nattered on about the responsibilities that came with being a brother, Cadogan stared at the duke's mouth as it moved.

Raina deserved more—*so* much more.

Perhaps he'd cut out the depraved bastard's throat?

Or his heart?

Maybe both?

With absolutely no idea how close Cadogan was to ending him, the duke, returned—glass in hand.

After he'd seated himself, Argyll studied him with a bemused expression. "You appear surprisingly eager for me to call you out."

"*You* appear surprisingly relaxed after discovering your sister deflowered with her lover still in her arms, *duke*."

A slight twitch at the corner of his mouth revealed the first crack in Argyll's composure.

Having knocked Raina's brother off-balance, Cadogan struck.

"What do you want, Argyll?" Everyone wanted something. "Come to the point."

"What do I want?" Raina's brother rested his forearms atop his enormous desk. "Given you took what you wanted, I trust I should be asking how *you* intend to remedy the situation."

"As I see it, there *is* no situation. No one is any wiser as to what may have happened—"

"What *did happen*," the duke gritted out.

"There was no audience," Cadogan continued over that interruption.

The other man's surprisingly sturdy patience at last cracked.

"How conveniently you exclude the audience of one made by me, the lady's *brother*," he sniped.

Here it was. The fight he'd been anticipating and preferring. Cadogan dealt best when all the cards were laid out.

Cadogan carefully chose his tone and words. "As I promised earlier, she is still a virgin, Your Grace."

He'd left her maidenhead perfectly intact for some other *proper*, marriage-minded gent to claim. No man would bring her the level of surrender that he could, but with Raina as passionate and eager as she was, she'd still mightily enjoy some other fellow's efforts.

A sharp, murderous rage ran through him. He tasted the metallic bite of it on his tongue. He felt the bitter, bone-deep twisting of it low in his gut.

With his next question, Argyll yanked Cadogan from the deep abyss of indecipherable emotion he'd found himself falling.

"Did you have your fingers in her, Cadogan?"

Did he…?

Still momentarily slack-witted, it took a moment for that blunt query to fully register.

For the first time in Cadogan's life, he felt a rush of heat climb his neck and splotch his cheeks.

He'd maim the bastard so bad, that Argyll would spend the rest of his days *wishing* Cadogan had done the mercy of killing him, instead.

A growl built in his chest. "Need I remind you the lady you are speaking about, is in fact, your sister?."

"*You* of all people are reminding me of that detail, Cadogan?" The other man's features froze, and then tossing his head back, he roared with laughter. "Now, *that* is rich," he said, with a single, hard, clap of his palms.

The duke's forced and fake hilarity died quick; his eyes darkened. "With your expertise, I expect you don't require me to point out how easily that scrap of flesh can tear, and if she enters into a union with some chap believing she's a virgin only to find some other fellow…" he paused and skimmed a pompous glance down the length of his straight-bridged, Patrician nose at Cadogan, "relieved him of that endeavor, there will be hell to pay, and not only me, but more importantly, Raina would pay the price."

The vivid visual of Raina suffering for perceived sins by a brutal bastard she found herself bound to, briefly blinded Cadogan. Visions of Raina: with those goddamned tears that gutted him, streaming down her cheeks. Raina, stretching out a hand and bowing her head in supplication. Raina, explaining there'd been a man—Cadogan, being the one—who'd awakened her to pleasure and left…because leaving was what he did. Because he had to. Men like him didn't and couldn't put down roots.

His mind in vast, riotous tumult, he found Argyll shrewdly eying him.

Cadogan rolled his shoulders.

The hell if he'd allow this libertine to paint Cadogan as the lone villain in this farce.

"What does it say about you, Your Grace," he said quietly. "That you'd tie her to a man whom you can't be confident would treat her with due reverence and respect?"

Argyll pounded a fist so hard onto his neat workspace, the crystal and gilt-bronze inkwell set jumped.

"The bloody ballocks on you, speaking about *my* character," he thundered. "You come before me and speak about some fictitious dastard and his *lack of respect* for Raina. All the while *knowing*, this was hardly the first and only transgression on your part."

Caught off-guard, Cadogan drew back.

Argyll blazed ahead with his scathing castigation. "As if after barely a day in my household, you didn't have her against the kitchen wall?" Or further indulge of her charms at Craven's club."

Cadogan narrowed his eyes to razor slits.

The duke lowered his eyebrows and pinched them together. "And now *this* latest transgression."

His mind spun. How the hell did the other man know all that?

"Why don't you just tell me what you want, Your Grace? Or call me out. But do so quickly, because I'm running out of patience."

The duke lifted his head. "Very well. Given the circumstances, it is only fitting you do right by my—"

"No."

"Sister," the duke continued over his interruption. "She is a lady—"

"I'm *far* from a gentleman."

Argyll scoffed. "By the nature of *my* work, the same could and *is* said about me." Dropping his elbows on the neat surface of his desk, he leaned forward. "The fact remains, despite the unconventional nature of our career, we are still members of the *ton*, and will make matches with respectable la."

"You misunderstand," he said coolly. "I am not saying I'm unworthy of your sister." Which he was. But that was neither here nor there, where this matter and discussion was concerned.

Raina's brother thinned his eyes. "You're saying you will not do right by her."

"I'm saying I won't marry her." In that, he'd be doing right by Raina. He wouldn't marry any woman. He'd enough enemies that he'd not subject a wife to a fate where she and any children they bore were in constant threat.

The duke frowned. "This is unexpected."

Which meant, the other man had *expected* other things…

Cadogan went motionless.

"Given your title and birthright, Killburn," Argyll was saying. "I don't have to tell you what your obligations are to my sister following all of this."

Argyll, however, proceeded to do just that.

While Raina's brother went on enumerating each and every reason he'd an obligation to marry the lady in question, Cadogan went over his meeting with Argyll.

Cadogan recalled: Every. Single. Moment.

Raina, as she'd been, despite the late hour at their first meeting. Paraded before Cadogan in a diamond-studded crown and a satin gown with its plunging neckline that accentuated every lush curve.

Argyll willingly leaving Cadogan alone with the man's *beloved* sister, whom he sought to protect above all else.

Raina's cheery disposition and offer of friendship throughout that exchange.

Each and every seemingly piddling detail, came together to form one profound picture of how he'd been played by this crafty, cunning brother and sister.

Raina happening to come *upon* Cadogan alone, drinking ale in the kitchens, long after she should have slept.

Her sad, doe-eyes.

Her self-recriminations.

The claims she'd been *bullied* by society.

Cadogan's pulse throbbed in his ears. He saw the duke's mouth moving as he spoke, but he heard not a single word falling out of those Machiavellian lips.

And then, there'd been tonight.

Two leches had been conveniently passing where he and Raina had just been together; that pair speaking crass about her. Only for Raina to return and find him avenging her. The over-the-top adoration in her eyes as she'd kissed him.

…I'd ask what is going on…Alas, the moment I discovered you gone, and your bodyguard missing, I'd already determined what was at play…

Had he not been seated, Cadogan would've been knocked hard on his arse.

My God, what a bloody, fucking, fool he'd been.

She'd taken his cock into her mouth and swallowed down his

seed. When they'd at last both been sated, she'd erupted into tears, perfectly timed for her brother's arrival.

Likely those tears had been disgust, after all, at the things she'd been forced to do with him, all to benefit whatever twisted plot she and her brother had cooked up.

And then, that last, telling, guilty admission from the lady's own lips before she'd dutifully followed her scheming brother...

"I am s-sorry," she whispered. "I am s-so sorr—"

Cadogan's rage briefly blinded him.

Maybe guilt had found her in that minute

Cadogan hardened his jaw.

Whatever it'd been mattered not, only her deception did.

I'd already determined what was at play...

All along, the bloody bastard had done just that, the director and orchestrator of the unlikeliest deception, and he'd been joined by the most delicious, delectable leading actress.

The pieces of the earlier puzzle, at last, fell into place.

This is why the other man had exuded calm before—he'd trusted Cadogan would marry Raina. Only when it'd become apparent that'd be the last offer he'd make this night, had Argyll lost control.

There remained but one question now: *why?*

He fixed a dogged gaze on the Argyll.

Only Cadogan knew. He'd just realized it too late. There'd been, first, the duke's offer of employment as head guard of *Forbidden Pleasures*. Cadogan's declination. Then a new offer, this one, an unlikely one.

But Cadogan had been *so* blinded with his hungering for revenge against the enemy who'd marked him, he'd failed to see he'd been embroiled in another plot, with a *different* opponent.

Argyll finished his lecture and stared expectantly at Cadogan.

"You were aware of prior exchanges between your sister and myself," he said carefully, "and yet, you kept me in your employ." Cadogan's wasn't a question.

The duke tensed. Several lines creased his forehead, in that moment Argyll realized he'd *truly* slipped up.

A slow, but deathless rage spilled through Cadogan: with Argyll, Raina, and worse, himself. He'd dealt with manipulators before.

He'd never, however, let himself be manipulated. This time, he'd his cock rule his head.

"You orchestrated it."

"Oh, come," the duke scoffed. "I brought you in with the hope that you'd form an attachment with my sister, but ultimately, you're the one who went falling for Raina."

He didn't even deny it.

"My God." He whistled through his teeth. "You not only knew, but *hoped*, I'd fuck your sister." Here he'd discovered a match, in his ruthlessness, after all.

"Hey, now." Argyll bristled. "There is no need to be crude."

Cadogan climbed to his feet. Pressing his palms on the duke's desk, he leaned in.

"You who used your sister like one of the molls at your club would speak to *me* about being crude?" he whispered.

The bumptious bastard shrank.

With a nervous laugh, Raina's brother yanked at his cravat. "This doesn't have to be all bad, Cadogan. In fact, what I'm proposing is something that will benefit you greatly."

"Benefit *me*?" he asked bluntly.

Argyll had the good grace to flush. "Benefit the both of us."

The other man took Cadogan's silence as permission to continue with his proposition.

"You have something I want. And I have *someone* you want."

He narrowed his eyes. "Do you believe I'd give you anything of value in exchange for a *woman*?"

Although for the tempting, clever, Lady Raina you could almost be tempted into making an exception, that lustful voice in his head taunted. Almost. But not even that fair Helen of Troy could make him trade his freedom and power.

The duke matched Cadogan's frosty gaze with one of his own. "My sister is not some woman. She is not a trollop."

"Funny with your reasons for putting me to work guarding her, *you* should make that claim."

Argyll didn't take the bait. "She is the most sought-after Diamond in several Seasons. She comes with a fortune to her name."

"Do I strike you as a man in need of fortune?" he asked bluntly. "I'll spare you answering, I'm not."

"Yes, yes." The duke waved his hand. "Your business as a hired assassin is quite lucrative but it is not something you can or will do forever." He gave Cadogan a canny look. "And knowing what I know about you, when you are done, the *last* thing you'll want is to retire onto some country estate keeping books."

"I'll die doing this work." He'd rather chop off all his limbs and with his teeth gnaw off the last unsevered appendage.

"Ah," Argyll gave a waggle of his eyebrows, "but if you are as good as you claim to be, then, you won't be taken down by anyone. You'll carry on with the business of killing until you've got the gout and your eyes and ears fail. Something also tells me, you're too proud to let some younger, stronger, man take you down as a way of dying doing what you love."

That detailing of a very plausible future gave Cadogan pause.

He'd never thought into a future, because for men in his line of work, no tomorrow was promised, but eventually all men, aged. Time leant a frailty and humility that made them easy marks for the younger, stronger, men—as the duke described them.

The idea of being one of the former left him in suspended in a state, confronting a horrifying prospect he'd not considered until now.

He'd hand it to the crafty peer; the *gentle*man was quite adept at manipulation.

As if he'd sensed an unlikely opening, Argyll seized on it.

"Marry my sister," he said, putting forth his proposal. "In exchange, she'll be yours. I'll—"

"I'm afraid your efforts have been for naught," Cadogan cut him off.

The duke had whored out his sister for his ends and now sought to make a whore out of Cadogan, too.

Fighting the urge to pull another blade and this time, bury it right between the bastard's eyes, Cadogan made himself turn and took a quick, clipped, path to the doorway.

There came the scrape of wood scraping wood as the duke shoved his chair back. "Then you'll never have the name of the man who marked you," Raina's brother vowed.

Fury brought Cadogan spinning back around. In the face of the other man's cavalier attitude, Cadogan's anger spiraled to a murderous rage.

"You bloody bastard," he hissed. "With your intentions for me and your sister, you gave me an assignment that could never be completed."

Argyll revealed a slow, triumphant smile.

Checkmate.

Fuck.

Cadogan was across the room and on the duke in an instant.

He closed a hand about Argyll's neck and the pompous duke's gasp died in Cadogan's grip.

"Bastard," Cadogan whispered.

He propelled Raina's brother against the wall behind that big, lofty desk of his.

Argyll rasped and twisted in a futile bid to escape Cadogan's hold.

To the libertine's credit, however, not a speck of fear glittered in his eyes.

Cadogan held him pinned, controlling when the duke breathed—and didn't. He relished each and every second of Argyll's fight for life-saving air. Red, ruddy, color flushed the gentleman's cheeks and his eyes bulged, but at no point in his desperate search for breath did Raina's brother bleed fear or desperation.

The proud bastard would sooner die than beg him. He'd deny Cadogan even that small satisfaction.

He'd get nothing out of killing him. That was, nothing other than the satisfaction of wearing Argyll's blood on his person.

With a silent curse, Cadogan released his hold.

The duke collapsed onto the floor and taking support against the same wall he'd come very close to dying against, Argyll alternately choked and sucked in great, heaving, gasps.

"I'll c-confer a portion of *Forbidden Pleasures*—the Duke of Craven's previous fraction—to you," the duke rasped, between each struggled breath he could manage. "I'll make you an even richer man, with power the likes of which only kings know."

Cadogan would hand it to the man. He had a sizeable pair of ballocks on him—he did *not* easily concede defeat.

Cadogan shook his head, and again, turned to leave.

"I'll give you the name you seek," Argyll wheezed.

He didn't break stride. "I'll sooner slit my own throat than marry." Not even for the pleasure of possessing Raina in every way would he sell himself.

When Cadogan's fingers touched the door handle, Argyll called out, in a hoarse but somewhat steadier, voice. "I'll ruin your business," he spoke conversationally of his plans for Cadogan.

With a sneer, he turned and faced Raina's bastard of a brother. "You might *try*."

"I'm not a man who '*tries*' at anything."

Infuriatingly blasé, Argyll tugged off his wrinkled cravat and gave the rumpled silk fabric several sharp snaps. "I simply deliver on my promises, Killburn...*and* my threats." He paused and cast a pointed look Cadogan's way.

Cadogan stiffened.

"Think about it," the duke continued matter-of-factly, and came out from behind his desk. "You insist we're different, and yet, in our determination and ruthlessness, we are very much of a like personality. But that is not the only way in which we're similar."

"Oh, and in which world—"

"We share the same clients," Argyll interrupted. "Yes, the services we offer may differ—in my case, I provide those blackguards and villains with their libidinous pleasures while *you* act as either their hired hand or deliverer. Either way, we both deal with the soulless, the depraved."

Cadogan met that perceptive commentary with only silence.

"Furthermore," the duke continued, "let us say, *if* I regaled my clients with details about the failed work you'd done for me, who do you believe *they* would trust, hmm? You, a man, who for the right price is their worst nightmare waiting in the shadows?"

Argyll inclined his head. "Or *me*, the generous, affable, proprietor who plies them with drinks and extends their credit so they might keep their homes and...continue feeding their *love* of gaming?" The calculating peer wasn't done. "Me, the man who provides the finest, most skilled, seductive, Cyprians throughout the kingdom, for their pleasures?"

The corner of Cadogan's right eye twitched.

He'd been wrong before. This moment, with the vow made by Argyll and the supercilious grin on his bloody smug lips, was the true checkmate.

Bloody fucking hell.

"We'll marry at dawn," Cadogan said quietly, reclaiming what little power he found himself in possession of. "No witnesses."

Raina's brother put up a protest. "There has to be—"

"That is none of *your* witnesses. I'll secure the body and the man of cloth." Men whose silence he did, could, and would control. "There'll be no formal announcement. By all intents and purposes no one will know we are married."

The duke frowned. "Surely you aren't so naïve as to believe the news will not be made public by *someone*—servants, dressmakers, any—"

"I'm not. But the longer our marriage remains secret, the safer she is from the danger she'll face as my wife."

Several creases marred, Argyll's impeccable brow.

Cadogan relished the first signs of apprehension from the cocksure proprietor. "You hadn't thought of that?" he taunted the duke over his belated fears. "My enemies are now your sister's."

A healthy amount of color slipped from the duke's cheeks.

"You were so obsessed with having me on your staff that you didn't give a shite about what fate awaited the wife of a former agent of the Crown and assassin," Cadogan said in grave tones.

The slight Adam's apple in the other man's throat moved. And while Argyll remained locked in the terrifying, but very real, picture Cadogan painted for the big brother's benefit, Cadogan found himself…also caught.

He'd never planned to take a wife for the simple fact he didn't want one or need one. As such, he'd not dwelt on the thought of the uncertain fate facing any woman he took to wife.

The faint stirring of unease took the place of the fury and hate that'd plagued him since he'd fallen for Argyll's trap.

The bloody worries kept coming.

In addition to his *wife*, there'd, of course, be children too whose safety and lives he'd be responsible for. Given all the times he intended to bed Raina, the risk he'd sire children on her was great. No matter the precautions he took…

Sweat slicked his palms.

The duke's murmur cut across Cadogan's racing thoughts. "I can only hope, for my sister's sake, that you are as good at your work as I believe you are, and that you've been credited with."

"And if not?" Cadogan said in sober tones. "What then?"

Argyll's features tensed. "I'm not going to think about it."

The bastard wouldn't *think* about it? Another curtain of rage fell over Cadogan's vision.

"Why *should* you?" Cadogan jeered. "It's only your sister's life."

The duke flinched.

Without another word, Cadogan turned on his heel, and quit the duke's offices.

When he returned four hours from now and left for a final time, it'd be the last time he'd ever set foot inside this household, and the last time his bride saw her brother.

CHAPTER 18

I'm beginning to forget what happiness is.
~ The Duchess of A

SEVERAL HOURS LATER, RAINA, ATTIRED in her finest gown of pale blue, crystal-encrusted silk and with her diamond studded tiara affixed to her artfully arranged curls, stared blankly at her brother's office door.

The irony of this full-circle moment was not lost on her.

Just days ago, she'd stood in this same way, outside this same panel, elegantly dressed at a godforsaken hour. Then, Raina knew only an eager excitement for the relationship she'd conjured up between herself and the man her brother would make her bodyguard. He'd have been a friend and confidante.

Now, he'd be…her husband.

Her brother, the duke, would stand for nothing less. If Raina *didn't* go through with this, Severin and Gregory, two men, so very alike in their ungodly amount of power, wealth, and pride *would* duel.

One man would die.

Sweat slicked Raina's skin.

An image slipped in—of Severin and Gregory on a misty field, while someone called out the pace count. She squeezed her eyes shut, but the play in her mind could not be stopped.

The signal to fire and then Severin and Gregory wheeling around.

The morbid, sickening thoughts came so fast, they couldn't be stopped.

The loud report of flintlock pistols and then, the smoke clearing to reveal Severin, with a hole blown through his chest. A slow expanding, dark stain, that begins small and widens. His hard mouth parting with shock…and then, collapsing to his knees.

Raina's breaths grew shallow and shaky.

Stop.

She squeezed her eyes shut and curled into herself to will the vision of Severin's life-blood slipping from his broad, powerful frame, gone.

Then, the image contorted and twisted and reversed to that hated beginning and played out all over again—this time, with Gregory, his crooked, confident, cheer-filled smile frozen on his mouth.

Raina pressed a fist against her mouth to stifle a sob. Either way, be it Severin or Gregory who fell, she'd never recover from a bottomless grief.

And it would be Gregory. Rumored to be a great shot, with a number of duels to his name, he still stood as no match to Severin. Self-serving and personally driven and distant as her brother had become, Gregory still was her older brother, and she'd love him forever.

There also wasn't the insignificant worry as to what would happen to both she *and* her younger sister were Gregory to die.

The idea of being married to the earl *should* horrify her.

Not because she feared Severin or was disgusted by him. He'd been blatantly open with her about his violent and dark past, but she could separate, even when Severin could not, the things he'd done in service to the Crown to the man he was.

For Severin, he'd done the manner of work he had for so long, it'd become entwined with his person, and he couldn't separate the two.

No, any and all horror stemmed from the fact that Raina *pathetically*, and against all her better judgment, had fallen hopelessly in love with Severin Cadogan, the Earl of Killburn.

An aching sorrow filled her breast.

To Raina, Severin, though blunt—albeit, grudgingly—in a

short time, had become what she'd dreamed he might be—a confidante with whom she'd shared things she'd never shared with anyone else, and also…the only real friend she'd ever known.

A sizeable knot formed in Raina's throat and when swallowing proved impossible, she rubbed a hand at her neck in a bid for air.

What a sad commentary on the state of your life, a cruel voice in her head needled. Nearly twenty years of age and the closest Raina had ever come to a friend was a dour, pitiless man whose only interest in her, as he'd claimed and proven, was purely carnal in nature.

Made of steel, Severin wasn't one who could be made to do *anything*, yet somehow, Raina's brother had managed to bring him around to marrying her. Despite the shock, disgust, and horror she'd spied in his eyes earlier that morning, the last thing he wanted was Raina as his wife.

It was why this wedding between she and Severin—a man who disavowed love and detested intimacy, outside of the physical—*would* proceed.

Grounded by that practical reminder, Raina gave her head a shake to clear the lingering scenes in her head.

But then, what else could she expect when the only two men in her life were possessed of ghastly amounts of power, money, and connections?

She closed her eyes.

Livingstone, the kindly, handsome footman to the right of the door cleared his throat. "Ahem. Should I…open the door?" he ventured.

It is time.

Raina nodded.

The moment Livingstone announced her, Raina stepped inside.

For a moment, with the dim lighting of Gregory's office and the absolute silence, Raina believed she must have been mistaken; that she'd been directed to the wrong place.

Gregory's booming and effusive greeting put an end to that possibility. "Ah, my sister, the beautiful bride."

She looked to where he stood at the hearth.

As her smiling sibling headed to greet her, Raina's gaze

however, of its own volition, flickered past Gregory, and over to the unsmiling trio. Each of big, sturdy builds and broad frames positioned as they were, near one another, managed to blot out the light cast by the fire.

Each man bore a scar of some sorts. Only one, she knew.

And he, could not even bring himself to look at her.

Instead, Severin kept his flinty, emotionless, eyes trained over the top of Raina's head.

Look at me, Severin. Please.

But, he didn't.

Raina caught the inside of her lower lip, hard, between her teeth.

For the arctic glaze upon his person, her husband-to-be, the dark, frosty, earl may as well have been chipped and chiseled from the coldest glacier.

"You had us all in suspense, dear sister!"

Dumbly, Raina looked to her brother. At some point, he'd joined her at the entrance of the room.

"The groom has been positively restless," he chided, his affable grin erasing all hint of rebuke.

Positively restless…?

She cast a brief dubious glance Severin's way in search of some hint of any form of movement and found none.

"*I,* however," Gregory continued on, bringing her attention whipping back his way, "assured the earl I did not doubt you'd be here, and that you wished to make a grand entrance, not that meant to worry your groom."

A grand entrance?

Worry her groom?

Was he *mad*?

Feeling like she'd stepped onto the stage of farce and found herself the only one without the benefit of the script, Raina allowed her brother to slip his arm through hers and escort her over to her husband-to-be.

When she stood before him, Severin didn't so much as spare Raina a glance…until the big, black-clad fellow between Severin and another stranger snapped open a book.

"Let us begin." The man, who upon careful inspection of

the book in his hand appeared to be the one performing the ceremony.

"Wait!" Raina's voice emerged shrill.

For the first time since she stepped foot inside the room, Severin, finally looked at her.

And she promptly wished he hadn't.

An apoplectic rage and dark, black hate emanated from those blue-black irises.

She gasped and stumbled away from him.

That same murderous rage, he'd previously leveled on the men who'd slandered her, he now fixed on Raina.

Given his volatile response and a startling display of desperation after they'd been discovered in their host's parlor, she'd known Severin didn't want to marry her—that much, couldn't have been clearer.

What she'd been wholly unprepared for, however, was *this*. The measure of hate he directed her way. It blazed from his eyes and seared her skin.

She'd witnessed that lethality before when she'd found him pulverizing her detractors.

Never, however, had she herself been victim to that terrifying emotion.

This was the supernatural god of mortal men's nightmares.

Raina took another step back and collided with something solid.

Frantic, she cast a desperate look over her shoulder.

Gregory.

Stationed close. To offer support? To ensure she not run?

Or, knowing her brother it was likely both.

"What is it, Raina?" Gregory gently asked.

What was it? Was he serious? She strangled on a panicked laugh.

Did her brother not see, or worse, not care—about the antipathy Severin carried for her?

Then, Gregory angled his body in a way that shielded Raina from Severin's death stare.

He did so with all the same tenderness he'd shown Raina when she'd been a girl. Tears formed in her eyes.

How much simpler life had been then. How much—

"Raina?" Gregory urged this time, with such a sense of urgency and impatience. "Any and all doubts and regrets you might have—"

"*Might* have?" she choked out on a whisper.

"Ceased to matter the moment you allowed Cadogan liberties reserved for your future husband," her brother spoke on a hush. He carried on over her quiet gasp. "It is time to do this and *now*...before Cadogan has a change of mind."

As Gregory delivered that last, and, clearly, most important part, he directed it not to Raina but to her stony bridegroom.

Fury mixed with pain and resentment, into a potent storm of blistering rage. "No," she said, not even bothering to mask her bitterness. "That wouldn't do at all," she spat, her voice climbing. "In fact, if he doesn't marry me, it would be a veritable disaster."

"Have some pride, Raina." Color splotched Gregory's cheeks. "Lower your voice."

Horrified, she glanced back at Severin, and here she'd believed the hate emanating from his eyes couldn't have burned more.

"Now, Raina," her brother snapped.

She stared at the elbow he extended.

Raina found herself reminded all over again that Gregory was no longer the loving brother out to protect a beloved sister. But then, he wasn't just her sibling. He was the all-powerful Duke of Argyll. And she, just like every other woman in the world, existed for the sole purpose of serving men.

That reminder sent a fresh wave of bitterness coursing through her.

To hell with him and his indifference.

"Where is Millie?" she clipped out.

A perplexed-looking Gregory shook his head, as if he'd never heard the name before. As if it was the most natural thing in the world for their youngest sibling to be absent from her sister's wedding.

"*Mil-lee*," she repeated, enunciating each syllable through gritted teeth. "I know it is early, but I want her to be here—"

Severin spoke his first words since Raina's arrival. "For the happy occasion?" His low baritone oozed such condescension and mockery and loathing, her heart and everything else within her being ached.

Knocked off-balance once more, Raina could only manage a bob of her head that emerged as something between a nod and a shake.

But at least he'd spoken to her.

Raina held his hate-filled gaze. "F-For the c-ceremony," she amended, her voice barely reaching her own ears.

"Millie is not here."

It took a moment to register what her brother just said.

Raina whipped her gaze over to Gregory. "I...don't... where...?"

All her thoughts went unfinished, and she hated herself for that weakness. She despised that she'd been reduced to a stuttering, woundable miss. No, that she'd *let* herself be reduced to such a pathetic state.

"You'd keep her from me?" Raina whispered.

"I thought given the situation it was the wisest course," he murmured.

Given the situation? The wisest course?

Anger proved a welcome emotion over her misery and dejectedness. Raina whipped about to face him completely.

"What are you talking about, Gregory? No one is any wiser to..." She slid a look to the pair of mutes. With their having failed to make so much as a single inhalation or exhalation, she'd forgotten their presence—until now.

When she again spoke to her brother, she did so in even quieter tones. "Millie needn't know anything about the reason for my marriage—"

"*Our* marriage," Severin put forward in mockingly cheerful tones that could never be confused with genuine affection on the groom's part for his bride-to-be.

It mattered not that she'd whispered; he heard *everything*.

"After all, my dear bride," he jeered, "the sole purpose of *your* union requires *my* complete and full cooperation."

His cooperation.

Somehow, Raina managed to go even colder.

Gregory had somehow wrangled Severin, a man who cowed to no one, to this make-shift altar to do right by her.

It mattered not that he'd been as much as a willing participant as she, Severin would hate her forever for landing him in a position he did not want.

Gregory touched her lightly on the arm. "Cadogan would rather keep your union a secret as long as possible," he explained.

Confused, she stared at up at him.

"A secret?" she repeated.

Again, Gregory glanced Severin's way, and then nodded.

Even more befuddled, Raina looked to her bridegroom, and searched his face.

He'd set his stubborn jaw at a mutinous angle. His deadened eyes contained nothing more than an icy cold.

And then, posed with his pitiless expression and what her brother had said, the realization of what it actually *meant*, hit Raina like a blow to the chest—Severin didn't want the world to know he'd married her.

Her neck, cheeks, and chest grew impossibly hot, and she had to fight to keep from clawing at the fabric of her dress.

The idea Severin's only love—and the sole thing on earth he'd commit to—his career, was *one* thing. Him not wanting to publicly acknowledge having her as his wife, was entirely *another*.

Raina stood exposed—on full-display for her brother, bridegroom, and the two, big, strangers he'd arrived with—feeling so very small.

She wanted to flee. She wanted to get away from her brother and Severin and this moment and continue running so fast backward that she landed herself at a time long before this one.

"Raina," her brother said quietly, but firmly. "It is time to begin."

Time to begin...

Raina couldn't go through this. She and *Severin* couldn't.

Taking her brother by the arm, she forced him to follow her, putting some distance between Raina and Severin and the men he'd arrived with.

"I can't," she whispered, imploring her brother.

His eyes instantly hardened, and she knew the very moment

when Gregory disappeared, and the Duke of Argyll emerged in his stead. "You have no choice, Raina," he said, his voice muted and coolly matter-of-fact. "The decision was made when you allowed Cadogan liberties."

Fire scorched her cheeks. "As if you haven't done far more, and far worse with a legion of—"

"*I'm* not a woman," he cut her off. "We are not held to the same standards and be it fair or not, that is the reality. You'll be ruined."

Raina gripped him by his arms and gave him a slight shake. "How?" she implored. "How when you are the only one who knows—"

"Because I know," he interrupted. This time, there hung an air of finality and warning upon his words.

Her shoulders sagged. "He doesn't love me."

"He will."

A laugh burst from her lips. "He doesn't even like me."

"He likes you enough, and in time, will grow to feel even more for you. I do not doubt it."

He didn't doubt it.

Because why would he? Her brother, as a duke, was all-powerful. The world bowed and bent to his wishes and whims. No one challenged him in any way, leaving him so arrogant, too arrogant to imagine he could ever be wrong.

And he was—wrong. Dead wrong.

With a growing sense of hopelessness, she registered the duke taking her by the arm and steering her over to the stoic men who waited.

The moment they returned, the tallest, biggest, man snapped his book open and got on with it.

Dearly beloved, we are gathered together here in the sight of God, and in the face of this congregation, to join together this man and this woman in holy Matrimony; which is an honorable estate, instituted of God in the time of man's innocency, signifying unto us the mystical union that is…"

While the most unconventional, but surprisingly, sonorous, man-of-cloth droned on over the Book of Prayers, Raina's gaze drifted about the equally unlikely place of her wedding.

"...and is commended of Saint Paul to be honorable among all..."

She had grown up believing the day she married would be a grand event. It would be held in St. George's Cathedral, resplendent in floral decor to rival the late Queen Charlotte's gardens. The king and queen were to have attended, along with all the *ton's* most powerful peers, so the vestibule pews were full to overflowing.

That'd been Raina's expectation, not because it was the dream *she'd* carried for herself. Rather, her ostentatious parents and equally sensational brother saw the Goodheart family as one grand exhibition.

They always insisted Raina's eventual wedding would befit a duke's daughter.

The only dream she'd carried, the only hope she'd held in her heart, was that she'd stand across from a loving, devoted, bridegroom who could not take his eyes off her.

Of course, what *she'd* dreamed of, *her* wants, *her* wishes, they'd never mattered—not even to the brother and parents who'd sired her.

It was why, she found herself face to face with a man who hated her so much, he wouldn't even look at her.

Raina squeezed her eyes shut to keep from weeping and made herself focus on the moment and not misery at what would never be.

"...therefore," the minister murmured, *"it is not by any to be enterprised, nor taken in hand, unadvisedly, lightly, or wantonly, to satisfy men's carnal lusts and appetites, like brute beasts that have no understanding..."*

Raina's toes curled reflexively into the soles of her slipper.

Without even looking at Severin, she could feel the heat of his mocking gaze.

"...First, it was ordained for the procreation of children..."

Children.

Raina's heart leapt at the word; at the prospect, at that which she'd only and always wanted—a loving family, for who each spouse, each child, was enough for one another.

Just another thing that will never be...

Her chest constricted sharply.

There came the crisp snap of the minister turning his page.

"*...Secondly, it was ordained for a remedy against sin, and to avoid fornication; that such persons as have not the gift of continency might marry...*"

This time, she did lift her gaze to Severin's, and with her eyes, she willed him to see the love she held for him, she willed it to matter.

"Severin," she mouthed his name, turning it into an entreaty.

His silence and opaque stare said nothing and everything all at the same time.

"*...Therefore, if any man can show any just cause, why they may not lawfully be joined together, let him now speak, or else hereafter forever hold his peace...*"

He doesn't want this. Surely, in Gregory's witnessing Severin's antipathy toward Raina during their ceremony, he would stop this. Surely, he'd see this could not continue.

Desperate, she turned to her brother.

"That's the last place where you'll find objection, sweet," Severin whispered.

"And I take it the first place I'll find it is with you, dear husband-to-be."

Where did she find the strength and will to issue that spirited, impertinent, rebuttal?

He smirked. "That would be correct."

Had he gutted her with a dull knife it couldn't have hurt more than his icy rejection.

Lest he see the fresh tears that sprung to her eyes, Raina lowered her gaze to the floor, and distantly listened on as the ceremony continued...on and on...and on.

"*...At which day of marriage, if any man do allege and declare any impediment, why they may not be coupled together in matrimony, by God's Law, or the Laws of this Realm; and will be bound, and sufficient sureties with him, to the parties; or else put in a caution...*"

Raina began to wonder if Severin, in fact, *chose* the minister he had in the hope Raina would die of boredom before the wedding concluded.

The vicar's oration grew increasingly robust, as it appeared to climb towards a crescendo—and then it did.

"Severin Constance William Cadogan,"

His name in its entirety—strong and bold and all-powerful as he—she'd not even known until now.

"Wilt thou have this woman to thy wedded wife, to live together after God's ordinance in the holy estate of matrimony? Wilt thou love her—"

Something welled in her throat.

"—comfort her, honor, and keep her in sickness and in health..."

Comfort her? Keep her in sickness and in health?

Raina giggled.

And wonder of wonder, she managed to silence the ceaseless vicar.

Her skin prickle with the feel of five annoyed stares upon her.

Raina turned the rest of her droll amusement into a cough. "Forgive me," she demurred. "If you'll please, continue."

The vicar inclined his head and resumed from the beginning of Severin's vows. *"Wilt thou love her—"*

As if Severin could. The whisper of Severin's earlier promise became tangled with the vicar's words.

"I don't make love to women...I fuck them."

She choked back another giggle.

"...Wilt though, comfort her..."

Never.

"...You do not mean anything to me. You are a job, my lady. That is all, that is it. A job just as every other I've taken, and not a thing more."

Then, the man of God's words seemed to come faster and faster. *"Honor her...keep her in sickness and in health...forsaking all others, keep thee only unto her, so long as ye both shall live?"*

It was too much.

A raspy laugh exploded from her with such force her body shook, and tears streamed down her cheeks—this time, these tears, were ones of utter mirth and amusement.

All the strangers present for Raina's wedding day stared on.

Good, let them stare.

Let—

Someone—her brother— took Raina firmly by her forearm and led her away.

Not releasing his hold on her, Gregory spoke her name with a quiet insistence. *"Raina."*

She erupted into a rueful snort of hilarity. No doubt he absolutely despised he couldn't control her emotions. Through her blurred vision, she caught sight of her brother's worried gaze.

Worried. That thin line she straddled between amusement and despair grew frail, and she teetered on the edge of madness.

Through the maelstrom of emotions, she felt Gregory's grip grow firmer.

And then it was gone.

A deep baritone penetrated Raina's confusion.

"The next time you put your hands on her, I'll cut them off," Severin warned.

At some point, he'd removed Gregory's hand from Raina's person. He now held Gregory in a hold so punishing, even her stalwart brother's cheeks had gone a sickly white.

Wide-eyed, Raina stared at the two men, so different in every way: Gregory fair, and slightly taller but several stones lighter than a black-haired, dark in every way, heavily muscled Severin.

"Am I clear?" Severin whispered and squeezed Gregory harder.

Raina's lungs cinched. No one had gone toe-to-toe with the Duke of Argyll, and most certainly not because of or for Raina.

Her brother's mouth tightened in furious annoyance, but still, he proved no match for the earl.

Gregory gave a jerky nod.

Severin released him so quickly, Gregory stumbled, then caught himself.

"Leave us," Severin said flatly. He directed his command at the duke, but his unswerving eyes remained on Raina.

His gaze would never not cause her to tremble.

Smoothing the lapels of his jacket, a ruffled Gregory gave another terse nod.

He rejoined the silent pair at the hearth, and Raina and Severin were alone with an illusion of privacy.

This had been the closest they'd come to being alone since he'd made love to her at Lord and Lady Rutherford's ball. How strange, a woman could be so close as she'd been to Severin, in every way, just hours ago, only to find herself at sea and shy and unsettled before him now.

"I know the reason for your laughter, Raina," he said quietly.

Raina hugged her arms tightly at her middle. "You have no idea, Severin."

Absent of his earlier vitriol she could almost believe he didn't hate her.

His next statement disabused her of any such delusions.

"You're thinking about all the ways I resent you…"

She flinched. How coldly impassive and matter-of-fact.

"And yet, when we wed, regardless of the," his eyelid twitched, "the *circumstances* surrounding our union, I will protect you and see you safe. I'll cut a man's hands off if he so much as attempts to put a finger on you." Severin paused. "And your brother is included in that list of men I'd not even blink at killing." His eyes flashed fire. "I protect what is mine, Raina, and make no mistake, going forward, you belong to me."

You belong to me.

I am his…

Raina shivered. Only, it wasn't fear that coursed through her, but rather, a feverish, breathlessness at having this man's fierce, male, protectiveness promised to her.

This time, it was not her brother who escorted Raina over to the ceremony, but the man who'd be her husband—until death did part them.

CHAPTER 19

My heart is forever broken...
~The Duchess of A

SEVERIN DIDN'T INDULGE IN SPIRITS. He ate only out of necessity. And he certainly, did not sleep.

With a lengthy list of enemies who could be waiting in the shadows, and the recollections of the things he'd done...and not done in the course of his career, a mindless, restful, deep, slumber wasn't a luxury afforded him.

So, he worked.

Cadogan seated at his desk, going over a pile of letters that'd arrived; even his wedding night, proved no exception.

Then, why *should* it?

Yes, he'd married a spirited, clever, breathtaking beauty who awaited him upstairs. That didn't change anything.

Oh, Cadogan intended to bed Raina. He was neither monk nor eunuch—he'd have to be to resist Raina's charms.

If he sought her out now, if that was his first, or even, second, third, or fourth, order of business, what the hell did that say about Cadogan and the power his wife, a woman who'd connived with her brother, have over him?

He stared darkly at the page in his hands.

Eh, but who are you really hurting though, the devil in his head tempted. *Go to her.*

Regardless the circumstances around the union, she belonged to him now. Nor would any force be required. She was as hot for Cadogan as he was for her.

Whether he liked it or not—and in Cadogan's case, the latter definitely held true—she was now *his*.

His to care after.

His to protect.

His to provide for.

His to bed.

Cadogan inhaled slowly.

Now, he needn't suppress his base urges. He was free to both take what he wanted and give the lady what she hungered for.

His shaft again stirred.

Give her what she hungered for?

Cadogan hardened his jaw. After Raina's betrayal, the *last* thing she deserved was to have him service her. Alas, his career had seen him bring vipers with intent to harm the Crown to the heights of pleasure. If he could bring himself to sate those schemers, he could certainly do the same for his wife.

And you'll enjoy it; you'll enjoy ringing mindless orgasm after mindless orgasm from her, too. Because something in you, no, something about Raina's blend of innocence and uninhibitedness in matters of the carnal, drives you mad with lust.

His body hardened.

Cursing roundly, he shook his head, and focused his attention on the letter in his hands.

My little brother,

"Bloody splendid. A perfect end to a godforsaken day," Cadogan mumbled.

I often hear your name talked about. You have made a life for yourself and I trust you are proud to have your services sought by the most powerful peers in London. Bravo, little brother.

It has been too long.

"Little brother," he muttered and crumpled the parchment into a ball.

Nothing to kill a cockstand faster than reading correspondence from one's distant, stranger of a brother.

Knock-Knock-Knock

"Enter," Cadogan called out.

Cadogan's de-facto *butler*, Mauley, didn't waste time with greetings or pleasantries.

"Per your request, Mr. Cadogan," he said, when he'd pushed the door shut behind him, and started over with a silver tray in hand. "I've sorted the folders by arrival date."

Mauley set the platter down before him.

"I've also organized them by assignment," the other man continued, pointing to each as he spoke. "And as you like them: by level of danger, power of clients, and payment, last, of course."

Of course.

Because having been his secretary and aide, Mauley knew firsthand what did—and did not motivate—Severin.

Wordlessly, he collected the closest stack and while Mauley gave an overall report of the men employed by Severin throughout London, Severin skimmed through the prospective jobs.

Familial battle over property.

Non-peers calling in debts against elevated nobles.

With every request, his frustration mounted, he tossed one after the other aside, the way a real gentleman would cards in a game of hazard.

One gave him pause.

Sightings of notorious, lethal, gang leader believed dead. Confirmation sought.

"Confirmation," Cadogan muttered to himself, and tossed aside the proposition from *R. Black*.

As long as Cadogan could help it, he'd take an assignment that required not only some investigating on his part but also, one that allowed him to see it through to its *conclusion*.

Giving his head a shake, he kept on sifting—and then stopped as his gaze caught the opening of the next note.

I'm not above fratricide.

Fraternal blood-battle.

Sitting up straighter in his chair, Cadogan lifted his focus to the detail made at the top of the page in his secretary's hand and underlined several times to grab Cadogan's attention—and interest. Mauley did his job and did it well. He knew the assignments Cadogan craved—and did not crave.

Cadogan sat up in his chair and carefully read the bold, angry, strokes of the one who'd wielded that pen.

Someone attempted to kill me. I strongly suspect my brother. I will not bore you with the details. Needless to say, I want names. I want every last servant, friend, family, or whoever else, who supported his efforts.

And then, you can… do with him as you see fit.

MCB

For the first time since he'd been caught with Raina, Cadogan found himself diverted, away from enraging thoughts about the Goodheart siblings.

Now, this was something that resonated—a ruthless family, where one brother thought nothing of taking down the other, only to have the wronged one return, for proper vengeance.

Justice had nothing to do with that, and by the bluntly written letter, this particular client knew as much, too.

"This one," he said, handing the missive to Mauley. "I'll call just before dawn tomorrow, at his residence. That will be all."

His secretary took the note, bowed his head, and turned to go.

Severin's lips quirked in a wry smile. *Another* dawn meeting. The one he'd take with his mystery client, however, proved vastly different than today's business, and he found himself reminded all over again the maelstrom of events that'd seen him trapped.

With a bride upstairs.

In the bedroom next to his.

At this hour, changed out of a gown that'd hugged her every curve, and into a thin, chemise.

It'd be white. Modestly made for a virgin.

He went hard.

His grin faded.

Cadogan stopped the other man from leaving. "Mauley?"

The stoic secretary turned and faced him.

"Mr. Cadogan?" his secretary asked when Cadogan didn't speak. "Is there something else you require?"

Yes. Cadogan needed to have his bride under him, her legs parted, and his cock buried in her hot cunny. Because his body didn't give a damn about anything other than having what he wanted—and what he'd wanted since the day she'd sauntered into her brother's office, all doe-eyed innocence.

"Not a goddamned thing," he snapped. "I don't need anything. I—"

His secretary's expressionless features managed to say both nothing and everything at the same time.

Bloody hell. She's got me losing control—again.

"Where's…where's…" Mrs. Cadogan. As his wife, Raina now carried Cadogan's name. Something in joining his name with hers set him to squirming.

"The countess?" Mauley helpfully supplied.

"Yes, *her.*" That title and formality were precisely what Cadogan needed to maintain a distance between himself and the schemer. "The *countess.* Where is she?"

"She is in the suites next to yours." His secretary hesitated. "And has been there since her arrival. I saw that trays were sent for the afternoon and evening meal, but both were returned."

That gave Cadogan a different pause.

Bold, spirited, unapologetic Raina, who excelled in sneaking about had confined herself to her new rooms? That hardly fit with everything he knew about his bride. Though the circumstances of these past ten or so hours had already proven Cadogan knew less than nothing about her.

"Would you like me to pass word to the lady that you will be joining her for your meal, Mr. Cadogan?"

"If I wanted that, I'd have asked you," he said, frostily.

As annoyed by the idea of Raina cowering in his household as he was by the disapproving glint in his secretary's eyes, Cadogan chose to latch on to the latter.

"Do you have something you wish to say, Mauley?" he asked warningly.

For Mauley's part, well, the man knew his value and worth to Cadogan. It'd take anything short of an ultimate betrayal or act of violence against Cadogan to see the man fired.

The insolent way Mauley inclined his head said he knew it, too.

"Not at all, Mr. Cadogan. Is there anything else you require?"

"No," he said, dismissing the servant for a second time. "That will be all."

And as his secretary took his leave, Cadogan couldn't help

but frustratingly note the absolute only one who could meet his current needs at the moment was none other than the little deceiver.

In fact, a visit with sweet Raina was overdue—*long* overdue.

With a feral grin, Cadogan made to stand and go find his new bride.

Rap-Rap—Rap

This gentle and uneven rapping on the panel came distinctly different than Mauley's assured, one that came as an announcement. For that matter, this delicate cross between a scratch and a knock, wasn't the way a single man in Cadogan's employ would declare their presence.

Falling back into his seat, Cadogan joined his fingers and lay his hands upon his chest. "Enter."

The door opened slowly, and she stepped inside.

His wife.

Raina, attired in the crystal-encrusted gown she'd worn to their *wedding*, hovered at the entrance. Her artfully arranged pale blonde curls had since loosened so that a number of those tresses hung about her delicate shoulders and trim waist.

And Cadogan despised himself for drinking in the sight of her the way a starving man consumed food.

Raina was the first to move. She drew the door shut behind them.

An unpleasant taste settled in his mouth.

What a moment when his young bride should find the ability to move when he sat lost in the sight of her.

"Wife," he greeted with false joviality. "I trust you are finding your new residence to your standards."

Raina rested her palms on the panel behind her and leaned against the door. "It is…lovely," she said softly.

"And the staff, my lady. Are they seeing to your needs?"

"Undoubtedly so," she was quick to assure. "Your staff has been attentive and courteous."

"Have they?" he asked silkily.

She nodded. "They have seen to my every need."

No, they hadn't. Not a single man Cadogan employed would dare.

"My staff has carefully seen to you, and yet you are here, wife." She flinched ever so slightly.

An unpleasant sensation—an unwelcome one—pitted in his gut. The sight of her, hurt, *no*, the sight of her *wounded* because of *him*, caused a sharp, twisting sensation in his chest. Like Cadogan had been the one who'd done something wrong and not she and her bloody bastard of a brother.

He silently raged at himself for giving a damn either way that she should appear offended. She was, after all, nothing but a bloody skilled actress.

That reminder firmed his resolve and chased away all sense of misguided guilt.

"Why are you here, Raina?" he asked quietly.

That way, he needn't have to look at those big, hurt-filled eyes or the pain bleeding from those azure depths.

"What is it you've come to say?" The sooner he knew, the sooner he could send her away. "What exactly is it you need or want?"

She spoke in those dulcet tones that had fascinated him from the start. "I thought we might talk."

"*Talk.*"

His wasn't a question, but Raina nodded, anyway.

"I understand you did not wish to marry me, Severin," she said calmly.

A muscle rippled along his jaw. How easily and naturally she wielded the Christian name his own parents and siblings hadn't.

Raina stepped away from the door and started forward. "I know you are a man who doesn't have a place for a family," she went on, continuing her approach, "and your love and devotion is reserved for your career."

She stopped several steps away from his desk and searched her gaze over his face. "But Severin, whether you like it," she grimaced, "or not, we *are* married."

His blood boiled by several degrees. "And? We are married, Raina. Just what is that supposed to mean? How is our being married in any way relevant to—"

"We are to spend the rest of our lives with one another, Severin," she cried out, her calm of moments ago, breaking.

"Wrong." He surged to his feet. "We are to spend our lives sharing a name and nothing more."

She recoiled. "You hate me so much?"

Hate her?

For the love of the Savior and Satan's armies combined. The fact that she'd worked her way past his defenses and left him knotted up was proof that she'd some kind of bloody hold over him.

That *hold* was what he hated.

He started to drag a shaky hand through his hair, caught himself, and let his arm fall to his side.

Raina's eyes grew sad, once more. The fight slipping from her being.

"I see," she said, tiredly, taking his silence as confirmation.

She did a search of his office.

No one had stepped inside these hallow halls, and now Raina stood here; this woman, who would share the same walls and staff and name—

You share more than a name, the voice of reason within, reminded Cadogan. They shared a life. Raina belonged to him, in name, and body. As he'd pointed out to her brother when attempting to avoid marriage, Cadogan's past, was now Raina's present and future, an idea that left him nauseous.

Sick at the prospect of the potential peril she, through her connection with him, had inherited. A detail, which when he'd been bent on self-preservation, had been secondary.

His stomach churned as it had during his first passage across the Channel.

Raina clasped her hands and stared down at the interlocked digits. "I'd just thought—"

"What did you think, *sweet wife?*" he asked, an edge of something very like desperation creeping in. "That I'd settle happily into a bucolically blissful married state with *you* as my bride?" He didn't allow her a chance to answer. "That we'd, what? Live some goddamned happily ever after?" A bitter laugh tore from his chest.

Raina's lower lip quivered.

Bloody hell. Even with the treachery her family carried out against him, the sight of her sadness cut him to the core.

Fake. It was all...

Then it hit him.

He stormed out from behind his desk. "My God, you did."

Raina tripped with the speed with which she bolted away from him.

His nostrils flared. "Do you think I'd hit you?" he snapped, somehow even more annoyed by that than...than...any other bloody part of this hellish day.

"N-No." Her eyes shimmered.

Oh, shite. Don't look at me like that. All wounded and hurting.

Her tears. They were a flimsy weapon, but to Cadogan, they were somehow his blasted Achille's heel.

That's precisely what'd landed him here.

Had he not, time and time again, let himself be weak for Raina Goodheart, she wouldn't be standing before him as Raina Cadogan, Countess of Killburn.

Cadogan chuckled. "Fearing your new husband hardly denotes the happy union you speak of."

"I d-don't fear you."

Even with that slight tremble, her avowal came so passionately, he could almost believe her.

"You're a shite liar." Which made it all the bloodier infuriating that he'd been so blind as to see what was at play from the moment she'd stepped into Argyll's office with that regal crown.

Raina drifted closer. "I *don't*. I—"

God, she would not quit.

"Let me spare you time and suffering, wife," he snapped. "The happily-ever-after's you're clearly in search of? They don't exist, and they certainly don't exist for jaded souls," of which he was, "and liars and schemers." Of which she—and he—was.

Not for beasts such as Cadogan. Not for anyone. He was just one of the few who realized as much.

"I know you likely believe that because of the things you've done, Severin," she said, beseechingly. "And maybe that is why you are so resistant to the idea of us—"

His coarse laugh cut over the rest of her ridiculous utterance. "The idea of '*us*'? *Jesus*, Raina."

A blush burst upon her high, radiant, cheeks, but she was unrelenting.

"You are so accustomed to being alone, the thought of you letting anyone close, terrifies you. It doesn't have to be that way, Severin. Our relationship, it's all been rushed, but there is nothing saying we cannot, at least, find peace, and maybe even… happiness."

There it was again.

Happiness.

He drew back as it hit him like a full ton of weight.

Shock chased away his anger. "You truly do believe all that."

Unflinching, Raina tipped her chin back and nodded.

He whistled. "You've somehow convinced yourself you and I can have some loving future together."

This time, her beautiful features, wavered.

"Why *can't* we, Severin?" she whispered.

Then, Raina lifted her smooth, unblemished palms up, as if in supplication.

It was her hands.

Cadogan fixed on those flawless, pure, lily-white hands, which, unlike his that'd been made for killing and done just that, hadn't seen an inch of hardship in her almost twenty years.

Incapable of words, Cadogan stared at her. After the way she'd colluded with Argyll to ensnare him, she was still naïve enough to think Cadogan would welcome a future with her.

The air sizzled and seethed with tension; and the silence stretched on so long, Raina's hands fell.

Her throat wobbled. "Won't you say something?"

"You want me to say something?" he repeated. Cadogan paused, not trusting himself to speak. "Did you truly believe after being trapped into marriage, I'd embrace a future with you?" he asked when he'd gotten himself calm.

Raina winced.

An odd expression settled over her face, and she shook her head slowly. "Poor Severin."

Cadogan stiffened.

He'd have to be deaf to fail and detect the irreverent quality of those otherwise soft murmurings.

"You, who doesn't believe in love and doesn't want to marry and who doesn't make love to women," she continued, icily, "but, who—how is it you referred to it?—*fucks* them, now finds yourself stuck for life with me, because we were discovered in flagrante delicto."

Raina trained an impressive glare on him, breathtaking in her fury.

"Need I remind you, Severin," she jabbed a finger at his chest, "you were an all-too-willing and eager participant, not only *last* evening but many times before."

With every word she'd spoken and vision she'd laid out, his anger, frustration, and fear built until it all exploded to the surface. Damned if in her challenging him, he didn't find himself wanting to drag her into his arms.

"Are you done?" he asked silkily.

Raina's bow lips formed a perfect bow. "No. No, I'm not. Your wounded party act, Severin? Is both tiresome and *juvenile*."

The air sizzled and crackled with tension.

"Tiresome and juvenile," he whispered, taking a step closer.

She gave a shaky nod, that sent the remainder of her ethereal blonde tresses cascading about her shoulders.

The sight of her, all indignant rage and pietistic hurt, shredded the last of his self-control.

"Wounded party act, Raina? You paint *me* as the irrational one and not say…*you*. *You* who casually waltzes in here as if there's nothing unordinary about our marriage and the circumstances of our being together is born of mutual consent and not *coercion*?"

Another harsh laugh exploded from him; this time one borne of actual ironical mirth.

Raina flinched. "I didn't coerce you," she spoke, her voice barely audible.

"No," he conceded. "Your brother did that part all on his own. Argyll attempted to bring me in as a partner and head of security of his bloody iniquitous club." He seethed. "I'd sooner make a widow of you than have *anything* to do with Argyll."

CHAPTER 20

I remember the day we married. The sun shone. The church was filled—but I only saw him.
~ The Duchess of A

When Raina set out to speak to Severin, she'd expected he'd still be angry as he'd been during their wedding ceremony.

A man as proud as Severin, and as committed to his career and bachelor state, would chafe at the bounds of matrimony. For that matter, a man as strong as her husband would lash out at being forced into doing *anything* he didn't wish.

She'd known all that when she'd made her way downstairs to find him.

Still, she'd hoped they could establish some semblance of peace.

What she'd found was anything but. What she'd met was bitter resentment, horrid accusations, and his burning hatred for Gregory *and* herself.

Standing just three feet apart, they may have been three worlds away.

His opaque gaze dared her to say something.

For a moment, she feared she wasn't as brave as she'd credited herself as being. But if she shrunk before him, if she ran away, she'd be the one who laid a foundation in their marriage of inequity—one where he was in a position of strength and she, cowed by him.

As he'd pointed out before, the very important truth she knew—he'd never hurt her. That gave her the courage to meet his gaze directly, and at last, speak.

"The way you love your work," she said, trying to strike some kind of accord between her brother whom she loved and the husband whom she also loved, but who hated her brother. "Is the *same* way Gregory loves his."

"I'm *nothing* like your brother."

She bit her tongue to keep from pointing out when it came to temperament, personality, and pride, Severin had more in common than he could ever know.

She'd not be side-tracked.

"Gregory offered you a share of ownership in his club, Severin—a venture he began with his oldest and closest friends. Is it so very bad he offered to make you a proprietor, as well? That he did so, long before you," *Were part of my life,* "worked in my family's house…"

Her words trailed off and she realized too late; she'd said too much.

Fury burned from within Severin's eyes; a blistering, black, rage.

Raina hugged herself tight around the middle in a futile attempt to hide from his hate.

"He robbed me of choice," he hissed, taking a furious step towards her. "From the moment I entered your household, and he offered me a post to serve as your goddamned bodyguard, the only intention he ever had was for me to fall under your spell."

Her cheeks went a fiery red. "You make me out to be some kind of object," she cried.

"That's precisely what you were to Argyll. A means, to my end."

She gasped. "How dare you? Gregory—"

"You'd make excuses for him?" he shouted.

Her pulse pounded. Never in all the times she'd challenged Severin had Raina witnessed him lose control.

He retained his grip so quickly; she might have merely imagined the slip in his composure. "I should have expected nothing less," Severin intoned, icily indifferent.

Raina frowned and tried to make sense of it all. "What is that supposed to mean?"

"The entire plan all along." Severin's hard lips peeled into a hateful sneer. "Was to force my hand and bend me so I was another lackey in his employ. What your brother failed to realize, however, is that I'd sooner end myself than work for or with him."

She drew back. Her mind whirred under those accusations.

What he suggested...No, what he actually maintained, was that Gregory had used Raina as bait to lure and trap Severin.

Raina struggled to find her voice.

Her brother wasn't the affectionate, fully devoted sibling he'd once been, but he'd not sell her like a trollop—not even in the name of *Forbidden Pleasures*.

She found strength in her outrage. "You'd accuse my brother of making a whore out of me for his own gains?"

His silence rocked the room far more than any verbal or concurrence.

"How dare you, Severin?" she hissed. "How—"

"You can stop with the theatrics, Raina. Argyll didn't even attempt to conceal what you'd both done. He owned the scheme completely."

She furrowed her brow.

Her brother *owned* the scheme? He wouldn't...He couldn't...

Couldn't he? Driven, ruthless, and single-minded in his obsession with his gaming hell, Gregory, would put it above everything and anyone—including his own sisters.

She squeezed her eyes shut as the weight and horror of that betrayal threatened to double her over.

"He wouldn't," she whispered, her voice raspy.

"He would and he did." Severin flicked another one of those contemptuous stares over her person. "The same, however, cannot be said of his loyal sister."

Wait...another admission Severin made registered.

"...Argyll didn't even attempt to conceal what you'd both done..."

The realization hit Raina hard, robbing her of breath.

"Surely you do not believe *I* helped him, Severin?" she whispered.

When he didn't say anything, she rushed over and gripped him by his upper arms.

His muscles jumped under her touch.

In disgust.

She released him quickly.

Severin, her husband, thought so little of Raina, he actually believed she'd aided and abetted some scheme masterminded by Gregory?

"Severin," she demanded, her voice climbing and pitchy to her own ears.

"The act grows old, Raina," he said impatiently. "That first meeting when you arrived in your diamond tiara—"

She sputtered. "My b-brother insisted on it!"

Which now made even more, horrifying, sense.

"I don't doubt that." Severin mowed ahead. "Argyll allowing me to be alone with you when any other devoted brother would have sooner seen me dead than stand for a private meeting with his precious sister."

Except, she wasn't precious to Gregory. Maybe she never had been. To him. To Severin. To no one.

Severin wasn't done with her. "Then there was all your talk about our being *friends.*"

Hearing him recite the naïve hope she'd carried, sent a blush burning across Raina's face; a blush he undoubtedly took as a sign of guilt.

"You sent me on a merry chase throughout London; leading me to areas you had no place being, all the while knowing I'd follow you into those salacious venues."

"No," she whispered, shaking her head. "I did *not* want you to follow."

Severin snorted.

That scoffing sound set her teeth to grating. "I didn't. I didn't want a nursemaid. I wanted..." She bit the inside of her cheek hard. *A friend and confidante.* Just as he'd just moments ago, mocked her over.

"There was the night you found me in the kitchens, Raina."

"I couldn't sleep and you happening to be there was—"

"A coincidence?" Severin quirked a menacing black eyebrow.

Raina cast another desperate glance about.

He'd already found her guilty of the false crimes he now charged her with. Trying to convince him otherwise, was nothing but a waste of time.

Severin brushed hard knuckles along her cheek with such

a tenderness it threatened to completely fracture her already splintered heart.

He guided her face to meet his. "What about last evening, Raina?" he quietly asked. "How do you account for your returning to that hallway and your surrender to me in the parlor?"

She'd gone back because she'd intended to profess her feelings for him. But he'd only see that admission as another lie.

Severin drew in a slow, shaky breath, through his teeth. "I thought so."

A fresh onslaught of tears pricked her eyes.

Here she'd believed nothing could hurt more than his derision and hate. But seeing him vulnerable, his eyes strained and glittering with disbelief and pain threatened to level her. For it meant…she'd hurt him.

How could that be possible if he didn't care about her?

Once again, a kernel of hope stirred. "Severin—"

"Your tears," he said in deadened tones that also killed that innocent dream. "Your brother's timely arrival." He paused. "Your apologies…"

"*I am s-sorry…I am s-so sorr—*"

She remembered all too clearly, as clearly as Severin, what she'd said, and how it would now appear given the circumstances.

"It all makes sense *now*," he said, toneless. "And it did then. I was just too blind to see why." For the first time, Severin's anger emerged more directed at himself.

She needed him to know the truth. "I didn't do those th–things, S-Severin," she whispered, her voice catching. "That is, I did, but I did not…"

She closed her eyes.

For…she had, though inadvertently. Given what Severin revealed, she'd been as he'd said, an instrument to help Gregory attain what he'd wanted most. In so doing, Severin had gotten what he'd wanted most, but stuck with that which he wanted least—Raina.

Neither of the two men in her life wanted her or cared about her.

Strangely, only the rejection of this man, the one she'd spend the rest of her days with should inflict the greatest hurt within.

She hugged herself hard.

When she opened her eyes, she found Severin staring at her with that opaque gaze she couldn't read.

"You aren't a man who can be made to do anything, Severin. You rejected my brother's offer of proprietorship." Her throat moved up and down. "Why then, did you agree to marry me? *Why?*"

Maybe some small part inside him that he'd not yet acknowledged—

"Argyll presented me with that which he and I both knew, I would never be able to refuse," he said somberly.

What was he saying?

Through an all-encompassing misery, hope blossomed.

Raina dampened her lips. "And what exactly was that?"

For a long while, he just peered at her with an inscrutable expression.

"The man who ended my career with the Home Office," he said, his gaze went all the way through her. "The duke learned his identity and hung it over me so that I can hunt down the man who consigned me to this empty, purposeless, existence here in London."

Before Raina stood a man who'd ceased to see her.

She went hot and then cold inside. A vicious crawling sensation eased along her skin.

The sole reason, Severin had married her was so he might have revenge.

Bile burned the back of her throat.

It hadn't been some gentlemanly sense of guilt and obligation that'd compelled Severin to wed her—which, though, awful in its own right—was nothing compared to *this*.

Her thoughts continued to spin, wildly out of control.

Preserving her honor and reputation hadn't been enough to—as Severin called it—compel him to marry Raina. Her brother had been forced to tender an even greater enticement.

Feeling like she'd become an outsider looking in on her real life, Raina did a frantic, empty sweep of Severin's office. The walls and ceiling grew smaller. Everything was closing in.

I'm going to be sick…

Through the fog, she detected a flash of movement as Severin moved away from her and returned to the place behind his desk.

"As you're here," Severin shifted so quickly onto a new topic, she suffered whiplash, "it would be best to outline the parameters of our union," he said, as he sat. "As you pointed out, we are," he grimaced, "whether we like it or not, joined forever. Ours will be nothing more than a business arrangement. You won't find me a cruel husband. You'll enjoy your freedom and the benefits which come with your role as countess. You'll have a sizeable alliance, and your dowry, per the contracts drawn up, will remain in your control for you to do with as you see fit.

"For your protection, I still expect a detailed list of your daily plans. You're never to leave without an escort or bring outsiders into this household. Is that clear?"

Was that clear?

Was *anything*, anymore?

Through the humming in her ears, she gave a small nod.

"You're dismissed, Raina."

With that, Severin returned to whatever work he'd been seeing to, and she was forgotten—just as she'd always been.

Just as she would always be.

Turning jerkily about, Raina headed for the door, and then stopped; her gaze fixed on the sturdy, stark, unadorned panel, so perfectly suited the austere king of this cold place.

"For what it is worth, Severin," she called out softly. Nothing. It would be worth nothing to him. Still, she had to say it anyway. "Gregory *did* use me. He used us both."

Raina let that truth sit in silence, and when it went answered, she left.

CHAPTER 21

*I've learned there's someone I love more than Wallace.
My son. I want a true family.
~The Duchess of A*

AS USUAL, CADOGAN DIDN'T BOTHER with sleep.

The evening had been a productive one—at least, as far as work went.

As soon as he'd accepted his latest assignment, Cadogan poured himself into drafting a series of interview questions for his newest client and preparing for his meeting with the nobleman later that morning.

He'd already met with three of the men he'd taken from the Home Office. Per his instruction, each had gone in quick search of whatever details they could ascertain about his latest client: the man's family, his friends, and any and every secret, scandal, or peccadillo carried by the lot of them.

Unlike in the past, even this particularly ruthless, campaign, hadn't posed enough of a distraction.

Then again, he'd not required distractions. Nothing but his craft and killing had occupied his thoughts.

In one fell swoop, almost overnight, however, Raina Goodheart had swept into his life, and nothing had been the same since.

Not Raina Goodheart: Raina Cadogan, Countess of Killburn.

His bride.

His wife.

Is she really your wife, if you haven't seen to the exquisite business of bedding her? The devil on his shoulder nudged. *She's up there, waiting for you, there for the taking.*

Teary-eyed though she may have left, she'd proven time and time again, how easily she'd surrender to desire.

His cock hardened…as it would until he'd finally buried himself ballocks deep inside her.

And he wanted her, somehow, with an even greater ferocity.

The forbidden, at last, belonged to Severin; the apple, free to sample and devour.

Bloody, bloody, hell.

All intentions of work at an end, Cadogan cursed and tossed his pen down. Ink splattered upon his hands and the stained surface of his desk.

He did not need these complications. He did not need Raina. He did not need any of this.

He'd made it a point to continue the Cadogan family ways— one lived one's own life, without inside or outside interference from anyone. Be it those who shared one's blood or one who pledged fealty, one didn't let them close or in—for the simple fact, he didn't need it.

Now, there was, Raina.

Splendorous, breathtaking, Raina who was his for better or worse, richer or poorer, sickness and in health, until death did part them.

Lust. It was the only thing he felt for this woman.

Lust could be slaked, and it would.

If that was the case, however, why did he find himself besieged by the memory of her exquisite features, twisted in shock and pain?

For the dozenth time since she'd tiptoed into his office and then quietly marched out, the memory of their exchange, possessed his thoughts.

"…You'd accuse my brother of making a whore out of me for his own gains…"

"…He wouldn't…"

Every question, statement, and demand rolled together.

"…Surely you do not believe I helped him, Severin?"

"…Gregory did use me, but I did not willingly or knowingly help him in his deception against you…"

"Fuck," he thundered, hurling a folder.

Cadogan surged to his feet and began to pace.

She'd intended to make him feel guilty, and guilt was a bloody emotion he needed even less than love.

His strides took on a greater urgency.

She was a liar. An actress.

But was she really? All the skills he'd attained as an agent for the Crown spoke to the contrary. Her eyes revealed too much, as did her lips.

The alternative, however, that she hadn't—

Knock-Knock—

He stopped in his tracks.

"Enter!" he boomed.

His secretary stepped inside.

"Mauley," he said, stupidly.

"These have already arrived, my lord," the other man said, coming to meet Cadogan.

Cadogan took the folios his efficient staff had already put together. He proceeded to sift through the first information to come in.

Yes, this was good; a productive diversion Cadogan needed from his bride.

"This also came," Mauley handed over a thick sheet of ivory vellum. "A note from Lord de Grey, indicating he is available to meet with you now."

Perfect. He could start now—this is what he wanted. This is precisely what he needed.

Cadogan braced for the familiar rush that accompanied the most mercenary jobs—which, strangely, did not come.

Why? A jittery panic formed in his gut. Why wouldn't he want to immediately commence an actual assignment? One that didn't include watching over young ladies or chasing down debts, but real, actual work to address an injustice.

"Or…later," Mauley, murmured.

Unnerved, Cadogan picked his head up and looked at his inscrutable secretary. "Hmm?"

His secretary gave him a peculiar look.

Bloody hell. Get your wits about you, man.

Cadogan grunted. "Reply to the marquess. Inform him I intend to review the information I have and…"

And, then what?

Going over the folders his men already supplied him with, hardly take him any time, at all.

The most important details Cadogan could gleam rested with the gentleman, not only ready but so eager to meet, he'd grant Cadogan an audience in the dead of night.

This night, however, also happened to be Cadogan's wedding night, which should mean less than absolutely nothing; which *did*, mean, absolutely less than nothing.

"Inform the marques I'll call at the specified location thirty minutes past five, Mauley," Cadogan said, with a cool he didn't feel. "As soon as I finish reviewing the notes assembled thus far, I'll pay him a call."

Mauley nodded and then let himself out.

Only after he'd gone and closed the door behind him did Cadogan scrape an uneven hand through his hair.

What the hell is wrong with me?

Here he was, presented by his secretary with an opportunity to set to work immediately on a new—and involved interesting—assignment. What had he done instead? He'd opted to remain here and delay his work.

From across the room, his gaze caught and locked on the harried figure reflected in the walnut gilt, Chippendale mirror—Cadogan's eyes bloodshot. His cheeks covered in a day's worth of growth. His hair disheveled and out of place.

That mirror which he'd directed hung so he'd have eyes on the front and back of any guests who stood before him, now exposed Cadogan as a man no different than the listless, ineffectual people he'd come across in his career.

"*Fuck*," he shouted, uncaring the guards carefully stationed around his office and connecting parlors heard.

Gritting his teeth, he sat down hard and dragged over the folders his men had left.

He made an angry grab for the nearest one and snapped it open.

Cadogan proceeded to read.

"*...During the marquess's disappearance, his younger brother, ascended to the title, where he accumulated a sizeable debt...*"

He flicked his gaze quickly over the page—rapidly taking in each word.

"*...betrothal between the marquess's brother and former betrothed...*"

"*...wedding to take place...*"

Wedding.

His mind strayed.

There'd been a wedding this day—his and Raina's. And with each wedding came the wedding night.

Abandoning all intentions to work until his meeting, Cadogan snapped the folder closed, stacked all the materials for his new case, and deposited them in the top, right-hand drawer.

Yes, I am going mad.

Cadogan knew as much, just as he knew the source of his insanity—the five-foot, seven-inch, Junoesque woman; a woman who at this very instant occupied the chambers across from his.

Waiting.

Alone.

The man of logic within him warred with the man of lust who wouldn't be sated until he'd devoured and consumed his wife.

Cadogan set his jaw. He'd never be weak for anyone, not even, Raina, a goddamned queen in her own right.

With that, he gave up on work and went to find his bride.

It was time they had their wedding night.

CHAPTER 22

I have told Wallace I wish to stop our debauched ways.
~ The Duchess of A

LYING IN HER NEW BED, Raina didn't bother to turn when she caught the slight *click* of the doorway; a click so faint, had the fire in the hearth crackled just a smidge louder, she wouldn't have detected his arrival.

Instead, she stared blankly at his visage in the mahogany pivoting mirror positioned near her—his—bed. This was, after all, *his* household. One she wasn't wanted or welcome in.

At some point, he'd shed his jacket, cravat, and boots. He'd untucked his white lawn shirt and the sight of this always cool, collected man in such a state of *complete* dishabille left Raina's mouth dry.

"Why are you here, Severin?" she asked tiredly; drained not from exhaustion but emotionally depleted.

"I think that should be quite clear, my love," he rejoined, in silky tones that carried more than a promise of what was to come.

She bit the inside of her cheek so hard, her teeth shred the flesh. She hated him. She hated him for blaming her for what they'd done and shared and for being discovered. But she hated herself even more for responding to him and wanting him still.

And she knew, after they consummated their wedding night, she'd never be the same. Once he laid masterful possession of her body, she'd lose an even larger part of herself to Severin Cadogan, and from that loss, she would never, ever recover.

She'd be her mother in the worst way—wanting a man who didn't truly want her in the same ways she yearned for *him*.

"You married me and got the information you sought, Severin," she said, unable—and not even trying— to keep the pleading from her voice. "There is no need for a wedding night."

"Ah, but a different 'need' is what brings me to your bed," he purred silkily. "Mine…and yours."

His coarse, unemotional pronouncement should repulse her. Instead, a wanton heat pooled between her legs, and she squirmed in a bid to lessen that misery.

She cursed her body's reaction to this man.

A slow, small, arrogant grin curved his lips at the corners. His smile said he'd witnessed her reaction, knew her thoughts, and reveled in them.

Then, barefoot and impossibly primal like a sleek, feral, black panther, Severin started toward her.

Raina closed her eyes.

He wanted her. That was, he wanted her *body*.

Those were two very different things.

He'd been clear, however, from the start, his feelings on lovemaking—there was no love nor feelings actually involved. There was just the raw lust all wild animals felt.

Not even a fortnight ago, she would have agreed with him. She would have said she'd discovered, after all, that human emotions were not involved in carnal matters. That was why men and women visited her brother's den of sin and why her late mother had accepted there wouldn't be the love she'd dreamed of with the duke and took lovers whose skills in bed, she'd marveled over in her diary.

But Raina had been wrong. She'd not been moved or wanted to join in the debauched acts with the gentleman she'd observed at *Lucifer's Lair* or sneak off to kiss a random gentleman at the masquerade.

She wanted…Severin. She ached to do all those indecorous, naughty things she'd witnessed other men doing to their lovers, but with Severin and only Severin.

She blinked back tears.

"There will be no tears this night, Raina," he whispered.

Severin didn't take his piercing gaze off Raina. With precise, tempting, and taunting movements, he pulled the garment up and over his head, tossed it aside, and stood bare-chested before her.

Unable to look away from the sight of him as he shed the rest of his garments, Raina boldly drank her fill.

His chest lightly matted with tight black curls and each muscle perfectly defined, he was a chiseled masterpiece of God's finest work.

Then, his hands went to the waist of his perfectly tailored black wool pants that clung to the corded muscles in his thighs and calves.

With another sarcastic grin, he dared her to look away.

Raina couldn't if she wanted to—and she did want to. She didn't want this man—or any man—to have this level of power over her.

While she watched on, Severin edged his trousers down and then in one swift movement, he rid himself of the garment, until he stood naked before her.

And as she drank her fill of him, a yearning the likes of which she'd never known—even in all the passionate exchanges she'd had with Severin, before now—sent such a keen, painful ache between her legs, Raina squirmed and twisted to be free of it.

The mattress dipped as he climbed onto the bed.

He came over her and she wanted to resist. With his previous and loyal work for the Crown, and the rage with which he'd avenged the men he'd overheard insulting her, he'd not force himself upon an unwilling woman. He possessed too much honor and pride to ever do so.

He'd stop if she but spoke even a single word of protest.

Instead, as he slowly, seductively divested her of her night rail, kissing each swath of bare skin he exposed, Raina shifted so he could free her of the garment.

Then as weak as Eve, she parted her legs for Severin, and he settled between them like the conquering king claiming his rightful place upon the throne.

He lowered his head to claim her lips in a bold possession, she opened hers and welcomed him inside.

Severin ravaged her mouth and Raina returned his violent kiss with a like fervor, tangling and twisting her tongue with his, against his.

He grunted his approval, and she swallowed that low, primal, rumble.

"Severin," she rasped between each kiss.

Then, he slipped a hand between her legs.

She moaned in anticipation of his touch, knowing what he'd find, and too hungry to care.

As expected, as soon as Severin slipped his fingers into her thick, slippery wetness, he chuckled.

"You asked why I'm here, sweet." He teased her nub and Raina cried out.

The look in his eyes darkened. "This is why I'm here. I'll not punish either of us from taking what we both need, for doing your brother's bidding."

That is truly what he believed. His ill-opinion speared her all the way through.

With his spare hand, Severin gripped one of Raina's palms. He guided her fingers to his cock and wrapped her palm around his silken, steel-hard shaft.

Shamefully eager, she gripped him hard.

A shuddery hiss escaped past his gritted teeth, and Severin arched into her touch.

She moaned and, relishing the feel of his length and his lack of control, she tugged and squeezed his length the way he'd shown her.

Raina rocked her hips in a bid to ease that ache at her core from the simple pleasure of touching him.

Severin's breath emerged raspy and graveled as death. "It is as I said, sweet love,"

Sweet love. Raina wept inside at that endearment.

His next words put a quick end to all hints of romanticism. "Neither of us truly wanted this union, but neither does that mean we should not seek and take our pleasure with one another."

Severin gave her several more strokes with his fingers that chased away Raina's misery and centered her on the one thing he could promise her. "We both need this. We both want this. And then we'll both be free of our desire for one another."

"You said that already at the m-masquerade," she said, and then gasped as he stroked her in a place that nearly brought her to surrender. "And yet, h-here you are." Raina wanted to cry when he stopped touching that oversensitive flesh.

He smirked. "Ah, but we didn't fuck then, Raina. This will be different, and this will leave us both sated and able to move on from one another."

Never, she answered in her mind. While he'd tire of her, she'd never have enough of him. She wanted all of him. But for now, she'd take all he was capable of—and likely would only be capable of—offering her.

He drew his fingers from her body so quickly, she cried out.

"Shh, I'm not punishing you, sweet," he said in soothing tones that were, in the face of her persistent and irrepressible desire, infuriatingly composed. "I'm rewarding you for letting us have what we *both* want."

Then, he slid slowly down her body and guided her to open her legs wider for him. "I'm going to eat you again, little love. I'm going to feast on your nectar and suck you and finger you until you're screaming my name to the rafters. And then I'm going to bury my cock inside you."

His depraved promise brought Raina back to the first and last time he'd made love to her in that wicked, wonderful way. She whimpered as another rush of warmth and wetness flooded her core.

He chuckled.

His salacious promise alone brought her hips arching up and pulled another smug chuckle from him. "Lovely," he said, conferring more of his roughened praise.

Severin slid his hands under her buttocks and raised her hips close to his mouth. Her breath hitched and her eyes slid shut as he buried his nose in her humiliatingly drenched curls. Of course, he'd never allowed her to feel shame in her body's response to him.

Severin slipped his tongue inside her.

Her hips shooting off the bed, Raina cried out.

She closed her eyes tightly and sinking into the mattress, Raina surrendered herself to just feeling and living in this moment. Making love with him would never be enough, but like a pitiful creature, she'd take what he offered.

Over and over again, Severin slipped his tongue inside her. He sucked her nub until all coherent thought and words failed Raina. The wicked sounds of her wetness as he laved and drank, filled her ears and she thrashed her head back and forth upon the bed.

Only, there was no end to his torture.

"You taste so good," he extolled, wickedly

Her breath came in short, hungry spurts.

Of a sudden, Severin stopped, and Raina wept. "Please," she begged. "Do not stop."

"Never." Sealing that brusque promise with a hard kiss upon her mouth, Severin lowered himself between her legs. "I'm going to bury my cock so deep inside you, sweet, and you're going to love it," he panted.

She whimpered at the titillating scene he painted.

"Don't be afraid, little dove," he crooned, misunderstanding the reason for her cry. "You were made for this. I've stretched you every time I slipped my fingers in your sweet cunny. Your body will take me."

It did not escape her notice that he did not tack on the very important 'easily' at the end of his vow.

But she didn't care.

She wanted him deep inside her; so deep one could not say where Severin ended and Raina began; so that their souls fused and their hearts beat in time.

Severin nudged the plum tip of his penis to the entrance of her womanhood. Inch by agonizing inch he pushed himself inside Raina, further and further. Until he'd seated himself; his entire thick, long, length, stretched her, filled her.

As he'd promised, with all the ways he'd touched her before, he'd prepared her for his entry.

She squeezed her eyes shut and relished the full sensation of his being inside her.

And as he'd also promised, there was no pain, just an exquisite bliss. At least in this union, she and Severin were joined as one, in the way ordained by God in that fated Garden of Eden, when he'd known Adam and Eve could never deny themselves this most forbidden of fruits.

"Look at me," he commanded sharply, but it was the faintest edge of softness in that directive which brought Raina's lashes fluttering open.

"Have I hurt you?" he demanded, sounding almost angry at the prospect of having brought her pain.

Which was preposterous. He'd already hurt her in every way that mattered most, and he remained indifferent to that suffering.

But she understood what he asked.

She shook her head.

"No," she said softly, and slid her fingers through his hair, damp with perspiration. "You did not hurt me."

And to prove as much, and to urge him on, Raina lifted her hips.

His cobalt eyes turned a shade of black, and then, it was as if Raina had freed the savage beast from its cage.

He began to move.

They began to move *together.*

He lowered his hips and she lifted to meet his downward thrust.

While their bodies moved in perfect harmony, their bright gazes remained locked. No words were expressed between them. Aside from the ragged and harsh respirations spilling from their lips, not a sound was uttered.

They didn't speak, because no words were necessary.

Raina didn't want to look away, because in this moment, while she rose to meet each, powerful, drive of his strong thrusts, there existed only she and Severin.

Here, in this moment, didn't live lies and deceptions and wrongly reached conclusions. Hate couldn't be found here.

Only, she and Severin.

Which was how she wanted it to be.

Surrendering fully to the dream, Raina closed her eyes and fixed on the exquisiteness of each powerful stroke. Each downward drive of his hips sent her closer and closer, teetering to that edge he'd taken her soaring over in times before.

So close.

So close.

She bit her lower lip so hard, the metallic tinge of blood filled her mouth.

Severin swept his lips over hers and continued a quest of kisses lower, to her neck where he suckled and nipped that flesh.

Their rhythm took on a greater urgency; their undulations grew frenzied, more frantic.

His muscles quivered against Raina; under her; tensing and tightening.

"Come for me, sweet Raina," he rasped harshly.

Her name, twined with an endearment, in the form of a desperate plea from *this* man sent her hurtling toward the edge

He wants me as much as I want him…

That truth sent her flying all the way over.

Raina cried out.

Wrapping her arms about Severin's back, she sobbed and screamed as she came.

He rocked inside her over and over again, ringing every last drop of pleasure from her. "You feel so bloody good," he rasped. "So. Bloody. Good."

Severin gripped Raina's hips hard, positioning how he most needed her, and anchoring her in place, he continued pumping his hips harder, and faster.

His harshly beautiful features froze. And with a hoarse, triumphant, shout, he poured himself into Raina in long, powerful waves.

Through his climax, Raina held him more tightly, clinging to him.

Closing her eyes, she rode another wild, wonderful wave of ecstasy, before collapsing into the mattress.

There, replete and framed beneath Severin's strong, capable arms, Raina, with a sated smile on her lips, slept.

Some hours later

A faint and distant whimper penetrated the vast, emptiness of Raina's slumber.

Her eyes too heavy to open, she shifted and squirmed to escape that doleful mewling.

Wrapped in the safe, reassuring folds of the warmest blanket to ever cover her, Raina wanted to remain here forever, but the whineling of that wounded creature sent coldness seeping in.

Only, Raina didn't want to leave this feeling and seek out the source of that far off suffering.

Then, blessedly, that whimpering stopped and Raina slipped deeper toward that place of beautiful oblivion.

Just as she would have drifted off completely, a guttural sound so terrible, and filled with such sorrow, snatched Raina from sleep.

With her head thick from the fog, and lashes heavy, Raina fought to open her eyes.

An inky black darkness hung over an unfamiliar room. As she attempted to sort out where she was, the loud hum of silence, filled her ears.

Pushing herself up into a seated position, she blinked and gave her eyes an opportunity to adjust. A rush of cool night air touched her bare skin as she moved, and she glanced down.

With a gasp, she grabbed the nearby satin sheet and dragged it close.

Her gaze first alighted on the garments littering the hardwood floor, and then, her focus shifted until it caught and landed on the mirrored doors of a blue and cream painted armoire.

Raina stared dumbly at her naked, disheveled image reflected within those glass panels and the broad body pressed against hers.

Thoughts about what'd taken place crept slowly in—her and Severin. The masquerade. The discovery.

She gasped and jumped back.

Severin, dead to the world, flipped onto his other side and continued sleeping.

Raina's heart knocked in a sick, slow, thud against her ribcage as it all came rushing back. Severin believed she'd colluded with her brother to betray him. He'd married her against his own volition and desire, all so he might have the name of a man who'd wronged him.

They'd made love.

And now, Raina was to spend forever with a man who openly despised her.

Cupping together her shaking hands, Raina buried her face in her palms and took in a shaky breath.

How peculiar. Just weeks ago, she'd have believed love need exist for the intimate things she and Severin had shared.

Her husband, however, had shown Raina that for him, and many, the emotion of love could be all too separated from lust.

Her anguished whimper filled the quiet, and blared like a horn in an empty, cavernous, room.

She stilled.

That hadn't been her moan.

Then, it came again, an wounded animal's plaintive wail; it grew more insistent.

The cobwebs of sleep lifted in an instant, Raina did a sweep for the owner of that sorrow—and stopped.

Her gaze locked on Severin.

He rolled onto his back, taking the sheet Raina used to cover herself with, about him.

Her heart twisted as she found her husband's unblinking, cold, eyes upon her.

As if she'd needed any reminder of Severin's antipathy, the icy vacantness in those sapphire blue depths sent another chill through her.

What did one say to a man who'd made not only her heart yearn, but her body sing? What, when he despised her so?

She dampened her mouth.

"Severin," she said softly, stretching a hand toward him.

Severin's unflinching stare, however, remained locked at a point beyond Raina.

He could not even look at her…

Another spasm wracked that organ beneath her breast.

An unnatural, animal-like growl came from him.

Severin flipped his head so quick to the left and then right, and back to the left, with such a rapidity, there wasn't a way in which his neck muscles would not ache the following morning.

Raina froze and then it hit her.

He is sleeping.

Only, this was like no slumber she'd ever had, witnessed, or known man was capable of.

Her sorrow forgotten, Raina crawled over to her husband's side. Kneeling over him, she searched her eyes over his prone form.

Even in sleep, the harsh, scarred, plains of Severin's face were taut; like the demons he carried would not allow him an escape even in rest. Bestial growls, mingled with excruciating anguished moans left his slightly slack lips as one—like the warring emotions each vied for freedom from within Severin.

His wide, furrowed brow gleamed with sweat.

He remained trapped in some hell only he could see.

Severin stilled—but only for a moment. His nostrils flared giving him the look of a wounded beast and he resumed whipping his head wildly, back and forth.

Oh, God.

Her chest tightened.

"Sev—" Raina's imploring cut off on a gasp, as his long, powerful, fingers caught her wrist in a punishing hold that brought tears to her eyes.

In sleep, he proved as strong as he did in the waking hour.

"I-It is me, R-Raina," she pleaded, attempting to tug free.

His hold grew tighter.

Helpless, Raina glanced frantically about.

Where are you looking for? A voice in her head taunted. *For someone to help him? Or you?*

Suddenly with a torture moan, Cadogan released her. He collapsed into the folds of the mattress and his thrashing grew more fitful.

Raina scurried to the furthest corner of the bed.

All the while, Cadogan battled his demons—alone.

With every low, sorrowful groan he emitted, she bit her lip.

No doubt, proud man that he was, he'd want his silent suffering to remain private. No doubt, he'd want Raina—or anyone, for that matter—as far away as possible from him.

Of a certain, there'd been no one—until Raina—who'd seen him this way.

I am his wife. Regardless of everything that transpired before, how he felt, or didn't feel, none of it mattered.

She loved him. True love was not contractual, as had been the case with her parents. She wanted Severin with all his flaws and imperfections that made him complicated and guarded and perfectly *real*.

Strengthened by that, Raina eased herself against Severin's side.

Without rousing from his nightmare, he bucked and thrashed.

"Shh," she whispered." Undeterred, Raina pressed her body closer to Severin's harder, bigger form, slicked with sweat from his nightmare. "It is all right, Severin," she crooned and folded her arm over him. "I am here."

Then, it was as though the feel of her touch and the sound of her voice combined managed to penetrate whatever grim, horrible memories that gripped him.

"Shh," Raina whispered, stroking the sweat-slicked black hair away from his brow.

His movements grew less jerky until they stopped altogether, and Severin fell into a smooth, even, peaceful slumber.

As Raina lightly stroked her fingertips over the jagged scar that ran along his cheek, she studied him at rest—at a true rest—with the muscles of his face relaxed and his lips softened. She could imagine a world in which he'd never suffered or been used as a weapon of war in the name of King and country.

She smoothed her hand lower and only stopped when her palm kissed his tight pectoral muscles, which formed like a man-made armor over his chest.

Underneath her palm, however, his heart beat steadily and solidly, a reminder that underneath the granite exterior he'd constructed, dwelled a man, capable of hurting and laughing, and loving.

Severin had dwelled within that protective casing so long, he'd ceased to believe himself human.

How else *could* he have done the ruthless work for the Home

Office and continue in an equally perilous career if he believed himself fallible?

While he slept, Raina ran her eyes over the light growth upon his cheeks; his impossibly long, dark lashes, the stubborn curl that continued to fall over his brow, softening him all the more.

This time, Raina left that strand.

Despite what he'd let himself believe, in the name of self-preservation, Severin Cadogan wasn't an automaton made of steel or rock or granite. The marks he wore upon his body and the invisible scars inside that robbed him of rest, were both reminders.

It'd likely take her an entire lifetime to make Severin see he was a flesh and blood person, as the rest of them. Fortunately, she'd just pledged that lifetime to Severin this morning.

Raina burrowed herself against Severin's side.

His arm immediately came up and over to draw her nearer, closer, and this time, before she followed him into sleep, Raina smiled.

CHAPTER 23

Some days I wonder if I'll ever truly be happy.
~The Duchess of A

FROM SOME PECULIAR STATE, CADOGAN dimly registered… *nothing*. He existed within a big, black state of nothingness—empty and foreign and oddly, welcoming.

Where ordinarily, the faces of the men he'd slayed returned to pay a visit and promised to greet Cadogan when he joined them in the fiery flames of hell, this time, no one paid visit.

A flickering light pricked his vision and like a kaleidoscope constructed of day and night, the flashing glow dimmed, darkened, and then brightened once more.

What the hell?

Cadogan went absolutely motionless.

He angled his chin down and took in the lithesome beauty draped over his chest; her whiteish-blonde curls cascaded about them.

This wasn't the first time he'd awakened with a woman in his bed.

This, however, was the first time in which he'd been dead to the world, awakening when the goddamned sun was high in the sky and the pavement down below bustled with the distant laughter of passersby and the rattling of carriage wheels, and—

Fuck.

His heart pounding, Cadogan moved so quickly, Raina slipped off him. Her slender body hit the feather mattress and barely bounced.

Numbed by panic, Cadogan, on all fours, inched away from the slumbering Raina. When he reached the end of the mattress, he climbed down with such force, it interrupted his wife's heavy torpor. She muttered something incoherently, then rolled onto her back, and proceeded to snore.

His pulse hammering away, he stared dumbly at a thoroughly enervated Raina, curled on her side. With her long hair all tangled about her naked body, she had the look of a mermaid who'd been tossed about a tumultuous sea and washed ashore.

Granted, after all the ways you made love to her and her enthusiastic response, what did you expect?

Instead of that devil on his shoulder knocking Cadogan out of his horror-struck state, the dark beast of temptation only led Cadogan further down the licentious path of all the depraved things he'd done with and to his bride.

Before he'd left her sated enough to sleep, he'd relished every single second spent waking her, and making love to her again, with his mouth.

Cadogan's breathing grew ragged.

Then again, a third time, when he'd shown her how to ride him.

Then, a fourth time when he'd buried himself ballocks deep inside erasing where he ended and Raina began.

Blood surged to his already impressive morning erection and Cadogan gritted his teeth.

Last night had been pure, unadulterated lust.

But Cadogan's slipping into a dead sleep? Now, that was as unforgivable as it was unexplainable. He didn't rest, and certainly not soundly. He'd been trained specifically on how to function without sleep.

Is it really that you're concerned about? Or was it the fact he'd left himself vulnerable, and in doing so, he'd left the delicate slip of a woman who now shared his name, even more vulnerable?

His body broke out in a cold sweat.

In sleeping beside Raina, anything could have happened. If not an intruding enemy, he could have awakened in a fit as he'd done too many times in the past. It's why he didn't sleep on damned cozy mattresses, but hard floors.

Another one of those endearing, bleating snores of hers split the quiet.

Endearing.

He recoiled and backed away from the bed—her bed, which happened to occupy a space in Cadogan's residence, directly across from his rooms.

And...

His meeting.

Fuck.

What the hell time was it?

Except, even as he hurried around the room, snatching the garments he'd hastily shed hours earlier, he knew.

The floorboards no longer contained a chill from the night's cold, but rather a warmth from where the sun's rays had touched the wood.

He found his trousers and grabbed the timepiece.

Twenty-six minutes past eleven o'clock?

Bloody hell, he'd not only *slept*, but he'd also missed his damned meeting with the marquess.

Fuck. Fu—

"Severin?"

Cursing roundly, Cadogan spun about.

His heart pounded.

Raina, her glorious blonde tresses framed her face in a way that accentuated her big, languid, eyes sat upright in bed, watching him.

Her head tilted at an adorable angle, and she studied him through sleep-heavy eyes.

With that same sheet he and she had left thoroughly rumpled through their exertions, clutched close and her knees drawn up, she portrayed an entrancing display of modesty.

As if he hadn't made love to her nearly every way there was to make love to a woman.

As if he didn't want to now complete the remainder of the ones they hadn't yet.

His breaths became shallow.

From any other woman those actions would have been an artful show.

But there was no reason for games—at least, not any longer.

"Good morning, Severin," Raina shyly greeted.

Sleep had leant her sultry contralto an even deeper husk that fired his blood.

And for a moment he forgot the source of his earlier panic. For an even longer moment, he wanted to join her in that billowingly soft mattress, and pick up precisely where they'd left off before he'd fallen a—

"Morning," he mumbled.

As Cadogan stuffed his legs into his trousers, one at a time, he felt Raina's eyes upon him.

He made a grab for his shirt when her halting voice reached him.

"Are you…all right?"

He grunted. "I'm fine." *I just need to get the hell out of here.*

His nape prickled.

Cadogan stopped and refaced his wife.

Her eyes, those windows into her soul, radiated a tender concern.

"You aren't talking about now?" he stated, dumbly.

Something flickered across her face. "Well, I am speaking about now, too," she allowed, fiddling with the edges of her sheet.

Too. That single syllable, almost an afterthought, said more than all the other ones to come before.

A chill eased along his spine.

He narrowed his gaze.

"Drop the sheet," he demanded.

"S-Severin?"

He stalked over to the bedside. "I said drop the bloody sheet."

"Severin," she entreated.

"Drop the sheet, Raina," he hissed.

This time, Raina complied.

The material fell in a whispery pool about her waist, before pooling upon the mattress.

Cadogan looked Raina carefully over; forcing aside his hungering for her. He searched for any indication—

His gaze snagged on the awkward way she attempted to carefully angle her arm away from him.

His pulse thudded a sick beat.

"Let me see your arm," he demanded.

Raina hesitated.

"Now!" he thundered.

Raina quickly showed a long limb, for his inspection. He skimmed it over.

"The other one," he barked.

This time, Raina reluctantly revealed the other arm.

Then, he found it.

A buzzing filled his ears.

Stark and vivid upon her slender, impossibly delicate wrist; the dark, angry, imprints left by his fingers. She'd not sustained those bruises while they'd made love, but…after.

Cadogan sucked in a breath through his nose.

Christ.

"I'm fine, Severin," Raina hurried to reassure him.

She was reassuring *him*?

"No. *I'm* fine," he gritted out.

Her regal brow furrowed in confusion.

Cadogan took an angry step towards her. "There is nothing wrong with…" His remaining words trailed off. For there was something wrong with him. Some nights, he became a beast.

He took a slow deep breath through his nose. "You on the other hand, wife, wear my marks upon you."

Her mesmerizing blue-green irises glittered with worry. "It is—"

"Do not say 'it is fine,'" he bit out each syllable through gritted teeth.

"But *it is*!" Bold and undaunted, she'd never take orders from him. "We all have demons. You helped me to see my past does not ma—"

"It wasn't *your* past, Raina," he shouted. "It was your *parents*. Your parents. The things I've done—"

"You did them in the name of King and country, Severin," she entreated.

"And when I returned—"

"When you returned, it was all you *knew*, Severin. My God,

Severin, they gave you the title '*Killburn*' so you wear it as a reminder. It why you insist on being known as Cadogan."

He shook his head. "You're inventing things. Things that aren't true. Things I've never even thought."

"Only because you've never allowed yourself to freely think them."

Before he gathered her intentions, Raina took his hands and drew them to her chest. Her bare skin, warm under his hands; her heart, it raced—like his.

"It was all you knew," she repeated. She lifted adoring eyes to his, and he reeled under the power of emotion reflected in those depths. "But now, you know me," she said softly. "I love—"

"*No*."

"You," she finished over his rough declination. "I love you," she repeated, with a warmth that slipped through cracks he'd never even known existed in the icy walls of his being. "I love you for who you are, and for surviving things no other man could and...."

A caustic laugh burst from inside him. "My scar tells another story."

"Your scar, I do not even see, Severin. I see a man who is brave. A man who'll sit for

"It was my job," he gritted out.

"Your job was to sit for Millie's endless portrait session?" she said, gently. "You stayed, because you enjoyed her company."

Lies. "I didn't."

He may as well have saved his breath.

"And because you are not a man who believes himself above speaking with a child."

Cadogan swiped a hand through his hair; and darted his gaze about. Then, it hit him. "I know what you're doing," he breathed. "This is the next part of your and Argyll's plan. You'll pretend to love me and convince me I want a family with you, so I give up my work and take on ownership at his club.

"Oh, Severin," she whispered. "You've gone through so much of your life believing everyone is possessed of an ulterior motive, second-guessing, and triple-guessing people, that you can't even see the truth before you."

"You lied to me," he rasped. "*Deceived* me."

"No, I didn't," she said, with the kind of calm not even the greatest agent could fake. "You want to *believe* I betrayed you because you think it will be easier. But you know the truth, Severin, and somewhere inside, you do, too. You're scared of us and—"

"I'm afraid of *nothing*," he snarled.

"*This* you fear," she insisted like the bold queen she was.

"And there is no us!" Cadogan hissed, his panic redoubling.

This was too much. *Get control of yourself, man.*

"I'm late for an appointment," he said, flatly. He resumed gathering up his things. "This will be the last time we sleep together."

Cadogan issued that reminder for himself as much as her.

Her features twisted into a paroxysm of such grief it nearly brought Cadogan to his knees.

Lies.

"Please don't push me away, Severin," she beseeched.

"Push you away?" Why would he ever do that? Unless she mattered to him. Which she couldn't. She didn't.

Raina gave a shaky nod.

"*Push you away?*" he jeered. "Have I ever been anything but clear my only interest in you is of a carnal nature?"

She winced but remained otherwise proudly stoic. "I don't believe you."

It wasn't enough. They'd shared entirely too many intimacies. He needed to disabuse his whimsical wife of any fanciful dreams she had about the life they'd have together and sever whatever this power she held over him.

"You don't want to believe everything you said to be true because it makes you feel better." He looked down the length of his nose. "If I *needed* to push you away, it would mean I cared about you in some way beyond the physical." He locked eyes with hers. "And I don't, Raina."

Raina jerked like he'd dealt her a death blow, and in this instant, he'd have been all too happy to have someone deliver *him* a fatal strike.

The visible recoil of her pain caused all his muscles to clench and tighten and ache inside him.

Not bringing himself to look at her, *unable* to look at her, Cadogan finished dressing, turned on his heel and left.

CHAPTER 24

I pray my children are nothing like their parents.
I pray they know real love.
~The Duchess of A

WHEN FACED WITH CURLING INTO a ball and weeping until she broke or finding a well-placed outlet for her anger and resentment, Raina opted for the latter.

If she allowed herself to relive all the hard, cruel, statements Severin had flung earlier, she'd break into a thousand million pieces.

Instead, while her maid attended Raina's hair, Raina stared at her ravaged reflection and seethed.

How dare he? How *dare* her brother destroy Severin's life and saddle him with that which he'd never wanted—Raina as his wife.

Along the way, Gregory had become so obsessed with his gaming empire, Raina and Millie had become an afterthought. Even then, however, Raina never doubted his love or his desire to protect her.

Until he'd trapped her and Severin and revealed the treacherous lengths, he'd go to achieve his end, by whatever means possible.

Gregory's work, the life he lived—a depraved one like their late parents—had changed him—and in no way for the better.

She pulled in a breath.

Inversely, Raina wanted a man who loved and desired her and *only* her—but Severin would never be that man.

But, how, I wish he was.

Raina bit the inside of her lower lip to keep it from trembling.

The irony was not lost on her. In the ultimate fraternal ultimate betrayal, Gregory had both joined her with the only man she'd ever love, but also a man who'd hate her forever.

Except, silently raging over Gregory's duplicity, reminded her all over again, of Severin's disdain for *her*.

She squeezed her eyes shut, and willed thoughts of her recent exchange with Severin away—to no avail.

"*…Have I ever been anything but clear my only interest in you is of a carnal nature?*"

However, that hadn't been entirely true. He'd also seen her as a business assignment.

Tears formed in her throat. Whether he'd spoken about his lust for her or obligation to watch *over* her, both realities of how he felt—or rather, didn't feel—about Raina, nearly crippled her with grief.

"There you are, my lady," Lucy announced.

Yet another irony, she'd spent so many years worrying she possessed her mother's wicked streak. Only to find she was just like the late duchess, after all, in the worst possible way. Raina loved a man who'd never love her.

That had been the greatest tragedy surrounding her mother's life. Not the things she'd *done*, but what she'd not *had* in her marriage to the duke.

Raina let the sob building in her chest, free, as an ugly, pain-filled laugh.

"My lady?" Lucy spoke, haltingly. "I've finished…w-with your hair."

Her hair.

Raina blinked at her reflection. "Yes, thank you, Lucy." She pushed back her vanity chair and stood, when a firm knock landed on her door.

The maid rushed over and drew the solid oak panel open enough to duck her head out.

"Her Ladyship's carriage is waiting," the gentleman said to Lucy.

Ah, yes. The servant she'd been greeted by on her wedding day: Mauley. Not a servant, but a guard.

Whatever the charmer said next, drew a giggle from a smitten Lucy.

A sour taste filled Raina's mouth. How glib of tongue these agents were. They knew just what to say to attain whatever information it was they sought.

As Raina made her way to the quietly conversing pair, she detected the minion's muted words.

"Where should I direct the countess's driver, fair Lucy?"

Raina coolly interrupted before the young girl could speak. "The countess is more than capable of advising my driver of my destination, Mr. Mauley."

Lucy jumped, dropped a curtsy, and stepped aside so Raina could exit.

"Fair Lucy," she said drolly, as she fell into step; Mauley kept pace beside her. "I must confess, you might speak to your superior, Mr. Cadogan, about more *inspiring* endearments. I'd suggest you use a bit more tact if you'd like to ascertain my movements."

Mauley's mouth tightened—only for a moment. "Pardon me, my lady. I did not mean to upset you."

"Mr. Mauley?" Raina stopped so abruptly, Cadogan's minion had to double back. "How long have you known my husband?"

He kept tightlipped.

"Oh, come now," she scoffed. "He *is* my husband," No matter how much Severin despised the fact. "I'm aware of his history."

Surprise lighted the handsome guard's eyes.

"My brother, the duke, shared some," she reluctantly confessed. "Mr. Cadogan shared more."

Mauley hesitated. "I was appointed Mr. Cadogan's secretary with the Home Office the moment I left university. I've been with him since. Eleven years come June."

She detected something in his tone but could not make it out. "You are loyal to my husband."

A muscle spasmed at the corner of his right eye.

"I am not questioning your loyalty," she said matter-of-factly. "I'm pointing out that given your relationship, given the fact you witnessed our wedding, you're likely also aware of the circumstances surrounding our marriage. As such, it is no secret to you, that my husband did not want this u-union." Her voice broke and tears pricked behind her eyes.

She increased her strides.

Mr. Mauley cleared his throat. "Be that may, Mr. Cadogan pro—"

"Protects what is his?" she volunteered.

"Yes, my lady."

They reached the foyer, where the second butler, Falston, stood in wait.

She flashed Mauley a smile. "Well, that is splendid, but I belong to no man."

Color skimmed along the skin just above the line of Mauley's beard.

To Mr. Falston's credit, he didn't seek his superior's permission and went ahead opening the front door.

With a word of thanks to the tow-headed servant, she headed outside.

"His Lordship will be displeased," Mr. Mauley called after her.

"Ah, but His Lordship isn't here," Raina rejoined, without glancing back. "As such, he isn't around to *be* displeased."

Raina reached the gleaming black carriage. The surly driver looked as thrilled by Raina's apparent show of defiance as Mauley.

When he made no attempt to help her inside, Raina firmed her jaw.

They could all go to hell. "Men, you'd rather order women about and tie us on leading strings like children based on nothing more than an assumption that your lord and master will be displeased."

"Oh, I assure you," Mauley drawled, "make no doubt about it, Cadogan *will* be displeased."

"You spend a good deal of time worrying about displeasing Mr. Cadogan," she mused.

"You'd be wise to do so, as well."

"Ah," Raina patted his arm, "I don't scare easily. And fortunately, as I'm not a small child, I'm entirely capable of opening my own door."

With that, she let herself inside and pulled the door shut behind her.

Once seated, she drew the black velvet curtain back.

Mauley looked to the driver and when he didn't find any help there, he glanced back at Falston.

The second butler returned inside and shut the black-painted doors.

Raina laughed.

Severin's right-hand man, swung his focus back to where Raina sat, and glared.

She waved; then thumped her fist on the roof. "If you'll please, Mr. Barlowe. *To Forbidden Pleasures.*"

The two men exchanged a few words, and then her driver nodded, and climbed atop his box.

The moment the expansive conveyance dipped, she glanced over to find Mauley climbing inside.

"I'm going with you, my lady."

"You needn't—"

"It's not a request. Cadogan will have my head if I do not follow you."

"Then you can either get in the carriage, Mauley, or get the hell out of my way," she said tersely, tired to her soul of being manipulated and treated like a pawn on a chessboard.

It wasn't long before Raina and Mr. Mauley arrived at *Forbidden Pleasures*. The carriage just completed a full stop, when Raina tossed the door open, and jumped down.

She faltered, her left ankle shifting slightly from that uneven leap.

Squaring her jaw, Raina righted herself.

Ignoring Mauley's shouts behind her, Raina took off running for the front doors of Gregory's beloved establishment.

She ground her teeth.

It was all Gregory was capable of loving. Not she. Not Millie. No one.

"My lady," Mauley shouted, more insistently.

The guards stationed outside didn't bother to mask their surprise at finding the duke's sister storming the club. Also in their favor, they drew the doors as wide and welcoming as if she were herself a patron.

The moment she stepped inside, they shut the door, locking Mauley out.

The guard's muffled shouts penetrated the heavy panels.

Raina ignored them.

Seething, she did a sweep of the nearly empty gaming floors.

Stationed on a small dais, Rex DuMond caught sight of Raina first.

The handful of gentlemen playing cards throughout seemed to notice her the same time as the dealers and serving women did.

DuMond said something to the other partner, head of security, Lachlan Latimer, who stole a quick glance at Raina.

"My brother," she called. "The duke. I want a meeting. *Now.*"

She needn't have bothered finishing her demand. The towering guard, and third partner, Latimer, had already let himself out through a paneled door behind the dais.

While she waited, gentlemen continued to stare.

Let them.

Severin had taught her that. None of them mattered. The one man who did, however, hated her for perceived crimes—because of her brother.

"Gregory," she thundered. By God, she'd find him herself.

She headed for those not-so-secret doors. As she did, DuMond shouted orders to his staff.

Within just a handful of moments, the marques had dispensed of all the revelers and the staff.

"My brother will be displeased with your sending the patrons away," she noted when she'd reached him.

"Yes," DuMond acknowledged gently. "But that's not more important than you. I know Argyll agrees."

Her eyes blurred. "You think, do you?" If her brother felt the same way his friend did, then she and Severin would not be in this quagmire.

There came the thundering of footfalls.

Her barefoot brother, dressed in nothing more than his trousers and untucked lawn shirt, crashed through the doors. Just like their father, he was.

His frantic gaze immediately found her. "Raina!"

"My apologies." Curling her lip, she gave him a scathing once over. "By the look of it, I've taken you away from your busy afternoon of whoring."

Flummoxed, Gregory staggered.

From the corner of her eye, she caught DuMond and Latimer exchange a look. Together, they took their leave.

When his partners had gone, Gregory found his voice. "Raina, you shouldn't—"

"What?" She cut him off. "Say 'you were off whoring?' Be inside your…" She ran a caustic eye over his beloved institution. "*Gauche* club. Nothing at all like Craven's."

She returned her focus to Gregory and found his frown had deepened.

"You went to Craven's?" he asked, his voice sharp.

In mock surprise, Raina pressed a hand to her breast. "Never tell me you weren't aware of my visit?"

"I wasn't," he snapped.

"Tsk. Tsk. And here, I'd believed you'd neatly planned all of this. How heartening to know the minute Severin was in our household, you ceased to worry about where I went or what I did."

He flinched.

"Hmm. If I didn't know better, big brother, I'd believe you have a conscience buried somewhere deep inside your ruthless being."

Gregory didn't let her incite him.

His hard lips went white at the corners. "Going forward, Raina, you are not to go anywhere near Cra—"

She tossed her head back and roared with hilarity.

"My God," she rasped, between great, big, heaving fits of laughter. "One could almost be convinced you care about me, Your Grace."

"I *do* care." There crept a faint thread of desperation into Gregory's usually imperturbable voice.

She clasped her hands before her and made her gaze adoring. "You are such a devoted, loving, considerate, big brother."

Raina dropped the melodramatic act. "Only you would be

able to speak that so convincingly, Your Grace," she said coolly. "Either way, you needn't worry. I'm no longer your problem. Remember? You whored me out so you could—"

Gregory went ashen-faced, and she followed his frantic gaze over to the door his partners and friends exited through moments ago.

Raina lowered her voice. "You whored me out, trapped Severin in a marriage he did not want."

Gregory dragged a hand through his loose, angel-like golden curls. "I didn't."

More like the Devil.

"You *didn't* use me that way, Your Grace?"

"Raina," he beseeched. "I didn't want…What I thought…"

She clicked her tongue. "I never thought I'd see the day; the glib-tongued, Duke of Argyll finds himself unable to speak."

Her brother rubbed a palm over his haggard face.

Then, it dawned.

"Oh, my God." A quiet laugh, built this time. "He wasn't supposed to just fuck me, he was supposed to *fall in love* with me."

His features twisted. "*Raina!*"

She smoothed her features. "Ah, how could I forget? A lady mustn't curse, but when it comes to gentlemen, whoring about, and selling a sister, it is very much aboveboard."

Fire blazed to life in Gregory's eyes. "Do *not* speak so." He strode angrily the rest of the way towards her. "You are *no* whore."

"No, I'm not." Raina knew that now.

She considered her brother for a long moment. "Do you know, I spent my entire life worrying I was wicked and immoral, a whore like mother, father, *you?*"

He flinched.

"I realize now, our mother was a good woman," Raina said, more to herself. "She deeply loved a man who didn't love her. At least, not the way she wanted or deserved."

She gave him a pitying look. "I feel badly for you, Gregory. For you, in every way, are cut of his cloth. My only prayer is whichever unfortunate woman you wed, doesn't have her heart broken as our father did to our mother."

He stayed uncharacteristically silent through her address.

Raina gave her head a clearing shake. "Either way, that's not why I've come here. I want something from you."

"Anything," he instantly vowed.

"I want the information you promised to my husband."

"Anything except that."

Raina drew back. "Do not tell me you lied," she whispered.

His eyes darkened. "You are my sister, Raina. I love you, but do not call a gentleman a liar."

If she could manage a laugh, this would have been the moment.

"Yes, well when I see a gentleman, Your Grace, I will take care."

A flush climbed his neck and splotched the rugged line of his cheekbones.

Frustrated at her inability to get another rise out of him, she sighed.

"Forgive me, Gregory," she said softly.

He inclined his head like a benevolent lord.

"I did not expect a man with so little honor to draw a moral line at flat-out lying. Are you *more* comfortable with lies of omission, hmm?"

"Bloody hell, Raina," he said, exasperatedly.

The fight within her began to fade. She couldn't stand to look at this man she'd called friend. He'd been her hero for so long; the adoring older brother who'd wiped her tears and welcomed her in his life.

Her throat moved spasmodically.

"In addition to your trustworthiness," she said softly, without any of her earlier acrimony, "given the recent events, even your claims of loving me, are also highly doubtable."

His body jolted. "Raina," he implored, his voice ragged.

Raina made herself take several breaths. "As I said, it's done. *Our* relationship," she motioned between them. "is over, but I *can* try and salvage a future with my husband. If you give me what Severin so desperately seeks."

A flush climbed his neck and splotched the rugged line of his cheekbones. "I can't," he finally said, his voice agonized.

Her frustration mounted all over again. "You can't? Or you *won't.*"

Gregory touched a hand to her shoulder. "*Ray.*"

Raina shrugged off his touch. "Do *not* touch me and do *not* call me by that name."

In a rare display of desperation, Gregory scrubbed both hands over his face. He let his arms fall uselessly at his side.

"Raina," he said, and when he spoke, this time he was back in full control of his emotions. "The earl intends to hunt down the ones who betrayed him. His quest would put you in danger."

She snorted. "It's a little bit late to be worrying about my safety, isn't it?"

Then, what he'd said, registered.

"You *never* intended to fulfill your end of the arrangement," she breathed.

Gregory's hesitation served as his confirmation.

"You bastard," Raina hissed.

Curling her hand into a fist, she brought her arm back and punched him with enough force to snap his head back.

Excruciating pain radiated from her fingertips to the length of her palm. She cried out. Sucking in sharp, jagged, breaths, Raina drew her injured appendage close.

Even with the crimson mark she'd left upon his cheek, her brother gave no indication of any physical hurt.

"DuMond," he thundered.

The marquess and Mr. Latimer came racing in so quickly, there could never be a doubt they'd been just on the other side of that doorway, waiting for their partner and friend.

Friend. Pfft.

Gregory didn't know a thing about truly loving or caring for anyone other than himself.

"Summon the surgeon," he barked, in full ducal command.

Lachlan was the first to move.

"Do not, Mr. Latimer." She stayed the enigmatic head guard. Not because she didn't need a doctor, per se. "I'm not staying. This will be the last you see of me."

Giving Gregory her shoulder completely, Raina continued to hold her smarting hand and looked to the two gentlemen.

"Rex," she said softly. "Thank you for everything." She would miss Rex. He'd always been hard, dark, and cynical, but with her he'd been patient and kindly towards.

He winked. "No need to thank me, Mopsy."

Mopsy. It'd been years.

His eyes bore the sadness of one who knew this was goodbye.

Raina turned next to Latimer. "You came into my life, far later, and I am grateful you were in it, at all."

"Aye, you're still a sister to us," the towering guard promised, his meaning clear.

She could always rely upon he and DuMond.

Not so much as looking Gregory's way, Raina straightened her shoulders and headed for the door.

"Raina!" her brother called out, stopping her when she'd neared the front of his precious club.

"You say I trapped Cadogan in a marriage *he* did not want. Perhaps I can take that to mean, it was a marriage *you* wanted, and you have feelings for the earl."

Feelings for Severin? She loved him, madly, deeply, and beyond all reason.

It was the *only* marriage she'd wanted.

Raina squeezed her eyes shut to keep the tears falling, and when she had them in check, she faced Gregory. "Unfortunately, what *didn't* occur to you was in using me to entrap Severin, you've ensured he will *never* love me."

Pain ravaged his features. "Raina, I've *seen* the way Cadogan watches y—"

"Stop!" she cried. Her voice pinged around the vast, high-ceilinged gaming hell floors. Raina stretched an unsteady hand. "*Just stop*. You couldn't possibly see anything, Gregory, because you were never around."

Latimer headed for the opposite doorway, to take his leave.

Gregory swung a frantic gaze between the heard guard who'd been a best friend to him, and Raina.

Ah, a choice: between friend and business partner, or sister who no longer served a purpose.

The moment he took a step toward Latimer's retreating figure, Raina started for the exit.

"*Raina!*"

She didn't stop this time, quickening her pace, lengthening her strides.

"Hold that door, Knight," Gregory barked to the guard when she reached the front entrance.

An unfamiliar, younger, dark-haired, man positioned himself between Raina and her exit.

"*Argyll*," DuMond censured.

Behind her, a quarrel broke out between the men.

Raina tilted her chin. "Mr. Knight, are you aware of who my husband is?"

His large Adam's apple bobbed.

He nodded jerkily. "Aye, m-my lady."

Heady at witnessing the fear her husband's name evoked, Raina became more emboldened.

"I can promise, if you keep me here against my will, Mr. Cadogan will return, and you'll regret ever having followed a single one of His Grace's—"

She didn't even need to finish.

The darkly clad, uniformed servant yanked one of the panels wide, allowing the sunlight to come streaming through.

Squinting, Raina blinked several times. When her eyes adjusted to the change in setting, she found Mauley pacing alongside Severin's carriage.

Her husband's secretary stopped in his tracks.

She hurried to meet him.

"Please, Raina," Gregory entreated from the doorway.

The moment Raina drew close, Mauley withdrew a firearm from under his jacket.

Her heart lurched.

A barefoot, half-naked, Gregory, staggered to a stop. Even though he raised his palms, the flint in his eyes oozed with violence.

"Mauley," she said sharply. "Put your weapon down."

All around them, passersby took in the titillating display unfolding.

"Now," she snapped when the guard didn't move fast enough.

With a palpable reluctance, Severin's man returned his gun to its holster.

Gregory immediately rushed over. When he reached Raina, he opened his mouth to speak, and then stopped.

"I'm speaking with my sister, *Mauley*." Ducal authority rang in her brother's. "Get the hell out."

Mauley remained steadfast. "*The countess* is also my employer's wife and that supersedes any authority you *think* you may have over Her Ladyship."

Snarling, Gregory charged.

Bloody hell. Raina placed herself between them, preventing the battle each craved.

"That will be all, Mauley," she said swiftly before the two obstinate men came to blows. "I would like a moment with His Grace."

When he'd retreated, giving Raina and Gregory some distance, she looked to her brother.

"I'm sorry, Gregory." As angry as she would forever be with him, she loved him still. "I would never allow him or any of Severin's men—"

"Do not apologize," he interrupted, gruffly. "Severin's job is to protect you, and his man did just that today."

Silence fell; the calls of vendors hawking goods and the steady clip-clop of horses highlighted the quiet between them.

"I never wanted to hurt you," he said simply. "I decided Cadogan would be a good protector and husband to you long before I even considered how that union could and would benefit me."

Gregory skimmed regret-filled eyes over her face. "I don't expect your forgiveness, but I would have you understand, the feud between Craven and I—" His mouth tightened. "You weren't safe. Now you are." Pain ravaged his features. "Even if that means I'm never permitted to see you."

Her eyes burned. She'd always love her brother, but he'd betrayed Raina's husband, and there was no going back from that.

He took her hands in his and lightly squeezed. "I promise, I will not allow Killburn to keep you and Millie apart."

"He wouldn't." Just as Gregory would be no match for Severin. Several tears fell.

Releasing her, he wiped those tears away with the pads of his thumbs.

"Hmph." Gregory wore a bemused expression. "Seems to me, you have hope for Cadogan, after all."

With that reminder of his perfidiousness, the tender moment was cut quick.

"Goodbye, Gregory," she said hoarsely.

He unexpectedly hauled her into his arms and held her just as he'd done the day, he shared the news of their parents' deaths.

Fighting back a sob, she hugged him back.

"I didn't want to give this over for a host of reasons," he said, even against her temple, his voice scarcely audible. "One being a desire for your husband to put his fraught career behind him, for your sake—"

"And yours," she drolly reminded.

"Fair enough." His chest shook with quiet laughter. "And mine."

His mirth faded. "The other because I believed there couldn't be anything good to come from him knowing what's in here."

He pressed something into Raina's palm, and deftly guided her fingers closed around a scrap of paper. "I realize now, that isn't my place to decide."

Raina attempted to draw back and see what he'd shared

"Not here," he whispered. "When you're alone."

Then, dropping a kiss against her temple, he set her from his arms.

Only after she'd asked Mauley to ride with the driver and sat alone on the carriage bench, did she do as her brother instructed.

With the steady sway of the carriage, she carefully unfolded the tiny scrap and froze.

Her breath lodged painfully in her chest, and she stared at the information written there, willing it to change.

But it didn't.

Raina's eyes slid shut.

No.

CHAPTER 25

As Cadogan urged his mount along Wimpole Street, he glared at the path ahead.

While he'd been off, taking the first meeting of his latest assignment, Raina, now Raina Cadogan, *his wife*, had fled to see her brother.

He heard nothing beyond the furious beat of his pulse in his ears. The cacophony of everyday street sounds came as if Cadogan were submerged ten meters underwater.

What was more, she'd chosen to meet Argyll at *Forbidden Pleasures*.

Coming out of his stirrups, he urged the stallion faster.

Forbidden Fucking Pleasures—in the *seediest* part of London, where any gruesome fate could have met her.

Cadogan breathed in and out through flared nostrils.

She'd revolted against the men he'd assigned her.

The moment the mount drew to a halt in the cobblestone courtyard, Cadogan jumped down and tossed the reins to the waiting groom.

"My wife, Ainsworth," Cadogan demanded; already heading for the main house. "Lady Killburn?"

"Returned she did, Mr. Cadogan," he called after him. "Can't say where she is now. Mauley brought her…"

With the distance Cadogan quickly built between them, the rest of Ainsworth's explanation grew faint and then turned to nothing.

The groom didn't know Raina's location at this precise moment and neither did Cadogan; because this morning, he'd run off like a scared, fucking, child and gone to attend *important* matters.

She is here, he reminded himself.

Safe.

The closer he got to his residence, however, Cadogan's pulse continued to race.

My God, the infuriating, brash, minx. What had she been *thinking*?

"She wasn't," he muttered under his breath.

"...Please, don't push me away, Severin..."

His chest tightened. Didn't she know, if any harm befell her, he'd be destroyed?

At the side entrance of his house, Cadogan staggered to a stop.

He put his palms upon the green-painted door panels, to keep himself from pitching face-first, and stared blankly at his badly shaking hands. These same hands that'd taken lives and saved them, that were now useless to him.

When...? How...?

But he knew.

Now, he did.

His sage, spirited, wife though, knew all along.

"...You want to believe I betrayed you because you think it will be easier. But you know the truth, Severin. You're scared of us...you fear this..."

From the first moment she'd outwitted Cadogan, he'd lost himself completely to Raina, Proud Princess, now Queen of his once useless heart. That organ whose only purpose before her, had been to sustain his bleak life, now beat entirely, *for* her.

He waited for the rush of terror that didn't come. The only dread he'd known this day had been when Chase forced his way into Cadogan's meeting with the marquess to say Raina had rushed off to *Forbidden Pleasures*.

Cadogan hadn't cared about her defying his orders—ones she'd never followed, anyway. Or been angered that she met with Argyll.

He'd worried only about her and her safety.

He loved her.

All the rest: his goddamned business, his irate client, his feud with her brother, could go straight to hell.

Steady for the first time in his miserable, lonely, life, Cadogan straightened.

Ripping the side door open, he raced inside.

The guard stationed there immediately trained a weapon on him, until he realized who'd stormed the house. "Mr. C-Cadogan. My apologies."

"Worry not, my good man. As long as you lower your pistol."

The younger man, Ross, eyed Cadogan like he'd lost his mind, and maybe he had.

If so, he never wished to be sane again.

He nudged his chin pointedly.

Ross followed Cadogan's gaze downward; his cheeks, flushing, Ross promptly dropped his weapon.

"Where is my wife?"

"In your rooms, Mr. Cadogan."

He took off running.

"...Have I ever been anything but clear my only interest in you is of a carnal nature?"

A piteous moan spilled from his lips. God, what a bloody bastard he'd been.

Moreso, it hadn't been this day only.

"...I am not your friend. We never will be. I'm not here as some confidante you can talk to about your hopes and dreams and wishes or gossip..."

Severin tried—and failed—to swallow.

In his head, he went over every last minute he'd spent with Raina.

"...You're nothing but an assignment, Princess..."

He flinched.

"...Next time you have an urge, I'll be more than happy to take that on as another job. Just so you don't have to go dashing about London to get your itch scratched..."

What exactly should she, or could she, have known with everything that'd come to pass between them?

He hated himself.

He abhorred the things he'd done.

He loathed what he'd become.

But most, he *despised* himself for having hurt a woman he'd give his soul for. She'd been the only person who'd ever loved him, who *hadn't* feared him, who didn't expect him—and want him—to be a monster.

She saw him as a *man*, to be teased, and loved, and one deserving of happiness.

Of an absolute certainty, *he* didn't deserve *her*.

A bloody lifetime later, when he reached the hall that led to his rooms, the guard stationed there briefed him.

"Her Ladyship is in your rooms."

"Is she—?"

"Walked in on her own two feet."

Oh, God, thank you.

He finally released a breath.

"Mr. Mauley is—"

Cadogan blew ahead. "I don't give two shites what Mauley is doing at this moment."

Breathing hard, he came to a stop outside his rooms. He couldn't allow her to see him like this, all half-mad and blustering. When he admitted what an unmitigated ass he'd been and told her how she owned every part of him, and how much he loved her, he'd be calm.

Composed once more, he slipped into the room.

His calm went up in a blazing flame of smoke.

A softly smiling Raina sat perched upon the leather sofa in the offices he'd had constructed in—

Cadogan's nostrils flared.

Mauley on a knee beside Raina, cradled one of her delicate hands in his larger ones. They remained oblivious to his presence.

Unlike this morning when Cadogan left his new bride in tears, for Mauley she wore a smile.

There came a burning sensation in Cadogan's chest and gut neither of which had anything to do with his mad gallop through Town and flat-out sprint to reach Raina.

He'd lied to the guard stationed in the hall. Cadogan *did* give a shite.

Raina glanced up over the top of Mauley's head and noticed

Cadogan's presence first. The cheer-filled smile on her pillowy-soft lips, wilted. "S-Severin."

She'd gift her smile to another man. *No, you allowed her to gift her smile to another man.*

Pain built in his jaw from how tight he clenched his teeth.

Mauley, always on alert, with fucking hearing and scent to rival a bloody hound, turned belatedly, because he'd been transfixed by the sight of Cadogan's wife.

Cadogan pinned a death stare on his secretary. "Get your fucking hands off my wife, Mauley, before I cut them from your person."

Mauley went white as a cadaver. He released Raina quickly and stumbled to his feet.

"F-Forgive me. I was tending—"

"*No one* puts their hands upon my wife, Mauley," he warned on a fierce, sibilant whisper. "Not unless he wants to be fed his fingers for lunch. Is that understood?"

"Ye—"

"Get the hell out," Cadogan issued the virulent directive, lest he do something mad like tear his secretary apart.

The other man bowed deep at the waist and hied it past Cadogan.

As soon as his secretary had both feet outside the room, Cadogan shoved the heel of his boot hard into the wood panel.

The doorframe shook from the force of that drive.

Staring at him with stricken eyes, Raina cradled one of her soft palms, in the other.

When he'd spied Mauley touching her and Raina's sacred lips tipped up for another man, Cadogan had wanted but one thing: to throw his young, virile, secretary out so Cadogan could be alone with his wife.

Alone in the quiet, they openly stared at one another.

He opened his mouth to speak but nothing came out.

His brave, bold, wife always had words enough for the both of them.

"You are upset," she said softly.

He grunted. "I am not happy."

"Yes, but in fairness, you, yourself said that you neither laugh nor smile. Therefore, couldn't we agree there's no difference between this day and others?"

The panic and rage that'd sent him into a tear finally eased now that he had his own eyes on his wife.

He rested his back against the door and folded his arms at his chest. "I'm not upset, though."

Raina dampened her lips.

"I'm furious."

She lowered her gaze to her lap.

"With myself, Raina," he said somberly. "*With myself.*"

Raina whipped her head up quickly; surprise filled her big, blue, expressive eyes.

He eased next to her on the sofa. "I—"

Cadogan's carefully planned profession died on his lips. Rage blackened his vision.

Raina followed his stare to her bruised and swollen hand. She moved her other palm to conceal her injury, but it was too late. The image of those marks would be forever seared in his brain.

That's why Mauley had been tending her. Just as Mauley had accompanied her to Argyll's. Two instances too many of when Cadogan hadn't been there for his wife, and another man had.

Never again.

"Argyll put his hands on you," he said emotionlessly. "I'll kill him."

"No," Raina explained on a rush. "I put *my* hands on *him.*"

Cadogan stared perplexed at his beautiful bride.

Lifting the bruised appendage Raina formed a light fist and made a slow show of demonstrating what she'd done to the duke. "Like that."

An all-pervading wave of pride unfurled in him.

Cadogan fell into a place he'd been before—that of *surgeon*. The difference being, he'd only before tended his own wounds. Now, he cared for Raina, his wife.

While he carefully probed searched for indication of any breaks, he felt Raina's gaze on him.

"Mr. Mauley indicated it is not broken," she murmured.

He stole a peak at his wife. "*Mr. Cadogan* is going to verify for himself."

A smile twitched at her lips.

God, he could watch her do nothing but smile all day.

Cadogan finished his examination. "*Your husband* has confirmed there are no breaks."

Fetching a cloth from the porcelain bowl, *Mauley* had called up, Cadogan rang the cold fabric out. He continued to wrap and unwrap the cool dressings until the frigid water went lukewarm.

Cadogan tossed the last cloth into the bowl.

They sat next to each other with the quiet.

"So, you hit Argyll?" he finally said.

She nodded. "In his cheek."

Oh, God. She'd gone to confront her brother.

Raina cleared her throat. "I went to call him out for the lies he told, and the games he played with you and with me. I know you don't believe me, but—"

Cupping her cheek, Cadogan angled Raina's face toward his and touched his lips to hers in a gentle meeting.

He drew back.

"I believe you, Raina."

Desire and confusion left a cloud in her eyes. "You believe me?" she repeated back slowly, like she was afraid to believe the words he'd spoken.

"I believe you." A swell of emotion so great filled him, he struggled to get out all the things he needed to say. "You were right when you said, I knew the truth. It was easier for me to believe the lie because I was afraid. I have never felt anything like this, nor cared for…"

No.

He held her tear-filled gaze. "I have never loved before you, Raina."

"You *love me?*" she whispered.

"I love you beyond belief," he said hoarsely. "With all I am, and everything I have, and everything I hope to be—"

Raina touched her lips to his and he kissed her in return, sweetly, softly.

"I haven't been tender enough with you when we've made love," he said between each time their mouths met. "I'll fix that now."

"But I like it when you are rough," she breathlessly reminded.

His body ached. "God, you are a gift in every way." He drank of her mouth. "Why don't we agree, I'll make love to you in every way?"

Raina eased away. "You said you don't make love, that you—"

"Yes, I did say that," he cut in, not wanting to hear her use that crude word he'd taught her to describe what they'd done. "And I didn't. *But,*" Cadogan cupped her tenderly by the nape, "I've only ever made love to you, because you're the *only* woman I've ever, or will ever, have loved."

Tears shimmered in her eyes.

"Mm. Mm." He gently scolded. "No tears, love. Only happiness, now."

"Only happiness," she agreed.

"Though, I should warn you, no one else will bring you to smile, because I plan to see your days filled with such happiness, this expression you wear now, never leaves your face."

Half-laughing, half-sobbing, Raina twined her hands about Cadogan's nape and touched her brow to his.

Too quick, the light in her eyes went out. Worry creased her brow.

"A frown?" He teased the tip of his index finger against the corner of her mouth. "I'm failing miserably. I muse try harder. Very well, I accept your challenge and will find much pleasure in doing so."

"Sev—"

Cadogan kissed the rest of his name from her lips, as he did, he palmed one of the perfect swells of her breast. Through her gown, he teased the pebbled tip.

Raina panted softly. She wanted him. And he, he'd never not burn for her.

Never breaking contact with her mouth, he drew her skirts up, exposing her limbs, inch by inch.

She brought her hands up between them, stopping him. "There is something I must speak with you about, Cadogan," she said, winded.

"Are you not enjoying my touch, love?" he purred, nuzzling at her neck.

A whispery sigh filtered from her lips. "No. I am. Very much s-s-so." Raina's voice climbed a pitch as he palmed her between her legs. "B-but you'd mentioned your brother—"

There it was again. The killer of all great cockstands—mention of his brother. Cadogan removed his hand from that sweetest place.

"I don't want him here between us," he breathed, making to take her mouth once more.

Raina edged away. "He must be."

With an air of finality, Raina stood.

Cadogan stared at her.

The emotion and desire that'd gripped him faded at the grim set to Raina's features.

Suddenly registering the gravitas of the moment, he joined her, on his feet. "What is it, Raina?"

"I spoke to my brother."

"Yes, I'm aware." He took a moment. "And did...something happen?" Her answer would determine how the other man died.

"He didn't hurt me, Severin."

"I didn't say he did."

"I know what you're thinking."

Yes, she did. He'd claimed to know her thoughts, when in truth, this slip of a goddess knew him even better than he knew himself.

"I went to Gregory and demanded he give me the information he'd promised you."

Her words penetrated.

"The name," she said, when he didn't respond. "Of the one who betrayed you."

His blood ran cold. "Raina," he said quietly. "I need you to listen to me carefully. I do not want you involved."

"I already am, Severin." Raina looked him square in the eyes. "I am your wife. Until dea—"

"Forever," he said tightly. "Leave it as: 'until forever'." He'd not be able to live in a world without her in it.

"Forever, then," she murmured her ascent. "Gregory *did* have the information you wished for, but never intended to share it, because he believed knowing would do you no good."

Cadogan followed along closely.

"My brother indicated he always intended for us to marry."

Before, that'd grated. Now, he owed the other man a vow of fealty for the gift he'd entrusted to Cadogan.

"But he agreed, it wasn't his place to withhold from you the name of your betrayer. I expect he, at last, realized the harm he'd put you—and indirectly, me—in by not sharing."

She knew the identity of his betrayer.

Where only eager bloodlust would have filled him before, a steady dread lived in its place.

"Raina," he urged, his heart thundering. "Who—?"

"I am so sorry, Severin," she whispered, her voice breaking.

Raina held out a piece of folded paper from her pocket.

With a calm he didn't feel, Cadogan took the tiny scrap and opened it.

Blood rushed to his ears.

"I love you so much, Severin. *I* am your family. Me, and Millie, and the children you and I will one day have, and *Gregory*, even, if you so wish."

"Carnell," he said dumbly. His own voice came like it traveled down a long corridor and reached his ears on a delay.

"This is why you didn't wish to speak to your brother," she wept softly. "He is a monster."

No, he wasn't. Something didn't fit in his brain. He shook his head. "No. It doesn't make sense."

There came a knock outside the door. "Mr. Cadogan? There is someone insisting to see you."

Dazed, he glanced from the handful of words written on the page, that'd upended his world, to the door. "Tell whoever the hell it is I'm not receiving visitors."

"I've tried, but he insists he'll..." Mauley coughed. "Burn the townhouse down if you don't see him this instant."

With a frown, Cadogan stalked over and yanked the door open. "Who is *he*?"

Mauley's skin had a pallor unlike Cadogan ever witnessed of the unflappable secretary. "The Marquess of Carnell."

Cadogan's brother.

Raina gasped.

This visitor, he'd receive.

"I'll be down shortly, Mauley. Have two men positioned outside my office, one at the base of my office window, one—"

"I've already stationed six men around the inside perimeter, four on the outside with His Lordship's conveyance, and the remainders scattered throughout the halls leading to yours and Her Ladyship's chambers."

Of course, he had. Mauley didn't miss a thing.

Feeling Raina straining to listen, Cadogan dropped his voice another octave. "I want *you* to be the one at my wife's door."

Carnell hadn't possessed the level of evil Cadogan had and certainly not the skill he did in matters of fighting, but Severin also knew never to underestimate a person. His glorious wife had been the one to best hammer home that reminder.

After Mauley left, Cadogan faced Raina.

"No." She shook her head. "I'll not let you see him."

Oh, he would do more than see him.

The fog lifted, and his head cleared of everything, restoring Cadogan to his former role of agent. "I must, Raina. Surely you see that."

He started for the door.

She cried out. "Please, you cannot see him."

"Raina, for your safety, you are not to leave this room."

In a beautiful blaze of fury, she stormed between him and the door, barring Cadogan from entering. "I forbid you to go."

"Raina, I must."

She knew that. Cadogan saw that from the grief in her eyes.

He took her lips in a gentle kiss. "I love you, Raina."

"I love you, too." Tears filled her voice, and her sorrow threatened to cut him up inside. "Please, let me go with you," she begged.

"Anywhere," he vowed. "But not this time."

Her tears, those most virulent of weapons against him, freely fell.

"I see." With an uneven nod, she stepped aside so Cadogan could pass.

The sight of her suffering, and because of him, threatened to take him down. He could not afford this. Not when Cadogan needed his wits about him.

"I'll return, Raina. Mauley will be waiting right outside your door," he promised when she still didn't say anything.

Raina gave him a small, sad, smile. "I don't want Mauley. I want my husband."

With that anguished vow following Cadogan in his wake, he left Raina, and went to face the man who'd betrayed him.

CHAPTER 26

IT'D BEEN A LIFETIME SINCE Cadogan had seen his eldest brother; or, for that matter, *any* of his siblings.

Now, brother studied brother.

Time had changed the new Marquess of Thurso, and also, it hadn't. The tall, gangly, quiet-spoken boy had grown into a tall, wiry, somber-looking man.

At some point, he'd shed the wire-rimmed spectacles the late marquess tormented the then-young man, for needing.

Thurso had been bookish and skilled with musical instruments.

And though Cadogan had been well-read, and mastered six languages by age ten, he'd also boxed, fenced, and rode.

There stirred in his mind, the far-off echoes of their brutal sire's rantings…

"…why can't you be strong and savage and ruthless like your little brother…"

Though broad across the shoulders, and now several inches taller than Cadogan, it didn't appear he'd become strong, savage, or ruthless.

In a telltale displease of unease, Thurso shifted ever so slightly on his feet, rocking side to side.

Of a sudden, Cadogan's brother snatched the hat off his head, as if he'd only just recalled he still wore the fashionable article and dragged his spare hand through his slightly curling blond hair.

Yes, from their outward appearances to their ability to hide or conceal their emotions, Cadogan and the marquess couldn't be more different.

Cadogan went first. "Hullo, brother."

"Severin."

Severin.

How strange that two of just a handful of people in his life who referred to Cadogan so, should now stand under the same roof.

Thoughts of Raina and the terror and sorrow on her face as he'd left reminded Cadogan of his goal—ascertain whether Argyll's information was in fact, accurate. Whether, in his years apart from Thurso, they'd become a real-life Cain and Abel.

"My secretary informed me, that during my absence, you've taken to arson?"

"No." Color flooded Thurso's sharply chiseled cheeks. "I play cello now."

Now...?

"*...you pathetic boy, with your instruments...I already have two goddamned useless daughters...*"

Disturbed by the intrusion of that long-ago memory, Cadogan shoved those reminiscences aside and more carefully studied his brother.

He inclined his head. "I see your sense of sarcasm remains... off, big brother."

"Yes, well, I sense sarcasm in your words *now*, so one might say it's not quite as abjectly poor as it once was." Thurso gave a weak smile and took a glance about.

While the marquess swept his gaze over his office, Cadogan peered intently at him.

Was Thurso's gaze distracted? Nervous?

What was it?

Cadogan swept an arm over to the pair of armchairs in front of his desk. "Would you care to—?"

"I've written over the years," Thurso said.

He mentally tacked impatient to his brother's peculiar behavior.

"I wondered if..." the marquess mused aloud. This time, it was Cadogan's turn to be examined.

"Did you not receive my notes?"

"I did," Cadogan said.

His brother frowned.

Either the speed with which he'd answered, or the confirmation he'd given, or maybe both, had upset Thurso.

Cadogan took advantage of his brother's distractedness. "What is this about, Thurso?"

Visceral hate flashed in the older man's eyes, such vitriolic rage that confirmed, Thurso, too, possessed a hard streak.

"Do not call me that," Thurso—*Cadogan's brother*—ordered. "I may have been born to the title, but I'll be damned if I'm called by that bastard's name." His square jaw hardened. "March. I'm March."

Cadogan remained still during that crack in his brother's composure.

Thurso—*March*—beat his hat against his leg. "Forgive me."

Severin waved a hand about. "No. No, apologies. He *was* a bastard. Getting away was…"

His eldest brother lifted a blond eyebrow. "The best thing you ever did?"

March's response didn't contain any hint of bitterness. Sadness, yes. But not resentment.

Perhaps Raina had completely shattered the armor Cadogan had built, for he felt the sting of regret at having celebrated leaving when all his other siblings had been left behind.

His brother turned his hat up. "I do not blame you, Severin."

It appeared now two could read his thoughts.

"If fact, I wished I could be like you," March mused. "I believe if I could have, he'd have been less of a bastard."

"Psst. No, he was rotten to the core."

He'd believed the same of himself, until Raina.

Thoughts of her refocused him.

"Did you resent me?" Cadogan put the question to his brother that needed asking.

"Resent *you*?" March laughed. "God, no. Envy?" He lifted a finger. "Yes, very much so. But I did not envy all your life, just that you were free to leave."

"… *I don't need a useless heir*…"

"Time did not soften him, I take it?"

His elder brother answered with a question of his own. "Does it soften anyone? Or just make them harder, angrier, and uglier?"

"Is that what it did to you?" he quietly asked. "Is that why you attempted to have me killed?"

March took a deep, pained, breath, and closed his eyes; telling Cadogan everything he needed to know.

Oh, God.

"It's true," he said, his voice somehow flat, when his stomach churned. "You attempted to have me killed."

"N-No!" His brother's voice broke. "Never. I would never. I didn't mean…"

Reeling, Cadogan stumbled away. He praised a God, he'd not believed in until Raina, that Mauley had secured the house and remained in control, because Lord help him, Cadogan was lost.

"You didn't mean, 'what'?" he rasped. "To send someone to murder me."

"To leave you marked."

Cadogan gripped the sides of his head and sucked in deep lungful's of air. "What did I ever do to you?" he cried. "Was it not enough you had the marquessate? Was it because our father took great pleasure in reminding you, I was your superior in every way. What?" he begged. "What was it?"

Fear should bleed from the older man's eyes. "You believe I cared about how the duke viewed me?" March asked on an aching whisper. "I didn't need him to remind me, Severin, I always knew. I loved you. You were my hero. You were the big brother, in every way except age. As children, you protected me, as long as you could."

March's shoulders shook with an empty laugh. "As an adult, I tried to protect you, and of course, I fucked it up, in every way."

"What are you talking about?"

"Through a close connection at Parliament, I learned of an assignment you'd been slated to take."

Cadogan's ears sharpened. "Go on."

"The mission was doomed before it'd even been handed you. The outcome ended with you dead. In France, back in '25, there was the—"

"Yes, Yes. I know." He'd been so busy wallowing in the misery of his career being over, he'd not paid attention to details coming out about either the failed or successful missions at the Home Office. He'd taken a dull desk job and simmered all the while with bitter regret.

"I know you loved your career, Severin," his brother said quietly, pulling Cadogan back. "But I loved you more." He shook his head. "I cannot and I *will* not ever be sorry that you survived, even if it means you hate me."

Cadogan's head continued spinning. He tried to sort through everything March just revealed.

His career *had* been everything; the whole basis of his existence. It was all he'd needed and wanted and known.

That's what he'd believed from the moment he'd entered the Home Office, until the moment he'd taken on one unwanted assignment of guarding London's leading Diamond.

Had Cadogan not been marked, he'd have been dead years ago. There'd have been some other man Argyll picked to guard Raina, and be her husband and—

He lifted his stunned gaze to March. "Why didn't you tell me?"

"Oh, yes, let us imagine how that would go. Me, your elder brother, who last you knew was afraid of his own shadow, telling you to give up your career, because of dangerous assignment. I expect that would have gone over well."

Cadogan drew back. "Sarcasm, big brother. Well-done."

They shared their first smile, ever. Any ones that'd come and gone during their earliest years were now too distant to remember.

"You're not enraged," his brother noted. "I'd expected you'd snap my neck, or, at the very least pulverize me."

"I'm..." Cadogan shook his head. "I'm not. I'm happy, March," he said simply. "I'm in love with a woman I've just married."

"Yes, Lady Raina Goodheart. *Well-done*, little brother."

"Mrs. Raina Cadogan *now*. I forget, gossip travels quickly."

His brother nodded. "Particularly when it unfolds in one of London's most debauched gaming hells." March's expression turned serious. "As I said, I don't expect you to forgive me," he held out a hand, "but I—"

Cadogan caught his brother's palm and drew him into his arms. "You're forgiven."

"You hug now?"

"My wife's influence," he explained, thumping March on his back. "Which you should be grateful for, as this exchange prior to her presence in my life, would have gone a great deal differently and badly for you." He squeezed him hard.

His brother grunted. "I will be sure and express my appreciation when we meet," he wheezed.

Releasing his hold, Cadogan let March go.

Bemused, Cadogan shook his head. "My big brother saving me."

"Only once. Unlike you, who did so countless times from—"

"Do not mention him. He's dead to us."

Cadogan stilled, as a thought stirred in his mind. "Who—"

March accurately anticipated his question. "I cannot tell you the name of my contact in Parliament. I gave my word."

He inclined his head. Cadogan respected that. Something continued to pick at his brain.

March knew of the doomed assignment, but he'd needed the help of someone who could get close to Cadogan, but Cadogan didn't let anyone close.

He'd fought Raina's efforts, tooth and nail.

"Who is responsible for my scar?" he asked quietly.

"I was given contact information for a man who worked under you," his brother explained.

No. A slow-building dread unfurled slowly within him. *No.*

"Your secretary at the Home Office," March was saying.

No. No. Please, don't say it.

"...*I don't want Mauley*..."

"Mr.—"

"Mauley," Cadogan whispered.

"...*I want my husband*..."

"Yes, yes, that is his name."

A tortured moan spilled from Cadogan's chest.

"*Severin?*" his brother shouted after him.

His lungs burning, Cadogan kept running.

She had to be all right. There was no life without Raina in it. There was no reason for living.

She was the reason.

She was his reason for being.

And God help Mauley. If he so much as touched a hair on her head, Cadogan would spill the bastard's guts and let rabid dogs feast upon his bloody carcass.

CHAPTER 27

THE GREAT, BIG, LUMMOX.

In all the time he'd known her, Raina's husband hadn't learned a single thing about her.

Not. One. Thing.

Locking her in rooms. Ordering her to stay there. Assigning Mauley to guard her. Stationing men on either side of the hallways, while he marched off to meet the brother who'd ended his career and attempted to have him killed?

The list went on and on.

"Oh, I think not, dear husband," she muttered under her breath.

Raina, did a slow walkthrough of Severin's rooms and contemplated her latest prison cell.

Alas, with no Millie to rely upon, Raina would need to find her own way out, which was fine, as she'd learned from the best.

She paused beside the doorway connecting her and Severin's chambers.

Dropping her arms akimbo, she drummed her fingers, and continued to think.

There were guards around the perimeter of Severin's office, but most of her husband's men were outside.

She frowned.

Why would Mauley send so many of Severin's men out?

Raina ceased her distracted tapping. A slow smile curled her lips up.

The fact Mauley moved so many guards out, also meant there

were less inside to *protect* her. Or…say, notice if Raina slipped out.

Knock-Knock-Knock

Her heart leapt.

Or even better, perhaps Severin's meeting hadn't taken all that long, after all.

Maybe, there'd been some kind of misunderstanding. She frowned. *Or your brother lied.*

As high as her heart climbed in thinking Severin had returned to her, was as low as it fell thinking Gregory might have betrayed him a second time.

Knock-Knock-Knock

That pounding grew more incessant.

She furrowed her brow. Severin wouldn't know. He might kick a door down, but he'd never knock, especially at his own door.

And he'd absolutely announce himself.

But…she hadn't locked the door, and Severin hadn't actually locked the panel. He'd just instructed her to remain inside.

Her senses went on immediate alert.

Intuition taking over, she slipped inside her connecting rooms. Instead of shutting the door, she carefully drew the panel wide until her back touched the wall.

Lucy chose that moment to appear from Raina's closet. "My—"

Raina touched a finger to her lips. "Shh," she mouthed.

Wide-eyed with fear, the young girl nodded frantically, and swiftly retreated back inside.

Click.

Whomever knocked, had now breached Severin's rooms.

Not even daring to breathe, she waited for them to declare themselves, prayed it would be her husband, but knew it would not.

"Where the hell are you, you bloody, bothersome, bitch?" he muttered so faint she would have never heard him, had she not been listening so closely.

Closeted away in her own room, Raina, drew back.

Mauley. But Severin's charming secretary as she'd never before heard him.

The…the audacity of him to speak so about her.

It took everything in her to not tell Mr. Mauley *exactly* what she thought of his foul mouth, horrid manners, and shockingly bad temper.

The secretary's footfalls, usually very deliberate, rose and fell loudly and clumsily.

"Raina, your husband, is hurt," he called.

Reflexively, she took a step.

Mauley stopped.

"*Rainaa*," he said, in a sing-songy voice; chills scraped along her spine. "Where are you, dear? I understand you're scared. Let me take you to Mr. Cadogan. The doctor has been summoned, but he is asking for you."

There was an almost franticness to his movements, further emphasized by his increased mutterings.

Mauley's steps drew increasingly nearer. "You probably heard me curse and that was unpardonable, but I'm worried over His Lordship."

The hell he was.

Nothing had befallen Severin. Her heart would know; the organ would have ceased to beat.

Holding her breath, Raina tiptoed closer to the wall.

She'd never complain about slippers again.

"*Fuck!*" Mauley whispered.

And then, his steps were moving away from her rooms, and further and further.

Raina edged away from her hiding place, and slunk closer to the hearth.

The floorboards groaned.

Bloody hell.

Raina squeezed her eyes shut, and prayed he'd not heard.

But he, like Severin, had served the Home Office.

Mr. Mauley stopped.

"Lady Raina?" he called, his steps drawing nearer.

Biting the inside of her cheek, Raina pressed her back against the wall, and stretched her fingertips towards the fireplace poker.

He froze at the entryway.

Creeaaak.

"Hullo, sir," Lucy emerged from the closet, wearing a flirtatious smile. "You looking for Her Ladyship? Because," she dropped her voice to a whisper. "I'm happy to share she slipped off a bit ago. Something about a meeting His Lordship was attending…"

Lucy ran a fingertip over the modest neckline of her uniform. "We'll have even more time than—"

Mauley's curse cut off the rest of Lucy's promise.

"What, sir?" she cried. "Tired of me already, you are?" As Lucy chased the secretary from Raina's room, the girl gave Raina a sly wink.

They shared a victorious smile.

Their triumph proved short-lived.

Severin's thundering baritone shook the walls of both rooms. "Raina!"

Severin!

Did he know Mauley was up to something nefarious?

Mauley let fly another curse.

Shooting Raina an unwarranted, apologetic look, Lucy took flight, and headed right back to the closet.

Raina grabbed the fireplace poker the same moment, Severin stormed his chambers.

"Mauley."

The hate and lethality coating her husband's voice, indicated not only had he deduced some manner of treachery from the man, but that it'd be the last greeting Mr. Mauley every received.

"Mr. Cadogan," Mauley greeted.

"Where is my wife?"

"She's gone. Snuck off, as is her way."

She wrinkled her nose.

Severin growled like the beast Mr. Mauley had turned him into. "Quit the fucking games,"

The floorboards shifted, as Severin stepped into the room

There came the click of a pistol being cocked.

Oh, God. No. Please, no.

Nausea burned in her belly and bile burned her throat.

"Not a step more."

"I vow before God, Mauley, if you hurt her—"

"If I hurt her," His voice tipped up, in a mark of his rising hysteria. "You'll what, *Cadogan?*"

Raina bit her lip so hard, she drew blood. Severin had the disadvantage. He no doubt carried a weapon, but by the time he drew it, Mr. Mauley's bullet would have found a place inside her husband.

"The arrogance of you," Mauley chortled; his maniacal laugh raised the gooseflesh on her arms. "I've got a gun trained on you and your hands are empty, and you *still* come in here threatening me."

Raina breathed in slowly through her nose, and concentrating on her steps, she tiptoed towards the ensuing fight.

"But that is your way, isn't it," Mauley sneered. "You're infallible, unstoppable, there's nothing you cannot do, including getting yourself somehow married to the most exquisite beauty London's seen in decades."

"I don't understand."

Severin was stalling; waiting for his men to arrive.

"Why, Mauley?"

"Because I'm a bloody fool," Mauley spat. "Upon learning your next assignment, would lead to you dead, Lord Thurso came to me. He asked me to help end your career. You had me stuck behind a desk as your goddamned minion. I wanted the field and had I not intervened I'd be in an intelligence role."

As she inched closer, Raina's mind raced with each discovery. Severin's brother hadn't been a complete villain. If Mauley was to be believed, the marquess's intentions had been good.

"I couldn't see you d-die." The secretary's voice warbled. "But I admired you. I wanted to be you. I saw you as a brother and friend," Icy steel reentered his voice, "but you kept me back for selfish reasons."

"You didn't want me dead then, Mauley," Cadogan said, in a calming, quiet way. "You don't want me dead now."

This time, Mauley roared with laughter. "The *ballocks* on you."

Raina tightened her grip on her makeshift weapon. "I know your every method, Cadogan. Don't try them on me. It's a—"

Raina surged forward.

Both men, distracted by her entrance, turned at the same time.

With a cry, Raina clubbed Mauley in his legs.

Severin's betrayer let loose a bestial cry and collapsed in a writhing heap. The gun slipped from his fingers.

The moment his weapon hit the floor, it discharged.

Plaster came tumbling from where the bullet struck. Raina kicked the weapon away. In the hall, shouts went up.

As Severin rushed over, Raina's fingers went slack; the iron bar fell from her fingers on the back of an agonized Mauley's head.

The secretary collapsed and his sounds of misery stopped.

There came a beat of silence.

"My God, Raina," Severin cried, running his hands all over her. "Did he—?"

"He was going to hurt y-you," she whispered.

Several guards spilled into the room; the trio formed a tight circle around Mauley's prone form.

The reality of how close he'd come to death and her entire body began to tremble. "I hit him in the legs," she whispered. "I didn't want to kill him."

Severin hauled her into his arms. "He deserves killing, love."

"Alive," Chase announced, sounding morbidly regretful.

"Alas, he lives," her husband murmured, kissing her temple.

How blasé. How casual. And yet, this is the world her husband had once belonged to. Never again. No more.

She and Severin were now the institution to be preserved.

Raina curled her fingers into his chest. "You almost d-died. H-He would h-have shot y-you. I—" Her teeth began to chatter too bad for her to finish the rest of the horrifying possibility.

"Shh, love," he whispered.

Severin drew her in closer and held her tighter. He massaged her back. Until, those smooth, rhythmic circles, combined with the warmth and weight of him drove away all terror.

The moment Severin's team carried off a stirring, and handcuffed, Mauley, a tall, wiry, stranger she'd not noticed until now, stepped aside so they could exit.

Raina made a grab for the poker, but Severin intercepted her efforts.

The handsome blond man blanched.

"Worry not, love," Severin murmured, gently prying the

weapon from her fingers. "This gentleman is my eldest brother, March."

She opened her mouth and closed it several times. "Oh. It is…" She looked to Severin for help. "Uh…?"

"You may say 'lovely to meet you'." He nodded towards the distinguished figure at the entryway. "March came to explain his role in saving me from a doomed assignment years ago, and now, for a second time, in revealing Mauley's' role, he's saved me, and possibly you."

"Given what I've heard on the way upstairs, I believe Her Ladyship is quite adept at saving herself."

Raina found her first smile since the events. "I see where my husband receives his charm from."

Severin growled. "A moment with my wife, brother."

"Yes. Uh…it was lovely to meet you, my—"

"Raina," she said gently. "Please, call me, Raina."

Severin and his brother locked gazes for a long while; some unspoken communication happening between them. Then, exchanging nods, the marquess quit the rooms.

Her head continued to spin under the dizzying turn of events.

"We went from a 'treacherous betrayal to a family reunion," she said bemusedly. "I must know the entire story, my—" the rest of her lighthearted words were consumed by the heat of Severin's kiss.

Sighing, she kissed him wholeheartedly into return.

Raina's lashes fluttered.

"I promise, we'll speak about all of it later, love," he said huskily.

The force of emotion emanating from his eye touched every part of her being and soul with a beautiful, healing, warmth. How different he was, from the man who'd first interviewed her.

"For now, the only story I want to share and celebrate, is the one of you and I, my Queen, and the love we found in one another."

"Mmm," that dreamy exhalation slipped out. "Shall we begin with the tales of my subterfuge,"

"Which you learned from, dear Millie."

She gave him a playfully arch look. "Which proved very helpful today, I'll add."

Severin smiled. "*Very* helpful, as my you, my dear wife, saved me." His levity faded.

He moved a somber gaze over her face. "You saved me in every way, Raina." His eyes gleamed with emotion.

Raina twined her arms about his neck and lifted herself up until their gazes met. "You promised a celebration of our love, my husband," she said, throatily. "I would like to know more about this celebration."

Desire darkened his eyes. "I can do better than that, love."

He slipped his hands under her buttocks and drew her hard against his length.

That familiar ache only this man wrought, settled between her legs,

"C-Can you, now?" she asked, breathless.

Severin's lips curled into a slow, tempting, smile. "Allow me to show you."

And he proceeded to do just that.

The End

BE SURE AND CHECK OUT Christi Caldwell's next scorching Regency romance, exclusive to Amazon, coming October 2024.

THE WOLF OF MAYFAIR

USA Today bestselling author Christi Caldwell weaves a sensuous tale of innocence lost in this blistering romance about a young woman on the run and the lecherous cad she can't seem to resist.

WANT MORE?

Want to know the stories about other characters you met in
Lust-The Bad Earl?

Wrath: The Devil Duke
Seven Deadly Sins Series
Book 1

Featuring Miss Edith Caldecott and Edward de Vesy, the Marquess of Malden, Duke of Craven.

An Eye for An Eye

Once a respectable, sought after bachelor and do-gooder, Edward deVesy, the Marquess of Malden, took a fall to rival Satan's. A single decision cost him everything, including the gaming hell he helped build. From past betrayals has sprung a new man—one who is merciless, cruel, and incapable of pain. Now, Malden is applying every lesson he learned from his partners on the art of ruthlessness and raising a fortune to build an empire. And he will have revenge against those who wronged him.

Righting a Wrong

Having watched her eldest sister perish, Miss Edith Caldecott is no stranger to loss. Society may be content to accept Evie's death as an unfortunate twist of fate. Not Edith. She spent years digging to discover who was responsible. Now, she's taking matters into her own hands. To avenge her sister, she'll require the help of a man who has his finger on the pulse of evil.

An Unlikely Partnership

What begins as nothing more than a relationship born of vengeance slowly dissolves into something sinful, decadent, and dangerous as Edith falls deeper under Lord Malden's spell. When further betrayals come to light, Edith realizes she's crossed a bridge too far. But the damage is done as she's found herself falling for the last man who'd ever give Edith his guarded heart.

Heat level: Scorching!
Length: Novel

The Devil and the Debutante
The Heart of a Duke Series

Featuring: Lady Faith Brookfield and Rex DuMond, the Marquess of Rutherford.

A Dastardly Villain
Rex DuMond, the Marquess of Rutherford, rules over London's most wicked gaming hell Forbidden Pleasures. His black-hearted peers might spend their evenings in polite society, but they spend their nights gambling their wealth, land, and secrets away at his tables. No man can turn him from his chosen life of decadence and debauchery, not even his domineering and disapproving father.

A Daring Young Woman

Lady Faith Brookfield hasn't forgotten the night she entered Forbidden Pleasures and crossed paths with the dark, seductive gaming hell owner. That night, however, she discovered more than a dangerous attraction, she also uncovered dangerous secrets—ones that can avenge past wrongs against her aunt and save other young women from suffering a similar fate.

A Dangerous Gamble

In order to save his gaming empire, Rex has no choice but to pursue the innocent debutante for the secrets she holds. Can true love ever be born in treachery and deceit? Accustomed to a world where the house always wins, Rex must wager all he owns on the greatest gamble of all…love.

BIOGRAPHY

Christi Caldwell is the *USA Today* bestselling author of the Sinful Brides series and the Heart of a Duke series. She blames novelist Judith McNaught for luring her into the world of historical romance. When Christi was at the University of Connecticut, she began writing her own tales of love—ones where even the most perfect heroes and heroines had imperfections. She learned to enjoy torturing her couples before they earned their well-deserved happily ever after. Christi lives in Charlotte, North Carolina where she spends her time writing, baking, and being a mommy to the most inspiring little boy and empathetic, spirited girls who, with their mischievous twin antics, offer an endless source of story ideas!

Visit www.christicaldwellauthor.com to learn more about what Christi is working on, or join her on Facebook at Christi Caldwell Author, and Twitter @ChristiCaldwell!

Printed in Great Britain
by Amazon